BRETWALDA

BRETWALDA

PHILIP KETCHUM

ILLUSTRATED BY

V.E. PYLES

ALTUS PRESS
2015

© 2015 Steeger Properties, LLC, under license to Altus Press • First Edition—2015

EDITED AND DESIGNED BY
Matthew Moring

PUBLISHING HISTORY
The stories contained in this edition originally appeared in the February 25, March 18, April 15, May 13, June 10, July 8 & 29, August 19, September 23, October 14, November 4, and December 23, 1939 issues of *Argosy* magazine (Vol. 288 No. 4, Vol. 289 Nos. 1 & 5, Vol. 290 No. 3, Vol. 291 Nos. 1 & 5, Vol. 292 Nos. 2 & 5, Vol. 293 No. 4, Vol. 294 Nos. 1 & 4, and Vol. 295 No. 5). Copyright © 1939 by The Frank A. Munsey Company. Copyright renewed © 1966, 1967 and assigned to Steeger Properties, LLC. All rights reserved.

THANKS TO
Richard Hall, Chris Kalb, and Gerd Pircher

ALL RIGHTS RESERVED
No part of this book may be reproduced or utilized in any form or by any means without permission in writing from the publisher.

ISBN
978-1-61827-184-6

Visit *altuspress.com* for more books like this.
Printed in the United States of America.

TABLE OF CONTENTS

I

THE AXE BITES DEEP

'Twas the mightiest weapon the eyes of man had ever beheld; its mystic name meant "Ruler of Briton." And from over the Northern Sea came a Viking's thrall—the only man in the world who could wield that fearsome steel—to save good King Alfred and the homeland he scarce remembered.

CHAPTER I

FOR SIX DAYS Caedmon the Briton had labored at his forge and now, on Easter-eve, his work was about finished. Perspiration glistened on his bald pate and his great shoulders heaved as he thrust the metal into the coals of the fire. "Blow, lad. Blow," he commanded the bellows. And while the fire grew red, Caedmon watched the metal closely.

A large crowd had gathered around his forge for word that Caedmon was nearing the end of his work had spread throughout the village. It was a motley crowd; a curious crowd. For the time being, all thought of rank was forgotten. Thane, churl and slave mingled; questioned one another about the great axe Caedmon was making, for Caedmon was close of mouth and had talked little of his work.

To one side stood Ethelred, *ealdorman* of the village, a tall, heavily bearded man, broad of shoulder and with arms almost as thick as Caedmon's. Near him was Regnault, close friend and companion of King Alfred, who was now in hiding from the Danes somewhere in the woods of Somersetshire. Regnault was as tall and as broad of shoulder as Ethelred, but he was much younger and his eyes strayed often from Caedmon to Lady Ethelda, Ethelred's youngest daughter, who stood just beyond her father.

There was a stir among the people as Caedmon drew the great axe from the fire and bent over it. The crowd moved closer. And then suddenly one of the thanes at Caedmon's shoulder

1

"In this axe," Caedmon intoned solemly, "rests all the future safety of England. Its name is Bretwalda.*"*

uttered a startled cry and pointing at the axe, shouted, "Look! Look! The name!" Others took up the cry and looked at one another with wonder in their eyes. For every man there was ready to swear that no name had been inscribed on the great axe when it had been thrust into the fire.

Ethelred pushed up close to Caedmon. "I would see the name," he announced.

Caedmon stepped back, a broad smile on his face. "The name," he answered, "is *Bretwalda.*"

Others in the crowd gathered around the axe which now lay on the huge block of iron before the forge and even as Caedmon had said, the name *Bretwalda*, could clearly be seen. It was deeply inscribed just above the cutting edge of the axe.

"*Bretwalda*," Ethelred muttered. "Such was the name given to Briton's kings, long before our time. Its meaning is *Ruler of Briton*." Then turning suddenly to Caedmon, he asked, "For whom has this axe been made? Who ordered you to make it?"

Caedmon shook his head. "I do not know for whom the axe

*The stranger lifted Regnault
and flung him to the ground.
A mighty shout went up.*

is intended. I was ordered to make it in a vision. I was told by a voice which came to me that in the axe which I would make would rest the future safety of all of England."

"But such an axe, man," Ethelred answered. "Who is there that can wield it?"

Caedmon made no answer and there was no answer from the crowd. That same question each man there had asked himself for the axe was like no common axe. Head and handle were of steel, welded into one piece through the heat of Caedmon's forge. And the steel which had gone into the making of the axe was of a fine, bluish quality, seldom before seen. None knew where Caedmon got it.

The head of the axe was a full six hands broad and its curved, cutting edge, might have struck off four heads at once. Above the name *Bretwalda*, a dozen blood-red jewels were deeply imbedded in the steel. The handle was long and curiously engraved.

THERE was a sudden commotion at the edge of the crowd. Staring that way, Ethelred caught his breath and reached a hand to his sword. A dozen paces away stood a tall, fair haired stranger. Over his red woolen shirt he wore a coat of mail and his helmet was adorned with the wings of the raven. A long sword was belted at his side. Everything about the man labeled him as one of the hated Danes, who two years before, in 876, had overrun all Wessex, defeating King Alfred and driving him into hiding.

The men who had drawn away from the stranger were glancing about, searching for his companions; Ethelred looked from side to side. He saw no other strangers and that surprised him. Danes did not usually venture alone into communities like this, where loyalty to Alfred still ran high.

Ethelred was about to move toward the stranger when Regnault caught his arm and whispered, "Let me handle this."

The *ealdorman* hesitated. As the person of highest rank in this village, the responsibility was his. But Regnault was close to King Alfred, and his hatred for the Danes was a consuming fire. His prowess as a fighter was a matter of legend, and this stranger looked no weakling.

The *ealdorman* nodded and, moving over to where his daughter stood, said to her, "Watch, Ethelda. You have heard stories of Regnault. Today you may see how he fights."

Striding swiftly forward, Regnault stopped before the stranger, stared into his face. "Why have you come here?"

The stranger looked down at his questioner. Though Regnault was tall, he was the taller and his shoulders were just as broad. He stood very straight and there was a touch of arrogance in the set of his head. His eyes were level and direct and as he answered Regnault, a slight smile curved his lips.

"Why have I come here?" he repeated. "Why because this is my home."

There was a faint Danish accent to the words. Ethelred caught it; and Regnault, too, must have noticed it for he laughed tauntingly, dropped a hand to his sword and cried, "Your voice betrays you, Vandal. I would see the color of your blood."

SWIFTLY Regnault drew his sword. It flashed in the air, cut viciously at the stranger's neck above his coat of mail. But the blow was short. The stranger had stepped back out of reach.

With an angry shout, Regnault charged and what followed happened so swiftly that Ethelred caught only a blurred impression of the struggle. It was quickly ended. Ducking under the slashing sword the stranger laid his hands on Regnault's body, lifted him aloft, whirled once, and then threw Regnault to the ground much as a man might cast a sack of grain.

A sharp cry escaped from Regnault's lips. He seemed to try to get up but before he could make it the stranger had moved over to where he lay, had drawn his own sword and held the point of it above the stunned man's chest.

The crowd had started to surge toward him but as they saw the stranger hesitate, the movement stopped.

Staring from side to side, the stranger asked, "Who is there to claim the *wergild*—the atonement money for this killing? Who is his next of kin?"

Ethelred moved forward. He was a little dazed at what had happened but not so dazed that he wasn't more surprised at a Dane referring to the *wergild*.

"Who are you?" he bluntly demanded. With his free hand the stranger removed his helmet. Sunlight glinted against his hair, turning it bronze. There was a sharpness to his features, Ethelred noticed, but not the sharpness of the Vandals from the north. His face bore the look of a man whose sole reliance was in his own strength.

"Who am I?" repeated the stranger. "Not a Dane surely, though I have lived with them for many years. As a boy I was carried away a captive. That accounts for my manner of speech, for my clothing."

Ethelred frowned, Such a story might be true, he knew, for the Danes had harried the coast of England for years and had carried off many captives. Few captives, however, had ever returned and those who had, brought back such stories of hardship and slavery that it seemed unlikely that any man such as this would have been allowed a chance to get away.

A sudden thought struck Ethelred and he said, "If you are not a Dane, what think you of King Alfred?"

"I am hunting for him that I may give him a message."

"That man at whose breast you hold your sword is one of his followers," said Ethelred.

The stranger immediately sheathed his sword, "Then I am sorry for what I have done."

The people were pressing closer, now, curiously following every word of their conversation and Ethelred, suddenly conscious of his responsibilities as *ealdorman* and liking the stranger in spite of his suspicions, said to him, "Suppose you come to my house? I would question you further. What is your name?"

"Wilton," answered the stranger.

Ethelred nodded. Wilton was a good Saxon name but that alone told him nothing. "Come," he suggested.

But Wilton shook his head and answered, "In a moment." Then pushing forward he walked up to Caedmon's forge and stared down at the axe which the Briton had made. As he looked at it his eyes brightened and the fingers of his hand twitched as though itching to clutch the handle.

"What think you of it?" asked Caedmon.

Wilton smiled. "There," he murmured, "is a weapon for a man. A truly great weapon."

For several minutes he looked down at it while the people in the crowd watched him breathlessly, half expecting, perhaps, that he would try to lift it. But he didn't. Turning away at last he walked over to Ethelred's side and said, "I am ready. Which way do we go?"

CHAPTER II

AS THEY TURNED down the road toward the *ealdorman*'s home, Wilton could not get his mind away from thoughts of the great axe he had seen at Caedmon's forge. In him there was a love for fine weapons. The sword which he wore had been given to him by Ragnor Lodbrok, whose whim had lifted him from a position of servitude in the country of the Danes and made of him a warrior. It was a fine sword, a mate to the swords Lodbrok had given to each of his sons, Halvdan, Hubba, Ivar Boneless and Hrothgar. But it was still not so fine a weapon as the axe which Caedmon had forged. He felt a sudden longing to get his hands on that axe, to feel its power as he swung it.

The house of the *ealdorman*, though larger than the rest, was a low, crudely built structure; but inside, rich tapestries covered the walls and the furniture was of the finest. In the front room there was a sturdy table and several high-backed benches. Fresh reeds covered the floor.

Turning to him there, Ethelred said, "I should like to hear your story, Wilton. It is not often that slaves have escaped from the Danes."

Wilton shrugged. "But I was not a slave for long. For some reason or other, just why I do not know, Ragnor Lodbrok, the man to whom I was sold took a liking to me and had me raised with his own sons. They were older than I, of course, but as a youth I was quite tall and strong. With them I have been many places."

Ethelred frowned. "Ivar Boneless," he said slowly, "is the name of him who defeated King Edmund at Hoxne; who captured him and, when he would not submit to his demands, had him tied to a tree and shot to death with arrows."

Wilton nodded. "I have heard the story."

"And Halvdan and Hubba are two of the men who have led the Danes into Wessex and who have driven King Alfred into hiding."

"I know that too," said Wilton, "And Guthrum is with them. But was not Halvdan killed?"

"Yes, but a few weeks ago."

Wilton stared across the room. "Perhaps," he said, "my story is hard to believe. Let me tell you more. My father, also named Wilton, was the *ealdorman* of Donnershire, two hundred leagues up the coast. When I was but six the Danes landed on that coast and my father and all my family were killed. The village was destroyed.

"I, with a score of others, was carried away into captivity, and but for Ragnor Lodbrok, might have spent my life in the fields of the Danes. Instead, Lodbrok made of me a warrior. Perhaps he thought it a good joke. Perhaps he thought someday to send me against my own people. I know not what was in his mind. Yet, through all the years, but one thought has stayed with me and that thought was that some day I might come back to my native land and take my place with my own people. And with them strike a blow for the freedom of Briton."

For a moment Ethelred was silent. Then he said, "You spoke of a message for King Alfred."

"Yes," Wilton answered. "I must see him."

"What is the message?"

"That, I prefer to give him myself."

Ethelred looked a little doubtful, then suddenly excused himself and left the room.

AFTER he had gone, Wilton moved to the door and stared outside. Beyond the houses across from the *ealdorman*'s, as far as he could see, stretched the green hills of England and the sight of them deeply stirred him. From other captives he had heard them described, but they seemed more beautiful today than words could have pictured. Merely staring out at them brought a peace to his soul, and under his breath he murmured, "It's good to be home—good to be home."

A sound behind him caused him to turn and he saw the tall, slender girl whom he had noticed near the *ealdorman* at Caedmon's forge. She had a long drinking horn in her hands and she held it out to him.

"My father," she said, "thought that you might like to quench your thirst."

The tone of the girl's voice was pleasing to Wilton's ears and he liked the expression in her eyes and on her face. He felt a sudden desire to talk to her, to hear the sound of her voice again and as he crossed the room and took the horn he heard himself saying, "Please wait here until your father returns. I cannot remember ever having talked to one of the women of my own country."

A faint smile touched the girl's lips. "You speak as though you were glad to return,"

"I am glad. Though things seem strange to me, behind the strangeness there is a familiarity which I can feel as definitely as I can sense a storm in the winds of the sea. I was born not far from here, you know,"

The girl nodded. "The walls of the house are thin. I heard what you told my father from the next room."

"And you believe my story?"

"Yes, I think I do."

"Why?"

"Your story would not have sounded so strange had it been a lie. And besides, in spite of your armor you do not have the look of one of the Vandals. Are you not going to try the drink? You will not find a better mead in Somersetshire."

Wilton sampled the drink and found its sweetness pleasing. He said, half humorously, "I will have to learn things all over again, customs, ways of life, even ways of speaking for my words must show a trace of the language of the Danes."

Before the girl could answer, Ethelred came back into the room. He frowned at his daughter; looked suspiciously at Wilton. "I will show you to a room," he said abruptly. "Tonight we will talk about arranging to send you to see King Alfred."

DURING the remainder of the afternoon, Wilton waited impatiently in the room to which Ethelred had taken him. Part of the time he stared out blankly toward the sea, his eyes sweeping the horizon and on those occasions he thought mainly of Hrothgar, the youngest son of Ragnar Lodbrok. Though not so well known in England, Hrothgar was by far the most merciless and the strongest of the brothers. In a way, he was an outcast.

When Guthrum, several years before had laid before him and the other sons of Ragnor Lodbrok his plan for the conquest of England, Hrothgar alone had refused to have any part in it. Conquest, he favored. But he was not pleased with the idea of settling in the country and making it a part of the Danish lands. There was in him a streak of ruthlessness and a love of battle. Quick raids, fighting, pillaging and then escaping with the loot of a place was more to his liking.

Between Wilton and Hrothgar, since boyhood, there had been a bitter antagonism, yet in spite of that, Wilton had elected to go with Hrothgar on his piratical expeditions in preference to accompanying his brothers on a conquest of England.

When he had made that choice, in the back of his mind there had been the notion of leaving Hrothgar and of making his way to the land of his birth, there to take his stand with his own people. But such escape hadn't been easy. Though apparently one of Hrothgar's companions, he had always been closely watched. His first chance to get away had come a week before, coincident with the arrival of a messenger from Guthrum who had brought Hrothgar word from England and an appeal for the type of help dear to Hrothgar's heart.

Recalling that message, Wilton's lips tightened and he knew a sudden impatience to find King Alfred. It was a clever plan which Guthrum had worked out and unless he reached the king, there was a good chance that the plan would work.

One of the slaves finally summoned Wilton to the evening meal and there he met Ethelred's wife and the daughter with whom he had talked that afternoon.

There was little conversation at the meal and as soon as it was over the women left the room. Wilton followed Ethelda with his eyes. She had hardly spoken to him, but once or twice he had looked up from his food to find her eyes fixed on him and her expression, each time, had caused his heart to beat faster.

When the women were gone, Ethelred said, "I tried to see Regnault when I left you this afternoon but he had left the village. He could have taken you to King Alfred."

"Regnault? The man with whom I fought?"

"Yes."

"He was not hurt, then, by his fall."

"No, He was not. I have sent a messenger after him, asking him to return. I expect him at any time."

"Is there no other way to find King Alfred?"

"No other sure way."

Ethelred moved to the door and Wilton followed him. The *ealdorman* lifted his arm, pointed to the forests to the north. "In that direction, somewhere, lies King Alfred's camp. Only those close to him know just where it is. You could never reach it alone. Bands of Danes have tried to find it but without success."

Wilton shrugged, then asked a question which had been bothering him for some time. "Since the Danes have conquered Wessex and all of south England, how is it that they have not bothered you here?"

"They *have* bothered us," Ethelred answered, "but none has been stationed here, permanently. The *jarl* in whose territory this village lies is named Igor and is at Exanceaster. In the north he has great estates. Today, Wilton, the Danes control all of England. The only hope of the Briton lies in King Alfred. He defeated the Danes once, turned them back. But tonight he is a fugitive with only a few loyal followers."

Wilton knew all that to be true. He knew, too, how exacting the Danes could be and how hard must be the lot of the conquered people.

TURNING again into the room, Ethelred related in more detail the story of King Alfred's defeat and the conquest of Wessex and Wilton listened and awaited impatiently the arrival of Regnault.

A sudden knock on the door startled him. Ethelred came to his feet, hurried to the door and opened it. But it wasn't Regnault who stood there. Nor was it Ethelred's messenger. Instead, the man who had knocked was Caedmon, the smith. There was a bright look in Caedmon's eyes and his body was trembling.

"The stranger? Is he here?" Caedmon gasped.

Ethelred nodded. "What is it, Caedmon?"

"The axe is finished," Caedmon answered. "It was finished only a moment ago and as I was about to turn away from my work I had another vision. A bright light shone suddenly from the twelve jewels in the axe, a light as red as blood. And from the light a voice spoke to me."

Wilton had joined the *ealdorman* at the door. He felt strangely excited. "What did the voice say?" he heard himself whispering.

Caedmon looked at him. "The voice said first, 'Find the stranger who is at Ethelred's house. Say to him that *Bretwalda* is ready.'"

Wilton heard Ethelred gasp. "Was there more?" he asked.

Caedmon nodded. "The voice added, 'But warn him that to him who holds *Bretwalda* will come great sorrow and great joy, great victory and great defeat.' That was all. The voice said no more."

Ethelred turned to Wilton. In a low, husky tone he whispered, "Then it is for you. The axe is for you."

Wilton shook his head. Deep in his heart he had the feeling that Ethelred might be right, but he wasn't sure. He was aware of a tingling sensation in his arm as though even now it were feeling the weight of the axe.

Caedmon turned and stumbled away. And Wilton, drawing a deep breath, swung to face the ealdorman. "I would like to think that *Bretwalda* had been made for me," he said slowly. "But right now one other thing is more important. I must see King Alfred."

Ethelred looked at him curiously. "Aye, King Alfred," he nodded. "And you will see him if it is his will."

CHAPTER III

THE NIGHT MOVED slowly on while Wilton waited impatiently in his room. Ethelred had left the house to see why no word had come from Regnault; but something in the *ealdorman's* attitude caused Wilton grave concern.

A knock on the door startled him and he went to open it. Ethelda stood outside. She was wearing a gown of some dark material and he could hardly see the outline of her body. Her features were a vague blur.

Surprised, Wilton only murmured her name and stood gaping at her foolishly.

The girl moved a step into his room. In a voice hardly above a whisper she said suddenly, "You must get away from here. At once."

"Away from here?" Wilton gasped.

Ethelda nodded. "Every man in the village has heard of Caedmon's vision. Some still think that you are a Dane. Others, though granting that you are no Dane, think that it is your plan to kill the king. Caedmon's vision has strengthened that belief. The axe is named *Bretwalda* and that name means *Ruler of Briton*."

"But why must I leave?"

"Because there are in this village many men still loyal to King Alfred. It is their plan, as soon as Regnault returns, to have him lead you to a certain place in the forest where they will lie in wait. Strong though you may be, against so many you would have no chance."

Wilton swiftly considered the girl's words. He could understand how news of Caedmon's vision would have alarmed the loyal supporters of the king. Thinking that the axe was for him, knowing the meaning of its name, and already suspicious of

him, it would have been easy for them to assume that it was
his plan to kill King Alfred and take Alfred's place.

He nodded his head slowly. "Yes, I must get away from here.
But I must also get to the king. There is no more time to be
lost."

"But why? Surely—"

Wilton laid a hand on the girl's arm. "I know this much
already," he told her swiftly. "King Alfred is hidden somewhere
in Somersetshire forest. The exact place is in the center of a bog
formed by the junction of the Tone and Parrett rivers. There,
on some firm ground, he has built up a fortification, but his
greater safety lies in the fact that the paths across the bog are
treacherous and are unknown to any but his trusted companions.
The name of this place is Aethelingaeigg. It is north from here,
I know. Could you tell me how I might come to that place
quickly?"

For just a moment the girl hesitated, then she answered, "I
cannot tell you but I can show you the way."

"You trust me so much?"

Ethelda nodded. "Wait here a moment," she whispered, and
hurried away.

The girl was back a moment later and over her arm was some
clothing. She carried, also, a plain, unadorned, helmet.

"Change your clothing for this," she suggested. "It is the garb
of a Briton and while it will not serve as a disguise, it will at
least, not draw so much attention as the clothing you are
wearing. This clothing is my brother's. He is now with the king."

Wilton changed quickly in the darkness of the room and a
moment later joined the girl in the hallway. Her hand was cool
on his arm. "Guards have been placed around the house," she
whispered. "I will try to draw them off. Wait at the door for a
moment, then slip outside. I will meet you beyond Caedmon's
forge."

The girl's tone did not betray any unusual excitement. Her
hand slipped from Wilton's arm and she was gone.

Wilton waited. He heard, suddenly, a great commotion from behind the house, shouting, the trample of feet. Opening the front door, he stepped outside. A dozen swift paces took him to the road. Suddenly a vague figure loomed up before him and a voice commanded that he halt. Moonlight glistened on the naked blade of a sword.

Wilton backed away, his hand reaching for his own weapon. He jerked it free of the scabbard, lifted it to meet the blade of the man blocking his way. Twice did he fend off a slash from the guard and once did he strike on his own account. That blow of his, delivered with all the strength of his body, smashed the sword from the guard's hand.

Voices sounded from behind him and Wilton realized suddenly that others must have heard. He half turned to meet those who were coming to their comrade's aid; then, recalling the necessity that he reach King Alfred quickly, he changed his mind and fled down the road.

There were men at Caedmon's forge, men who were standing around the great axe, staring at it in wonder. An almost irresistible impulse came over Wilton to turn aside and shoulder the axe but with an effort he put it aside. Beyond the forge he waited in the darkness.

Ethelda found him there a few moments later. The girl was breathless and her black hair had come unloosened and hung down almost to her waist. "You got away," she gasped. "I was afraid—"

"Yes, I got away," Wilton replied.

The girl turned into the forest and Wilton followed her.

WILTON was never to forget that journey by night through the green hills of England. Sometimes, in the years to come, a curious, undefinable scent was to bring it rushing back to his memory and always, the soft murmur of rustling leaves was to give him a strange, tingling sensation. Somehow or other, as they hurried through the forest and across meadows and streams and over little knolls, he came to identify himself so closely with this countryside that he almost forgot that he had been a stranger to it for most of his life. Twice he said to the girl, "Stop for a moment." And when she inquired the reason, his only answer was, "I just wanted to look around."

He was to remember the dawn, too, the sun coming up in the east and slanting its rays down through the budding trees while he and the girl rested.

"It's Easter morn," she said to him soberly.

"Easter morn?" Wilton asked.

"Yes. On this day did Christ arise from the dead."

Wilton flushed. His memory of the religion of his people was dim and shadowy in his mind. The Norsemen worshiped Thor and Odin and a whole family of legendary gods.

"Tell me of Christ," he said to the girl. And while she told the story, he listened. Once his hand slipped to his sword. Through a leafy bush his keen eyes had caught sight of a man's face, a dirty, bearded face. But the man withdrew and didn't bother them.

When she was done, he stood up. "We must go on," he said abruptly.

The girl nodded, got to her feet. If she was tired she gave no sign of it but moved ahead rapidly on the trail.

IT WAS about an hour later that the girl suddenly stopped and Wilton heard her call out, "Ethelnoth! Ethelnoth!"

Moving up beside her he saw a tall, dark-featured man standing in the trail some dozen paces ahead. "He is my brother," said the girl swiftly, and then hurrying on, she cried. "Where is the king, Ethelnoth? I have brought a messenger."

Ethelnoth bore a marked resemblance to his father. He was broad of shoulder, long of arm. And his dark eyes shifted from his sister to Wilton, angrily.

Ethelnoth stepped forward. "The king," he said abruptly, "has gone to our village. There is a certain axe there which he would like to examine."

Wilton scowled. "You mean he has gone to the village which we have just left?"

Ethelnoth nodded.

Stepping forward, Wilton said swiftly, "Then we must go after him. There could be no more dangerous place for him than there."

Ethelnoth put his arm around his sister, drew her aside. And then suddenly arising from behind sheltering bushes, a dozen armed men circled Wilton. Wilton heard Ethelda gasp, saw her turn to her brother and start speaking rapidly to him. He saw Regnault step from behind a tree and move toward him, a bared sword in his hand. There was a stubborn determination in the man's face. Angry lights showed in his eyes.

For a moment Wilton didn't move. What had happened he could easily guess. Word of his escape had reached these men and also word had come to them of Caedmon's vision. King Alfred, hearing of the axe, had started for the village to see it. These men, sure that he planned the death of the king, had waited here to trap him.

As Regnault moved forward, Wilton realized that nothing but the truth would sound real enough to these men to make them forget their suspicions. He lifted both hands up before him, empty and palms out. "Wait," he said sharply. "Let me tell you why I have come to see the king. Has it never occurred to you that it is strange that Guthrum sits idly at Ethandun while Alfred, his enemy, roams this forest at will and plots against him?"

Regnault paused, frowning, and one or two of the other men looked suddenly interested.

"I will tell you why Guthrum has done nothing," Wilton continued. "I will tell you what I came here to tell King Alfred. Off the shore of England, just beyond the horizon, lies the fleet of Hrothgar, brother of Ivar Boneless, Hubba and Halvdan. Spies sent out by Guthrum brought him maps of the way to this place but Guthrum knows that your own spies watch his every move and he sent the map to Hrothgar. A great storm which damaged some of Hrothgar's ships has delayed him but soon now, tonight perhaps, his men will land and will sweep this way. They think to find you unprepared. That is what I would have told the king. That is why you must go after him."

For a moment, Wilton thought that his story had convinced these men. He could see a puzzled indecision in their eyes. Then he heard a short laugh from Regnault and heard Regnault say, "A good story, Vandal, but there is no need to hurry after the king. Were all the Danes in Wessex in yonder village, they could never find him. Dressed as a minstrel, our king not long ago visited Guthrum's camp, was even entertained by Guthrum himself. Disguised as a swineherd he has traveled from one end of Wessex to another. Though your story were true, we would not need to fear for him."

Others of the men nodded and Regnault moved even closer to Wilton. Under other circumstances, perhaps, his better judgment would have overridden his suspicions of Wilton; but there was, Wilton could see, a deep pride in the man and his defeat the day before must have rankled bitterly in his heart.

"Do you wear that sword only as an ornament?" he asked sharply.

WILTON'S hand dropped to the weapon at his side. Despite the faith these men had in their king's ability to escape detection, Wilton knew what Hrothgar and his men were like when once unleashed on a community. Guthrum had promised him, as an inducement, whatever slaves and booty he could carry away and Hrothgar was a thorough worker. In Alfred, Wilton knew, rested the only hopes of England. Alfred was a capable ruler. He was well liked, popular. Every report which had come to him about the king had led him to that belief; and he knew, now, that regardless of what these men thought, it was his responsibility to warn the king of Hrothgar's plan.

He gave no warning of his intent.

At one moment he stood silently in front of Regnault, in

another he had bared his sword and had leapt forward. It flashed up and down, knocking away the weapon which Regnault held and staggering him to his knees.

Another of the men rushed forward and Wilton's sword struck down again. He whirled, swinging the sword around with him. His feet were as the feet of a deer. Rushing first one way and then another, he engaged half a dozen men at once. It was broad and double-edged, this sword which Ragnor Lodbrok had given him, and it was heavy and sharp. The arm which wielded it was like iron. Men gave way before him or went down.

A shout rose to Wilton's throat, a shout which he could not hold back. Out of the corner of his eye he caught sight of Ethelda. Pale-faced, she was clinging to her brother's arm, holding him back from the fight. And then above the cries of all others he heard her voice calling, "Go, Wilton. Go to the king."

Wilton whirled around. There was but one man behind him. He ran toward him but the man fled out of his way, and Wilton continued—back over the way which he and the girl had come.

He was unmarked from the fight. His very quickness had taken the men by surprise. Another time he might not have come off so luckily. He realized that, as he ran along the trail. He realized, too, that those men would follow him but that fact bothered him not at all. Once he could reach King Alfred and talk to him, his mission was over. After that, what happened to him mattered little one way or another. He would have struck his blow for England.

The sun reached its zenith and started down the western sky. Shadows lengthened. How far he had to go, Wilton wasn't sure. But suddenly he topped a little hill and staring south his eyes caught sight of the sea. At first he saw nothing more. Then, just as he was about to move on, the top of a square sail caught his attention. For a long moment Wilton stared toward that sail and as clearly as though he had been six paces away, he knew the ship.

It was the ship of Hrothgar. The Danes were moving in from the sea.

Wilton was never afterward sure whether he really heard the voice or only imagined it, but whichever the case may have been, three words went singing across his mind: "*Bretwalda* is ready."

He straightened, drew a deep breath, opened and closed his hands. Already, it seemed to him, he could feel the weight of the great axe. With a grim smile he hurried onward.

CHAPTER IV

IT WAS FARTHER to the village than Wilton had supposed and long before he reached it, darkness had crowded down from the sky, thickening the shadows of the forest. Twice he lost his way and blundered into thickly wooded places where passage was almost impossible. He had hoped, shortly after sighting the distant square sail of Hrothgar's ship, to reach the village before the Norsemen could disembark; but a shaft of light, reaching up into the sky just ahead of him, made him realize that Hrothgar had already landed. For Wilton knew what that light meant.

Always, when raiding a town, one of Hrothgar's first measures was to set some building afire. It accomplished two purposes. It helped strike fear into the people of the village and it gave the Vandals light by which they could continue their work of destruction.

Shortly after sighting that light the faint, distant sounds of battle came to his ears, hoarse shouts, weird screams, the clamor of sword against shield.

Wilton ran faster, down the trail through the forest. By the sounds which came to him he could measure the course of battle. For a few moments it raged fiercely, then the sounds, though louder, took on a thinning note and he knew that the defense was broken. The light from the burning building was now directly ahead of him and its flames were visible through the branches of the trees. Suddenly, a little to one side, he could make out the shape of Caedmon's forge and a moment later he came to a spot from which he could see into the main part of the village and beyond it, to the harbor.

Hrothgar's *dreka*, or dragon ship, was anchored close to the crude pier which stretched out into the bay, and around it were the other ships of his fleet, fully thirty of them. More than a thousand fighting men were carried on those ships, more than a thousand chosen warriors who followed Hrothgar's example with a ferocity that knew no bonds. From several of the ships, men were still landing but most of the Vandals were already on shore and as Wilton paused far just a moment breathing deeply, he saw flames lick up the sides of several more buildings and he heard the clarion sound of Hrothgar's horn as the chieftain blew it, summoning his men to general assembly. That meant, Wilton knew, that the resistance in the village was indeed at an end.

The leaping flames threw the picture before him into a strange relief. Here and there he could see raving groups of the Danes turning in and out of the houses. Bared swords were in their hands. Where there was any kind of resistance at all, those swords were put to immediate use. But the men, women and children who did not resist were being herded into the center of the village, for Hrothgar was a canny man and in his fleet he numbered three *kjolls*—high, broad ships with halfdecks in the prow and stern. In the undecked middle part of these ships he would load his captives, later to sell them into slavery in some Gothic or Mediterranean port.

All that picture, Wilton's eyes caught during the moment of his pause at the edge of the forest. He saw here and there the silent, motionless figures of those who had been slain and his thoughts turned to King Alfred. There was a chance, he knew, that the king might not have reached this village, or that it he had, there was a chance that he might have escaped slaughter or capture. But it was up to him to discover just what had happened and with that in mind, Wilton hurried on toward Caedmon's forge.

NEAR it, the body of a man lay across the trail and as Wilton was about to pass, the man moved, made an attempt to drag himself onward. The movement caught Wilton's eye and something familiar in the figure made him pause. He saw then, that the man was Ethelred, the *ealdorman*, wounded near to death.

Bending over him he called the *ealdorman*'s name and turned him so that he could look into his face. "Where is King Alfred?" he demanded.

Ethelred stared up it him blankly.

"It was because I knew of this raid that I wanted to see the king," Wilton said swiftly. "I knew that it would come soon but not so soon as this or I would have warned you, too. In he forest I learned that the king had started for this village. Where is he?"

Ethelred's lips moved and bending closely over him, Wilton heard him say: "He was taken captive with others—here near the forge. I tried to get away. I wanted to bring help. I thought—"

"How shall I know him?"

"He is clothed as a swineherd. There is a bit of red on his hat. His staff—"

Ethelred's voice choked. His eyes glazed. A tremor ran over his body and then he was still.

Standing, Wilton looked toward the center of the village. There, in a group, the captives had been gathered. They were under heavy guard. Soon they would be transferred to a ship, and then all hope of rescue would be past.

Hrothgar's horn sounded again; near the place where the captives had been herded, the Vandals were gathering, bearing armloads of loot, rich tapestries, heavy boxes, a miscellany of things which had caught their fancy.

Wilton moved on to the forge. The huge axe Caedmon had fashioned still lay on the block of iron. It had either remained unnoticed thus far in the raid or had proved to be too heavy to be moved. For a moment Wilton stared at it, at the curious carvings on the handle, at the twelve blood-red jewels set deep in the head, at the engraven name *Bretwalda*. Then, as naturally as though the axe had always been his he reached out his hands and took hold of it.

CLOSE behind him sounded an angry shout and to his ears came the shuffling of feet. Wilton whirled around. A group of Norsemen were hurrying forward. Grim, black-visaged men. In their eyes was a wolfish light, and blood dripped from the swords in their hands.

Wilton was unaware of the great weight of the axe as he swung it above his head and sprang forward. He did not hear the shout which burst from his own lips. But he saw the first bite of the axe, saw three of the figures which were before him go down under its swing. Again he swung it aloft and again he sprang toward the Norsemen. They gave way before his charge. Swords were as straw before *Bretwalda*'s keen edge; armor was little more protection than cloth. The Norsemen broke and fled.

Lowering the axe, Wilton stared after them. He saw others join the fleeing group, saw them slow down, look back; saw them stop and saw still more men join them.

A rush of footsteps from the forest behind caused him to turn. Coming his way, breathless with their haste, were Regnault and Ethelnoth and a score more Britons.

He gave them no time to speak. "Men of Wessex," he shouted, "your king is a captive of yonder Vandals. Which of you will follow to his aid?"

The road through the village was black with Norsemen and more were coming up from the shore. For all that any of the Britons might see, only a quick death lay ahead for them if they followed Wilton.

Yet, with scarcely any hesitation at all, Ethelnoth and Regnault stepped forward to Wilton's side and following after them, came the others.

Wilton jerked around to face the Vandals. The thought came to him that this one moment was worth all the bitterness of the past. Here he stood on English soil and at his back were a group of Britons ready to follow his lead. Raising *Bretwalda* aloft his voice sang out, "For Alfred and for country!"

Regnault and Ethelnoth took up the cry and charged after him as Wilton ran forward. Other Britons hurried abreast of them. Not a single man in that group knew that they were making history this night, not a man of them could have known that this fight of theirs was, in the years yet ahead, to be made the topic of many a minstrel's lay. Wilton had one thing only in his mind and that was that if they could make this attack threatening enough, King Alfred might possibly escape.

ONCE more the clash of arms sounded above the crackling of the flames from the burning building.

Norsemen blocked the road but a V-shaped wedge cut into the heart of the Vandals. At the head of that wedge, *Bretwalda* slashed the way, driven by Wilton's powerful arms. Strength seemed to flow into him from the handle of the axe. And with each sweeping blow his shout sounded above the din of the battle.

Somewhere or other he had lost his helmet and his yellowish hair, bronze-tinted by the fire, streamed to his shoulders. To the right and left of him, Regnault and Ethelnoth were striking mighty blows; Regnault, grim-lipped and scowling, Ethelnoth grunting with deep satisfaction every time his sword cut through a shield or struck sparks from a helmet.

Through that mass of men, more quickly than he had ever dreamed possible, Wilton and the Britons cut their way. Over to one side stood the chieftain Hrothgar, his horn now silent, a heavy scowl on his ugly face. Beyond him the prisoners were huddled in a group, still closely guarded. Those guards had started away, drawn by the fight in the street, but Hrothgar had ordered them back. Wilton had seen as much but a few moments before.

Turning now toward Hrothgar, Wilton shouted his name and pressed forward, *Bretwalda* clearing a path before him.

Hrothgar stood before a low roofed building. He might have waited there to meet Wilton but the press of men giving way before the Britons gave him no chance. He was swept to one side.

Wilton turned again as an angry chorus of voices arose from behind him. A new group of warriors, he saw at once, had charged into the fray. Under their assault, first one and then another Briton gave way. At his side, Ethelnoth staggered and Regnault was puffing heavily from his exertions.

Swinging *Bretwalda* aloft, Wilton shouted, "Back, Regnault! Back Ethelnoth! Against the building. The rest of you, too."

From every side at once the Danes seemed to be charging forward. The edge of a sword gashed Wilton in the scalp and a spear cut into his thigh. He laughed mockingly at the two men who had succeeded in wounding him, and with *Bretwalda* ended their lives at almost the same instant. That great axe of Caedmon's became as an armor around him and again the rush of the Vandals stopped.

Hrothgar's bull voice arose above the cries of the wounded and the angry shouts of the Norsemen; at his command, the Norsemen backed away, lowering their swords. Wilton shot a look behind him. Grouped against the building were five of the Britons. Some were sorely wounded but no fear showed in any man's eyes. Wilton lowered his axe and with one hand pushed his hair back from his face. Its natural yellow was now streaked with blood, and crimson from his wound stained his face and the shirt which Ethelda had brought him to wear over his coat of mail.

Leaning heavily on *Bretwalda*, Wilton stared around at the men facing him. They had not quit, he knew. They were not of a type to quit. They had drawn back only because Hrothgar had ordered it, and knowing Hrothgar, Wilton knew what to expect. Hrothgar might have let his men continue the fight, it could not have lasted much longer. But since he had stopped it, Wilton knew that some devilish plan had entered the man's mind

He waited grimly to learn what it was. Behind him he could hear the heavy breathing of the Britons and over to the side he could see the prisoners. A deep scowl came to his face. Several men were dragging a girl forward to be added to those under guard. The girl was tall and had long black hair and as her face turned his way Wilton recognized Ethelda. She must have followed the men back here to the village, arriving almost as quickly as they. And now she was in Hrothgar's power.

Still looking over toward the prisoners Wilton's eyes suddenly were attracted to the stooped figure of one man, dressed in ragged clothing. He carried a staff and in his battered hat there was a bit of red cloth. Ethelred's dying words came back to Wilton's mind. Instinctively he straightened. That stooped figure, he knew, could be none other than King Alfred—his king.

Hrothgar's voice cut sharply across his consciousness and turning back, Wilton faced his old enemy.

CHAPTER V

IN MANY WAYS, Hrothgar and Wilton were much alike. Both were tall, and if Wilton had a slight advantage in height, Hrothgar's shoulders were more broad. A golden helmet worked into the figure of a raven covered the Vandal chieftain's head, and a gold rim circled his leather-covered shield.

Moving forward Hrothgar said sharply, "I once pledged my father never to lift my hand against you. Tonight, however, if Ragnar Lodbrok were here he would be the first to bid me fight. Wilton, make ready."

With the suddenness of a striking serpent, Hrothgar's sword slashed through the air. So quick a blow might have caught another man unprepared despite the warning. Wilton, however, sprang backward and laughed. With the same movement he raised Caedmon's axe and brought it down. Hrothgar's shield raised to meet the blow but *Bretwalda* bit through it as though it had been paper. The tip of the axe cut the Vandal's arm to the bone.

A gasp of astonishment went up from the men crowding around. None had a shield so fine as Hrothgar's. It had withstood many a stout blow, yet before the axe in Wilton's hand it had been of no avail.

The two parts of the shield fell uselessly to the ground as Hrothgar released his hold. A startled look came into his eyes, a look which might have been the mirror of fear. Again his sword swept up and down. Legion were the men who had fallen before that sword of his and before the might of his arm still, in mid-air *Bretwalda* met that swinging steel and the sword broke in two, half of it flying over Wilton's shoulder and falling to the ground at Regnault's feet.

Wilton's laugh had a deep, mocking note. He took a step forward and raised the axe again. For a moment he held it poised high above his head. He could bring it down before Hrothgar could manage to get out of the way. And Hrothgar knew it. In the Vandal's eyes, Wilton could read that knowledge. Wilton moved forward again, as though to make the blow more sure. But he did not strike. Instead, his voice rasping harshly, he commanded, "Hrothgar, order the guards to turn the prisoners free."

Hrothgar straightened. There was a cunning look in his eyes. He shook his head. "I have no fear of death, Wilton. Hrothgar listens to the command of no other man."

Wilton still hesitated. If he killed Hrothgar, all was lost. Against so many enemies he had no chance. It would be merely a matter of time until they cut him down.

Then Hrothgar spoke again and the cunning of the man was clearly shown by his words. No one had ever before vanquished him in battle and his hate for Wilton sought some deeper satisfaction than Wilton's death.

"I would make a bargain with you, Wilton," he said clearly. "If you think so much of these miserable prisoners, I will let them go in exchange for you and for your pledge to take their place."

Wilton blinked at the man standing before him. He well knew what was back of that offer. Should he agree to it he need have no fear of death. Hrothgar would take an insane delight in selling him into servitude in some foreign port or perhaps an even greater delight in placing him with the slaves in the Norsemen's country. He could hold to no thoughts of escape, either, for Hrothgar would see to it that he would never again have a chance to escape.

Wilton lowered *Bretwalda* and moved a step backward. There was no point, now, in holding the axe over Hrothgar's head.

He could see that the thought of the exchange had gripped the Vandal's imagination and he knew even then what his answer would be.

"These men who fought with me, too?" he asked bluntly.

Hrothgar nodded. "Those too."

Turning his head, Wilton glanced at the prisoners. The stooped figure with the bit of red in his hat was looking at him and for just a moment, Wilton stared into the face of his king. There were kindly lines around the man's mouth, yet his face was stern and there was a square, stubborn ruggedness about it which made Wilton feel the worth of the man's character. England would be safe under the rule of such a man, he thought, and as he stared at him, Wilton had the feeling that someday King Alfred would triumph over his foes; that some day again, all of southern England would be freed from the yoke of the Dane.

"Well, how about it, Wilton?" Hrothgar asked.

Wilton turned his eyes away from the prisoners. "Release them," he commanded. "You have my pledge."

SITTING on a box in the space between the two halfdecks on one of Hrothgar's merchant ships, Wilton watched the dawn of another day. His wounds troubled him sorely and a great weariness had settled over him.

From time to time he smiled; and had he been asked, on such occasions, why he smiled, he might have told the story of the releasing of the prisoners. For Hrothgar had kept his word and had let them go; and King Alfred was safe. In spite of the greatest odds, Wilton had struck a blow for England that was to change the course of history. For, a short time later, King Alfred was to meet with the men of Somersetshire, Hampshire and Wiltshire and was to lead them to a great victory over the Danes at Ethandun, a complete triumph that which was to free the south of England from the invader.

Wilton couldn't have known that but he must have felt it deep in his soul for he had no regrets for the course he had taken. And now, as the first rays of the morning sun reached down into the ship and touched him, he turned his glance toward Caedmon's axe. He had brought it with him when he had been taken to the ship, hardly conscious of the fact that he carried it. What use he would find for it in the life which lay ahead for him he didn't know. But his eyes brightened as he looked at the axe and he got up and walking over to where it leaned against the side of the ship, he rested his hand against it.

The sound of voices caught his attention and glancing toward the stern of the vessel he saw a figure being lowered to the space between decks. At the first sight of that figure Wilton thought that he must be dreaming for it looked like Ethelda, the daughter of the *ealdorman*. A moment later he saw that it was she, for casting off the ropes by which she had been lowered, the girl moved toward him. Her cheeks were slightly flushed.

Wilton stared at her first in amazement, then with a sudden anger, directed not toward the girl but toward Hrothgar.

"You were with the prisoners," he said sharply. "You were to have been released. How came you here?"

The flush on the girl's cheeks deepened but she looked directly into Wilton's eyes. "I am here because I chose to come," she answered, "because I asked to come."

Wilton's astonishment deepened. "You asked to come? You know what it means?"

The girl shook her head. "Perhaps. I am not sure. But with you I will not be afraid."

ETHELDA laid a hand on Wilton's arm and Wilton found himself trembling. He had felt a strange compulsion drawing him to this girl since the first moment when he had seen her. Deep in the forest the day before he had felt very close to her, and the same feeling of closeness gripped him now.

"The axe—you have it with you," the girl said suddenly.

Wilton nodded.

"Do you remember the warning which came to Caedmon and which he brought to you?"

Again Wilton nodded. "He told me that to the man who held *Bretwalda* would come a great victory—"

"You saved your king."

"—and a great defeat—"

"You have sacrificed your liberty."

"—a great sorrow—"

"Never again to live in the England you love."

"—and a great joy."

The girl was silent for a moment, then looking up at Wilton she said, "I cannot answer that promise but perhaps together we can find the answer—even if we are together for only as long as the voyage may last."

Wilton drew a deep breath. What other woman, he wondered, would have followed a man along the road which lay ahead for him. He reached out and covered Ethelda's hand with his own. "I know the answer," he replied. "You have brought it with you."

Ethelda's eyes had again dropped to the axe and she suddenly exclaimed. "Look! One of the jewels is gone."

Glancing down, Wilton nodded. Where there had been twelve jewels before there were now only eleven. One had somehow or other been lost during the fight the night before. He thought little of the lost jewel, however. "It is a great axe," he murmured.

Looking at him, Ethelda said, "A weapon for a man."

Wilton smiled and again his hand rested against it. He stared out to the north. Ethelda was still watching him. There was nothing of the look of a captive or the look of a slave or of a defeated man in Wilton's eyes and she knew suddenly that there never would be. No matter what might lie ahead for them, Wilton would always rise above any defeat.

The girl smiled and turned and stared with him to the north.

II

VANDAL

Storm clouds over Norway, for a kingdom stands in jeopardy. But jarl and churl alike, take warning! A slave's son has grasped the mystic axe Bretwalda—and he holds all the warrior strength of a nation in his hands.

CHAPTER I

FROM A FOREST clearing not far from the great hall of Jarl Lodvessen and close to the Trondelogan road there came a sound of steel clashing on steel and the murmur of men's voices, now sharp and commanding now caustic or in laughter.

Rolv Haarfagre, one of the younger sons of King Harold of Norway, reined up his horse and glanced at his sister.

"I wonder what that means," he said frowning. "Surely men do not laugh if the battle is serious."

Sigrid Haarfagre looked toward the sound of the clashing steel. She was tall and fair haired, and she sat on her horse with ease of one much accustomed to riding. A white mantle, embroidered in scarlet and gold, was fastened at her throat. Beneath it there was a coat of mail and at her side she wore a sword.

"We might go and see what it is, Rolv," she suggested. "The fighters cannot be many for I hear only two voices."

Rolv Haarfagre glanced back over the Trondelogan road. Far in the distance he could see a cloud of dust which marked the approach of his father's retinue and after a moment's hesitation he nodded.

Sigrid swung to the ground. She tied her horse to a tree at the edge of the road and then turned toward the sounds coming from the forest. Only a few paces from the road she came to a clearing in the forest and from behind the shelter of a bush she looked out at two men, engaged in a duel with great, double-edged swords.

"What is it?" whispered Rolv, moving up to her side.

"Look!" answered Sigrid. "Perhaps it is not serious, but never did I see two men fight with such earnestness and call it play."

In the forest clearing, two tall, broad-shouldered men protected only by coats of mail, belabored each other with flashing swords, slashing, parrying, stabbing, now and then rushing to the attack or falling back in a desperate defense. And as they fought, one of the men, the elder of the two, kept calling advice to the other one.

"Faster there, Alfred," he would cry. "Move your feet. Keep moving your feet. Dance! Dance! And throw less weight on the lunge. Even in your attack you must defend yourself. Watch now for your head."

With great slashing strokes, the older man cut at the head of the youth. How those blows were parried, Sigrid couldn't see, yet in some way or other the younger man turned them aside and then with a bewildering burst of speed, charged at his antagonist.

But the older man, too, blocked the attack and despite the fury of the fight, continued calling out advice.

"Never did I see two such men," breathed Rolv. "I wonder who they can be?"

Sigrid laid a hand on her brother's arm. "Hush. They are stopping. Perhaps we will find out."

THE YOUNGER man had stepped back and had lowered the point of his sword to the ground. He wiped a hand across his face and then removed the leather band which had held his reddish hair in place. "Never will I be able to stand against you, Father," he said slowly. "No matter where I strike, your blade is in the way. No matter what trick I try, you have it figured out before I can move."

The older man laughed, then stepped forward and dropped an arm around his son's shoulder. He shook his head and said, "Nay, Alfred. Three times, today, I escaped your sword only

As they fought fiercly, the older
man kept calling out advice.

through luck. You are better, lad, than I was at your age. There
is little more that I can teach you."

"Did you bring the axe, Father?"

"Aye, lad."

"You said that some day you would tell me the story of the
axe. Will you tell me today?"

The older mar seemed to hesitate, Then he nodded and said,
"Yes, Alfred. I will get it and tell you the story."

As the older man turned away, his son moved so that Sigrid
could see his face. It was a square, ruddy-colored face. There
was a look of strength about it. The eyes were wide-spaced below
a high forehead. The young man was, Sigrid judged, about
twenty-five.

Sigrid turned to her brother. "Hadn't we better go?" she
whispered.

Rolv shook his head. "No. I want to hear this. Look!'

Sigrid glanced back to the clearing. The older man was
moving forward from a row of trees across the way and over

his shoulder he carried a great axe. Sigrid had never seen such an axe. Both handle and head seemed to be made of steel and the cutting edge was a full six hands broad. Red jewels set in the head of the axe caught light from the sun.

Pausing near his son, the older man lowered the axe to the ground "Lift it, Alfred. Swing it," he suggested.

Alfred reached for the handle of the axe. The muscles in his arms corded like rope, perspiration stood out on his forehead. He lifted the axe shoulder high, lifted it until it was even with his head but he could get it no higher though his face and neck were crimson from the effort.

The older man smiled. He reached for the axe and, handling it as easily as though it were made of wood, he swung it through the air, cutting at imaginary enemies.

Then lowering the axe again to the ground, he said slowly, "You are stronger than I, Alfred, yet you cannot swing *Bretwalda*. However, do not be impatient. The strength to swing *Bretwalda* comes not from the arm and shoulder but from the axe itself. If the time ever comes for you to use it, do not hesitate."

Alfred sank down on the ground. "The name of the axe, *Bretwalda*. What does it mean?"

"*Bretwalda* means *Ruler of Briton*," replied the older man, sitting down near his son. "The axe was forged by a man named Caedmon. The name was burned into it in his forge as were the jewels in the head of the axe. There were once twelve jewels but one was lost in the fight near Athelney in England."

"When you saved the life of Alfred, the King of England?"

"Aye, lad. The man for whom you are named. For you are a Briton. Never forget that. And some day, son, I want you to return to England and to take *Bretwalda* with you."

For a while the two men were silent and Rolv whispered to Sigrid, "I know him now. The older man is Wilton. He and his wife were brought here many years ago on a slave ship of Hrothgar's."

"Then they are slaves?"

Rolv shook his head. "Wilton did something for our father and was granted his freedom and the right to own land. The young man must be his son. Listen!"

Alfred had reached for the axe and was examining the handle. "What is the meaning of this inscription?" he asked.

"According to Caedmon," said the older man, "it means, *To him who holds Bretwalda will come great sorrow and great joy, great victory and great defeat.*"

"Great sorrow and great joy, great victory and great defeat," Alfred repeated.

The older man nodded.

Though what she had heard fascinated her, Sigrid had the feeling that she was eavesdropping on a conversation sacred to the two men in the clearing, A flush of embarrassment came to her face and she started to back away, but Rolv caught at her arm.

"Look!" he whispered, pointing to the left.

SIGRID glanced that way. A group of armed men was entering the clearing. They were led by a broad-shouldered figure clad in a glistening coat of mail, a figure whose helmet was made of gold and silver, adorned with raven wings, She recognized the man immediately as Jarl Lodvessen, the man who had been appointed by her father to maintain order and collect taxes in this distant part of the realm.

The father and son who had been sitting on the grass had come to their feet and Sigrid saw that the younger man had half drawn his sword. The older man turned toward him and whispered something in his ear. Then he moved forward alone.

Lodvessen and his men had stopped, and as the older man approached him, Sigrid heard the *jarl* say. "We've come for you, Wilton."

"Why?" asked Wilton, quietly.

Lodvessen made no direct answer. To his men he said, "Take him. Bind his arms and watch him closely."

The men who laid hold of Wilton were not gentle about it. They threw him to the ground and knelt about him. Some man produced a rope and started to wind it around his body.

Before Alfred made a move, Sigrid knew what was going to happen. She saw his muscles tighten, saw him spring forward.

A thin, cruel smile showed on Lodvessen's face. He drew his sword and slashed at the charging man. How Alfred evaded that blow Sigrid could never understand, but with one swift movement he twisted aside, and in another moment his own sword flashed in the sunlight.

Lodvessen stepped forward confidently. He struck out twice more, but Alfred had side-stepped again; now he attacked. Lodvessen's sword was torn from his hand by the power of that blow and with a startled cry he backed away.

The men who had been binding Wilton left him and reached for their weapons. Once again steel rang upon steel in that little clearing not far from the Trondelogan road. Only this time the battle was in earnest.

Rolv left his sister's side and hurried forward. "Stop!" he cried. "Stop! In the king's name, I command it!"

Sigrid, too, had moved after her brother, her heart pounding. But it was not fated then that either she or Rolv should engage in the fight. For Jarl Lodvessen recognized them and called his men back.

Alfred lowered his blade and turned to stare at Rolv and Sigrid. His face showed no surprise. Sigrid looked away from him toward Lodvessen who was hurrying forward.

"What is this all about, Lodvessen?" Rolv demanded.

Lodvessen's face darkened. He stared at Wilton who was sitting up, unwinding the rope from his body and then he looked over at Alfred. There was a deep anger in his eyes.

"This man Wilton has refused to pay his taxes," he said bluntly. "And his refusal has encouraged others to refuse to pay theirs. I meant but to bring him to trial."

Rolv nodded. He said, "Jarl Lodvessen, my father and his

court are but a little way behind us. It would be well for you to join them. I will be responsible for these men."

Lodvessen glanced at Sigrid. "I did not expect you so soon, but all is in readiness. As for these men, let them go. I can deal with them later."

Neither Rolv nor Sigrid made any answer. After a moment's hesitation Lodvessen turned to his men and ordered them to follow him to the Trondelogan road.

CHAPTER II

ALFRED, SON OF Wilton the Briton sat on a high cliff overlooking the sea. Far to the left he could see torchlights marking the location of Lodvessen's great hall, and in the bay near it were the vague outlines of some of Lodvessen's ships.

A strange restlessness troubled him, a restlessness which he could not understand. Vaguely he realized that many things were responsible for it. Today, for the first time, he had heard the story of his father's axe and today for the first time he had raised his sword against the sword of another in an engagement which was not just practice. Today, too, the son and daughter of a king had talked to him and to his father and had gone with them to the hut where they lived.

Staring to the south, Alfred's thoughts turned to England. He had never been there, yet he seemed to know England as well as he did this great rugged country where he had been born. One of his earliest recollections was of his father and mother sitting on this cliff and talking of the green forests of Somersetshire, and on many a quiet morning he had heard his mother say, "This is like a morning in England." All his life he had felt that some day he would see this land which his father and mother loved so well. Now, for some reason, he had the feeling that the time was close at hand.

A footstep sounded on the rocks behind him and turning, Alfred caught sight of his father. He could see at once that his father was excited and he asked swiftly, "What has happened? Did Lodvessen—"

Wilton shook his head. "I have seen Harold Haarfagre," he answered. "He has asked that we come to the great hall tonight."

Alfred stood up. "To the great hall?"

"Yes." His father nodded. "What he wanted he did not say. He only asked that I come and that I bring my son."

Alfred's thoughts turned to the girl Sigrid and her brother Rolv, son and daughter of the king, After the trouble in the forest they had gone with him and his father to their hut, ostensibly for a drink of water. Neither one of them had referred to Lodvessen's charge against the Wiltons. Rolv had tried to handle the great axe and had been chagrined when he could barely lift it. The girl had said little, but Alfred had noticed that she seemed quite interested in his father and in the few things his father had said. And he wondered, suddenly, if some report from Rolv or Sigrid was behind this request that he and his father come to the court.

Looking out toward the sea, his father said slowly, "In many ways, son, Harold Haarfagre is a great king. Thirty-five years ago there were many kings in this north country. They bickered and fought among themselves. They outfitted boats and went on raiding expeditions to the English coast. A man's strength was the only law and his only security. Then Harold Haarfagre conquered the other kings one by one, and finally in a great sea battle at Hafrsfjord he overcame the last of their opposition.

"Since then he has tried to weld this country into an empire; he has organized trading expeditions to take place of the former raids, He has been a friend of England and since he has been in power no great Viking raids have been made on the English coast. His road has not been an easy one. Time and again the former kings have revolted, thinking of the old days when the sacking of a town filled their chests with gold and furnished them slaves for their fields."

Alfred nodded. "Was not Jarl Lodvessen once a king?"

"In the Orkneyjar, yes."

"Why should he have tried to bring you to trial, Father? You have paid the taxes as demanded."

Wilton frowned, shook his head. "That I do not know."

"Why has the king come here?"

"One of his daughters, the one we saw, is to be married to Lodvessen. The king is here to celebrate the marriage."

Again, Alfred's mind turned to the girl he had seen that afternoon. The thought of her as the wife of Jarl Lodvessen disturbed him more than he was willing to admit. Lodvessen, he knew, was brutal and despotic; his court was a mockery, for the man had only a cynical contempt for justice.

The gray shadows of night were sweeping in from the sea and a deep haze clung to the distant horizon. Through that haze it seemed to Alfred that he faintly distinguished the broad, square sails of a distant fleet of ships. He leaned forward, straining his eyes against the gathering shadows.

His father touched him on the arm and said, "Come, son. We must not be too late to the court of King Harold."

Alfred nodded, turned away and followed his father along the path away from the cliff.

THE GREAT hall of Jarl Lodvessen was ablaze with lighted torches. On benches around the walls were members of King Harold Haarfagre's court who had come north with him and *jarls* and *hersers* from the surrounding country, The tables before them were piled high with food, and slaves scurried back and forth with steaming platters and huge flagons of wine, In the open space before the tables, *hirdscalds* sang stories of battle and of victory, of valor and of heroic deeds.

In the high seat, midway down the hall, King Harold Haarfagre listened to occasional petitions from various members of the court. His was a tall, imposing figure. He was well past middle age, broad of shoulder and keen of eye. There was a blunt stubbornness in the set of his jaw. One or two of his closest counselors stood at his shoulder and whispered to him from time to time, but he seemed to pay little attention to their words.

In the second high seat, across the room from the king, sat Jarl Lodvessen, occupying that place of honor because this was his territory.

There were a score or more women in the room, most of them women who had come north with the court, wives of various *jarls*. Like Sigrid, many of them wore coats of mail beneath embroidered finery. Their positions were almost as exalted as their husbands' for they accompanied their men in battle and on expeditions across the sea.

Guards stationed at the door stopped Alfred and his father for a moment while a messenger was sent to the king, and as they awaited permission to enter, Alfred was aware of a tingling excitement.

"What do we do when we get inside, Father?" he whispered.

Wilton lowered his great axe to the ground. "We see the king, son. That is all."

Alfred straightened the cloak around his shoulders. It was of blue *baldakin*, a cloth imported from the east. It dropped almost to his heels, hiding the sword sheathed at his side. A leather band around his head held his hair in place.

The guard at the door, apparently having received his orders, stepped away and Alfred followed his father into the hall. His first impression of the great room was rather confused. Near the entrance a *hirdscald* was playing a harp and singing the story of the battle of Hafrsfjord; near him several men were arguing in loud voices. Someone called Alfred's name and turning, he saw Frode Thorfinn. Thorfinn was the captain of a merchant ship. He was a small, heavy-set man with dark, ugly features and long, matted hair. Tonight there was a deep scowl on his face.

Alfred nodded to him and Thorfinn said in an undertone, "I'd like to see you later, Alfred, in the cove of Ljome."

"Tonight?" Alfred asked, surprised.

Thorfinn nodded. He said no more but turned abruptly away.

Alfred wondered what was on the man's mind. The cove of Ljome was several miles to the north. The coast around it was rugged and desolate. Why Thorfinn should have asked him to come there, Alfred couldn't understand. But he had a liking for the surly old sea captain whom he had come to know pretty well. There would be a reason behind that request to meet him, Alfred knew.

Moving up the great hall toward the raised platform before the high seat, Alfred glanced quickly from side to side. Some of the men in the hall he knew. An instant later he saw that Jarl Lodvessen was looking in his direction and that there was a mocking smile on the man's lips. Alfred felt a sudden stab of uneasiness; his hand brushed against the hilt of his sword. Then, turning to look toward the other wall, he caught sight of Sigrid and her brother Rolv.

Sigrid, too, was looking toward him and his father, smiling a little. She had changed her cloak. The one she now wore was of blue and gold and was fastened at the throat with a sparkling, jeweled pin. Alfred instinctively straightened his shoulders. He nodded his head and Sigrid nodded in return.

Then suddenly they were standing on the platform before Harold Haarfagre.

THE KING leaned forward, clapped his hands for silence, and when the *hirdscalds* had stopped their singing and the men in the hall were still, he said in a deep, ringing voice, "Thirty years ago, one of these two men before me was brought here as a slave. When the Vandals led by Solve Kolfe raided this coast, he, a slave, took his axe and fought at my side against them. For that service I granted him his freedom but not the right to return to his home in England.

"Today, however, in recognition of that service and in celebration of the marriage of my daughter, I extend to him and to his family, full freedom and the right to return home if he so desires."

A thunderous applause shook the hall and the king smiled for he knew that gestures like this appealed to his people.

Alfred glanced at his father. It seemed to him that there was a new light in his father's eyes, and he realized that no honor which the king might have conferred would have meant as much as this. Then he heard his father sigh and saw him lift his eyes above the king's head.

"What say you, Wilton?" asked the king.

Alfred's father looked it Harold Haarfagre. He answered slowly, "I am deeply grateful. My only regret is that my wife did not live to see this day."

"She is dead, then, the English woman who was brought here with you?"

"She died two years ago."

There was a sudden commotion at the door. Harold Haarfagre frowned, glanced that way. Quickly the noise grew louder and Alfred swung around. Between where he stood and the doorway he saw men drawing their swords. Then through the doorway there came a throng of men, swords, spears and axes bared and already bloody from the fight outside.

Stepping down from the high seat, Harold Haarfagre cried, "To me! To me!" and the men of his court backed toward him.

Alfred remembered suddenly the fleet of ships he had seen from the cliff that evening, and he recalled his father's telling him that some of the *jarls* were continually rebelling against Harold Haarfagre's rule. These men must be some of those who were dissatisfied.

A tall, white-bearded man with an ugly twisted face seemed to be their leader. His head was thrown back now, for he had caught sight of the king, and, sword lifted, he was shouting "There he is. Take him!"

At his side Alfred heard his father breathe, "Hrothgar," and then before he could move his father was charging forward, swinging his great axe and shouting the man's name.

All over the hall, it seemed to Alfred, fighting had broken

out. Hardly aware of it, he had drawn his own sword. One of the invaders loomed up before him and went down under a slashing cut. Another took his place for a moment, but like his comrade he could not stand up against Alfred's sword.

Then Rolv Haarfagre was standing beside Alfred. The young prince's face was pale, but there was no fear in his eyes.

"Another," he grunted, slashing out with his sword. "And another!"

ALFRED'S eyes sought his father, and the picture of him which he caught that night was to remain etched in his mind. Pressing forward, swinging his great axe *Bretwalda*, Wilton the Briton fought where the battle raged most fiercely. So tall that he stood almost a head higher than any of the other men, his white hair unhelmeted, he seemed the leader now, the warrior king. More and more invaders were pressing into the great hall and in every other place King Harold's men were giving ground. But Wilton still strode forward. The great axe was like a wall of steel around him. Men pressed back, stumbling against each other, to escape its blade. And then, as Alfred watched, his father cut a path through the invaders, so that he was standing before their leader.

"Hrothgar," Wilton cried, "it has been a long time, but I have been waiting."

The tall, dark leader of the invaders stabbed out desperately with his sword but Wilton only laughed and swung *Bretwalda* aloft. It whipped down once and Hrothgar dropped to the floor. Then, almost in that same moment, Alfred caught sight of Lodvessen. Lodvessen stood over at one side of his father, a long spear in his hand. He drew back his arm—and Alfred screamed a warning.

His cry was too late, as it echoed in the great hall he saw Lodvessen's spear sink into his father's back; he saw his father fall to the floor, *Bretwalda* slipping from his hands.

What happened after that was never clear in Alfred's mind. He was never to be able to recall how he fought his way forward to where his father lay. But with Rolv on his one side and a man called Guttorm Hnuva on his other, he reached the body of Wilton the Briton. There he bent down and grasped the axe *Bretwalda*.

He swept it aloft, in his anger unsurprised that *Bretwalda* should seem no longer heavy in his hand. Swinging the great axe, he must have looked to the invaders like the reincarnation of the man who had slain Hrothgar. But Alfred only knew that men backed away from him in terror, and he felt a fierce joy as he drove them on.

Then quite suddenly they had reached the door and were outside. The cool night air cleared Alfred's mind.

Alfred looked at the men near him. A few others had joined Rolv and Guttorm in that drive for the door. He thought of his father lying dead in the great hall and a great bitterness swept over him.

To Rolv, he said, "Your father?"

Rolv shook his head. "He was overcome. Whether he is dead or alive I do not know, but I saw him being dragged away."

"Your sister, Sigrid?"

"Here," answered a low voice.

Alfred glanced that way. Standing with the men he saw Sigrid Haarfagre. Her cloak was gone. Without it, she looked at a casual glance, like one of the other men. A sword was in her hand and there was a bloody gash on her cheek. That she had come through the fight without a more serious injury was amazing.

She stood there, pale and biting at her lips.

Alfred's eyes swept the shadows near the great hall. From the direction of the shore he could hear the shouting of men's voices and could see moving torches. Guttorm and one of the other men stood at the door to the great hall, holding the invaders inside.

Turning to Rolv, Alfred said, "There is nothing to be gained through remaining here. Come. Follow me."

He waited for no answer but started running to the north and Rolv and the others followed him.

CHAPTER III

THE CAVE WAS an hour's journey north of Lodvessen's great hall. To reach it Alfred led the way across the valley and up the rugged side of the plateau and then through the depths of a forest to a place where a narrow fjord reached in from the sea.

It was not a large cave, but it was sufficient to shelter the half-dozen people who followed him. And they needed shelter for a storm was howling in from the sea bringing with it great sheets of rain. Besides, two of the men were seriously wounded.

Alfred built a fire in the mouth of the cave. He doubted that any effective pursuit could be organized until the next day. There was little danger that the fire would be seen.

The injured men lay down on the ground and without a word to anyone Sigrid Haarfagre bathed their wounds in rain water, caught in her brother's helmet. For bandages, Alfred ripped apart his sirk.

As the girl was working, Rolv drew Alfred aside. "We must get word to my brother Erick," he insisted. "Erick is at Trondelogan. He has there a fleet of a hundred ships and many warriors."

Alfred considered the possibility of getting word to Erick. He had never been to Trondelogan, but he knew that it was at least a week's journey to the south. It didn't seem to him that they could count much on Erick's help.

"Who were the men?" he asked Rolv.

Rolv Haarfagre scowled. He said slowly, "The man back of that raid was Solve Kolfe, a Vandal, and my father's greatest enemy. He has never recognized my father as the king and for years be has stirred up rebellions. He must have received word that my father was coming up here to hold court. I did not see Solve in the hall, but some of his men were there."

"And Hrothgar?" Alfred nodded.

"A Vandal and one of Solve's closest friends."

"It was Hrothgar," said Alfred, "who brought my father and mother here as slaves. I have heard the story many a time from my father. Once he had Hrothgar at his mercy but he spared his life to save the life of Alfred, the King of England. Tonight there was nothing to stay my father's hand."

Rolv nodded, his mind apparently busy with other thoughts.

Alfred glanced over toward the great axe which leaned against the wall of the cave. He pictured his father swinging it in battle with his old enemy, and through the sorrow and bitterness which had gripped his mind there came the realization that at least his father had known the final satisfaction of a just revenge.

"How can we get word to Erick?" Rolv insisted.

Alfred frowned and then suddenly he recalled the message Frode Thorfinn, the sea captain, had whispered to him. He did not recall having seen Thorfinn in the great hall when the trouble had started; perhaps he had escaped. It didn't matter now why Thorfinn wanted to see him; but Alfred realized that with the aid of the sea captain they might find a possible escape. Thorfinn might even take them to Trondelogan where Erick's fleet lay.

Turning to Rolv he said quickly, "Remain here. I will be back as soon as I can,"

IT WAS not far to the cove of Ljome, but the storm had increased in fury. It howled with the intensity of a gale. The rain was bitterly cold. Alfred plowed ahead in a stumbling run, now and then pausing for a breathing space in the shelter of a great rock or behind the trunk of a sturdy tree. He came, finally, to the place where a trail led down the side of the cliff and slowly started to descend.

He had a fear, now, that his journey would be for nothing. That Thorfinn would be waiting here seemed ridiculous in view of the storm. Yet, as he reached the foot of the trail and turned to stare out across the beach, he heard the faint sound of his name and a moment later the vague figure of a man left the heavy shadows of a sheltering rock and moved toward him.

"Thorfinn?" Alfred cried.

The old sea captain nodded. Rain had soaked through his hood and was running across his wrinkled face.

"I didn't know whether you would come or not," he shouted.

"You know, then, what happened at the great hall?"

Thorfinn made no answer. He took Alfred's arm and led him toward the shelter of the rocks behind which he had waited. Other men were there, Alfred saw, as he stepped around the rocks. There were a score or more of them, dark, vague figures pressed against the rough boulders, seeking protection against the driving rain.

It seemed quiet here after the open storm. Above them the wind still bowled and from the direction of the sea came the booming roar of the surf. Yet now it was not necessary to shout in order to be heard and Alfred asked again, "You know what happened at the great hall, Thorfinn?"

The sea captain nodded, "I know what happened. I was afraid that it would happen and I had warned the king. He said, however, that the fleet I saw was the fleet of his son Erick."

"Why did you ask me to come here?"

"I thought that you might want to join me. I could use a man like you. Besides, with a man like Solve Kolfe in power in Norway, this country will turn backward a hundred years. He cannot control it as King Harold did. Trade and commerce will be destroyed and once more the Vikings will take to the sea and raid the English coast. I had thought that we might sail to the south and find a new country where we would be welcome. Here there will be no future but death."

"Was the king slain?" Alfred asked.

Thorfinn shook his head. "No, but he might better have been slain. What Solve plans to do with him I do not know. He had King Harold taken aboard his *dreki* ship. Perhaps he plans to hold him for a ransom to be collected from his sons. But even so, Solve Kolfe will never let King Harold out of his hands alive."

"Where is your ship."

"It is beached over yonder across the cove."

"And how many men do you have?"

"Nigh to a hundred. Most of them are under the covering stretched over the ship."

For a moment Alfred was silent, considering all that Thorfinn had told him. A wild, impossible sort of plan had occurred to him. Then suddenly, he asked, "How long will the storm blow, Thorfinn?"

The old sea captain shrugged. "All night, probably all tomorrow."

"And Solve cannot well leave in such a storm?"

"No. But why do you ask?"

"Because," said Alfred, "I have decided to take over his *dreki*."

"What?" Thorfinn gasped.

"I have decided to take over his *dreki*," Alfred repeated.

Thorfinn shook his head, "Solve has more than three thousand men with him. How could you possibly take his *dreki*?"

Alfred leaned forward. He said slowly. "Most of Solve's ships will be beached during the storm, just as yours. When the wind abates it will take some time to launch them. If it is then night, the chances are that Solve will delay his departure until the dawn. His men, unless I misjudge them, will still be celebrating their victory. Four or five men, in the quiet of the night, might easily capture the *dreki* ship if they could reach it without being too much observed. Not many guards will be on the ship."

"But how would you reach it?" Thorfinn asked, still shaking his head.

"You will take me there. You can sail into the harbor and close past the ship."

"But—"

Alfred settled down to argue his plan, working out the details as Thorfinn brought up new objections.

IT WAS dawn before Alfred returned to the cave. A worried, anxious Rolv met him at the entrance. "I had begun to think you weren't coming back." Rolv greeted him.

Alfred ducked inside. The fire was out and over to one side he could see the figure of Sigrid. She was lying on her back, sound asleep. One of the wounded men was muttering feverishly. The other was silent. Guttorm was bending over the man who was muttering.

"How are they?" Alfred asked.

"One has died," Rolv answered in a low voice. "For the other there is little hope."

Removing his clothing, Alfred rubbed his body until his skin glowed. He wrung out the garments, waved them in the air, wondering how he could dry them without a fire, and at last put them back on. Then he told Rolv and Guttorm, who had joined them, of his talk with Thorfinn. Rolv's shoulders straightened at word that his father still lived and his eyes glowed when Alfred outlined his plans for rescuing him.

"Once we have overcome the guards," Alfred finished, "we will let the *dreki* drift out toward the sea. When the movement is discovered we will put up the sail and run for it. With luck we will succeed."

A deep laugh shook the sturdy body of Guttorm Hnuva. He was a middle-aged man with a wide scar on his cheek. Short and a little stooped, he was almost repellently ugly; but within him there was a deep loyalty to Harold Haarfagre. He said now, "Whether we succeed or not, the plan is worth trying. Briton, you have a head on those wide shoulders."

For a while the three men discussed the plan, then moving over to the side of the cave, Alfred lay down. He didn't think that he would be able to close his eyes but almost at once he fell into a deep sleep.

WHEN he awoke, Sigrid was sitting near him, looking at him with a strange, contemplative gaze. Alfred blinked, sat up. His muscles ached and he felt hungry and thirsty. As though anticipating his needs, Sigrid held out Rolv's helmet. "Rainwater," she said. Then as he took it she reached behind her and brought forth a sack made of cloth. From it she took a double handful of wild berries.

"They are bitter, a little," she remarked. "But at least they are something to eat."

Alfred took the berries. "You gathered them?"

Sigrid nodded. The cut in her cheek was inflamed and Alfred knew that the pain from it must be making her miserable. Her hair, which hung almost to her waist, was wet and tangled. Her face was haggard; and yet, he thought, it was still beautiful.

Glancing away from her, he noticed that Rolv and Guttorm were sleeping. He saw nothing of the other two men and asked about them.

"Dead," Sigrid answered. "I did all that I could, but they had lost too much blood. There are now just the four of us."

The girl's last statement stirred Alfred curiously. Without question she was including him in the group with herself, her brother, and Guttorm who had long been one of her father's warriors.

"Rolv told me what you had planned," Sigrid continued. "It is rash but it might succeed."

Alfred shrugged. He listened to the storm. It was mid-afternoon, he judged, but its fury seemed to have abated little.

He glanced at the girl and was surprised to near himself asking, "Why were you to marry Jarl Lodvessen?"

Sigrid frowned. She did not seem astonished at his question. Looking directly at him, she answered, "A king's daughter has little to say in such matters. It was my father who arranged it."

"You knew the man?"

"Yes."

"And would have married him?"

"For my father, yes. Perhaps you can't understand that, but all my life I have been led to believe in my father's destiny and in the future of his kingdom. He knew that Jarl Lodvessen was not particularly loyal to him and that he had a strong following. It was his thought that a marriage would tie Lodvessen into the family. When my father explained that to me, I agreed to the marriage."

"You do not love the man?"

A faint smile touched Sigrid's lips. "No. I do not love him. I love my father. I love Rolv. And Norway."

There was a deep seriousness to the girl's voice. Alfred stared into her eyes for a moment. Then he said slowly, "That's the way my father and mother felt about England. I think I can understand."

Munching the berries, Alfred thought how different his life had been from the life of this girl, yet now, a peculiar chain of circumstances had drawn them together. The past made little difference now, and he felt very close to this daughter of the king.

"I wish that your father might have lived," Sigrid murmured. "I wish that he might have returned to England."

Alfred's lips tightened. He recalled that last picture of his father wielding the great axe, and again he saw Lodvessen hurling the spear at his back. Some day that fatal blow would be repaid.

Getting to his feet, he reached his hand out for his father's axe. He swung it to his shoulder and strode to the entrance to the cave. The storm was still raging outside.

Nevertheless he turned to Sigrid and ordered, "Wake the others. It is time that we left for the cove of Ljome."

CHAPTER IV

TWO HOURS AFTER dark Frode Thorfinn's merchant vessel turned into the bay of Hrollaug. Close in near the shore could be seen the outlines of Solve Kolfe's fleet. A few of the smaller ships were beached, but a natural harbor had protected the fleet from the storm and most of the ships were afloat in the deep water offshore. Some had been lashed together, others rode at anchor alone.

Torches lighted up the small town on the shore and as the merchant vessel drew closer to the fleet the sounds of men's voices could be heard in snatches of song, in laughter, in sharp, angry quarreling.

The storm was over and the rain had stopped. Thin, gray clouds were scudding across the sky. To the east could be seen the yellow radiance of a moon, three-quarters full. And then suddenly a flaming light showed in the town and the steersman on the vessel called, "They have set fire to the great hall of Jarl Lodvessen."

On the front halfdeck of the merchant vessel crouched five silent figures, Alfred, Rolv and Sigrid Haarfagre, Guttorm Hnuva and Thorfinn. Others of Thorfinn's men had volunteered to accompany them on their venture, but Alfred had decided against it. He had agreed that Thorfinn might come because he realized that the man's knowledge of the sea would be invaluable in case they succeeded in getting away. There was, however, a fresh wind and Alfred counted on that wind and a sail and the lightness of the ship to carry them away from Solve Kolfe, if they could take the ship. Five men could take it, he was sure, if the surprise was complete.

Staring now toward the town, Alfred marked the progress of the flames as they crept up the walls of the great hall. He was gazing at his father's funeral bier, he knew, for according to custom all who had died in the fight were being committed to the flames of the building, But for the storm the hall would have been burned the night before.

At his side, Sigrid guessing his thoughts, murmured, "He was a great man, Alfred. You can well be proud of such a father."

Alfred glanced at the girl. He had tried unsuccessfully to

persuade her not to accompany them on this venture. Now he started to make an answer, but before he could speak the sound of a horn reached him from the shore, and looking that way once more he saw that the Vandals were gathering on the beach and that already some of them had started for the fleet in small boats.

"What does that mean?" he asked sharply.

Thorfinn turned toward him. "It means that Solve is putting out to sea."

"But I thought that he would wait until morning."

"There will be a moon most of the night," Thorfinn pointed out. "Perhaps he wishes to get away before there is any chance for Erick's fleet to sail up the coast. Do you still wish to go ahead?"

Alfred was studying the shore. There were more men now in the small boats heading for the fleet. Just ahead of the merchant vessel he could now make out the *dreki* ship. It was a long, graceful boat with the carved figure of a dragon on the prow and with a dragon's tail fashioned at the stern. There was a short deck at either end and along each side were rowing benches. The mast and sail were down. Some half-dozen men were standing in the mid section of the *dreki*, looking toward the merchant vessel.

"Well?" Thorfinn demanded.

Alfred nodded. "We will go ahead."

Swiftly, now, it seemed to him, their ship drew closer to the *dreki*, and on the *dreki* the men ran forward and shouted angrily at the steersman, warning him to turn aside.

Alfred's hand tightened on the great axe. He was aware of a sudden excitement coursing through his veins. He rose to his knees, moved forward to the edge of the deck. Thorfinn was at one side of him, watching closely, a sword in his hand. The water between the two ships narrowed and now more angry shouts sounded from the *dreki*. Thorfinn looked toward the steersman. "Over!" he called suddenly. "Over! Hard!"

The merchant vessel swung abruptly toward Solve's ship. There was a light bump. Alfred sprang erect. He leapt over the edge of the deck and dropped lightly into the *dreki* ship. Thorfinn landed just ahead of him and tripped over one of the rowing benches. Three more figures dropped down from the merchant vessel just as it sheared away

With a startled cry the men on the *dreki* came running forward, naked sword-blades flashing in the moonlight. There were more than six—at least a dozen.

ALFRED swung *Bretwalda* aloft. He choked off the cry which came to his lips. The first of the guards reached him and went down under the stroke of the axe. Another recoiled in sudden fear but not quickly enough to escape. At one side, Frode Thorfinn was grunting and slashing with his axe, and on the other side he could hear the clash of Guttorm's sword and of Rolv's. Out of the corner of his eye he caught sight of Sigrid. She stood beside her brother and her sword was engaging two men at once.

That one brief glimpse of the battle was all that Alfred had. As suddenly as it had started it was over. Guttorm was down, gasping from a wound in the throat, and Rolv's arm was bloody. Thorfinn, Rolv and the girl were unhurt.

"Quick!" Alfred snapped. "Find your father."

Rolv and Sigrid hurried forward. There was a bound figure lying on the floor of the ship between the rowing benches. Rolv bent over it, slashed the bonds which held the man's hands together. Moving that way, Alfred saw that the man was Harold Haarfagre. His hair was matted with blood but otherwise he seemed unharmed.

Alfred looked toward the shore and saw that the boats were quite near the fleet. Some half-dozen of them were heading straight for the *dreki* ship, and there were at least ten men in each boat. In that moment Alfred thought bitterly that his plan had failed. There was no time now to get up the sail and escape. If they could have come half an hour earlier they might have succeeded, but they had come too late. His mind fumbled frantically for some way out, grasped at the only course which seemed feasible.

Swinging to face Harold Haarfagre, he snapped, "Can you swim?"

The king nodded. He was still dazed by the suddenness of his rescue.

"Then take off your clothing," Alfred ordered, "and go over the side. Rolv, do you swim?"

"Yes."

"Go with him. He will need help. His muscles have been cramped by the ropes."

Rolv Haarfagre didn't question the order. He started to rip off his clothing.

Alfred then turned to Sigrid. He said. "You, too. It is your only chance."

He waited for no answer but moved over to where Frode Thorfinn was standing. "Solve and his men will be here in a moment," he said to Thorfinn. "If they discover at once that Haarfagre is gone they will naturally look to the sea. In some way or other we must prevent that."

Thorfinn moistened his lips. "How?"

"We must act the part of the guards."

"Two men to take the part of a dozen?"

"We can say that the others left the boat, went to shore. But you will have to do the talking. My voice would betray me. You know the language that men such as these might use."

Thorfinn hesitated but a moment, then nodded.

Alfred dropped a hand on the old sea captain's shoulder. He knew that in making his decision, Frode Thorfinn had chosen death.

A voice behind Alfred whispered softly, "I can't swim."

Alfred swung around, stared at Sigrid Haarfagre. He could think of nothing to say. If the girl could not swim she must

remain on the ship. That she might not be able to swim had
never occurred to him.

Rolv called him in a low voice and Alfred saw that the king
and Rolv were ready to go over the side. They were still wearing
their serks which were of a dark-colored cloth. These would
serve, Alfred knew, to help conceal them when they were in the
water.

To Rolv he whispered. "Once you get to the shore, head
through the woods for the Trondelogan road. In almost any
house along the way you will find people ready to serve the
king."

There was time for no more. Rolv and Harold Haarfagre
slipped over the side of the boat and after them, Alfred eased
the bodies of the slain guards. Guttorm Hnuva he did not lower
into the waters of the bay, even though Guttorm was dead.
Instead, carrying him to the center of the ship, he laid him in
the place once occupied by Harold Haarfagre. It was a fitting
place for Guttorm, he thought. Even though dead, for a while
he could play the part of the king he had loved.

A boat scraped against the side of the *dreki* and a harsh voice
called out, "Bjorn! Bjorn!"

Thorfinn mumbled some unintelligible reply.

A tall, heavy-set figure stepped over the gunwale and moved
toward Thorfinn. Other men followed him, clambering into
the boat, looping their shields over the edge and seeking places
on the rowing benches.

ALFRED saw the heavy-set man glance at the still figure of
Guttorm, kick it as he passed by. The moon, which had been
hidden by the clouds, broke through again, and by its light
Alfred could see the man's face clearly. It was a thin, cruel face.
The man wore a reddish beard and a long, twisted mustache.
His eyes were deep-sunken and small.

As he reached Thorfinn, Alfred moved up behind him. *Bretwalda* stood against the lowered mast, several paces away, but
in his hand Alfred held his sword.

"Where are the others, Bjorn?" rasped the man. "What was the trouble here just as we put out from shore?"

Thorfinn started to answer but at the man's sudden gasp, Alfred knew that he had guessed that Thorfinn was a stranger. The heavy-set man's hand reached for the weapon at his side, but Alfred grasped his wrist. In a low voice Alfred said, "Steady, there! Cry out and you die!"

When the man jerked around, Alfred half lifted his sword.

"Who are you?" gasped the man.

Alfred made no immediate answer. The boat was now half filled with men and there was much loud conversation. Near the bow two men were quarreling. Alfred was grateful for that quarrel; it was attracting the attention of most of the crew. Staring away from the boat and out over the waters of the bay, he thought that he could make out two bobbing heads. The swimmers hadn't gone far but were moving steadily toward the shore.

Thorfinn stepped forward, a short knife in his hand. He pressed the blade through a rent in the coat of mail the heavy-set man was wearing and Alfred heard him say, "One word out of you, Solve, and you'll never speak another."

Sweat beaded the forehead of Solve Kolfe. His eyes narrowed as he stared at Alfred. One or two of the men who had just clambered into the boat started toward him and Alfred snapped. "Tell your men to keep back. Order the boat out to sea."

Alfred didn't think that Solve would obey that order, but the man did. At his command, oars were lifted over the gunwale and fastened by straps into the tholes; a steersman stepped to the prow of the *dreki*; and the ship moved out toward the sea.

Alfred made Solve sit down. He took the knife from Thorfinn and squatted behind the Vandal leader. Thorfinn knelt down near him and close by Thorfinn was the figure of Sigrid Haarf-agre, stretched out on the floor of the boat as though asleep. She was trying to make herself unnoticeable.

Slowly at first and then faster, the *dreki* ship of Solve Kolfe glided across the bay. Other ships in the fleet moved after it. Alfred looked back and there in the moonlit waters he thought that he could make out two bobbing heads.

Thorfinn whispered, "We've done it, Alfred! We've done it!"

Alfred made no answer. He stared ahead toward the open sea, wondering how long it would be before the men on the *dreki* ship guessed that something was wrong.

CHAPTER V

THE MOON REACHED high into the sky and started its descent toward the waters on the western horizon. Behind the ship the shoreline of Norway faded from view. The wind had died out until there was scarcely a breeze and the men on the *dreki* still manned the oars, a second crew sleeping on the floor between the rowing benches.

Solve Kolfe long ago had quit his muttering and had ceased snarling questions. Now he sat staring moodily straight ahead. He had glanced a good many times at the silent figure of Guttorm, and Alfred guessed that the Vandal leader had figured out what had happened. Now he was only waiting for a chance to strike back without the danger of losing his life.

As it began to grow light in the east, Alfred turned to Thorfinn and asked in a low voice, "Where are we headed?"

"Orkneyjar," Thorfinn answered. "It's a group of islands to the west of Norway. From the position of the stars, that seems to be our course."

Alfred nodded.

"They got ashore," Thorfinn added.

"You mean Rolv and the king?"

"Yes. I saw them reach the beach just before our ship came to the open sea."

At a command from the steersman the rowers ceased their labors and woke the men sleeping between the benches. These took their places at the oars, and the men who had been rowing lay down to sleep.

The light in the east grew brighter and finally the sun crawled up from the sea. Alfred felt suddenly very tired. He glanced over at Sigrid. The girl's face was pale. It showed the strain she had been under, but her lips managed a smile. Looking beyond her, Alfred noticed one of the men at the oars staring wide-eyed at the girl. He saw the man whisper to his companion and saw the latter turn to gaze at the girl. Like the movement of a fire through dry grass, that whisper ran around the boat. Alfred's muscles tightened. All night he had anticipated this moment, and now at last it had come.

Two of the men who had been sleeping awoke, stood up, stretched and then turned toward Solve Kolfe. At the sight of Alfred, kneeling behind their leader, they stopped. Then one of the men reached for his sword.

"Tell them to keep back," Alfred whispered into Solve's ear.

Solve Kolfe moistened his lips. He winced from the prick of the knife in his back and then in a hoarse voice gave the order.

Sigrid moved closer to Alfred and Thorfinn bared his sword. The rowers had stopped work. Here and there more men stood up, reaching for their weapons.

Again Alfred's knife pricked the Vandal leader's back. "Order the boat to move on," he rasped. "Order the men to keep away."

Solve gave the order, his voice bitter. There was a moment while those men hesitated; then slowly, the command was obeyed. But now there wasn't a man on the *dreki* ship who didn't understand the situation. Someone had turned over Guttorm's body and had discovered that it wasn't the figure of the king. And those who couldn't see the knife Alfred was holding against Solve's back had heard of it from others. They had little respect for the value of human life, those Vandals Solve Kolfe had gathered; but the habit of obedience to his commands lay heavily upon them. Besides, they must have known that there was no chance in the world for the three who had taken the boat to escape.

The boat moved on.

Thorfinn drew in a deep breath. He said slowly, "I thought our time had come, Alfred. How much longer can we hold out?"

Alfred shrugged. He wondered, suddenly, what point there was in trying to hold out any longer. For the end was inevitable. There was no possibility of escape, had never been any possibility of escape from the time when they had taken command of the boat. All they had sought to accomplish had been accomplished by the time they had reached the open sea and when Rolv and Harold Haarfagre had climbed out on the beach.

Then Sigrid touched his arm and murmured, "I wish that there was something I could do for you, something to show you how much I appreciate what you have done for my father and my country."

Alfred smiled at the girl. "Those words are enough, Sigrid."

Near the stern of the boat one of the men was preparing food for the others. Great pieces of cold meat and a hard, dark-colored bread were handed out. Flagons of wine were passed from hand to hand. At a command from Solve, food was brought to him and to Alfred, Thorfinn and the girl.

THE SUN climbed higher into the sky and the fleet continued on to the west. On board the *dreki* ship there was little conversation. Harsh, sullen glances were cast toward those in the center of the boat, and now and again men fingered their weapons. At regular intervals the crew at the oars was changed and in mid-afternoon more of the same food was served.

Thorfinn had now taken Alfred's place behind the Vandal leader and Alfred, leaning back against the mast, recalled suddenly his father's charge that some day *Bretwalda* must return to England. There was no chance of that now. His hand touched the handle of the axe. He lifted it, smiled. Once more, at least *Bretwalda* would taste the Vandal's blood. A grim, tight feeling settled over him and he stared toward the west. Far in the distance he thought that he could make out land and he wondered if they had already come as far as Orkneyjar. His eyes strained.

Afternoon waned. The sun dipped down into the sea. Clouds swept over the sky and it began to grow dark. The land to the west was now clearly visible, and at a sudden order from Solve the boat stopped.

Without turning away from Solve, Thorfinn said, "The waters beyond here are shallow and dangerous. The boats can go no closer to the shore."

Alfred stood up. He glanced to left and right. From the other ships of the fleet, small boats were putting out to the shore. Several boats seemed to be heading toward the *dreki*.

There was a new, sullen tension on the *dreki* ship. The men who had been rowing released their oars and got to their feet. Swords were unsheathed. And though as at a command, every warrior faced Solve Kolfe and the three who stood behind him.

Alfred's hands tightened on *Bretwalda*. He glanced at the girl. There was no look of fear in her face, though he knew that she must realize what lay ahead for them.

"I'm sorry," he said in a low voice, "that you could not have gone with your father and brother."

Sigrid shook her head and, looking directly at him, she answered, "I'm not sorry."

Her words puzzled Alfred, but he had no time to think about them. Solve Kolfe's body was tense. With a sudden cry the Vandal leader threw himself forward. Thorfinn drove out his knife, then dropped it and seized his sword. The warriors on the boat surged forward. There was nothing now to hold them off. Solve, on hands and knees, blood welling from the wound in his back, tried to get to his feet but the Vandals swept past him. Alfred swung the great axe into the air and brought it down with a slashing stroke.

Hoarse cries filled the air and the din of battle spread over the waters. Alfred faced the prow of the boat and at his back stood Thorfinn and Sigrid. He could hear the old sea captain growling as he fought. From Sigrid there came no sound.

One of the small boats scraped against the *dreki* ship and several men clambered over the gunwale. In spite of the gathering darkness, Alfred could see that one of the new arrivals was Jarl Lodvessen and he shouted the man's name.

Back of him, Thorfinn coughed, staggered. For a moment longer his sword beat off the charging Vandals; then quite suddenly he fell to the deck. Alfred increased the sweeping strokes of his great axe. Sigrid, he knew, had been behind him, but he could feel her there no longer. He swung around. The girl crouched over almost at his feet. A man stabbing at her with a sword went down under a crushing blow from *Bretwalda*.

Blows from behind him rained on Alfred's coat of mail. He could feel warm blood coursing along the length of his body. Why he didn't go down he couldn't understand, but for some reason there was no weariness in him, and *Bretwalda* was light in his hands. Then suddenly he remembered that his father had told him the strength to swing *Bretwalda* came not from a man's muscles but from the handle of the axe. He knew now that this was true. The great axe was not just a weapon of steel. It was like something alive in his hands.

A hoarse laugh broke from Alfred's throat. To one side he caught a glimpse of Jarl Lodvessen, the man whose cowardly blow had slain his father. He turned that way. Lodvessen backed off but he could not escape. In one moment his sword was above his head in a desperate effort to turn the swinging axe; in another he had slumped over one of the rowing benches with the dead.

The surging battle carried Alfred to the side of the *dreki* ship and there with the sea at his back he made his final stand. The leather thong which had bound his hair had come undone and his long, blond locks streamed from his head like a banner. Again and again his taunting shout rose above the din of clashing steel. Blood from the slain made the deck slippery. Twice he almost fell but each time he recovered his balance. Then with a hoarse cry one of the Vandals charged forward under the swinging axe and the weight of the man's body carried Alfred backward. *Bretwalda* slipped from his grasp and his fingers sought the man's throat. Together they went over the side of the ship and the dark, cold waters closed in over them.

WEIRD dreams tortured Alfred's mind and strange visions haunted him. Through a foggy, semi-consciousness he seemed to be able, at times, to distinguish the features of Sigrid Haarf-agre. But he knew that those must be dreams, for Sigrid was dead.

Then, in the coolness of a quiet evening, he opened his eyes and saw the girl bending above him, For a long time he stared at her, afraid that as before she would fade from his sight. But this time she didn't. Instead, he felt her hand on his forehead and heard her voice saying, "Sleep, Alfred. We have at last reached shore."

He puzzled over those words until he finally dropped off to sleep and he was still puzzling over them when he again awoke. The girl was still at his side and he whispered her name. She turned to face him.

"Where are we?" Alfred heard himself asking.

Sigrid shook her head. "I do not know. We are on some land far to the west or north of Orkneyjar." Then, as though divining the questions in his mind, she added, "I was not badly hurt in the fight on the *dreki* ship. I was only stunned. When you fell into the sea, I dropped over the other side. I found you in the water and managed to get you into one of the small boats. It was dark and we were not noticed. We drifted out to sea and after five days we came to this land."

For a few moments Alfred lay still, considering the girl's words. Later they were to amaze him even more than they did now, and later he was to want to know every detail of the girl's struggle to save 'him and of the long trip in the open boat. Just now, however, another thought struck his as more important.

"You told me,'" he accused, "that you couldn't swim."

The girl flushed. "I can—a little."

Again Alfred was silent for a time, his thoughts turning back to the fight on the *dreki* ship. He wondered what had happened to the great axe, whether it had fallen on the ship or had been lost in the sea. He asked Sigrid about it but she couldn't answer him.

"I should have taken that axe to England," Alfred said slowly. "It belongs there."

"It did a service for England," Sigrid answered. "With my father in power in Norway there will be no trouble between England and my country. Under Solve Kolfe, there would have been."

Alfred nodded and a moment later he said, "You do not know this land?"

"No."

"Are there any people living here?"

The girl shrugged. "Does it matter?"

"How will we get back to Norway?"

Sigrid turned to look into his face. In a voice so low that he could hardly distinguish the words, she asked, "And does that matter, Alfred?"

Alfred felt the girls hand touching his. He drew a deep breath. Again he thought of his father's great axe, and he recalled his fathers translation of the inscription on the handle. "To him who holds *Bretwalda* will come great sorrow and great joy, great defeat and great victory."

He had held *Bretwalda* and he had known sorrow in his fathers death, victory in the release of Harold Haarfagre, defeat in the battle on the *dreki* ship, joy in the promised companionship of the girl at his side.

He tried to sit up but Sigrid would not let him. "Rest a while longer, Alfred," she insisted.

Her eyes were smiling.

Alfred, son of Wilton the Briton, stared up at the sky. Some day, he decided, he would build a boat and they would sail back to the east, find the great axe of his father's and return it to England. And thinking of that he closed his eyes and slept.

III

A SWORD FOR LEIF
THE LUCKY

Bretwalda, *mystic weapon of Britain's chosen
kings, is summoned once more to battle—and now
it must save the life of the son of England's enemy,
and clear the way for an epoch-making odyssey.*

CHAPTER I

A LONG ROW of trees marked the western edge of the field and between their gnarled trunks, Harald could catch a glimpse of the sea, sometimes so blue and quiet that it looked almost like the sky, sometimes angry and storm tossed by the heavy winds which swept out of the north. Occasionally he could make out the sail of a distant ship making its way up the coast line toward the Trondhjem fiord and the town of Nidaros. There was such a ship out there now in this late spring afternoon in the year 1000, and leaning on his plow, Harald watched it and wondered whence it had come and what strange cargo it might carry.

He was tall, broad of shoulder, deep of chest. Flecks of gold glinted in his long blond hair, and his gray eyes, as they stared at the ship, were the eyes of a dreamer.

A horseman, traveling up the road which skirted the field, drew rein and studied him thoughtfully, nodded and then rode closer.

Harald swung around, and the dreamy look went from his eyes as he saw that the man was a stranger, that he wore helmet and coat of mail, and that a long sword was fastened at his side.

"Like to be on that ship?" asked the stranger, his voice blunt and heavy.

Harald shrugged. "I know nothing of ships."

The stranger dismounted. Like Harald, he was tall and broad of shoulder but his skin was dark and his features were sharp.

He had quick, nervous eyes, and as he came forward they jerked over to the plow and noticed the sword which was tied in its scabbard to the handle. At the sight of it, he stopped and a curiously amused expression cane into his face.

"That looks like at good sword," he said.

Harald rested a hand on it and nodded, watching the stranger closely.

"I think," said the stranger, "that I would like to have it."

Harald withdrew the sword. "And you may," he said grimly, "can you take it from me."

Laughing, the stranger drew his own sword from its sheath and slashed out at Harald's arm. Harald jerked back. He whipped up his blade and engaged. A dozen times he caught and turned aside powerful, vicious blows. The other's thrusts he parried easily. And then he moved forward in attack. Farmer he might look in his leather kirtle and trousers, and farmer he might be. Yet in his handling of that sword he was a master. Its weight seemed not to trouble him at all, though the sword was a heavy, double-edged blade. With half a dozen swift strokes he beat down the strangers guard, then whipped up the sword for a final slash at the man's unprotected neck.

The stranger scrambled back. "Nay, Harald! Nay!" he shouted. "I have had enough."

THE SOUND of his name was startling. Harald lowered his sword, stared unblinkingly at the stranger. "You called me Harald?"

"Aye," said the stranger. "Harald, son of Rolf, whose other name was Wilton."

Harald caught his breath. "You know my father?"

"Aye, lad. And the moment I saw you, I knew you for his son. You are of the same giant stature. You have the same square face, the same stubborn chin, the same expression, calm and peaceful. Yet it is a deceptive peacefulness. I did not want your sword. I wondered only if you were as skillful as your father in its use."

*Another had joined the fray,
swinging his double-edged
weapon against the traitor crew.*

"My father," said Harald, "taught me."

"I can tell that."

"And my father? You have word of him?"

The strangers lips tightened. "Aye, Harald. I have a message from him for you and your mother. She is—"

"In the house across the field," said Harald.

"Then let us go there."

Harald ran across the field, calling his mother's name, and as he drew near to the house she came to the door, a tall woman, still slender and straight though gray of hair.

"It is a messenger from father," Harald cried, his voice betraying his excitement. "I—I fought with him, Mother. And then he called me by name, recognized me."

Harald's mother stared toward the stranger, her hands clenched at her sides, her eyes clouded.

The man came up to the door, bowed, then gazed into the woman's face. A brief smile touched his lips, "You are Thorhild," he said quietly. "I would have known you anywhere from Rolf's description."

"And Rolf?" asked Harald's mother.

The stranger turned back to the horse which he had led across the field and from one side he unstrapped a great axe. Lifting it with both hands he carried it back to the door. "Rolf sent me with this," he answered.

At the first sight of the axe, Harald had caught his breath. And now, leaning forward, his eyes could make out the curious markings on the long handle, the ten red jewels in the head and the letters deeply engraved above the curved cutting edge. "It is it," he cried hoarsely. "It is the axe Bretwalda. He has found it, mother! He has found it."

Harald's mother made no answer, and Harald looked at her in amazement. Pale, her eyes wide and frightened, she was staring at the stranger. One hand was clutched to her breast. In a voice scarcely louder than a whisper, she said: "This—this means—"

The stranger nodded.

A chill which seemed to come from a heart suddenly turned to ice, swept over Harald's body. Emotion choked him. He sought desperately for something to say but no words could pass the thickness of his throat. He saw his mother close her eyes, saw a rigidity as of marble settle over her features. He put an arm around her but she was unresponsive.

"It happened in Greenland," the stranger was saying. "We were planning to leave for Norway the next day. I have never seen Rolf in better spirits. Not only had he found the axe for which he had searched so long and for which his father before him had searched. But also the trip had been a success in other ways. Chests of gold coins were on our boat, rare silks from the Orient. Then an old enemy appeared and an old quarrel, long forgotten, was fanned alive. There was a fight, and Rolf—"

The stranger drew a deep breath. He said, "There was nothing I could do, nothing any of us could do to stop what happened."

Harald's mother opened her eyes. "When I saw you coming," she said steadily, "I think I knew what had happened. Will you not come in? This is Rolf Wilton's home and here his friends are always welcome."

THE STRANGER nodded and entered the house, bringing the great axe with him. His name, he said, was Bjarne Herjolvsson, and over a supper of bread, fish and curds, he talked of Harald's father, told the story of the finding of the axe *Bretwalda* and of their long voyage and search.

Harald listened to all that he said, making but few comments. Now and again he glanced at his mother and noticed how she hung on every word which Bjarne uttered. And his mind called up a picture of his father. It was hard for him to realize that he would never again see the tall, blond, happy faced man who had romped with him when he was a boy; who had taught him how to use a sword and staff as he grew to manhood.

He leaned forward and, interrupting, said with a sharpness which surprised him.

"Who was it? Who killed him?"

Bjarne shook his head. "Let me tell you something else first. As your father lay dying in my arms, Harald, he looked up at me and said, 'Bjarne, I was returning to Norway to cast my lot with Olav Tryggvason, to help him Christianize the country. Since I cannot go, I ask you to take *Bretwalda* to my son. I want you to tell him it is my wish that a Wilton should take his place at the king's side in his fight for the Christ I have loved.'"

Harald stared down at the rushes on the floor, blinking hot tears from his eyes. He well knew how difficult a time the king was having. A few years before, Christ had been almost unknown in Norway. When Olav Tryggvason, a Christian, had been made king he had set about evangelizing his people, with true missionary zeal. But there were many *jarls* and lords which still clung to their old beliefs. And of late it had been rumored that the more powerful of his enemies were combining all the opposition to the faith in a hope to overthrow him.

"My father said that?" Harald whispered.

"Aye, Harald. He did."

Harald stood up. He crossed over to the wall against which Bjarne stood the great axe, reached out to take it. He was deeply familiar with the mystic story of this huge weapon, brought to the north country by the first Walton, and then lost almost a hundred years before. It had been forged by a Briton named Caedmon; it was all of solid steel, both head and handle. Its almost unbelievable weight made it seem impossible for any mortal man to wield it. Yet the strength to swing the axe, so the story went, came not from a man's own power but from the axe itself.

"Lift it to your shoulder, Harald," said Bjarne.

Harald took a deep breath. He lifted the axe, rested it on his shoulder, then lowered it and stared at in surprise. It seemed to have had no weight at all. He lifted it again.

Bjarne laughed and in the laugh there was a note of deep satisfaction. "You handle it as your father before you. If he had had *Bretwalda* with him when he met Erik the Red—"

Harald whirled around. "Erik the Red! He was the one?"

Bjarne nodded.

"Erik the Red," Harald repeated with a strange grimness. "It is a name I will not forget."

His mother had gone to a chest across the room and now she came back, bearing a coat of mail, a long purple cloak and a raven-winged helmet. She held them out to Harald with a proud and terrible smile on her lips.

"Take them," she said quietly. "You most go. I knew that when I saw Bjarne coming toward the house. Today have I lost not one but two—my husband and my son."

Again, just as when he had stood at the door, a lump choked Harald's throat.

"You—you wish me to go?" he heard himself whispering.

"Nay, Harald," said his mother. "I cannot wish it. But I know that you must—for you are a Wilton."

"Should I leave you? All alone—?"

The smile on her face grew grave and steady but there was no smile in her eyes. Almost fearfully they gazed at him. There was something familiar in that expression and Harald suddenly remembered what it was. Even so had his mother looked at his father when he had left on his last journey. There had been a smile on her lips that day, too.

Once more, then, Harald lowered *Bretwalda* to the floor and stepping forward he gathered his mother into his arms, forgetting for a while that he had become a man.

Bjarne muttered something about finding another horse and went outside.

CHAPTER II

THE ROYAL HALL in Nidaros was long and wide and down the center of the building, on deep stone hearths, faggots blazed. Most of the smoke from the fires went up through a vent in the roof, but sometimes it would sweep across the room like a blanketing mist. There were long tables on each side and behind them benches for the men of the court. At the far end was a table piled with food and casks of wine and mead. Slaves were passing steaming platters and flagons of wine.

In the second high seat, midway down the hall and across from the high seat reserved for Olav Tryggvason, sat Svein Jarl, old and stooped, gray-haired and wrinkled. Except Olav Tryggvason, there was no more powerful man in Norway.

In the space before him, *hirdscalds* were singing the story of the battle of Hafrsfjord; and one after another, the men in the hall were going up to speak in whispers to Svein Jarl, or to consult with one of the other *jarls* who stood near him.

From a bench near the door, Harald kept glancing from side to side, drinking in the scene. A strange excitement pounded through his veins. He tried to hide it, forced a yawn and said to Bjarne, who was seated beside him, "So the king will not be here until tomorrow."

Bjarne had been very silent and when he made no answer, Harald glanced at him. The older man, he saw, was staring at the group around Svein Jarl. There was a deep scowl on his face.

"What troubles you, Bjarne?" Harald asked.

Bjarne Herjolvsson shrugged his shoulders. He said under his breath, "There sits the man who would be king, and from what I know, most of those here tonight would be happy to see him take Olav Tryggvason's place."

Harald looked at the group around the second high seat.

A slave girl stopped at Bjarne's side, filled his drinking horn and moved on down the table. She was one of the few women in the hall and Harald had noticed her before. She was young, slender and tall. Her hair was very dark and there was a sweetness and serenity in her face that made Harald look at her the second time. There was an unbroken pride in the set of her chin and in the level, steady expression of her eyes. Harald couldn't help but wonder about her.

"When I was here before," rumbled Bjarne, "I had trouble with some of those men. They have little liking for me." He had been alert to the hostile glances directed at them since the beginning of the feast.

One of the men who had been standing in the group around Svein Jarl, turned away and lurched drunkenly down the hall toward them. He fell heavily against Harald, laughed and dropped down on the bench beside him. Bjarne's hand reached for Harald's wrist, clasped it tightly. Under his breath he said, "Easy, Harald. Easy. This is aimed at me."

HARALD looked over at the man. He was young, stalwart, thick-bodied. There was a thin golden-brown beard on his face. He had sharp, dark eyes, long coarse hair. Reaching for a drinking horn he shouted for wine and started beating the table.

The slave girl came hurrying back. She tilted the flagon and started to fill the drinking horn. The man got up, knocking the flagon from the girl's hand. He had meant, perhaps, to spill the wine on Harald. But instead the flagon twisted around, spattering on his own trousers.

An angry shout roared from the man's lips. His hand snapped out to strike the girl across the face. It was a brutal blow that sent her reeling back against the wall. She leaned there for a moment, her legs bent, then slid limply to the floor. Someone laughed aloud.

Harald did not know that he was on his feet until he found himself staring into the man's face. He heard Bjarne's warning cry but he did not catch the shouted words. A hand pulled on his arm, but he shook it off. There was a mocking sneer on the other's lips. Harald drew a deep breath and said very slowly, "Where I come from, men do not strike women, even if they be slaves. But they sometimes strike other men. So!'"

With no other warning, Harald's fist jerked forward. It landed squarely on the man's sneering mouth. All the weight of Harald's body was behind that blow. No second stroke was needful. The man staggered, tripped and fell.

In an instant, it seemed, Harald and Bjarne were surrounded by a score of the fallen man's friends. Bjarne had whipped out his sword and Harald lifted *Bretwalda*. In another moment, blood might have been shed, but the harsh, rasping voice of Svein Jarl broke the tension.

"Put up your swords," he commanded. "The royal hall is no battleground."

Swords were sheathed and the men fell back. Two of them helped the fallen man to his feet. His lips were cut and puffed and anger blazed in his eyes.

"If Ivar Svarte is not satisfied," said Svein Jarl, "there is always the *holmgang*."

The *holmgang* was a custom often invoked in settlement of a dispute. It was a duel by swords ending with the first drawing of blood. A price was usually set on the contest, which the loser paid, if he lived.

"That will satisfy me," said Ivar Svarte. "Let us go to the beach. There is a full moon tonight. It will give light enough."

The men around Ivar Svarte moved with him toward the door. Harald glanced at Bjarne. Bjarne was scowling. "They know nothing of you," he said slowly, "but one of their number has already tasted the steel of my blade. Yet even that doesn't explain what has happened."

"I have no fear of that man," said Harald.

"Nor I for you," Bjarne replied. "Yet I still do not understand."

HARALD shouldered *Bretwalda* and turned to the door and Bjarne walked with him. Svein Jarl stood near the door. There was a look of satisfaction in the old man's eyes. Harald scowled. They passed outside and turned down toward the beach and as they moved that way a feeling of apprehension came to Harald Wilton. He couldn't fathom it. Never had he known fear. He did not think now that he was afraid, yet this apprehension, he knew, was closely akin to it.

Down on the beach a group of men were waiting for them. They were over to one side, near a row of boat-sheds, and it seemed to Harald that the group was larger than the one that had left the hall. He could count more than a score of men.

As he and Bjarne walked forward, Ivar Svarte turned to face him. He had removed his cloak. His coat of mail reached below the knees. He wore a horned helmet and on his left arm he bore a shield, iron rimmed and covered with leather, painted red.

"Is this place to your liking?" he asked bluntly.

Harald shrugged. The sand was hard packed and the footing sure. He removed his own cloak and dropped it to the ground. *Bretwalda* he gave into Bjarne's keeping. He unslung the shield from his back, slipped his left arm through its straps, drew his sword.

One of the men with Svarte came forward and whispered something to him. Svarte shook his head. "Let me finish this, first. The fool struck me."

"Feel him out," advised Bjarne. "Then finish it at the first opportunity."

Harald nodded, facing Svarte. And with a sudden rush, Svarte bore down on him. Steel clashed against steel, shield butted shield.

At first, almost by instinct, Harald parried Svarte's blows with his sword or caught them on the rim of his shield. This was a game that he knew well, one which he had often played with his father, even when only a boy. A vicious cut narrowly missed his head and Svarte's friends shouted encouragement. Harald ducked under another. He caught a third on his shield, parried a fourth. And then he suddenly found himself pressing forward, forcing Svarte to give ground.

The play of his sword in the few moments which followed was too swift for the eye to mark. Step by step he drove Svarte backward. Perspiration showed on the man's face and a startled expression came into his eyes. His breath grew labored; his sword slower. With three heavy, powerful blows, Harald battered down his shield. He might have killed him, then, for the way was open for a thrust at the throat. But instead, as his sword stabbed out Harald lifted it and touched Svarte on the cheek.

Blood spurted from that cut and Harald stepped back, lowering his sword. Such was the custom. The *holmgang* was ended. But with a sudden, wild cry, Svarte charged forward, his sword a silver streak in the moonlight. Barely in time did Harald thwart that blow, spring aside.

A cry startled him and he jerked around. Behind him, Bjarne was slumping over. There was a man at Bjarne's back, in his hand a bloodstained sword.

Harald's eyes widened. There was a concerted movement from the other men who had come down to the beach and who until now had been standing almost motionless, watching the fight. Bared swords appeared in their hands and they started forward.

HARALD understood then the vague apprehension which had troubled him. This had never been meant to be a simple *holmgang*. They had been deliberately planned to get Bjarne out here and slay him. And now Bjarne lay motionless, almost at his feet, his head half severed from his body.

With a cry, half sob, Harald dropped his sword, cast away

his shield, and stooped to seize the axe which Bjarne had dropped. He lifted it as the men closed in, slashing with it from left to right. Long was the handle and sharp the blade. Men went down never to rise again. Screams tore the air as those nearer to him scrambled for safety. Yet they did not flee. In a grim circle they surrounded him, now one darting forward, now another.

Turning from side to side, ever turning, Harald held them off. But the fight was hopeless and he realized it. Sooner or later they would tire him out, and then, despite *Bretwalda*, he would go down. Dark anger flamed through his body. Like a man gone mad he charged at the circle and broke it. It formed again. Swords stabbed at his legs; and someone picking up sand, threw it into his face to blind him.

A shout sounded from one of the nearby boat-sheds and more men came running forward. Harald could taste the bitterness of defeat. Sand gritted in his eyes until he could hardly see. Once more he charged the emboldened circle. And again *Bretwalda* drew its measure of blood.

Near him, then, Harald saw a strange sight. A tall, blond young man with no coat-of-mail or helmet, was wielding a mighty sword in battle with three others. There was a wide smile on his face and he laughed as he fought. Beyond him others were fighting; and suddenly Harald realized that the circle which had surrounded him had melted away. He saw men running toward Nidaros, others chasing after them. Two of those who had engaged the blond young giant, broke away and fled. The third went down under his sword.

Harold lowered *Bretwalda* to the sand. His deliverance had been so sudden and so unexpected that he could hardly understand it.

The tall young man turned toward him, still smiling. "We had come down to the boat-sheds," he stated. "I saw the fight and joined in, though I doubt you needed us."

"Had you not come when you did," Harald answered simply,

"I would be lying yonder on the ground with Bjarne Herjolvsson."

"Bjarne Herjolvsson!"

"Aye. Did you know him?"

The man nodded. "And I know these others. They are men of Svein Jarl's, the enemy of King Olav Tryggvason. We had best leave before they find others to help them and return here. Have you a place to stay? A place where you will be safe?"

Harald shook his head. He and Bjarne had planned on staying in the royal hall, but he could not return there now.

"Then come with me," said the man. "I have found lodgings here in the town where you need not fear trouble."

"Your name?" asked Harald.

"Leif Ericsson."

"Harald Wilton."

A shadow crossed Ericsson's face. "Son of Rolf?" he asked.

"Aye."

Ericsson nodded. He said slowly. "Come. It would not be wise to stay here longer."

CHAPTER III

THE HOME OF Torf Ungi was on the outskirts of Nidaros. It was a new building, larger than many of the others. Back of the main room was a smaller room for the use of Torf's family. The front room was often given over to guests who slept on mat covered benches around the walls.

Torf Ungi, himself, was a short, stooped man with iron gray hair and a wrinkled face which reminded Harald much of Svein Jarl's. He greeted Leif Ericsson and his men and Harald with a smile, but when he heard of what had happened on the beach his face grew thoughtful.

"Did they recognize you, Leif?" he demanded.

"I don't see how they could help it." Ericsson laughed. "Erling Syr was there. And Ulvsson and Ivar Svarte and others I know."

Torf Ungi scowled. He said slowly, "I have tried to play my part well. I am one of them, yet I am not in their confidence. Sometimes I think they suspect that I am not wholly with them."

Wine and drinking horns were brought into the room by the women of Torf Ungi's household; and from the bench which was to be his bed, Harald listened to the talk between the master of the house and Leif Ericsson. Much of what they said had come to him before as rumors. Here and there throughout all of Norway, various *jarls*, resentful of Tyggvason's domination, were planning a revolt. There was no question of it in Turf Ungi's mind. He, himself, had played the part of an enemy of the king.

"But does not King Clav know of it?" asked Harald.

"Of course he does," Torf answered. "But it does not seem to concern him. He is concerned only with those who refuse to accept Christ. His greatest enemies are among those who have been baptized, but who still plot against him,"

Leif Ericsson frowned, "Should I postpone my departure? If that would help—"

Torf Ungi shook his head. "It would be to no purpose. I do not think that the kings enemies are ready to strike."

Harald Wilton slept that night in Torf Ungi's house on a bench between Leif Ericsson and one of his men, He slept well and did not waken until the sun was high in the sky. When he sat up, Ericsson and most of his men were gone. Only a short, slender fellow whom Harald had met the night before and whose name was Tyrker, was still in the room.

Tyrker brought him a breakfast of bread and curds, prepared by one of the slaves. Then joining Harald at the common table, he said abruptly, "You are to stay here until Leif returns. He left me with that message for you."

Harald frowned. "Why?"

"I guess maybe someone's hunting for you. Twice men have called here, seeking word of you. Torf Ungi sent them away."

"The king has not arrived?"

"He is expected shortly after noon."

HARALD nodded and his mind turned back to the happenings of the night before. He thought of Bjarne Herjolvsson and the memory of the man who had been his father's friend brought a stab of pain to his heart. Bjarne hadn't had a chance. He had been struck clown from behind. And if it hadn't been for Leif Ericsson, he realized, he too might now he lying out there on the beach, stiff and cold.

"Tell me of this Leif Ericsson," he said suddenly, swinging around to face Tyrker.

Tyrker smiled. "What would you know of him?"

"Who is he? Why did he come to my assistance last night, when such a move could have gained him nothing but deeper hatred from the men he fought."

Tyrker shook his head. "I cannot answer that question excepting to say that it was like him to draw his sword when he saw another in danger."

"He did not know me."

"Perhaps not."

"What is this trip he was talking about last night?"

"He is going to Greenland. Olav Tryggvason had persuaded him to go there with the story of Christ. The king is sending missionaries along with us."

"To Greenland?"

"Aye. And if you would know Leif you should see him on his ship. There was never in all the world a sailor like him. As a boy, when other boys were playing with wooden swords and slaying imaginary enemies, Leif Ericsson played on the shore at Brattahlid in Greenland, carving toy boats and fitting them with sails and floating them in the water. He loves a storm at sea as a fighting man loves a battle. I have seen him stand for hours on the steering platform of a boat, laughing into the teeth of a gale, shouting his defiance at it. Someday, he has told me, he plans to sail west of the Greenland sea, where man has never gone. Someday he will."

Harald slowly nodded his head. Something in Tyrker's words fired his imagination. He recalled Ericsson's laughter as he had faced those three men on the beach and a smile came to his face. Such a man he would like to know better.

The day passed slowly. Sometime after noon, Harald heard the blaring of trumpets announcing the arrival of the king. The impulse came to him then to leave the security of Torf Ungi's house and seek out Olav Tryggvason, but he put it down. It would be the part of wisdom, he knew, to await word from Leif Ericsson.

Leif Ericsson returned at dusk and the moment that Harald saw him he knew that things hadn't gone well. There was a worried frown on his face, uncertainty in his manner.

"What is it, Leif?" Harald demanded.

Leif Ericsson sat down. He said slowly, "Your enemies had the ear of the king even before he reached here. Ivar Svarte and another went to meet him. Last night, aside from those slain on the beach, three others were killed, three men close to the king. And Tryggvason has been persuaded that you are the man who killed them. He has ordered you found and brought before him. I have little doubt what he will do in such a case."

Harald stared at Ericsson, amazed at his words. "It is as bad as that?"

"Worse. I tried to give him the truth in the matter but he would not listen. I will see him again tonight but I have little hope. He is a stubborn man and once his mind is made up, nothing can change it."

"I could plead my own case before him."

"Against lying witnesses you would not get far."

Harald paced across the room and back, his brow furrowed in thought. Coming here to enter into Olav Tryggvason's service, the king's enemies had placed him in a position that rendered him helpless. He was but being made the scapegoat, he knew. Personally, he was unimportant, either to the king or to those who wanted to displace him. But the king's enemies, still unready to strike, needed someone to blame for those they had killed. And they had selected him.

THERE was a knock at the door. Leif Ericsson jumped up, hurried to open it, held a whispered conversation with the person outside and then stood away from the door.

A slender, cloaked and hooded figure stepped into the room.

"The horses?" asked Ericsson.

"They will be ready sometime before dawn," came the answer in words so low that Harald hardly caught them.

"But he cannot wait here that long. Already this house is suspected."

"I have a plate where he will be safe."

Harald walked forward. The hooded figure turned toward him. Harald caught his breath, stared in amazement.

"You recognize her, perhaps," said Ericsson. "This is Mercia, a slave in the household of Svein Jarl. But despite that, she is to be trusted. There are few in Nidaros of whom one can be sure."

Mercia threw back her hood and for a moment a smile touched her lips. Slave she might be but she certainly didn't have the manner of one.

"You should not have resented that blow the other night," she said quietly. "I have received many that were worse."

Harald stared at her, glanced at Leif. "What was this about horses?"

Leif Ericsson frowned. "I could think of nothing else to do," he said slowly. "For a reason which you would not understand it is impossible for me to take you with me when I sail. If you stay here you will surely be found and killed. By horse you can escape. To the north, in Maeren, Torf Ungi's brother is *jarl*. Torf will send him word of your coming. Mercia, here, will see that you get safely away."

The girl stepped forward, laid a hand on Harald's arm. "We must hurry or I will be missed."

Harald nodded. He said to Ericsson, "I cannot thank you for all you have done for me. But perhaps someday—"

A curious smile came to Leif Ericsson's face. "Perhaps someday we will meet again. And now you must go."

Harald turned back into the room, put on his cloak and picked up the axe *Bretwalda*. He hurried to the door and followed the girl out into the gathering shadows of the night.

CHAPTER IV

MERCIA TURNED TO the left and moved off slowly, her shoulders stooped, her arms folded in front of her. The hood of her gown completely concealed her face. "Keep the axe under your cloak," she said to Harald, "and if we are stopped, let me to the talking. There is a mute slave about your size who sometimes accompanies me on errands. You may be mistaken for him."

Harald smiled but he hid the axe as the girl had directed and slowed his gait to her shuffling walk. It still was not dark and a clear, cloudless sky gave little promise of heavier shadows. Before midnight the moon would be up.

Through the outskirts of Nidaros the girl made her way. Here and there they passed unfinished houses and great piles of rough hewn boards. Several times Harald saw men at a distance but no one seemed interested in him.

Turning down a gentle hill, Mercia came to a broad meadow. To the right, at the end of the meadow near the town, and clustered together as though for mutual protection, were a score of crude, windowless hovels. Some were sagging crazily and looked as though a good push would send them toppling over.

Mercia stopped and pointed that way. "The quarters for Svein Jarl's slaves," she said to Harald.

"You are taking me there?"

"Yes."

"The other slaves—"

"All working. But even if they were not, you could find hiding there."

Mercia walked on and Harald, moving beside her, studied the slave quarters. Near one of the buildings he thought that he detected a moving shadow. His hand slipped under his cloak and fastened on *Bretwalda*. They drew nearer and again Harald thought that he saw a moving figure. He glanced at Mercia. The girl's head was still bowed and she shuffled along with the same slow walk.

The attack came even as they passed the first hovel—suddenly and without any warning at all. Out of the shadows sprang two hurtling figures. Starlight glinted from upraised blades.

Harald's arm reached out and swept the girl to the ground. He ducked a swishing blow, felt another slant against the helmet under his hood. And then he jerked erect, swinging *Bretwalda* in both hands. One of the men never knew what struck him. Under the cut of the axe he reeled back and fell to the ground. The other screamed, tried to flee, but with a swift step, Harald overtook him. Another blow, and the Fight was ended.

MERCIA sat up, got to her feet. She crossed over to the first man, looked at his face. Then she looked at the face of the second.

Harald waited, leaning on his axe, his ears tuned for the sound of danger. He saw Mercia looking up at him and in the faint half light her face was very pale.

"I know them," she said. "They were standing near me when Leif Ericsson asked for my help. I said then that you might be hidden here. They must have thought to gain favor with the king or with Svein Jarl through taking you."

Harald made no answer.

The girl frowned. "Don't you believe me?"

Her eyes were very direct. Harald heard himself saying, "Yes, I believe you."

From the town there came a sound of marching feet. It grew

nearer. Mercia jumped up, hurried to Harald's side. "They must be coming here," she whispered. "Perhaps these men told others."

To one side, a little distance away, there was a grove of trees. Harald reached for the girl's hand. He turned that way, running. As they left the shelter of the slave quarters, a shout sounded from the road and arrows winged over them. But they gained the trees in safety, hurried through them, came to a hill.

Catching at Harald's arm, the girl stopped him. "Beyond, the hill is bare and there is a great valley. No place in it could we hide. With horses those men would quickly overtake us."

"Back to Nidaros. Who would think that we would dare return?"

"And in Nidaros?"

"Half of the boat-sheds are empty and they are not far from where Guttorm was to bring the horse."

Harald swung to the right. He moved more slowly now, being careful to make no noise. They could hear the voices of the soldiers calling to one another as they came forward. They had spread out and were beating the underbrush as they moved through the woods.

Crouched at the edge of the woods, again within sight of the town, Harald and Mercia waited until they had passed. Two of the soldiers came so close that Harald could almost touch them. He caught a snatch of their conversation. "Others have gone for horses. If they passed through here, we will run them down in the valley beyond."

When the soldiers had gone, Mercia stood up. "I think it is safe to go, now."

"You are going with me?"

"I cannot go back. By now, Svein Jarl knows what I have done. There is little kindness in him."

"What will you do?" Harald asked.

"Can that matter to you?"

Harald was silent, considering the girl's plight. The lot of one who tried to escape was not easy. Death was the penalty to any man who harbored an escaped slave. A few, who had managed to get their hands on anything of value, had managed to buy passage on a boat, but such instances were rare.

MOVING again through the outskirts of the town, Mercia led the way to the waterfront and not far from where Harald had fought with Ivar Svarte the night before, she found an empty boat-shed. The smell of paint was heavy inside and the darkness was intense. Mercia closed the doors after them, fixed a bar in place and then dropped down on the sand.

Harald sat beside her and for a long time neither spoke. Faint shouts now and then reached Harald's ears and occasionally he could hear the strains of a fiddle. The steady slap-slapping of the waves against the beach was the only other noise.

"It is a strange feeling to he hunted," Harald said suddenly. "Now I know how a bear must feel when the chase draws close. It's funny, but I never thought of the hunted as having any particular feeling at all."

"You have done much hunting?"

"Yes. With my father."

The girl sighed, "In my own country I once went with my brothers on a hunt. I did not like it."

"Your country is England."

"How did you know?"'

"The first of my line was an English man. And like you, he was brought here as a slave."

"Then you—"

"He did not stay a slave."

The girl moved as though making herself more comfortable. Harald stretched out on the sand. "Tell me about yourself," he said slowly. "Who are you? How did you come here? What has your life been like?"

The girl started to talk. She told of her home in England, of her father and brothers. There was a deep, resonant quality in her voice which Harald liked. He couldn't see her face but he could imagine that she was smiling as she talked and gradually, the picture that she painted became so vivid to him that he could see it spread out before him. The girl told of the raid of the northmen, of her capture, of her trip to Nidaros and of her life here, She did not complain. And suddenly the conviction came to Harald that she was speaking of everything that had gone before as though it had all happened to someone else, not to her at all; as though is some way or other she had been able to detach her spirit from her body and rise above the suffering she had known.

"And now," said Harald, when she had finished, "you have cast your lot with mine."

"For tonight," said the girl.

"And after tonight?"

"I have not looked ahead."

Her voice was quiet.

"Were it not for what you have done for me," said Harald, "yon would not know be in danger."

"You did not consider the danger when you struck Ivar Svarte the other night."

Harald sat up. "Would you have offered to help me had you known where it would lead?"

For a moment the girl was silent. Then she said slowly, "That is hard to answer now, yet I think I would. Even before you struck Ivar Svarte I could see that you were not like those other men in the hall. You did not belong there. This may sound strange to you, but long ago my life ceased to be of any importance to me. Until tonight, when I was given an opportunity to strike back at the man whose slave I am, I lived only because it was easier to live than to die."

HARALD stared toward the girl. Outside, the moon had come up, and there was light showing through the chinks between the boards. He still could not see Mercia's face but he could make out the shadow of her figure. She was leaning back in the sand near him.

Harald got to his feet, moved over to the door, pulled it open and looked outside. He turned back to the girl. "Who is this man who has agreed to furnish a horse?"

"Guttorm. He is the master of Svein Jarl's stables. The court tonight will last until dawn, for it is in celebration of the departure of Leif Ericsson. Until then, Guttorm did not think it would be safe to lead a horse to the grove near the Maeren road. Too many men will be awake in the town."

"Could he bring two horses?"

"Two horses?"

"Yes. For you are going with me."

She shook her head then.

"Nay, Harald. I thank you for the offer but I will be an escaped slave and the penalty for you would be death. You came here to serve Olav Tryggvason and he badly needs your help. What you propose would only mean death for both of us."

Harald came back and sat down near the girl. He started to speak, but she stopped him, saying, "If you would do something for me, Harald, help me to forget for tonight that I am a slave and that tomorrow death is waiting for me. Tell me of yourself, of your life and plans. Talk to me as you would talk to the girl you will some day marry. That will mean more to me than anything else."

"Tomorrow you and I will be far away from here?"

"I can pretend, too. And what will we do?"

Harald smiled. "It is not pretense. I will tell you. Tomorrow..."

The moon rose swiftly. In the royal hall at Nidaros, Olav Tryggvason sat in the high seat, on each side of him a black-robed priest, near to him Leif Ericsson. From time to time he would beckon to Ericsson and would start a discussion of some new phase of Ericsson's mission to Greenland.

Across from the king, Svein Jarl sipped at a horn of mead.

From time to time, he, too, would beckon a man and give him whispered instructions. He kept looking toward the king, and in his eyes there was a mocking light which he could not hide.

Weary soldiers, afoot and on horse, returned to their camp in the square beyond the royal hall, after a fruitless search for an escaped slave and a murderer. They were very disgruntled when they reached the camp, but in the camp, wine flowed freely and they soon forgot all their troubles.

And in the boat-shed on the beach, Harald was saying, "That is what we will do, Mercia. And neither the king nor his enemies will stop us."

From outside the boat-shed came the sound of murmuring voices, of tramping feet. Harald slipped over to the door, opened it a crack and stared outside, one hand gripping *Bretwalda*. Men were marching past. Moonlight glinted on their helmets and coats of mail. They moved down the row of sheds to the one next to the last and opening its doors, disappeared from sight.

"Leif Ericsson's crew," whispered Mercia. "That is where his boat has been kept. They sail at dawn and have come to make the boat ready."

Harald nodded. "I should like to have gone on this voyage with Leif. He must be a great sailor."

"Men say that he is greater than his father, Eric the Red."

Harald caught his breath, stiffened. "What was that? Leif's father is Eric the Red?"

"Yes. Didn't you know?"

A confusion of feelings swept over Harald. From his throat there came a dry laugh. "That is strange—to owe my life to that man's son. You don't know how funny it is."

"What do you mean?" asked the girl.

There was a dry, tight feeling in Harald's throat, an emptiness in his stomach. To his mind there came the picture of Leif Ericsson. He laughed again, harshly, and swept the picture from his thoughts. Turning to the girl, he said, "That horse? Would it be ready?"

"I will see," Mercia answered. "You wait here. It will not take me long."

CHAPTER V

IT WAS QUIET and somehow or other, very lonely in the boat-shed after the girl had gone and Harald's thoughts were comfortless companions. He was aware of utter defeat—failure without having been able to strike a blow. And more, there was the realization of his obligation to the son of the man who had killed his father—the man whose life he had vowed to take.

Marching drearily back and forth through the heavy sand, Harald tried to look ahead. A few moments before, in talking to the girl, that had been easy. But now it wasn't.

Moving to the door, he stared outside. No sounds came to him from the boat-shed down the line. He frowned, bit his lips, turned back to his pacing.

As silently as she had left, Mercia returned, slipping through the door and closing it after her.

Harald crossed to her side. "The horse?"

"It is ready. It is in the grove where the Maeren road turns up the valley. You can find it easily."

"But you are coming with me."

"No, I—I must see Leif Ericsson."

There was a note of excitement in the girl's voice. Harald laid a hand on her arm. She was trembling and her breath was coming heavily.

"What is it, Mercia?" Harald asked. "What has happened?"

For a moment the girl hesitated, then she said swiftly, "Those men we saw going to Leif Ericsson's boat-shed weren't his men."

Harald frowned. "What do you mean?"

The door had sagged open and a narrow shaft of light sifted over the girl's face. There was a sharp tension in her features. She looked up at Harald and said, "I learned this from Guttorm, the man who brought the horse to the grove. He, too, is a slave,

but I know that he spoke the truth. There is little happens in
Nidaros we do not know of. People pay small attention to the
slaves. They talk freely before them. If a man is leaving his wife
we probably hear of it before anyone else. If—"

"What did you learn from Guttorm?"

"Those men who have come down to the boat-shed are Svein
Jarl's men. Ericsson's boat has been moved outside, ready for
the launching. But inside the shed are all his supplies and equip-
ment. Just before dawn, Leif Ericsson and his men will leave
the royal hall and come down here. The king will come with
them. In some way or other, Svein Jarl will induce the king and
Leif Ericsson to enter the boat-shed. They will never come out."

"But the kings soldiers?"

"They are back in the camp. All night they have been served
wine and mead until most of them are drunk. Though Ericsson's
men and a few others, faithful to the king, might put up a fight,
the soldiers would never get down here in time to help."

Harald frowned, He glanced through the door. The shadows
in the eastern sky were beginning to thin. It would not be long
now until it would start to grow light.

"Why would you warn Ericsson?"he asked of the girl.

Mercia bit her lips. She said slowly, "He is a Christian, just
as I. And so is the king, That is reason enough."

"You could never get to him. You could never get beyond the
guard at the door of the royal hall."

"I would reach him some way or other."

"It would mean your death."

Mercia smiled. "That is all that awaits me anyhow. Did you
really think that I could leave with you, Harald? There was never
a chance for us. In your heart, you know it."

ONCE more Harald stared out through the door. There was
really little chance, he decided, that the girl could reach Ericsson. And even if she did, a warning might fail to serve its
purpose. If Svein Jarl knew that his plot was uncovered, he

would only have to rearrange the details, call the men back from the boat-shed, make the attack nearer the hall or even in the hall. If he was ready to strike, he would strike. Discovery of the plot would not stop him.

"I must hurry," whispered Mercia.

Harald shook his head. "I was thinking of something. I was thinking of what happened here on the beach the other night and of a man without armor or helmet who came to the assistance of a man he didn't even know. Somehow or other I can't get that out of my head."

"Let me go," insisted the girl. "You can find your way to the grove. I—"

Harald laughed softly, and in the laugh there sounded a freedom of spirit and a lightness which he had not known since he had first sighted Bjarne Herjolvsson sitting on his horse and staring at him as he stood in the field near his home.

"No, Mercia," he answered. "I will never find the grove for I must go another way. It is strange, the way things sometimes work out. My father died at the hand of Ericsson the Red. The son of Eric the Red saved my life and now I must give my life for him—and for the king I came to serve."

"No," cried the girl sharply.

Harald smiled. "There is no other way. Perhaps it was for this purpose that I came here. Who can tell?"

"What do you mean to do?"

"I must go. There are some men waiting for me—at the boat-shed."

"No."

Harald lifted *Bretwalda* to his shoulder. "There is a curious legend concerning this axe. The inscription on the handle is supposed to predict for any who wield it, a great joy and a great sorrow, a great victory and a great defeat. I have known happiness tonight, Mercia, sorrow that it must end. And now I go to taste victory and defeat. You take the horse, ride to Macren. Here is money with which to purchase your passage to England."

From his belt, Harald took a leather bag. He pressed it into the girl's hands. They were icy cold and clung to his. "What can you hope to accomplish?"

"Noise of the fight will rouse the king's soldiers. They will not all be drunk. And the trap will be sprung ahead of time. With the king's soldiers, even a part of them, on hand, and with his picked murderers dead, Svein Jarl will be helpless."

"But—"

Harald put down the girl's hands and turned through the door. He started for Leif Ericsson's boat-shed. Her voice called after him but he didn't answer. From the royal hall he could hear shouting, suddenly louder than a few moments before, and the conviction came that Ericsson and the king were on the way to the harbor.

A thin smile touched Harald's lips. Beside one of the boat-sheds he could see a boat which had been taken out. Wooden rollers were laid near it, ready for moving the boat to the water. This was Ericsson's. Sturdy, well built…

HARALD passed the boat and came to the door of the shed. In the soft sand his feet had made no sound; his approach had been undetected. Low murmurs came from within the shed and for a moment he listened, Names were mentioned. Ketil Sebbason, Ebinar Ulvsson, Ivar Svarte. Harald drew a deep breath. These were no mere hired assassins. Within the shed were some of the most potent enemies of the king. That realization gave new point to the task ahead of him. He opened the door, stepped inside and closed it after him.

A sharp silence fell, to be broken suddenly when a harsh voice rasped, "Who are you?"

On all sides of him, Harald could distinguish vague, shadowy figures. He answered clearly, "A friend of the king's."

There was need to say no more. A blade slashed out at him from the darkness and there was a concerted rush toward the door. Harald swung *Bretwalda* over his head, slashed with it to the left, to the right, to the left again. Screams filled the air and hoarse shouts tore from men's throats. Those in the front were urged on by those behind them. Swords flailing, they rushed in, some to trip over bodies, others to fall before the keen edge of Harald's axe. The clash of steel on steel, groans, curses, shouts and screams mingled together to make the night hideous.

A spear broke against Harald's coat of mail, a sword thrust pierced his leg. A fiery pain burned across his neck. Shadows danced before him. To right and to left he swung the great axe and there were none who could stand against it, yet the end was near.

He could feel his strength draining out through a dozen wounds. His legs tottered. His vision clouded. No longer could he see those dancing silhouettes distinctly. Before him the darkness seemed to be growing more intense. Only in his arms lay any strength. The great axe still was not heavy.

Ivar Svarte's voice came to him. "This way," Svarte was yelling. "I have found a loose board. We can tear it free, get outside. Ketil! Einar!"

There was fear in that voice. Harald laughed drunkenly. He cut his way through to the spot from which that voice had come, He heard Svarte scream, felt a blade slice into his shoulder as he brought down the axe. Svarte went down. Harald couldn't see it but he could feel it.

The darkness was closing in more rapidly. He stumbled, fell, tried to get up but couldn't lift his body.

Across his mind flashed the vision of a girl riding through the dawn along the Maeren road. A smile came to his lips and his grip on the axe loosened, but he didn't know it. He didn't know anything more. The darkness had become complete.

AS THE FIRST rays of the morning sun touched the waters of the bay at Nidaros, Leif Ericsson's ship put slowly out from the shore. On the beach, flanked by the two black-robed priests and surrounded by his soldiers, stood the erect figure of King Olav Tryggvason. Near him was Svein Jarl, moody and stooped with dead, glassy eyes.

Leif Ericsson stood on the steering platform of the ship and Tyrker was beside him.

"We are well away from here," said Tyrker slowly. "Had it not been for this Harald Wilton—"

"I know.'" Leif nodded. "Had it not been for him, the king and you and I and others of our crew might now be lying where lie those who plotted to take our lives. You saw the dead?"

"Aye."

"Svarte, Sebbasson, Ulvsson, Syr—all the men on whom Svein Jarl counted. He must start his plotting all over. And perhaps, before he can get far, Olav Tryggvason will realize his scheme."

They did not speak further of the frustrated revolt, but the mind of each man was filled with the same thought: that, while the king himself might never know, Harald Wilton had saved the throne of Norway.

A strong breeze filled the sail and the shore fell rapidly away. After a long silence, Ericsson said, "Was he still alive when we left?"

Tyrker nodded. "He was still alive, though by what miracle I do not know."

"Tell the girl," said Ericsson, "that I want to see her."

Tyrker left the steering platform and a few moments later Mercia took his place. There was a quiet, calm light in the girl's eyes. "You sent for me?" she asked.

Ericsson nodded. "How is he?"

There was a deep assurance in the girl's voice. "He will live. Such a one cannot die."

Ericsson frowned. He said slowly, "When we hid him on the boat I had thought that there was little chance for him. If he lives, what shall I do. He would not be safe in Norway or on any of the nearby islands for Olav Tryggvason still believes him a murderer. The plotters Harald killed, the king counted as his friends."

"Would he not be safe in Greenland?"

"I cannot take him with me to Greenland."

"Why not?"

"Because of my father. I cannot think that he knew it, but Rolf Wilton, Harald's father, died not long ago at the hands of Eric the Red."

"He knew it," said Mercia.

"He knew it!" Ericsson gasped.

"Aye, and it made no difference to him when he discovered that you were the son of Eric the Red."

"Yet I still cannot take him to Greenland. He is a Wilton and to my father it would make no difference what he had done for me. He hates the very sound of the name."

"Then England?"

"Nay. I dare not risk it. What English port is there that the ship of a Northman could enter and leave unharmed?"

Mercia bit her lips, stared straight ahead to the west. "Somewhere there should be a place."

For a long moment, Leif Ericsson was silent. Then a smile came to his lips and he nodded slowly. "There is a place," he said almost to himself, "that lies west of the Greenland sea. Far across the broad and mighty water... No man has ever been there. Many there are who say that the sea is unending and that no more lands exist. Yet often have I faced to the west and felt in the winds which blew against my face the knowledge of a far off country."

"Why not go there?" whispered the girl.

Leif Ericsson turned then and studied the girls tense, eager face. Again, for a moment or two he did not speak; he seemed to be judging both the girl and this wild plan. But at last he said slowly:

"You would risk such a voyage, Mercia?"

"Aye."

Leif Ericsson threw back his head and laughed. His hand tightened on the tiller. "Then we will," he declared. "We will sail west—west into the sunset. Go now and watch over Harald."

IV

PATHS OF CONQUEST

*October 14, 1066… the day that changed the
destiny of the world. And toward that day,
across the channel from France, raced Hugh
of the house of Wilton, bearing the mystic axe
Bretwalda the Maker and Destroyer of Kings.*

CHAPTER I

THE SWINEHERD WAS tall and young, and he lounged against a tree near the Rouen road as though he had not a care in the world. None of the men-at-arms who passed that way bothered to do more than glance at him for a swineherd was unworthy of their attention. And that was as well, for though clad in rags and begrimed of face, this lounging man was no swineherd, as any who paused to see could easily have discovered. His body was well muscled and straight, and below his high forehead his blue eyes were cold and sharp.

A man clad in tattered trousers and wearing an old, gray jacket and a peasant's hat, came trudging up the road and as he neared the swineherd turned aside to talk to him. His words were strange for a Norman peasant; they were in English.

"Hugh, why stand you out here in plain sight? If you were recognized—"

The swineherd shrugged. "Small chance, Oliver. Those who pass seem in a great hurry to get to Rouen or away from it."

"Aye."

"What news have you?"

"None."

"The palace maid—"

"She did not come to the meeting place and when I inquired at the palace a queer look came into the eyes of the page boy. He hurried away and when he came back guards were with him. Had I not been quick to get away I would not be here. We

must give up this mad plan, Hugh. There is no chance in the world that we can rescue Duke Edward of Mercia from the dungeons of William of Normandy."

Hugh Wilton smiled and placed an arm around the shoulder of his friend. "We know where Duke Eduard is held. That much we have gained."

"But to what purpose?"

A long column of horsemen clattered up the road. Sunlight glinted from their armor and from the points of their long spears. At the head of the column rode the blue banner of the house of Anjou.

"More French to join with the Normans," Hugh Wilton muttered. "It is a strange army that William of Normandy is gathering. French, Bretons, Teutons, Vikings from the north. Before he is through the scum of all Europe will be at his command."

Oliver Sweyn shuddered. "Five years ago," he said slowly, "a sorcerer told me to beware the year 1066."

"I care not for sorcery," Hugh Wilton answered.

The Briton knew that if he and his companion were recognized, their lives would end in the dungeons of William of Normandy.

"Nor I," admitted Oliver Sweyn. "Yet this is 1066 and this year King Edward the Confessor died. You know what has happened since. Both Tostig, his brother, and William of Normandy have claimed the English crown, which, by the Witan, was granted to Harold of Wessex. Tostig has allied himself with Hardrada, King of Norway. And you yourself have seen the preparations William of Normandy is making."

HUGH WILTON made no answer. How serious a problem England faced, he knew full well. It was that which had brought him here on an apparently hopeless mission. Shortly after Harold had been named King, he had sent Duke Edward of Mercia to Normandy with gifts and a message which he had thought might appease the anger of William of Normandy. But Duke Edward had been seized and thrown into the dungeons; and in Mercia, Roger Montfort had usurped Duke Edward's place. Long an enemy of Harold of Wessex, Roger Montfort was spreading dissension at a time when England's united strength was needed to preserve the kingdom.

The release of Duke Edward, Hugh Wilton knew, and his return to Mercia in England, would result in the defeat of Montfort's purpose, would throw all the power of Mercia behind King Harold. And with such help, England need not then fear either an invasion by the Vikings or by William of Normandy.

Oliver Sweyn was short and sturdy, round of face. He made a better looking peasant than he dreamed. "What now?" he asked bluntly.

Hugh Wilton had no chance to answer. A score of armored horsemen riding up the road turned suddenly aside, scattering the swine in every direction. One of the horsemen drew rein near the tree against which Hugh Wilton was leaning.

"Whose swine are these?" he demanded gruffly.

"They belong to William of Normandy," Hugh Wilton answered.

The man laughed. He was a large man, heavy, thick-featured. There was a wide scar across one cheek which drew his lips into a perpetual sneer. "We will borrow a few," he announced. "I am sure William of Normandy will not object."

Hugh Wilton shrugged. He did not move from the tree but stood watching as the man ordered those with him to go ahead. The swine were quick-footed, tough-skinned and half wild. The trees and shrubbery were thick. Using their spears, the horsemen sought to impale the animals. One tusked boar, wounded and snorting with pain, charged at the horsemen, and a horse, rearing to get out of the way, unseated his rider. But for the armor which protected him that rider might have felt the tusks of the boar.

Seven of the swine were finally slain by the soldiers who then mounted with them and rode off without another word.

As the men clattered back down the road, Hugh Wilton drew a deep breath and slowly nodded his head. "I have it, Oliver."

"Have what, Hugh?"

"A plan. The leader of those men was Otto de Balse. He was pointed out to me once when went to Paris with my father."

"The Tuscan."

"Aye, and William of Normandy's champion. Tomorrow, Oliver, I enter the lists."

Oliver Sweyn gasped. He stared at Hugh Wilton as though the latter were out of his mind. "Do you know what that means?" he whispered.

"It will mean freedom for Duke Edward. For a week, now, no one has dared answer de Balse's challenge. Each day he is proclaimed as William of Normandy's champion. And William of Normandy would not dare to refuse the request of the man who conquers him."

"But even should you conquer him—"

Again Hugh Wilton smiled. "Come, Oliver. Let us get back to Rouen. We will let the remainder of the swine go free. We have no more need for them."

A GREAT crowd was gathered in the palace grounds at Rouen. To one side, under a sheltering canopy, a group of nobles in shining armor and ladies in fine raiment were grouped around the throne chair of William of Normandy and circling the wide grounds were soldiers from many lands. Here and there were a few people from the town.

To the left of the Dukes canopy there were several tents. In these, the contestants in the day's games, prepared for their exhibitions or for battle, and in them, those who had been hurt were cared for. Banners and flags at various points gave to the scene a gala appearance.

These afternoon games and contests had been started by Duke William as something to keep the soldiers and nobles occupied while they awaited the completion of his fleet, and the favorable winds which would carry them across the channel to England.

Archers from Norway vied against archers from far away Tuscany. There were duels with sword and spear, exhibitions of horsemanship, wrestling.

In these contests were the crude beginnings of the tournament which fifty years later was to come into full bloom with the beginnings of the Crusades.

Hugh Wilton and Oliver Sweyn reached the palace grounds late in the afternoon and at a time when three of the Bretons were showing their skill with the cross-bow. The rags which Hugh Wilton had worn the afternoon before had been replaced by a coat-of-mail and his blond hair was covered by a Norman helmet with a fixed nasal, protecting the nose. At his side he wore a long sword.

"This is a mad plan of yours," Oliver Sweyn said bluntly as they paused at the edge of the crowd not far from the Duke's canopy. "Forget it, Hugh. If you are recognized—"

Hugh Wilton shrugged. His friend had been talking in the same vein since the afternoon before. He stared over at the group under the canopy. Duke William, at tall, round-faced man with a very black mustache, leaned back in his throne chair, and at his side Hugh Wilton could see his wife, Matilda. At the Duke's shoulder stood Count Henri d'Anjou, a tall, thin man, gray of hair and beard. A brief smile touched Hugh Wilton's lips. He knew Henri d'Anjou, had met him long ago. There was little chance, he decided, that he would be unrecognized.

A shout from the crowd drew Hugh Wilton's attention away from the canopy. One of the cross-bowmen, he saw, had been proclaimed victor and several of the man's friends had rushed forward to bear him in triumph from the field.

Trumpets shrilled and the crowd suddenly grew silent. Again the trumpets sounded and as their last echo faded out a stentorial voice shouted: "Otto de Balse, the Duke's champion!"

The crowd at the far side of the field, parted, and through the lane they made there came a warrior mounted on a white charger. His armor was burnished until it reflected the sun like water and from his helmet, which was a duplicate of the one Hugh Wilton wore, there floated a plume of red feathers.

Twice around the field de Balse rode, sitting very straight in the saddle, his gold tipped spear held erect at his side. Then drawing rein in front of Duke William, he cast the gage of battle to the ground, bowed and waited silent.

Hugh Wilton turned to his companion.

"If I do not come back, Oliver," he whispered swiftly, "make your way to England and fight for me at our King's side."

Oliver Sweyn nodded and tears showed in his eyes as he said, "You're a fool, Hugh, but I love you for it. God go with you."

HUGH WILTON pushed forward and started across the open space toward the canopy. A great shout arose from the crowd. He saw Otto de Balse swing down from his saddle and turn to pick up the gage of battle which he had cast to the ground, saw the Duke's champion stiffen as de Balse noticed him.

He moved steadily ahead, reached the place where lay the glove which de Balse had thrown to the ground. He stooped over, picked it up, tucked it in his belt. Again the trumpets sounded and as their echo faded, a heavy voice cried out, "A challenger to meet the Duke's champion. Your name, sir?"

Hugh Wilton was standing not more than eight paces from the canopy and he stared straight at Duke William. Before he could speak, however, someone leaned over and whispered in the Duke's ear and William of Normandy turned his head. Hugh Wilton glanced at the man who had whispered to the Duke. He felt a sudden chill run over his body, became aware of a deep anger boiling in his veins. Tall, thin and dark was that man who had whispered to the Duke. He had a long, crooked nose, bloodless lips, deep-set, little eyes. Roger Montfort!

Hugh Wilton sucked in a deep breath. He could hardly believe his eyes. That Roger Montfort who had usurped Duke Edward's power in Mercia, hated King Harold of England, he knew. But that Roger Montfort would have dealings with William of Normandy was almost unbelievable. Yet there he stood at Duke William's side, a thin mocking smile on his lips.

Hugh Wilton stepped forward. He glanced over at Count Henri d'Anjou and saw that the old man had recognized him.

Now, however, that made little difference, because beyond doubt, Roger Montfort knew him.

A pace from the canopy, Hugh Wilton paused. "My name," he said bluntly, "is Hugh Wilton of Mercia."

Duke William jerked to his feet. His face was flushed with anger. "What do you here?" he demanded harshly.

Hugh Wilton bowed. "I am here, Duke William, to challenge your champion. I have taken up his gage."

"And should you win?"

"And should I win I ask of you the life and freedom of Duke Edward of Mercia who is held in your dungeons."

At that bold statement, a gasp ran over those people under the canopy. Roger Montfort scowled, moistened his lips.

From Hugh Wilton's side, a thick yoke said confidently, "He will not win, sire. I am de Balse."

Wilton glanced at de Balse. The man's eyes were narrowed and hard. His face, twisted by the scar on his cheek, wore its usual sneer. Looking back at the Duke, Hugh Wilton saw that Montfort was again whispering to him. And whatever it was that Montfort said must have pleased the Duke for the Duke laughed and waved his hand and cried, "Let the contest go on."

Otto de Balse turned to the lady seated at Duke Williams side. "Madame," he said boldly, "I dedicate this fight to you."

There was a flutter of applause from the women who were gathered back of Matilda's chair but one of them, Hugh Wilton saw, did not clap her hands. She was a tall, slender girl, fair of hair. Her eyes were as blue as his own. Something in her face seemed familiar to him but Hugh Wilton didn't know just what it was. She was frowning slightly and it seemed to him that she looked worried. On a sudden impulse, Hugh Wilton stepped toward her.

"And I, fair lady," he said boldly, "dedicate the fight to you."

Those standing near the girl drew away as though afraid of being mistakenly identified as the one Hugh Wilton meant.

But the girl, herself, showed no embarrassment and it seemed to Hugh Wilton that she was pleased.

HE SWUNG around, faced de Balse. De Balse's sword was out and with a loud shout the Tuscan charged forward. Hugh Wilton jerked up his blade. He parried the blow, took a cut at the Tuscan's head, parried another and then another. And suddenly his high laugh rang out above the sound of clashing steel and the shouts of the watching crowd. Champion this man might be and feared he might have been by all in the camp.

Yet Hugh Wilton knew that he was the better man. His stature was as great as the Tuscan's, his arms were as thick, his movements swifter. From the time when he was only a boy his father had drilled him in the use of the sword and the axe. He could recall now, as he faced de Balse, the long torturous hours he had spent in developing his skill. At times he had hated his father for driving him at it, yet now he had cause to be thankful.

Around and around they circled, now one rushing to the attack, now the other. Their feet churned up thick, black dust which gathered around them like a cloud. Through it, Hugh Wilton could see that de Balse was perspiring. He did not look so confident, now. Fear showed in his eyes and he was biting his lips.

Hugh Wilton moved forward. He slashed down with his sword. Again and again. Each blow beat de Balse's guard lower. Once more Hugh Wilton laughed. His sword swept up and down. There was a sharp crack and the blade broke off at the hilt!

A shout went up from the crowd and a new light came into de Balse's eyes. He rushed at Hugh Wilton, blade uplifted. But Hugh Wilton did not give back. Instead, hurling the broken hilt of his sword directly at de Balse's face, he moved to meet him.

Under that swinging sword he ducked and with both hands he grasped the Tuscan's body. Up into the air he swung it while the crowd gasped in stunned amazement. Three times, then, did Hugh Wilton turn around, de Balse's twisting body held above his head. And suddenly he threw it from him as a man might have tossed a heavy timber.

The Tuscan struck the ground heavily and lay where he fell, a scant pace from the canopy. Hugh Wilton glanced over at Duke William. The Duke was standing, his mouth wide open, amazement written on his face. "A new champion! A new champion!" the crowd was shouting.

But black rage suffused the face of William of Normandy. He lifted an arm and shouted, "The guard! The guard! Seize and hold that man!"

"Your pledge Duke William?" Hugh Wilton called.

"I will keep my pledge," William of Normandy answered. "But as for you—"

The Norman guards were rushing forward. They surrounded Hugh Wilton as a wall of steel. He had no weapon with which to defend himself. For an instant his mind turned back to the great axe which he had brought with him, the axe *Bretwalda*. It was an axe which had come down to him from his father. He would have given a lot, just then, to have held *Bretwalda* in his hands but the axe was hidden on the outskirts of Rouen.

"Seize him!" shouted William of Normandy. "He will take Duke Edward's place in the dungeons."

The Norman guard moved forward. Over the shoulders of two of them, Hugh Wilton caught sight of the girl to whom he had dedicated the fight. She was standing proudly erect, smiling at him. And then suddenly her place was taken by Roger Montfort and on Montfort's face there was a mocking sneer. The elation Hugh Wilton had felt at his victory and in the knowledge that Duke Edward would be released, was abruptly dampened. He stepped toward Montfort but the Norman guards closed in around him, seized his arms and dragged him away.

CHAPTER II

THE DUNGEON CELL was damp and bitterly cold. Foul, stagnant water seeped through the stone walls and gathered in a pool on the stone floor. Gaunt rats ventured into the cell. In the dim, half light, it sometimes seemed to Hugh Wilton that they sat around grinning at him, confident of his death and of a chance to fatten themselves off of what was left of him when he no longer had the strength to frighten them away.

There was no way of marking time save by his increasing hunger, thirst and weakness. There was no hope of escape. The door of his cell was heavy, barred and strong. When he had first been brought here Wilton had known that he would never leave. Eventual death came to all who had the ill fortune to be thrown into the dungeons under the Norman castle at Rouen.

All save one. Duke Edward of Mercia. It was here that he had been confined, and in the knowledge of his release, Hugh Wilton felt a grim satisfaction.

In the early days of his confinement, Hugh Wilton tried to imagine what the result of Duke Edward's release would mean. In his mind he could picture Duke Edward's return to Mercia and he knew that the fighting men of Mercia would rally to the Duke's command. Duke Edward had a deep loyalty to King Harold of England, and aware of the strength of William of Normandy, he would give King Harold his full support. Five thousand men he could summon in a few days and five thousand men might make all the difference between defeat and victory.

Roger Montfort would have no chance against him. Though he had usurped Duke Edward's authority, he could never stand against the rightful ruler of Mercia. Duke Edwards was too well loved by his people. Montfort might tell the people of Mercia that there was no danger from the invaders and that there was no reason to leave their fields and go to battle. But when Duke Edward appeared and summoned the men, there were none who would not answer his call.

At first it was easy for Hugh Wilton to reason all that out

and to understand that whatever else might be said of William of Normandy, he was at least a man of his word and would let Duke Edward go. But as time went on and as hunger gnawed at Hugh Wilton's stomach and as his throat cried out for water and as he could feel his strength slipping away from him, his mind grew clouded and the mocking smile of Roger Montfort came to torment him.

At times, then, he would imagine hearing a footfall in the corridor outside his door, would imagine the opening of the door, would vision Montfort standing out there, laughing at him.

A hand shaking Hugh Wilton's shoulder aroused him from the depths of a sodden lethargy and a voice said sharply, "Come on. Get up and follow me."

Hugh Wilton blinked. He sat up. The cell door was open and a soldier was bending over him.

"Come on," growled the soldier. "I have but little time."

Hugh Wilton got to his knees, to his feet. He leaned unsteadily against the wall. The soldier turned away, moved through the door and turned along a dim, narrow corridor.

For a moment Hugh Wilton didn't move. His mind was stunned by the suddenness of the soldier's arrival and by the open door of his cell.

"Come on," said the soldier gruffly.

He was alone. There were no others out in the corridor. And the abrupt realization that this might mean his deliverance from the dungeons went to Hugh Wilton's head like wine. With a strength which he didn't know that he still possessed, he stepped out into the corridor, started after the soldier.

Through one barred door and then another, the soldier led him. They climbed a long stairway, passed another door. Near it, three soldiers lay in a drunken stupor. Hugh Wilton stared at them.

Across a hallway the soldier had opened still another door. "Outside," he said sharply.

Through that doorway, Hugh Wilton could see the thin crescent of a moon and a star-studded sky! No sight which had ever met his eyes had seemed more wonderful. He crossed over to the door, passed through it.

Two men stepped forward, took him by the arms and started leading him away from the towering wall of the castle. Who they were, Hugh Wilton didn't know; where they were taking him, he didn't know. A sudden weakness swept over him. His body sagged against one of the men and again his mind clouded.

A SWEET, life-giving liquid warmed his stomach and from somewhere near him a voice said: "That's enough now. He can have more later."

Hugh Wilton opened his eyes. He was lying on a straw pallet in a dimly lighted room and a heavy, red-faced woman was kneeling at his side. In her hand she held a bowl and from the bowl came a delicious smell. Hugh Wilton reached for it but the woman drew away and from behind her the same voice which he had heard before said, "Not now. You can have more later."

Hugh Wilton turned his eyes that way. Beyond the kneeling woman stood the tall, slender figure of a girl. A dark cloak covered her body and the hood was pulled over her head. She turned slightly and the candlelight fell on her face. It was a small, round face. It was a face Hugh Wilton remembered. It was the face of the girl to whom he had dedicated his fight with Otto de Balse.

"You?" he said. "You did this for me?"

The girl looked at him steadily, shook her head. "I did it for a long-legged awkward boy who once came to Paris and whose father did a service for the Count of Anjou."

Hugh Wilton knew, then, why the girl's face had seemed familiar. This was the daughter of Count Henri of Anjou. She had been with her father in Paris on that occasion long ago just as he had been there with his father.

"Thyra d'Anjou," he murmured.

A brief smile touched the girl's lips. "You remember my name. I had not thought—"

The girl's voice broke off as there was a sudden commotion at the door. Hugh Wilton raised himself up on his elbow. The door burst open and Oliver Sweyn came into the room. He was breathless and there was a cut on his cheek. Blood dripped from a wounded arm.

"Hugh!" he cried.

"Oliver!"

Oliver Sweyn hurried over to where Hugh Wilton lay. "Thank God you are free," he said huskily, dropping on his knees. "I was afraid—"

"What has happened?" asked Thyra d'Anjou swiftly. "Have the guards—"

"No. It was not the castle guards."

"Then—"

"Have you told Hugh about Duke Edward?"

Hugh Wilton straightened up. He felt a little dizzy but his friend's excitement had gripped him. "What about Duke Edward?" he demanded. "Didn't William of Normandy free him?"

"Aye. He freed him, all right. But he freed a man who was almost dead. Had it not been for Count Henri d'Anjou I doubt if he would have lived. He had had no food for weeks, Hugh. He was thin, weak. Like—like you—"

A sharp fear gripped Hugh Wilton's heart. "Then he did go to England?"

"He could not go. Henri d'Anjou took care of him."

"And William of Normandy? Has he left for England?"

"He sailed with his army more than a week ago."

HUGH WILTON got slowly to his feet. He stared at Oliver Sweyn. All that he had tried, then, he suddenly realized, had gone for nothing. William of Normandy was already in England. Perhaps he had already met and defeated King Harold.

"I made myself known to Count Henri," Oliver Sweyn was saying, "and I secured a boat to take Duke Edward to England as soon as he was strong enough to make the journey. It is not yet too late, or it was not too late up to an hour ago. William of Normandy has not yet met the English. He landed at Pevensey and has been ravaging the coast, waiting for the English to march and meet him. A messenger brought me that word from England. He also brought me word that King Harold met and defeated his brother Tostig and Kind Hardrada, though at a terrific loss to his army."

"Then there is still a chance?" Hugh Wilton cried. "If Duke Edward can reach England, if he can rally Mercia, the cause is not lost. Where is Duke Edward, now?"

Oliver Sweyn stared at his wounded arm. "In the hands of men sent to take him to England—men sent by Roger Montfort."

"What!"

"Only a few minutes ago did they arrive. I tried to stop them but there were too many. They put him in a coach, headed for Le Havre."

Hugh Wilton's eyes turned from side to side. Over in one corner of the room he saw the axe *Bretwalda* and at the sight of it he drew a deep breath. He moved that way, reached for the long handle. A great weapon was this axe which had come down to him from his father. Both the head and handle were of the finest steel and the cutting edge of the axe was a full six hands wide, Above that edge was the deeply engraven name, *Bretwalda* and over those letters there were nine blood red jewels. Once there had been twelve, but three were lost.

So heavy was the axe that the average man could not wield it, yet to Hugh Wilton, the axe had no great weight. His father had told him its story—that to a Wilton, the strength to wield *Bretwalda* came from the axe itself, and not from any physical prowess. What truth there was in that Hugh Wilton did not know, yet this axe had become the symbol of his family. In its mystic powers, his father had believed and he half believed in those powers himself. Certainly, with it in his hands, he felt an assurance which nothing could shake.

The red-faced woman was bandaging Oliver Sweyn's arm and near her, Hugh Wilton noticed the bowl from which he had been fed. He moved that way, reached for the bowl, drained it.

"Duke Edward, and no other," he said slowly, "can arouse all of Mercia. It is not yet too late."

"Those men who took Duke Edward will see that he never reaches England," Oliver Sweyn muttered.

"Aye, but we will see that he does reach England. Get us two horses, Oliver. We ride after them, to Le Havre. They would not dare to slay Duke Edward here in Normandy after William of Normandy's pledge. They will wait until they are crossing the channel. If we can overtake them—"

DURING all this, Thyra d'Anjou had been standing to one side, glancing from Hugh Wilton to Oliver Sweyn, but now, as Oliver turned to the door, she moved that way and stood before it.

"No," she said sharply. "You are not going to La Havre."

Oliver stopped, frowning. He looked over at Hugh Wilton.

"What do you mean?" Hugh Wilton asked.

The girl's lips tightened and she lifted her head, proudly. "I am my father's daughter," she answered, "and my father, at the request of King Philip of France, fights at the side of William of Normandy." The girl looked over at Hugh Wilton. "I bribed the guards to release you from the dungeons to pay an old debt of my family's but I cannot let you escape to England to fight against my father, or to see that Duke Edward gets there to raise more men for the English king."

Hugh Wilton scowled. "I am an Englishman," he said bluntly. "What I have to do is clear. Oliver, find us two horses."

"No!" cried Thyra d'Anjou. "If you leave this room I will summon the guard. If you—"

Hugh Wilton stepped swiftly forward, seized Thyra d'Anjou and pulled her away from the door. The girl screamed. His arm went around her and his hand closed over her mouth. "The horses, Oliver," he said sharply.

Oliver rushed from the room while Hugh held the struggling figure of the girl who had been responsible for his escape from the dungeons. She was stronger than she looked and it was all he could do to hold her fast. Her hair came loose and tumbled around her shoulders. He could feel her teeth biting at the palm of his hand. From across the room the red-faced woman watched them uncertainly.

Wilton's emotions, during the moments which followed, were of a strange mixture. He felt deep regret that he couldn't better repay this girl for what she had done for him. He felt amazement at her strength, and at the same time he was acutely conscious of the softness of her body and of the scent of her hair. Yet beyond all this and more important than anything else lay the knowledge of his responsibility to his king and the realization of how essential it was that Duke Edward return to Mercia in time to arouse that part of the country to the king's support.

Footsteps hammered up to the door and the door burst open. "I have a coach," Oliver called from outside. "It will be easier on you, Hugh, and it will still get us to Le Havre before Roger Montfort's men can put out from the harbor. They will not leave before dawn."

Still holding the girl, Hugh Wilton moved to the door. He was thankful for Oliver's wisdom in securing a coach, not only because in his own weakened condition a coach would be better than a long ride by horse. But also because he knew that they didn't dare leave Thyra d'Anjou or the red-faced woman behind to give an alarm.

"Bring the other woman," he said to Oliver. "And my axe. Are the horses fresh?"

"They will make it."

Wilton nodded. He lifted Thyra and carried her to the coach.

CHAPTER III

THE ROAD TO Le Havre ran along the Seine. It was rough and the coach bounced along at a mad pace. Wilton braced himself in one of the two seats. In the other, facing him, were Thyra and the red-faced woman. The night was dark and Hugh couldn't see either of them. He felt a little thankful for that. As he had placed Thyra in the coach the expression of scorn on her face had cut him like a knife.

Oliver was driving with all the skill he possessed. Wilton wondered, several times, if a coach had ever before traveled as fast as this one. At times it rocked perilously on two wheels and seemed about to go over; and time and time again, heavy jolts almost threw him from the seat.

Bretwalda was on the floor beneath his feet and the knowledge that it was there gave him a deep assurance. Before they had left Rouen he had said to Oliver, "Get us to Le Havre before those men of Roger Montfort's can sail with Duke Edward. That is all I ask."

"And when we get there?" Oliver Sweyn had inquired.

"And when we get there," Hugh Wilton had said grimly, "we will take over the boat. With Duke Edward we will sail for England. There may still be time to rally Mercia behind the king."

He kept saying that to himself, over and over, as the coach rocked on through the night. And though he knew that Oliver was driving the horses to death, he kept saying under his breath, "Faster—faster—faster—"

He knew by what a narrow thread hung the fate of England. If they failed to overtake Roger Montfort's men before they sailed he knew that Duke Edward would never reach England alive. And without the help which Duke Edward could give to the king he was afraid that William of Normandy might conquer.

England was still not a united country. The old divisions persisted. Men of Wessex had few dealings with men of East Anglia; men of Northumberland dealt suspiciously with men of Mercia. Only their leaders could unite them. And with Duke Edward gone and Roger Montfort stirring up old enmities, King Harold's power was broken.

"Faster—faster—faster—" Hugh Wilton breathed. "There may yet be time! There may yet be time!"

The eastern sky was beginning to grow light and the stars were fading in the sky. Hugh could make out Thyra's face. She was looking straight at him without seeing him. If she felt any fear it did not show in her face. Proud and unbending, one hand clutched to the coach strap and the other to the seat, she held her place. The red-faced woman was no longer red faced. She looked pale and frightened.

With a series of sudden jolts, the coach stopped. Hugh Wilton flung open the door, stepped outside. His legs felt weak and a blinding dizziness assailed him. He leaned back against the coach, pressed a hand over his eyes.

Oliver clambered down to his side. "We're here," he said swiftly. "Yonder is the harbor and there is only one boat. There are none within sight on the water."

Hugh Wilton blinked, nodded. On the shore near the boat there was another coach and near it were several horses. Between them and the boat lay some score of wretched hovels in which lived the fishermen who made this place their home.

ON THE BOAT there were signs of activity. It is a small boat with only one tall mast and as Hugh Wilton looked that way, men working at the ropes began raising a square sail.

"Drive on down there," Hugh Wilton ordered. "Drive straight into the water, as close to the boat as you can get."

He climbed back into the coach, picked up *Bretwalda*.

"You are going to try to take that boat alone?" Thyra whispered.

"Oliver and I." Hugh Wilton nodded.

"You haven't a chance."

"Nevertheless we must take it."

The girl looked at him strangely. She bit her lips as the coach lurched on down toward the harbor.

As the horses splashed into the water, Wilton opened the door once more. It was a deep harbor and almost at once the horses were floundering beyond their depth. But because it was deep, the boat was also close to the shore, not more than a few paces from where the coach started to float. At the vessel's rail, six or eight startled faces stared out at the coach. Hugh Wilton threw his great axe directly at them and he saw the men scramble back.

He jumped into the water, splashed toward the boat, sinking once but kicking his way to the surface again. Near him was a rope. He grasped it, went up that rope hand over hand, sprawled to the deck, got up and rushed forward to where two men were bending over the axe. And hurling those men aside, he lifted *Bretwalda* into the air.

Those near him in that moment were only fishermen, owners of the boat, perhaps. They had been startled at the sight of a coach plunging into the water, at the axe flung on board, at his own arrival when he clambered up the rope. They fell back from him as he lifted the axe, surprise and bewilderment showing in their faces.

But those were not the only men on board for suddenly half a score, fully armored, burst around the side of the cabin and rushed toward Hugh Wilton with drawn swords.

In the instant before they clashed, Hugh recognized several of those men as men he knew for friends of Montfort. And despite the straggling beard on his face and his haggard appearance, some of them must have recognized him for he heard his name shouted and saw one or two of them fall back. The others, however, came on and the sudden, sharp clashing of steel sounded across the harbor as they met.

The details of that fight on the boat were never very clear in Hugh Wilton's mind.

Swinging *Bretwalda* above his head he met their charge and under the slashing strokes of his great axe he could feel them giving back. Screams, hoarse, agonizing cries, shouts and yells arose above the sound of the battle. Sword points pricked Hugh Wilton's arms and legs but closer than that, none of those men could get. The axe was like a protecting wall of steel. Of its great weight he was not conscious, but only of an exhilarating sense of power as he swung it and as men went down under its hungry bite.

Oliver Sweyn, a sword in his good arm, was suddenly at his side. How he had come on board, Hugh Wilton didn't know, but the sight of his friend brought a shout from his throat.

"After them!" Oliver yelled. "After them!"

The defenders of the boat broke and fled under their combined assault. Several sprang into the sea, others cringed away, dropping their weapons. And as suddenly as it had started, the fight was over.

Hugh Wilton lowered the great axe. He leaned back against the cabin. What had sustained him during that fight he didn't know. Now that it was over he could hardly stand erect and a great pain was tearing at his stomach.

Oliver came running up. "He's here. Duke Edward is here and is safe. And now—"

"And now for England," Hugh Wilton interrupted. "The women in the coach?"

"I will see to them and to men to sail the ship," Oliver Sweyn promised. "Duke Edward is in the cabin."

Hugh Wilton nodded. He turned and moved unsteadily toward the cabin's door.

UNDER the spur of a heavy wind, the fishing boat put out from the harbor. Gold, of which Oliver Sweyn had a goodly supply, bought the services of the men necessary to handle it. In the cabin, Hugh Wilton talked to Duke Edward, talked of Montfort, of King Harold, of the impending battle. He was shocked at Duke Edward's appearance. The man was but a shadow of his former self. Gaunt, haggard, pale, he looked as though he still stood on the threshold of death. But despite that, the character of the men still showed in his flashing eyes.

"A day to England, two more to Mercia," he said to Hugh Wilton. "You must get to King Harold as soon as we land. Given a week I will bring him ten thousand fighting men. Make him delay the battle, no matter what the cost."

And Hugh nodded. Someone brought him food and he ate it wolfishly, got up and staggered to the deck. The sea was choppy and rough and his stomach, unaccustomed to food, began churning up and down.

Oliver joined him and Wilton asked sharply, "When will we reach the coast?"

"Not before tomorrow dawn, so the fishermen tell me."

"We must get there sooner. There is no time to lose."

Oliver Sweyn looked judiciously at his friend and a faint smile touched his lips. "I know how you feel, Hugh," he said slowly, "A great impatience is driving you, Hugh. It is also driving me. But this ship will go no faster than the winds can carry it."

Hugh Wilton knew it was true. There was nothing for him to do until the ship reached England. He moved forward to the prow, stared out to the west. A salt spray dashed against his face but he was unaware of it. He sat down and leaned his head against the bulwark and began thinking of England; and fell suddenly asleep.

IT WAS dark when he woke and there was a blanket over his shoulders. He threw it back, sat up. The sky above him was clear and the wind had gone down. The boat hardly seemed to be moving. Near him, there was a vague movement in the darkness. Hugh Wilton glanced around. Not far from where he had been lying stood the slender figure of Thyra. Her hood had dropped back; and she was looking out across the sea.

"What do you here?" Hugh Wilton asked suddenly.

The girl turned to face him. "Your friend brought me on

board from the coach," she answered. And the tone of her voice told him nothing. She sounded neither angry nor wholly indifferent.

A deep frown creased Wilton's forehead. He recalled having told Oliver to take care of the women and he guessed that Oliver could think of nothing else to do but bring them on board.

"Where are you taking me?" asked the girl.

"To England," Hugh Wilton replied.

"Where you plan to join your King and where Duke Edward plans to raise the men of Mercia against the invasion of William of Normandy?"

"Aye, that is it."

"But to what purpose, Hugh Wilton? Did not Edward the Confessor promise the English crown to William of Normandy?"

"Perhaps. But the Witan, the English council, gave it to Harold of Wessex."

"Think you that William of Normandy would make a poor king? He is honest, just, wise. I know all that from what my father has said."

"But he is not a Briton."

"And who are your Britons? Are not many of them Danes, just as William of Normandy?"

Again Hugh Wilton frowned. He was silent for a moment and when he looked around, the girl was gone. She was back in a moment, however, bringing him bread and meat and a flagon of wine; and at the sight of the food, Hugh Wilton's hands trembled and he realized suddenly how hungry he was.

Mumbling his thanks, he reached for the food. Thyra knelt down beside him, watched him eat. And after a while she said quietly, "You are much like your father. I remember him well. That axe you have used to be his, didn't it?"

Hugh Wilton nodded.

"It seems so heavy that I wonder that you can swing it."'

A faint smile touched Hugh Wilton's lips. "It is an axe which has been long in our family. A man named Caedmon forged it in the time of the first great English king, Alfred. And it is said that the strength to wield it comes not from the man but from the axe itself."

"You would use it in defense of King Harold."

"Aye."

The girl stared out to the west, toward the still hidden English shore. And after a long time she said slowly, "Hugh Wilton, I would not have you change sides, even though you might meet my father on the field of battle. A man must hold true to what he believes, no matter what the cost. I could not help you come to England. So long as I could, I had to try to keep you from coming. But since I could not do that there is something that I would tell you."

"What would you tell me?"

"Only this. That if William of Normandy conquers he will become an English king. As Duke of Normandy, he owes allegiance to King Philip of France. That is one reason you oppose him, I know. But you need have no fears along that line."

"Why do you say that?"

"Because my lather says it, my father who was sent by the French king to help him. And my father knows."

"But why do you tell me this?"

Again the girl was silent for a moment. Then again speaking slowly, she said, "I tell you this, Hugh Wilton, because I have a feeling that you will fail to arrive in England in time to accomplish what you desire. I tell you because I believe that William of Normandy will defeat the English king."

"Never!"

The girl shrugged. "And if he does?"

"There will still be those of us to fight him."

"And lose your lives as outlaws or rebels."

A STRANGE, uneasy feeling came over Hugh Wilton. The assurance in the girl's voice was a thing he couldn't overlook. A sudden, deep bitterness swept over him. He had on this boat a man who could raise all Mercia to England's defense, yet if that man didn't get to Mercia in time to raise his army, it would avail them nothing. He stared out into the darkness ahead, scowling.

Thyra leaned forward, moved the blanket so that it was around his shoulders, and suddenly, for a reason which he couldn't understand, he was sharply aware of her presence and of the fact that she was a woman, beautiful, desirable and of a proud and noble line. It occurred to him to wonder what their fate might have been could their second meeting have come about under other conditions.

He leaned back, closed his eyes and smiled. And once more, then, he dropped off to sleep. Thyra moved closer to him, rearranged the blanket so that it covered him more completely. And when be turned restlessly in his slumber she lifted his head and rested it in her lap and ran her fingers through his long, blond locks of hair, smoothing it back from his forehead. Oliver Sweyn came forward once and saw them and tiptoed quietly away and left them alone.

CHAPTER IV

A LIGHT, CHILLY fog thickened the air during the early hours of the morning and as the boat drew near to the English coast, Hugh Wilton, with the blanket still around his shoulders, turned to Oliver.

"What point is this?" he asked.

"It is near the town of Hastings, so the fishermen say."

"Duke Edward?"

"He still sleeps. I had not thought to waken him until the last moment. It will be a long, hard journey to Mercia."

Hugh Wilton nodded. He said slowly, "You will go with him,

Oliver. You will find a coach. There is no one who can handle horses like you."

"And what of yourself, Hugh?"

"I go to find King Harold. To persuade him to delay the battle until the men of Mercia can arrive."

The boat was now closer to the shore and back away from the cove toward which they were headed, Hugh Wilton could now make out the cluster of houses which he knew must comprise the village of Hastings.

Oliver turned back to the cabin and a few minutes later the ship hove to and several of the fishermen lowered a small boat.

Wilton moved that way and Oliver came from the cabin, half carrying the gaunt figure of Duke Edward. Together, they got the man into the boat.

"We will go with you," said a voice at Hugh Wilton's shoulder.

He glanced around. Thyra and the red-faced woman were standing near him.

Hugh Wilton shrugged. He knew from the reports that Oliver had received from England, that William of Normandy's army was in the territory near this part of the coast. That meant that the girl's father could not be far away. It would not be difficult, he decided, for her to find him and he knew that Count Henri would see that his daughter and her friend would be safe.

The two women got into the boat and Hugh and Oliver Sweyn followed them. No one met them when they landed and as they reached the village it at first seemed deserted. A gangling youth, however, suddenly came running around the corner of one of the houses and Hugh Wilton hailed him.

The youth stared with wide open mouth at the three men and two women, at the great axe on Hugh Wilton's shoulder. He came closer to where they stood.

"Where is everyone?" Hugh Wilton demanded. "Where can we get a coach, horses?"

The youth blinked. "You are going to the battle?"

"Battle?" Hugh Wilton cried.

"Aye. On Senlac Hill."

Hugh Wilton felt himself gripped by apprehension. Perspiration broke out all over his body. "What battle, lad? What are you talking about?" he demanded.

The youth made no answer. As though suddenly recalling some mission which the sight of these men had interrupted but which was very important, he swung around and started running on down toward a house closer to the shore.

Hugh Wilton called after him but the youth did not stop and looking over at Oliver Sweyn, he asked, "What think you that he meant?"

Oliver Sweyn shook his head. "I do not know. There is a hill just beyond here known as Senlac Hill. It is high and could be well defended. If King Harold were ready to give battle to the forces of William of Normandy, he could pick no better place."

"But he must not yet give battle."

Oliver made no answer. There was no answer to be made. Hugh Wilton heard Duke Edward muttering, "If I but had a week. If I could but get to Mercia a full ten thousand men could I rally."

Thyra was standing near the duke. Hugh glanced at her and saw that her eyes were resting on him and that there was something of sadness in her expression. He recalled abruptly the prediction she had made on the boat the night before, the prediction that William of Normandy would be victorious.

DOWN the road which angled off to the west came a galloping horse and rider. The rider was swaying from side to side and as he drew closer Hugh Wilton could see that his whole side was stained with blood. Suddenly he lost his seat and fell heavily to the ground. The horse stopped, looked back, snorted and moved a little to one side.

Hugh Wilton looked at Oliver. "I'll take that horse," he said sharply. "Even yet it may not be too late to get King Harold to withdraw. Can you get Duke Edward to Mercia?"

"I'll get him there, Hugh."

"Horses? A coach?"

"I'll get horses and a coach if I have to take them away from William of Normandy himself."

Duke Edward drew himself up. "Find the king," he said to Hugh Wilton. "Tell him that I am here. Tell him that within a week, all Mercia will be marching to support him."

There was a ring in Duke Edward's voice, a note of challenge which straightened Hugh Wilton's shoulders. He glanced over at Thyra and he suddenly recalled the moment of his wakening that morning. His head had been in Thyra's lap and her hands had been warming his shoulders. The strange sweetness of that moment came back to him now. He took a step toward the girl, stopped. The shifting of the wind brought to his ears the din of clashing arms and the faint, distant shouting of many voices.

Abruptly, then, Hugh Wilton swung around. He started running toward the horse. It seemed to him that he heard Thyra's voice calling his name but he wasn't sure. He reached the horse, seized its bridle, threw himself into the saddle, wheeled around and started up the road.

ON THAT morning of the fourteenth of October in the year 1066, King Harold of England inspected the stockade and trench with which his men had fortified Senlac Hill. On Telham Mound and on the higher ground around Hastings, the Norman forces were encamped. All night long he had watched their campfires and with the coming of the dawn he had known that they would attack.

In the position he had chosen he felt a deep confidence. To the right the ground below the hill was marshy and impassable. To the left and on the hill were grouped his men. Staunch warriors they were. At Stamford Bridge near York a few weeks before they had turned back the forces of King Hardrada of Norway and now they would repel this other invasion, unless—

A momentary doubt crept into King Harold's mind, He had

lost many men at Stamford Bridge and were their force but a little stronger—

"Shall I plant the standard here, Sire?" asked a voice.

King Harold looked around. Near him stood a soldier who carried a banner displaying the Golden Dragon of Wessex.

"Yes," King Harold answered. "Plant the banner here. I will not leave this place until victory is ours."

Norman trumpets shattered the quiet of the early morning hour and through the gray dawn King Harold could see the Norman battle line forming below the hill. He watched quietly as they began their advance.

Before them rode a minstrel, tossing his sword high into the air and dexterously catching it as it fell. He was singing as he rode forward. The minstrel's name was Taillefer and the song he sang was the Song of Roland.

Nearer and nearer drew the minstrel and closer and closer came the line of Norman foot soldiers. A flight of arrows clouded the sky and hoarse, shouting voices broke in on the minstrel's song. Suddenly, then, the two forces met. Swords flashed in the early dawn and shield butted against shield. The minstrel's song was stopped by death.

From the left a charge of Norman horsemen was broken by the stockade on Senlac Hill and from behind that stockade poured English knights with sword, axe and spear.

WHILE still far off, Hugh Wilton saw the battle array. On the crest of the hill he could distinguish King Harold's banner and in the Norman ranks he could make out the pennant of the house of Anjou and flags from Breton and Tuscany. He made for the hill, whipping his horse mercilessly. And coming up behind the English ranks he threw himself to the ground and pressed forward. Beyond the stockade lay a score of silent, motionless figures. Here and there, wounded men were crawling and dragging themselves away from the field of battle.

King Harold stood near his banner, a bared, bloody sword in his hand. Hugh Wilton reached his side, bowed, straightened.

"I have just come from Normandy, Sire," he said bluntly. "Duke Edward came with me. He is now on his way to Mercia. In a week he can raise ten thousand men. In a week—"

"In a week," said King Harold, "we will not need them.'"

Hugh Wilton bit his lips. He knew something of King Harold's pride, of his stubbornness. He started to speak again but the king interrupted him.

"By nightfall we will have pushed the Normans back into the sea. What matters it that we are outnumbered? We will let them break their forces against this stockade, against our position here. Then, when they are weary, we will advance."

"But if we waited for the men of Mercia—"

"I have not the patience to wait," answered King Harold.

Someone hurrying up demanded the king's attention and Hugh Wilton turned away. The sense of failure was strongly upon him. He bit his lips, stared out over the Norman lines. How Harold could possibly defeat so great a number he couldn't see.

Again the Norman lines charged forward. Hugh Wilton's lips tightened, he straightened up. No matter what the result of this issue, here was his place at the side of his king. He lifted *Bretwalda* and with the others he rushed to repel the attack.

All track of time was lost by those defending the hill. The early fog thinned and the sun came out bright. It rose high in a cloudless sky. Again and again the Norman attack was broken and again and again their forces were hurled back. The dead and dying cluttered up the brow of the hill and the shrieking cries of the wounded beat monotonously against his eardrums. His axe was splashed with blood. In the press of one charge he saw Otto de Balse, the Tuscan, go down before the sword thrust of the king. And then, quite suddenly, he caught sight of Roger Montfort.

Tall, thin, and clothed in a heavy, protecting armor, Roger Montfort stood behind a group of the Norman warriors, urging them on with loud, sharp commands. His face was pale and tight with emotion. His sword was bright, unsullied.

A loud shout tore from Hugh Wilton's throat at the sight of him. He pressed forward, slashing from left to right with his great axe. Men went down or gave way before him. A few moments before he had felt the pressure of a heavy fatigue but he did not feel it now. There, beyond the fighting, securely protected, stood the man who, above all others, would be responsible for the defeat of the English if they lost this battle. Sure of William of Normandy's success, he was showing himself definitely on the side of the invader.

BEFORE the fury of Hugh Wilton's advance, against the great slashing cuts of his ante, no man could stand. Hardly had his shout died out before he had fought his way to where Roger Montfort stood. And Roger Montfort saw him, saw him and trembled with fear.

Hugh Wilton said not a word to the man. He swung *Bretwalda* above his head, saw Montfort bring up his sword in a desperate attempt to block the blow.

William of Normandy, his helmet off, his voice sharp and clear, was rallying his men. Archers and men with crossbows were hastening closer. From the left came a charging line of horsemen. And suddenly the fury of the battle there at the crest of Senlac Hill reached a fever pitch.

The crucial moments had come. In a final, desperate venture, William of Normandy was throwing the full strength of his forces against the English.

A wild, fierce cry came from Hugh Wilton's throat. He brought his great axe down with a vicious swing. Roger Montfort's sword was like a straw in its way. The blade of the axe crashed against his helmet and sliced it way through the steel as though it had been paper, sliced through flesh and bone to the man's shoulders and drew away as the body fell to the ground.

For a moment, then, Hugh Wilton rested. All about him raged the battle. He saw King Harold wielding his long sword in the midst of a score of Normans, heard the shout of the

French troops as they poured into the fight. He turned, fought his way to the king's side. A cry of horror came from a man near him and Hugh Wilton saw King Harold stagger back, the shaft of an arrow protruding from his eye.

Slowly, wearily, the king's figure sank to the ground. Hugh Wilton stared down at him. Death had followed the flight of that arrow he knew full well, death for the king, death for the hopes of England. A great bitterness seized him. All about he could hear men shouting news of what had happened and all about him, men were fleeing.

Hugh Wilton's hands tightened on the bloodstained handle of the axe.

All throughout the fight he had been sustained by the thought that if they met defeat here, they could still rally with the men of Mercia and engage the invaders again. But now that possibility was gone. The king was dead. There was none left to lead a fight against William of Normandy.

With a score of others, Hugh Wilton gathered around the king's body. Against them pressed the forces of the enemy. The man to his right went down under the thrust of a spear and the man to his left fell before the slashing blow of a sword. Grimly, desperately Hugh Wilton held his ground, the dead piling high around him.

A tall, gaunt figure pressed forward and through the haze which was gathering over his eyes Hugh Wilton suddenly recognized the man as Count Henri d'Anjou. Thyra's words came back to him. "*Even though you might meet my father on the field of battle....*"

He swung *Bretwalda* aloft, hesitated. Pain exploded in his head and a sudden, yawning darkness reached out for him.

ALL was lost.... Over and over in the delirium of the days which followed that thought outweighed every other thought which came to his mind.

All was lost!

Even as his wounds healed and as his body grew stronger

and his mind clearer, there was nothing else of which to think. Where he was he didn't know. By what chance he was still alive he didn't even care to guess. An old man and woman were taking care of him and from their conversations he knew what had happened. Completely victorious on the hill at Senlac, William of Normandy had marched by Canterbury upon London.

Hastily formed opposition to him had been crushed. The widow of Edward the Confessor had surrendered, the Bishops had submitted, London had fallen. And on Christmas day at Westminster, William of Normandy had been crowned King of England by Archbishop Eldred.

All was lost!

A Norman, a, foreigner, ruled the land. A man who was a vassal of the King of France.

Outside the small cottage where Hugh Wilton lay, a coach stopped and a tall, gray-haired man descended from it and came up to the door. He talked for a moment to the old couple who had looked after Hugh Wilton and some money exchanged hands. Then, passing through the door, the man closed it after him and looked down on Hugh Wilton.

"You are better, they tell me," he said slowly. "In fact, the old man said that you could leave."

Hugh Wilton looked up at the Count d'Anjou. "And to what purpose?" he demanded sharply.

The man pondered him a moment, and then he smiled slightly.

"I thought that you might like to go back to your home in Mercia."

Hugh Wilton made no answer. He must owe his life, he decided, to this man who stood above him. Undoubtedly it had been Count d'Anjou who had had him carried away from the battlefield and who had provided for his care here. He glanced over to the corner of the room. There stood the axe *Bretwalda*. The engravings on the handle, he suddenly recalled, were supposed to read: *To him who holds Bretwalda will came great sorrow and great joy, great defeat and great victory.*

A thin smile touched his lips. He stood up and said slowly, "Why should I go back to Mercia?"

The blue eyes of the Frenchman rested on him kindly. "You no doubt feel bitter, Hugh Wilton, but all is not so bad as you think. When King Philip of France agreed to help William of Normandy I said to him that once William of Normandy was named King of England, he would forget his allegiance to France. I was right. Though he is a Norman, he has become an English king. Perhaps he will even make a good king. But whether good or bad, this is still England and if you love your country as I love mine you will still find ways of serving it."

Hugh Wilton lifted his head, He felt suddenly ashamed of his bitter thoughts. In the Frenchman's words he could see a deep truth. No matter who the ruler might be, England was still England and would always have need of those men who loved her.

"Your friend, Oliver Sweyn, and Duke Edward await you in Mercia," Count Henri continued. "I am on my way back to France."

"Back to France?"

The Frenchman smiled. "You are not the only one who has lost a battle. In the past few days I have lost two. One to William of Normandy who is now William of England. I tried to remind him of what he owed the French king, The other battle I lost to my daughter."

"To your daughter?"

Hugh Wilton stared at him and then repeated slowly:

"Yes. I had wanted her to return with me to France. She insists that she is staying here. Hugh Wilton, can I leave her in England with safety?"

As Count Henri d'Anjou spoke the door opened and standing there, outlined against the clear sunlight of the early afternoon, Hugh Wilton saw the girl Thyra. A faint smile trembled on her lips. Her deep blue eyes were steady.

Hugh Wilton felt born anew in the breathless moment which

followed. "Aye, you may leave her here," he answered. "You may leave her here in safety."

He walked forward, then, and took Thyra into his arms. Count Henri went on talking but Hugh Wilton didn't hear a word that he said. His thoughts were racing ahead down the years which were before him.

V

DELAY AT ANTIOCH

*"Deus Vult!" The cry rang high above the
clangor of shields and scimitars; and the magic
of those words sent a meager, exhausted band of
Crusaders against the mightiest army of Islam.*

CHAPTER I

UNDER THE WIDE tent of Raymond de St. Gilles, the leaders of the crusade gathered for another council. All were there. Tall, red-headed Behemond, Prince of Taranto. Tancred, his cousin. Godfrey de Bouillon, in whose veins ran the blood of Charlemagne. Robert of Normandy, son of England's king. Adhemar, Bishop of Puy. Taticius, the Byzantine general. Peter the Hermit, Guy de Fortney, and many another.

Short of temper were they all. For six months the siege of Antioch had dragged on and they seemed no closer to taking the city today than when they had first sighted it from the top of the Taurus Hills. Food supplies were low and many of their men were ill. And toward them, along the road from Allepo, came a great Saracen army. It seemed as though the Crusaders were about to be caught between the forces of Yagi Siyan, Amir of Antioch, and the force coming to his relief.

One after another, the leaders spoke their minds. Some favored an immediate assault upon the city, others favored withdrawing until the army of the Byzantine emperor could join them. Some, no doubt, felt willing to give up the entire purpose of the Crusade, for here, in Antioch, they seemed to have come to a barrier which they could not pass.

In the midst of the discussion, Behemond got suddenly to his feet and turned to face Tancred. "Cousin," he said sharply, "where are the two prisoners your men took last night?"

Tancred frowned. "Why ask about them?"

Now the crusaders, shouting their battle cry, came
swarming over the crest of the great wall.

"They were taken when leaving the city by one of the postern gates on the hills, were they not?"

"Aye."

"And they are Saracens, are they not?"

"Again you are right, cousin."

Behemond leaned forward. Though he had not so many followers as some of the others in this council he was gradually assuming the leadership of the Crusade. Quick of mind, cunning, ambitious, he had in him all the attributes of a leader.

"We cannot fall back," he said earnestly. "We must strike. And we must strike before the Saracen army arrives to make the battle more difficult. For months, now, we have had word from Armenian spies within the walls of Antioch, yet no word have they given us of any weakness of which we could take advantage. Perhaps from these Saracens which my cousin has taken we can learn something to our advantage."

"From a woman and a boy?" asked Tancred sarcastically.

"I have seen the woman," said Behemond. "From her bearing

I would guess that she is more than a common prisoner. Have both of them brought here."

TANCRED shrugged and left the tent. Shortly he was back with the two prisoners. The boy was about nine or ten—a thin, ragged urchin, now very frightened. The woman, tall and slender as all Saracen women, was clothed in a gray cloak which reached almost to the ground. A shawl covered her hair and a veil hid all of her face but her eyes and forehead.

Behemond glanced around the group. "Where is Wilton of Mercia?" he asked.

A tall, young man separated himself from a group near Robert of Normandy and came forward. He wore a tunic of chain mail which reached almost to his knees and on his broad chest was the red Crusader's cross. An old, battered helmet covered his short blond hair. His face was thin, gaunt, and somber and his eyes were a cold blue.

"Wilton," said Behemond, "you speak the Saracen tongue. Question this woman. Find out who she is. See what she can tell us of the defenses of Antioch."

Wilton frowned, looked over at the woman. He had little liking for such a task. He had come on this Crusade to help re-capture Jerusalem from the infidels. Fighting, he understood. With his father's great axe in his hands and under the banner of Mercia, there were no odds he would not face. But he had no enthusiasm for questioning prisoners or dealing with spies. He felt only distrust for the cunning of Behemond, the cleverness of Tancred, the intrigues of Raymond de St. Gilles.

"Tell her," said Behemond, "that if she speaks, she and the boy will go free."

Wilton shrugged. Still looking at the woman, he said slowly, "You were taken as you were leaving Antioch. Where you would have gone I do not know but you will be released if you answer my questions truthfully. Do you understand?"

The woman made no answer. Above the veil her dark eyes stared at him blankly.

"How large an army is there still within the walls?" Wilton asked.

The woman remained silent. Her body was very straight and no fear showed in her eyes. One of her hands rested on the shoulder of the boy who stood beside her, his arms around her waist.

"Perhaps you did not understand me," Wilton said. "Unless you answer my questions—"

"Unless I answer your questions," interrupted the woman, her voice low and tense, "I will be degraded, killed. I know that. I expect it. It is thus that you treat all women who fall into your hands."

Wilton bit his lips. There was a measure of truth in what she said. The scum of Europe had followed the path of the Crusaders, and many of the knights themselves had forgotten their vows.

"Who are you?" Wilton asked abruptly.

The woman made no answer.

Wilton tried again. "Tell me," he said, "the number of men at the Bridge Gate."

The woman still did not speak and Behemond, pushing

forward, said sharply, "Well, what have you learned, Wilton? Was I right about her?"

Wilton glanced at Behemond and the other leaders. All were leaning forward anxiously. "I have learned nothing," he answered. "But I think that this woman is no ordinary prisoner. I would hold her safely. Perhaps later she will talk. Perhaps—"

"We have no time to wait," broke in the harsh voice of Guy de Fortney. "I will show you how to make her talk."

IN THREE swift strides de Fortney reached the woman's side. He seized the boy, threw him to the ground and bent over him, a knife in his free hand. The woman screamed and rushed toward de Fortney, but Tancred caught and held her in his arms.

"Ask her your questions now, Wilton," de Fortney cried. "She will answer them."

The knife in de Fortney's hand was only inches from the boy's throat. Behemond said, "Yes, Wilton. Ask your questions now."

Wilton stared at the woman. In her struggle to free herself from Tancred's arms the veil had pulled away from her face and he saw that she was hardly more than a girl. She was fair, too, almost as fair of skin as he, and her face was lovely, even now in its agony. "No! No!" she was screaming in the Saracen tongue."That is al-Hakim, the son of Yagi Siyan. Spare him! Do not kill him!"

Wilton moved forward. He gave no warning of what he intended to do, but suddenly his hand seized de Fortney's wrist. A tall and heavy man was Guy de Fortney, proud of his strength. Yet now without apparent effort, Wilton brought him upright, away from the Saracen boy. For a moment, while the tent grew still and the men leaned tensely forward, they stood together, chest to chest. Wilton's pressure on de Fortney's wrist tightened. He bent the man's arm sideways, twisted it lower and lower. Perspiration stood out on de Fortney's forehead. His dark eyes clouded. Then suddenly his fingers loosened, and the knife fell to the ground.

Wilton stepped back, "I do not make war on women and children," he said gruffly. "Leave the boy alone."

De Fortney made no answer, though his thin, hawk-like face was twisted with anger and there was hatred in his eyes.

Behemond pushed him away. "You are a fool, Wilton," Behemond growled.

"Perhaps a fool," Wilton answered, "but they will never say of me that I tarnished the cross I wear."

Adhemar came forward, a tall heavy figure in his full bishop's robes. "Wilton is right," he announced. "We must get our information in some other way."

The bishop's decision was not questioned. One and all, pilgrim or knight, Greek or Norman, the Crusaders had come to love this Churchman who marched and suffered and fought with them. Behemond and Tancred had nothing more to say. The two prisoners were taken away and the council continued.

WILTON of Mercia turned away from the council tent. He strode to a high point in that meadow where the Crusaders were encamped, and there he sat down and stared at the high-walled town of Antioch. Broad and strong was that wall which encompassed the city. For two miles it ran along the far bank of the Orontes River, then it clambered over a series of little hills and circled to the south. At intervals stood massive square towers, rising to a height of sixty feet. There were five main gates in this nearest portion of the wall and all of them the Crusaders had closed.

But up in the hills there were other gates through which food was taken into the city by night. Despite the great number of Crusaders, the army could not entirely surround the city and cut off the supplies. Their six months of siege had accomplished nothing. Antioch still stood as a barrier to Jerusalem.

Sprawled all over the broad meadow were the tents of the Crusaders. A motley lot they were: knights from Normandy, England, Italy, France; mercenary soldiers of every nationality; peasant pilgrims from all corners of Europe. It was a miracle that they hung together, a miracle wrought by a symbol and a phrase. The Crusaders' cross and the cry, *Deus vult* had welded them into an army which had fought its way across southern Europe, which had taken Nicaea, which had crossed the Taurus mountains and now stood at the gateway of Syria.

The spirit which had made all that possible was a continual source of wonder to Wilton of Mercia. It was like a living, breathing thing. It had sustained men through hunger and thirst, suffering and privation. The Holy City was in the hands of the infidel Turks and the call to free it had swept the Christian world. It was unthinkable that here their cause should fail.

Wilton's mind turned abruptly to a consideration of what had happened in the council meeting that morning, and a vague feeling of uneasiness came over him. He couldn't place his finger on just what it was that troubled him. He had made an enemy of Guy de Fortney he knew, but quarrels were common in the camp and that did not trouble him. As for the captives, he had helped them little if any. In the privacy of his own tent, Behemond could repeat the scene which Wilton had stopped, if the Norman so desired. Wilton scowled. He wondered what fate awaited the girl whom he had questioned. He could not get the picture of her face out of his mind.

A footstep sounded near him and Behemond's voice said caustically, "What troubles you, Wilton? The Saracen maid?"

Wilton looked around and saw that the tall, heavy Norman was smiling faintly.

"I have no interest in Saracen women," Wilton answered shortly.

"But you are interested in taking Antioch."

"Aye. What man of us isn't?"

"The council," said Behemond. "They still argue while the army of Kerbogha comes nearer and nearer to trapping us."

Wilton's frown deepened. Impregnable though the walls of Antioch might seem, he had long favored an assault rather than the months of delay which they had known.

BEHEMOND moved closer. "Wilton," he said, "I would tell you something in confidence. A week ago a Turkish officer who has been mistreated by Yagi Siyan, the Amir of Antioch, sent word to me that he would open one of the gates to us if I would pledge safety to him and his men."

"Others have made such an offer." Wilton shrugged. "It has come to nothing."

"Others who have made such an offer had not the authority to back their pledge. This man of whom I speak is one who can do what he agrees to do. When I tell you his name you will understand. I speak of Firuz, the Turk."

"Firuz!"

Wilton slowly nodded his head. From word which had trickled into their camp he knew that Firuz commanded the Turks who were helping Yagi Siyan in the defense of Antioch. If he had agreed to open one of the gates to the Crusaders, he could do it.

"Why did you not mention this in the council meeting?" he asked.

"And have the spies of the Saracens learn of it? Nay. Such would have been a foolish thing to do. Save for my cousin Tancred, you are the only one I have told."

"Why have you told me?"

"I need your help."

"In what way?"

Behemond drew a deep breath. "For three days now," he said slowly, "it has been impossible for me to get word to Firuz. All details of the assault have been arranged. The greater portion of our men are to leave camp for the hills as though they were upon a foraging expedition. Under cover of darkness we are to creep back to the wall at a certain place in the hills near the tower of the Two Sisters. Yet, though all plans are made, I have been unable to set a night for the assault and each day the Saracen army which is coming up the Allepo road draws closer."

Wilton stood up. "What would you have me do?"

"Would you dare venture into Antioch? You speak the Saracen tongue, Wilton. You could be trusted. The time is short."

"No man who is a stranger could get past the gates, no matter how well he speaks the language of the Moslems."

"You can get by the gates."

"How?"

"You recall the Saracen maid whom you questioned this morning? She can get you by the gate. She will get you by the gate and take you to Firuz if by so doing she can be assured of the life of—al-Hakim."

Wilton scowled. "You understood her? You heard her call the boy by that name?"

"I heard her call that name and I know that al-Hakim is the name given to the son of Yagi Siyan. The woman, I would guess, is the amir's daughter, Shajar. That is why I feel that she could get you in."

"You are sure that Firuz—"

"I pledge you by the cross of Christ that what I have told you is true, Wilton. I dare trust no common spy. Will you undertake this mission?"

For a long moment, Wilton was silent. Though he cared little for Behemond he could see how vital it was that someone reach Firuz. An open assault on the city would cost the lives of thousands of men. If an entrance could be made through one of the gates, many of those lives might be saved. And time was short. Antioch blocked their way to Jerusalem. Until it fell they could not go on and if they delayed much longer their cause might be lost.

"When would you make the assault?" he asked abruptly.

"An hour before dawn, tomorrow."

Wilton nodded. "Take me to the Saracen maid. I will be your messenger."

CHAPTER II

THE NIGHT WAS clear and cool and the light breeze sweeping down from the hills carried with it the scent of myriad wild flowers. Here and there in the rough, rugged country back of Antioch were groves of olive trees, great laurels, pines. The thin sliver of a moon showed in the sky, attended by countless stars. They gave but little light, and it was quite dark in the shadows of the shrubbery along one of the trails where Wilton and the Saracen maid waited.

They had been there now for quite a while. Occasionally they conversed in low tones. Most of the time they were silent. A long Moslem robe covered Wilton's coat-of-mail. A turban was wrapped around his head. To his chin and jaws was pasted a long, dark beard. By day that beard would not pass muster, but he felt that it would serve in the darkness. Touching it with his hand, he smiled.

"I would make a good Moslem, don't you think?" he said to the girl.

He received no answer, but despite the darkness he could see her turn to look at him. Her name was Shajar, he had discovered, and she was the daughter of Yagi Siyan. He had learned more. She and her brother had been captured when her father had decided to send them to Allepo where they would be safe if the Crusaders breached the walls of the city. But that didn't mean, Shajar had insisted, that conditions within Antioch were bad. Only her father's caution had prompted that step.

Leaning forward, Shajar said abruptly, "Why must you do this thing? Do you not know that only death awaits those who enter Antioch? Do you think that even to save my brother's life I would betray my city?"

Wilton shrugged. He could think of no adequate answer. He had not told Shajar why he wished to enter Antioch. He had asked her only to pass him through the gates and in return for that, he had Behemond's pledge that no harm would come to her brother.

"Why must you enter Antioch?" asked the girl again.

"I must," said Wilton. "Let us let it go at that."

For a long time the girl was silent, then she asked suddenly,"Where did you learn the Moslem tongue?"

Wilton smiled. "Six years ago I came to the holy land on a pilgrimage. I learned it then."

Shajar shook her head. "It is hard to think of you as a pilgrim."

"Why?"

"And it is hard to think of you as an infidel, as one of the horde which is despoiling my country."

"Again, why?"

"You asked a moment ago if I did not think that you would make a good Moslem. I can almost imagine that you are like one of my own people. Does that seem strange to you?"

WILTON stared over at the girl. He couldn't see her face, but something in her voice sent a strange excitement pounding through his veins. He had little knowledge of women. His youth had been spent under the rigid discipline of his father and its hours had been taken up with practice in the use of the sword, axe, bow and lance.

Hardly had he attained his manhood when he joined a pilgrimage to the Holy Land. And almost immediately after his return home Pope Urban's call had sent him off on this Crusade. Sometimes he had dreamed of finding some girl as fair as a princess, as wise as his mother. And suddenly, now, he wondered if he hadn't found her.

An instant of doubt flashed across his mind, but he put it aside. Moslem this girl might be—an infidel. Yet that did not matter. The hot blood of youth was in his veins and in his heart there was a deep yearning for this woman—a desire born so suddenly in him that he was frightened.

He leaned forward and said huskily, "Shajar—Shajar—"

The girl didn't move. His arms went out, grasped her. He pulled her close against him, his mouth eagerly seeking her lips.

"Stop!" The word was as sharp as a lash.

"Stop, infidel dog!"

Fingernails scraped across his face. The girl broke free, and by the faint light of the stars he could see that she held one hand across her face. She was breathing heavily.

Wilton stood silent a moment, confused by his anger and his shame.

"I meant you no harm," he said at last, sharply. "Come. By this time the guard should be changed. Let us get on to the city."

Shajar banked away from him. She lifted her veil into place. Without a word she turned and made for the trail which led to one of the small postern gates....

There was no difficulty at the gate. What Shajar said to the guards Wilton didn't know, but the gate was opened without question and they both passed swiftly through it.

Beyond the gate and away from the guards, the girl stopped and said, "I have done what was asked of me. And my brother—"

"You need not fear for him," Wilton answered. "I have Behemond's pledge that he will be safe."

The girl nodded and then stood silent, her eyes on his face. Wilton's expression was stony. He still felt a hurt and anger from that experience along the trail. He had told himself that what had happened was for the best; yet now once again he was almost painfully aware of the girl's loveliness. Straight and slender was her body and proudly erect was her head.

"There is yet a chance for you to escape," she said suddenly. "Beyond the gate—"

Wilton's eyes moved past the girl. They were standing near one of the high points of the city. Near them were only a few houses. The roadway was deserted. Below lay the town, marked here and there by the domes of its mosques, by narrow, finger-like minarets pointing up to the sky. Some of those streets down there, Wilton knew, were paved with marble. Qushani tile and mosaic work decorated many of the buildings. In that lower part of the city there was a hanging garden, a fairy wonderland of plants, flowers and bubbling fountains. Not far from it was a coliseum.

And down there the streets would be crowded with dark-browed Turkish soldiers, dusky Saracens, fair Armenians. A thousand torches lighted up the city, some stationary, some moving about as companies of men went from one place to another. To reach the place where he must go, Wilton would have to skirt the fringe of that populous center. Were he too closely questioned, there was little doubt as to what would happen to him.

"There is yet time to turn back," Shajar whispered.

A faint smile touched Wilton's lips and his fingers, slipping under his robe, touched the handle of the great axe strapped to his side. "Nay, Shajar," he answered. "I cannot turn back. Go at once to the house of your father. Stay there until tomorrow."

Then without waiting for an answer, he turned and started slowly down the hill, his heavy shoulders bowed, his feet taking the wandering pattern of an old man.

FIRUZ the Turk was a short man, middle-aged, swarthy of complexion. His eyes were keen, and a moment after his soldiers had brought Wilton to him he dismissed them and said bluntly, "How came you here? What word do you bring from Behemond?"

Wilton repeated Behemond's message and the Turk rubbed his hands together. "An hour before dawn," he nodded. "And at the tower of the Two Sisters."

"Aye."

"We will wait for the guard to pass, then lower rope ladders. When sufficient men are on the wall we will take the gate. Yagi Siyan has added Moslems to my own guard. He trusts me no longer."

Wilton could find in his own heart little love for the traitor. He sat down in a chair, tried to relax. The past few hours had been trying. It had not been easy to find the Turk. Time and again he had felt the sweat cold on his body, when discovery of his identity seemed imminent. And even now every nerve in his system was acutely aware of danger. Outside this room paced a guard. Around this building were hundreds more. He was thankful that it lacked but little time of the appointed hour.

"Come," said Firuz. "We will go to the tower of the Two Sisters."

Wilton got to his feet. At the side of the Turk he left the room, his body still bent, his feet still shuffling along their way. No one stopped them. They gained the wall, climbed it, turned to the east. Here and there, as they moved along the broad top of the wall, voices challenged their progress, but always at the Turk's answer they received the command to continue on their way.

In the shadow of one of the great stone towers on the eastern wall, Firuz stopped.

"This is the place," he said. "You are sure they will come?"

Wilton nodded. "They will come."

"I sent my son to Behemond only a few hours ago," Firuz muttered. "I told him to beg that Behemond make the assault tonight. Yagi Siyan watches me more closely each day."

"The gate," asked Wilton. "Where is it?"

Firuz pointed to the left. "Over there. We will first bring up as many men as we can, for the gate is well guarded and strong."

"The ropes?"

"Within the tower."

Wilton stared up at the eastern sky. It seemed to him that it was growing lighter, that the stars seemed fainter. Moving to the edge of the wall, he stared down into the shadows of the hills below it. They were heavily wooded. This was an ideal place to make a surprise attack. Under the cover of darkness and below the screen of the woods, a countless number of men could be assembled close to the walls. And if the gate were opened, nothing, he knew, could hold the Crusaders back.

A body of guards came marching down the wall, torches

lighting up their progress. Firuz drew Wilton through the arched doorway of the tower and the two stood there, silent, while the guards passed. Then when they were gone, Firuz said sharply, "The ropes! And if Behemond is here, Antioch is yours."

FROM a recess in the tower Firuz took a long, coiled rope ladder. He passed it to Wilton and reached for another. Wilton hurried outside. He fastened the ladder to one of the abutments on the wall and lowered it over the side. Firuz, working near him, lowered a second ladder.

The clanking sound of armor came to Wilton from the darkness below. The rope ladder went taut. Hoarse, whispered voices reached up to him and in another moment the tall, gaunt figure of one of the Crusaders appeared clambering up the ladder. Others were following him and more were coming up the ladder Firuz had lowered.

Wilton stepped back from the edge. He tore off the Moslem gown which he had been wearing, cast the turban from his head. From his side he loosened the axe which he had brought with him. A marvelous weapon was that axe which had been given to Wilton by his father. It was wrought entirely of steel and its handle was long and curiously marked. Above the broad cutting edge of the head was engraven the name *Bretwalda*, and above the letters were eight blood red jewels.

Though the axe looked awkward and heavy, Wilton lifted it easily to his shoulder and swung around to face the men who had clambered up the wall. Fully a score had gained the top and more were crowding up the ladders. Wilton caught sight of Richard Baliol, the Scot, of Arthur Bosworth of Essex. He saw the tall, thin-featured Robert of Normandy and near him Guy de Fortney.

Behemond scrambled over the edge of the wall, singled out Firuz and strode toward him, calling, "Where are the steps to the gate?"

Firuz hesitated. "You will need more men."

The sky had grown lighter, and now from a near-by tower

there came a sudden, warning shout. It was followed by the shrill, blatant note of a trumpet. Armored Moslem soldiers poured from the tower's arched doorway, started racing forward along the wall.

Eagerly the Crusaders turned to meet them. Steel clashed against steel as the curved Moslem scimitar struck against the long two-handled sword of the Crusaders. Hoarse shouts and screams arose above the din of the battle and louder still sounded the battlecry of the Crusaders, "*Deus vult! Deus vult!* God wills it!"

Wilton threw himself into the thick of the fray, swinging the great axe *Bretwalda* with ease and dexterity. To one side of him stood Robert of Normandy and to the other Arthur Bosworth, who yelled at the top of his lungs each time he struck out with his sword.

More men were clambering up the ladders, over-anxious to join in the fight. Almost together the heavily burdened ropes snapped and a half dozen men, part way up the wall, fell back to the ground.

Wilton heard the Turk's despairing cry. Other shouts told him what had happened. He drew back from the fight, turned to the stairs which led down from the wall to the gate. It had grown light enough now for him to see the space before the gate. Half a hundred armed men were down there, staring up at the top of the wall. They were standing motionless, stunned by the realization of what must have happened.

Wilton's eyes went swiftly from right to left. No more Crusaders were clambering over the edge of the wall. Behemond was yelling at Firuz, demanding more ropes. The Turk was shaking his head; he had no more. Fifty or sixty Crusaders had gained the top of the wall. They were not enough to storm the gate, yet this they must accomplish, for in taking it lay their only hope. Here they would be trapped and finally cut down like cattle.

"The gate!" Wilton shouted. "Follow me to the gate!"

BEHEMOND took up that cry, Richard Baliol echoed it, a score of men rushed for the stairs. Wilton heard them coming after him as he started down. A spear cast by one of the Moslems flashed past his shoulder and another narrowly missed his head. He gained the foot of the stairs, and slashing from one side to another with his great axe, he fought his way forward through the Saracens massed before the gate. Behemond was with him, Richard Baliol, de Fortney, Bosworth, Robert of Normandy, a score of others, their swords red in the gray dawn.

Wilton heard their shouts. He caught a confused impression of that desperate thrust toward the gate. He saw two Moslems fall at once from a slashing stroke of Behemond's sword. He saw Richard Baliol fighting with a grimness which took no measure of the odds. Foot by foot they pressed forward. The tip of a Moslem blade cut a thin, red line across Wilton's cheek and the man who swung that scimitar went down under the cut of *Bretwalda*. Suddenly the gate loomed up just ahead of them, defended now only by a handful of men.

"Open the gate, Wilton," Behemond called. "We will hold back the infidels. *Deus vult!*"

Bretwalda cleared the way to the gate, but the massive, wooden door was securely fastened. It shuddered under the blows and still held firm.

Wilton drew back. He swung *Bretwalda* against the heavy oak timbers and the head of the axe bit through the wood as though it had been paper. He swung the axe again, cutting through the braces across the door. The battering from the outside grew heavier and the door bulged, splintered. A loud shout tore from Wilton's lungs. Once that door was down the massed army of the Crusaders would pour into Antioch and after they were past the walls, nothing could keep them from victory. The road to Jerusalem would be open.

Once more Wilton lifted *Bretwalda*, swung it at the door. But what the result of that last blow was, Wilton did not see. A sudden, sharp pain exploded in his head and a thousand points of light danced before his eyes. He stumbled forward, stumbled into a heavy darkness which blotted out all consciousness.

Past his silent figure as the door went down came the charging army of the Crusaders. From tens of thousands of throats roared the cry, *"Deus vult!"* In the lower part of the town, before the citadel of Yagi Siyan, the Moslems formed to give them battle.

But the battle was a short one. Taken by surprise just before the hour for morning prayers, the Saracens and Turks had no organized plans for battle. Here and there groups of them made desperate stands against the Crusaders, but to no avail. And when the morning sun was bright, the Crusader's banners floated from the towers of Antioch. Only in the citadel of Yagi Siyan did the Saracens hold out.

CHAPTER III

WHEN WILTON OF Mercia recovered consciousness, he discovered that he was lying on a couch in a narrow, high-ceilinged room. Rich, colorful draperies covered the walls and on the floor there was a thick carpet.

For a long moment, Wilton lay without moving, his eyes turning from side to side. A steady, throbbing pain hammered in his head. His throat was dry and he was weak from hunger. Thinking required a huge effort, but he decided after a while that he must be in one of the buildings in Antioch. Since he was alive he knew that the Crusaders must have taken the city.

Behind the couch there was a rustling sound and the girl Shajar moved into the range of his vision. Wilton stared at her, blinking. "You?" he whispered hoarsely. "You? How came you here?"

Shajar knelt beside the couch. Her robe was of soft, white silk gathered at the waist by a scarlet girdle. She wore no shawl over her head and Wilton noticed that her hair was very dark and straight. A white silk veil reaching almost to her eyes was fastened by a band to her head.

"The man you call Behemond brought me here," Shajar answered. "I went to him two days ago to ask for my brother. He brought me here and said that he would send my brother to me. But he hasn't and I am afraid—"

Wilton tried to sit up, but the girl reached out suddenly and held him to the couch. She moistened a cloth and bathed his face. Relaxed, he studied the girl's eyes, but they told him nothing.

"You have cared for me?" he asked wonderingly.

"I and a man called Peter Bartholomew. He has gone now to try and find food. It is—it is very scarce. In the four days since the city was taken, all that we had has been eaten up."

Wilton lifted a hand to his head and felt of the bandage wrapped around it. That he had been unconscious for four days was hard to believe. It was also hard to understand why this girl had assisted in caring for him. He recalled her anger in the hills back of Antioch when he had tried to take her in his arms. He closed his eyes, opened them again and stared at her. And then, hardly realizing what he was saying, he whispered, "Shajar, remove your veil. Let me see your face."

Shajar lifted her hands to the sides of her head, unfastened the veil and dropped it. Twice before had Wilton seen the girl's face. Once, clearly, in the tent of Raymond de St. Gilles, again in the half light of that night in the hills. As he stared at her he knew that he would never forget the way her dark hair framed the oval of her face, nor the way her full, warm lips were formed in a wistful smile.

"Shajar," he whispered, "why have you helped to care for me? Surely you must have known what part I played in the taking of Antioch?"

The girl bowed her head. "It was Allah's will."

"But why have you helped to care for me?"

Shajar's head was still bowed. Without looking up she said slowly, "When I came into this room you were calling my name. I knew, then, that I had been wrong in what I had thought of you. I knew then that you needed me."

"Even though I be a Christian you felt that way?"

Shajar made no answer. She did not look up, but neither did she move away. And in that moment Wilton knew that the harsh differences of creed and of country did not matter now; something infinitely larger had swept them aside. The wonder of that realization went to his head like wine. He stretched a hand toward the girl's head, whispering, "Shaja—Shajar—"

"I do not even know your name," Shajar murmured, her voice low, unsteady. "Men call you Wilton of Mercia, but—"

"It is Henry," Wilton answered. "Thus my father called me. Let me hear you say it."

"Henry." The girl was looking at him now, her face radiant. "Henry. It is a strange name."

"Not strange when you say it."

"Then listen—Henry. Close your eyes. Rest. I will stay here, be here when you awake."

Wilton did not want to close his eyes, but with Shajar's cool hand on his brow he could feel a deep peace stealing over his body, and after a while he slept.

BEHEMOND, who had called to see Wilton, stormed back and forth across the room. This was the seventh day after the fall of the city and conditions within Antioch were rapidly growing serious. The food supply was exhausted and several of the hills within the walls were in the hands of the Moslems. Outside a great Saracen army was encamped. The besiegers had become the besieged. A Byzantine army was supposed to be coming to their rescue from the north, but there had been no sign of it.

Wilton was sitting up now. The wound in his head, a deep scalp wound, was slowly mending. Peter Bartholomew had been successful in securing a little food and the presence of Shajar had made Wilton's days glorious. She sat now on a couch across the room, watching Behemond anxiously, and Wilton knew what was in her mind.

"Where is the girl's brother?" he asked Behemond.

A heavy frown came to Behemond's face. "Dead," he said bluntly.

"Dead?" Wilton gasped. "But you pledged the girl—"

"I know it. The lad's death was an accident. Guy de Fortney was bringing him into the city from the camp. The lad tried to get away. One of de Fortney's men struck him down."

Wilton looked over at the girl. She did not understand Behemond's Norman speech, he knew, yet her face seemed unusually pale.

"I sent you the Saracen woman when she came to me to ask about the boy," Behemond continued. "After all, I felt that you deserved something for what you had done. And she's not a bad trick, is she?"

Wilton drew in a long breath. He fought against an impulse to smash his fist into Behemond's face. "Forget the Saracen woman," he growled.

Behemond shrugged. "All right, Wilton, but keep her out of de Fortney's sight. De Fortney wanted her. I told him she was dead. I want no trouble between you and de Fortney. After the way he helped you hack down that door at the gate the other morning, there should be none."

"After the way he what?" Wilton demanded.

"After the way he helped you break down that door. While the rest of us held the Moslems back, de Fortney joined you at the door."

Wilton lifted a hand to his head. How that wound had come there had been puzzling him ever since he had regained consciousness. It was a blade wound. He had about decided that one of the Moslems must have broken through the line of men protecting his back, just as the door went down. But now he wondered. He had not seen de Fortney at his side while he had been smashing away at that door.

"As soon as you are well," said Behemond, "we'll want you at our council meetings. Some of these fools want to make terms with the Moslems."

Wilton nodded. He watched Behemond leave then turned his head to glance at Shajar.

She came forward, rested a hand on Wilton's shoulder and looked steadily into his eyes. "My brother is dead, isn't he?" she whispered.

Wilton could not lie. He nodded, biting his lips and wishing that he knew of some way in which he could bear part of the grief which was Shajar's lot. Her father, too, was dead, he had discovered the day before.

The girl had closed her eyes. "It is the will of Allah," he heard her murmur. "But al-Hakim was so young, so—" Her voice choked and tears squeezed between the lids of her eyes.

Wilton stood to his feet. His arms went around her and he held her tightly while she sobbed against his breast.

CONDITIONS within Antioch grew no better. Bands of Crusaders which ventured into the hills in search of food, returned empty handed. Some returned not at all, having fallen prey to Moslem patrols. Each night new groups of men deserted the Crusaders' cause, slipping over the walls by means of ropes. Some of these escaped through the hills and made their way north, back over the path the Crusaders had followed. Many were trapped and slain.

Starvation and disease stalked the ranks of those who remained behind. Men faint with hunger dropped on the streets of Antioch and could not rise again. Nor were there any with the strength to haul their bodies away, and the stench of decaying flesh befouled the air. Bishop Adhemar proclaimed three days of fasting and prayer, and there were those among the Crusaders who laughed when they heard his order, for what man among them was not already fasting?

Wilton attended the meetings of the council, but these accomplished nothing. The Crusaders were too weak, too few, to risk attacking the army outside the gates. They could only look forward to the time when Alexius Comnenus, the Byzantine ruler, would arrive with his army.

Guy de Fortney was at the third council meeting which Wilton attended, and as Wilton came into the room he saw de Fortney's eyes lift toward his bandaged head. A thin smile touched Wilton's lips. He said nothing then, but when the council meeting was ended he crossed over to where de Fortney stood and said slowly, "I understand that I am indebted to you for help at the gate."

Guy de Fortney's pale eyes narrowed. He stood almost as tall as Wilton and was fully as heavy. He did not have the look of a man who had been without food. His cheeks were not sunken and there were greasy stains on his mantle.

"I did help you," he answered bluntly. "But for me that gate would never have been broken down. Your axe had slipped from your hands, had laid open your head. You—"

Wilton laughed. "You should learn to use your sword better, de Fortney," he said harshly. "When we reach Jerusalem I will undertake to give you a lesson."

"Why not now?" de Fortney sneered, his hand going to the blade at his side.

Wilton shrugged. He turned to Baliol who stood near by and said sharply, "Loan me your blade, Richard."

Behemond pushed forward, his face flushed with anger. "I will have no fights between my men," he shouted. "De Fortney, put up your blade."

De Fortney laughed and turned away. "We will settle this later, Wilton," he promised.

Wilton made no reply. He left the council room and walked back to his own quarters. Shajar met him at the door and came to his arms with a naturalness which always affected him strangely. He would never, he thought, get over the wonder of their love for each other. He seemed to have know Shajar always, for she was as much a part of him as his own right arm. And sometimes that feeling was frightening, when he thought of what his life would be like if he should lose her.

"What have you been doing while I have been gone?" Wilton asked, smiling.

"Waiting for you."

PETER BARTHOLOMEW came through the doorway. He was a tall, pale youth with wide, blue eyes and long, shaggy hair. "I have had a vision," he cried to Wilton. "In my dreams St. Andrew came to me. He told me—"

Wilton shook his head "Wait a minute, Peter. I don't feel up to listening to another one of your visions. Take it to someone else."

"But St. Andrew—"

"Go and tell the bishop."

Peter blinked. He seemed mightily crestfallen, but without another word he turned away.

"What had he to say?" Shajar asked.

"Nothing important. He wanted to tell me of a vision but right now I am interested only in you, Shajar, and in the army of Alexius."

Shajar frowned. "The Byzantine army."

"Yes."

"It has turned back, Henry. It will not come to Antioch."

"It has turned back? How have you heard that?"

"This morning I saw an Armenian woman I know quite well. I am part Armenian, you know, and I am accepted by them. This woman told me what I have just told you. Word was carried to their leader that all the Crusaders had been slain. This woman's husband saw them turn and start back north."

It didn't occur to Wilton to doubt the story Shajar had just told him. For several days he had been of the opinion that they could expect no help from the north. If he had been coming, Alexius Comnenus should have arrived long ago. Yet he had clung to the hope that he was wrong, clung to it desperately.

"It means the end, doesn't it?" Shajar whispered.

Wilton nodded. It meant the end. Outside the walls of

Antioch the Moslem host commanded by Kerbogha awaited. They might easily have stormed and retaken the city but they seemed to prefer to watch the Crusaders starve. Only a miracle, Wilton knew, could save them. His eyes rested on Shajar and he made himself smile. "Will you do something for me, Shajar?"

"Anything, Henry."

"I want you to take a message to Kerbogha, the Moslem leader. I want you to take it tonight. I will let you over the wall with ropes. You can reach him easily. The message is very important."

Shajar looked at him steadily, her eyes probing his. Wilton held the smile on his lips. He said lightly, "Then you can come back of course, if you want to."

Shajar shook her head. "You must not send me away, Henry."

"But this message—"

"There is no message. You know that if the daughter of Yagi Siyan were sent to the Moslem camp she could never return here."

Wilton shrugged. He felt little surprise that Shajar had guessed his purpose, though he had tried as well as possible to conceal it. Nevertheless he knew that he must send her away. Death hovered over all who remained in Antioch.

He crossed to the couch, sat down, leaned back against its cushions and Shajar came to his side. "Talk of yourself," he commanded her. "Tell me of your life before we came. Tell me what you did."

Shajar smiled. She began talking of her girlhood and while she talked Wilton planned what he must do. His lips became a thin, straight line, and his heart was like a piece of ice within his chest.

CHAPTER IV

THE ROPE WAS long and strong and its price was a hundred *dinars*. The Syrian who offered it for sale squinted knowingly at Wilton. He had little doubt as to its intended use. Men were still going over the wall each night, staking their lives and a chance for freedom against death in Antioch by starvation or at the hands of Kerbogha's patrols.

"Know you the way to Kerbogha's tent?" Wilton asked.

The Syrian blinked, nodded.

"And for another hundred *dinars* would you wait below the wall tonight and take to Kerbogha the woman I will lower to you?"

"A woman?"

"Yes. A woman for whom Kerbogha will pay a princely sum."

The Syrian hesitated but the thought of two hundred *dinars* and the promise of an additional reward overcame any scruples he might have had. The deal was made and details were discussed. Wilton paid the man two hundred *dinars*, took the rope and secreted it near the wall. He had no fear that Shajar would come to harm at the Syrian's hands. He had picked his man carefully. The Syrian, he knew, would deliver her to Kerbogha, and once she was there, Kerbogha would see that the daughter of Yagi Siyan came to no harm.

Wilton went back through the streets of Antioch. It was just growing dark and three hours remained before the time appointed for lowering Shajar over the wall. An almost irresistible impulse urged him toward his quarters. But he dare not go there, for Shajar, he knew, would be waiting for him and in her arms he might weaken.

The streets were thronged with people, Crusaders in their armor, pilgrims, priests. Here and there were even a few of the women who had followed them from Europe. Gaunt and haggard were their faces. Some of them seemed near to death. Wilton stared at them, blankly, wondering what their eventual fate would be. Many of them, he guessed, would die. Those who would live faced slavery.

Some man grasped him by the shoulder and cried, "Have you heard it also? Is it true? Is it really true?"

"Is what true?" Wilton asked.

"That the lance which pierced the side of the blessed Savior has been found?"

Wilton looked at the man stupidly. "What folly is this?" he demanded.

"No folly," shouted another voice. "It has been found. I have seen it. This hand," and the man lifted his right hand into the air, "this hand has touched it."

More people crowded around, shouting questions. They seemed caught in the grip of a surging emotion. Pale and thin their faces may have been, but in their eyes, there was an ecstatic light.

"Tell us of it," cried an old, white-bearded man. "Is it truly the lance?"

Still holding his hand high in the air, the man who claimed to have touched the lance, shouted, "It was found in the church of St. Peter which the infidels had made into a mosque. It was buried deep under the altar. Its hiding place was revealed in a vision to Peter Bartholomew. It was Peter Bartholomew himself who drew it from the hole which men had been digging all day. I have seen it, touched it. It is the lance."

A great shout went up from the crowd and here and there men dropped on their knees and began to pray. Others turned in the direction of St. Peter's church.

WILTON moved away, thinking of Peter Bartholomew and his visions. He had little faith in the youth, but he was suddenly glad for what had happened. From the scene in the street, the finding of this lance or whatever it was, would give the Crusaders and pilgrims something to take their minds off of their suffering.

Where he walked during the next two hours, Wilton was never to know. Occasionally he was conscious of shouting crowds, of throngs of people, occasionally he knew that he stood alone on narrow, deserted, side streets. In him there was a deep bitterness which he could not overcome. Death he had never feared, and even now he had no fear of death itself. Yet life had suddenly become precious to him.

Turning finally toward his own quarters, Wilton found himself hurrying, though there was still an hour before the appointed time. His breath was coming in swift gasps as he reached the door, and for a moment be waited, striving to regain his composure. Out in the street crowds of people were still milling around, but Wilton was not conscious of them. His thoughts turned suddenly to the axe *Bretwalda* and to a legend concerning it. To the holder of that axe, so the legend went, would come "a great sorrow and a great joy, a great victory and a great defeat."

His lips tightened and he made himself smile. Then he opened the door and stepped inside.

"I was worried about you," Shajar greeted him.

"Worried?"

"Yes. You were gone so long and there have been such crowds in the streets, and there has been so much shouting."

Wilton chuckled. "And our Peter is responsible for it. He has found, so it seems, the lance which pierced the side of our Savior as he hung on the cross."

Shajar unbuckled Wilton's sword belt and laid the blade on a table. She took his helmet, led him over to the couch. "Is our Peter really responsible?"

It suddenly occurred to Wilton that this discovery of the lance could be used to get Shajar out of the house and to a place near the wall. There he could bind her, carry her to the wall and lower her to the waiting Syrian. She would not go willingly, he knew.

"Would you not like to see the place where the lance was discovered?" he asked her.

"Tonight?"

"Aye. It would be an interesting sight."

"But—"

A loud banging on the door interrupted the girl. Wilton

came to his feet, but before he could move forward the door burst open and three men strode into the room.

Leading them was Guy de Fortney, a naked blade in his hand. At the sight of the girl his eyes brightened. "So the man was right," he said. "It is here that she has been kept."

Wilton's eyes narrowed. "What do you want, de Fortney? Why have you come here?"

Guy de Fortney laughed. "I have come for the Saracen woman. Stand away from her, Wilton. I have little time to spare. She is the daughter of Yagi Siyan and the man who holds her can bargain with the Moslems for his freedom."

How de Fortney had learned that Shajar was here Wilton didn't know, but there were many who might have told him, Without doubt, he could bargain with the Moslems for his freedom if he held her, and in de Fortney's eyes there was a look of desperation. He realized that only death awaited the Crusaders who stayed in Antioch.

"Stand away from her, Wilton," de Fortney cried again.

Shajar had come to her feet. She was clutching Wilton's arm. His eyes moved over to the table where his sword lay. It was more than three paces from where he stood. The axe *Bretwalda* hung on the other wall. He was unarmed and he knew that he could reach neither weapon before de Fortney struck him down.

"Do you not think I have tried to deal with Kerbogha?" he asked slowly. "'Tis no use. The Moslems—"

Guy de Fortney moved forward. "Wilton," he said savagely. "You told me once that I should learn to use this blade. It missed once. It will not miss this time."

AS HE faced the man, Wilton was conscious of no fear. He was aware only of the breathlessness of that moment. His eyes were fastened on de Fortney's. In another instant, he knew, de Fortney would swing that sword at him. Could he but escape that first slash he might be able to reach his axe before de Fortney or the other two men could strike again. There was no other chance for him. He loosened Shajar's hands from his arm, pushed her away. His muscles tightened.

A high, nervous laugh came from de Fortney's throat. His eyes widened. The blade in his hands whipped suddenly into the air, started downward. Instinctively, Wilton threw himself to one side, and then a sharp cry of horror burst from his lips.

"No. Shajar! No!" he screamed. "No—"

His hands went out to clutch the girl's body as she threw herself between him and the flashing blade. But though he touched her he could not stop her. The blade came down. It sheered deep into the girl's shoulder and warm, red blood burst like a fountain from the cut. A brief, piteous cry sounded from her lips, and then as de Fortney drew back she slumped to the door and lay motionless.

Wilton had no clear recollection of stumbling over to the wall where hung the axe *Bretwalda*, but he suddenly knew that he held it in his hands and that he was facing de Fortney and the two men. There was a stunned, bewildered expression on de Fortney's face. The other two looked frightened.

Whether he said anything or not, Wilton never knew. He moved forward, slashed out with the axe again and again. Swords cut at him, but they were as useless as straws, and one after another those three men went down, de Fortney last, with a wild screaming cry, to meet the death he had hoped to avoid.

But there was little satisfaction for Wilton in the death of those three men. He lowered the axe and went swiftly to where Shajar lay. Her shoulder was almost severed from her body and the carpet around her was soaking up her blood.

Wilton dropped to his knees. He lifted her in his arms, stared into her face. Tears blinded him until he could not see. His head dropped to her breast; he whispered her name over and over, "Shajar—Shajar—Shajar—"

"Henry."

The whisper was so faint that he hardly caught it. He raised his head, looked into her eyes. They had opened, were resting on his face. Shajar's lips moved and as though from a great distance away, Wilton heard her saying, "Do not grieve, Henry.

We have known more happiness in a few days than many people know in an entire lifetime."

"Shajar," Wilton whispered. "Shajar—"

The girl's figure relaxed in his arms. Her eyes closed. Wilton bent forward and kissed her and when he lifted his head he saw that there was a smile on her lips.

PEOPLE were still milling through the streets of Antioch in the gray dawn of the early morning. Before the church of St. Peter there was a great throng and on its steps stood Bishop Adhemar. He held in his hands the rusty blade of a lance which Peter Bartholomew had discovered buried beneath the church's altar. All night long had Bishop Adhemar stood there holding the lance while countless thousands of crusaders and pilgrims filed past him, stopping only to make the sign of the cross and to kiss the lance.

But then, though they moved on, none of them returned to their quarters. A religious frenzy had gripped them. They were massed in groups throughout the entire town. Here and there crowds of pilgrims knelt in prayer, here and there priests were exhorting great congregations. "It is the sign," men whispered. "It is the sign for which we have been waiting. The Byzantine army will come. Victory will be ours. *Deus vult!*"

Hunger was forgotten and men who were so weak that they could scarcely stand moved through the streets borne up by a nervous strength newly found. Peter the Hermit, who was un-surpassed in eloquence, had talked until he was hoarse. Behemond, Tancred, Robert of Normandy and other leaders forgot their fears. The discovery of the lance was a sign that the Lord was still with them. Hope was born anew....

Such were the scenes which met Wilton's eyes as he closed the door on the room where lay the body of Shajar. All night he had kept watch at her side, conscious of no other thoughts but of her. And gradually and very strangely a deep and quiet peace had calmed his nerves and brought order to the confusion of his mind. Shajar's love and devotion was as a mantle which covered him completely and which set him apart from all other men. It was a precious possession which he would never lose, and which would forever lift him above his companions.

As he moved down into the street and made his way through the crowd he heard on every hand the story of the finding of the lance. Over and over he heard men saying, "It is a sign. The Byzantine army is coming. The Byzantine army is coming."

Near the church of St. Peter, Wilton suddenly stopped, recalling an old story that he heard in England. Back in the year 1000, according to the story, men had expected the Second Coming of Christ and the Millennium. No crops had been planted that year, no work had been done. And on Christmas day, thousands had gathered at the churches to await His Coming. But He had not come. And the bitterness and disappointment which had followed had been so horrible that Christianity had almost perished from the face of the earth.

Remembering that story, Wilton knew what these companions of his were facing. For despite the sign of the lance, the Byzantine army was *not* coming. It had turned back. There was no hope for any of them, and in a day or two when this religious fervor had passed, starvation and weakness would take its dreadful toll; bitterness and disappointment would make a horror of the remaining days before the Moslems stormed the walls. It would be better, Wilton thought, to seek death on the field of battle than to wait supinely for such an end. It would be better to let the Moslems once more feel the cut of Christian blades, even if they were swung by weakened arms, than to await a cowardly death.

A tall, gaunt warrior grasped him by the shoulder, shouting, "The Byzantine army is coming. We will be victorious. We shall yet reach the Holy City."

Wilton smiled. "Why wait for the Byzantine army?"

The man blinked at him. "What do you mean?"

"If the Lord is with us, and the lance is a sign, how can we fail of victory if we attack the infidel?" Wilton asked.

The warrior's shoulder's straightened.

"Aye. How can we fail?"

Wilton moved on. To another and to another he asked the same question. "Why wait for the Byzantine army? Why wait for the Byzantine army?" He passed beyond the church, turned down another street, and echoes of that question reached him as he moved on. The thought took hold on the Crusaders' minds. It fitted in with the discovery of the lance. A sign had been given to them, a sign of victory. Swords gleamed in the morning air, axes flashed in the first rays of the sun. The crowds stopped milling about, turned toward the city's gates, shouting, crying, laughing, borne on by an excitement and fervor which stopped not to measure the odds against them.

TO THE TENT of Kerbogha, the leader of the Moslem army camped outside the walls of Antioch, came word that the Christians were moving out through the gates of the city and forming in a battle line. Kerbogha laughed. From his spies within the city walls he knew the conditions which the Crusaders had faced. He knew that they had been without food, that disease and death had stalked through their ranks, that their spirit was exhausted.

"It cannot be true," he insisted.

"But it is true," replied the messenger. "Many of the Christians have already crossed the river."

Kerbogha left his tent and saw that the Christians had indeed moved out of the city and were forming for battle. He saw, too, that most of them were on foot, that only a few had horses. And once more he laughed. A seasoned campaigner was this Moslem leader and under his banners he had the greatest Moslem force which had been assembled for years. He had horses for all his men, and all were well armed. It would be easy to defeat that straggling Christian mob.

"Have our men withdraw a distance of two miles," he ordered. "We will let the Christians walk to their death—as many as can walk."

DESPERATELY and earnestly did Behemond, Tancred, Godfrey de Bouillon and Robert of Normandy try to form the Crusaders' ranks into some kind of battle order, but as the Christians started forward, there was little of promise in their advance. To one side, Peter the Hermit led his following of pilgrims, some of them were not armed at all, many of whom were almost too weak to follow him. Before another body of men marched Bishop Adhemar, his standard a cross and fastened to it, the rusty lance which Bartholomew had found. In the center of the long line were the Crusaders, well armored, well armed. Lance, sword, axe and shield they bore, and if the weight of their armor was heavy to their weakened bodies, they did not show it. As the Moslems drew back, to many of them it seemed an advance sign of victory and the retreat was greeted with a shout.

Men started running forward across the plain, waving sword and shield and shouting, "*Deus vult! Deus vult!*" The battle line lost all semblance of order. Dust churned up by their racing feet spread behind them like a cloud, hiding the walls of Antioch from their sight. Here and there someone would stumble and fall, perhaps rise again, perhaps not.

Wilton ran with the others, and despite his knowledge of what lay ahead for all of them, a strange enthusiasm gripped him. He saw no ultimate victory, thought not of defeat, but in the cries around him he sensed a spirit which was greater than any force of arms.

"*Deus vult! Deus vult!*"

BEFORE him, suddenly, was the Moslem line. To the right and to the left lances pricked the sides of the Arab horses, riders were unseated and rearing, screaming stallions spread confusion through the Moslem ranks. Wilton continued moving forward, now and again slashing out with his great axe. A little way ahead the Moslems were forming on foot. Behind soldiers armored with shield and lance were file upon file of archers and bowmen. Beyond them were mounted regiments of Seljuk Turks, and now from the right and left in great flanking movements came thundering Arab horsemen, cutting into the pilgrims' ranks, riding them to the earth and moving on until finally stopped by the pressure of bodies around their horses.

Wilton ran forward, charging against that Moslem line. The axe *Bretwalda*, slashing from side to side, cut a wide pathway for him. Other Crusaders, following him, widened that pathway and made of it a wedge, ever broadening, ever moving forward. Nothing, it seemed, could stem their advance, nothing could stand against them. The Moslem lines broke under the fury of Christian sword and axe. Hastily re-formed, it was broken again. Panic spread through their ranks and men turned to flee. Crusaders caught up riderless horses and pursued the Moslems. The flight became a rout, and as the dust settled over the plains the weary Crusaders gathered at what had been Kerbogha's camp. There they found food in plenty. There they feasted that night, talking in low tones of the battle and now and then glancing reverently at Adhemar's standard, the cross with the rusted lance.

"A miracle," some whispered. And it had been a miracle. Few there were who realized it, but that day, not only had the Crusaders defeated a force many times greater than theirs in number, but also they had completely broken the resistance of the Moslems. For a while, as they marched on to Jerusalem, they were to be delayed at Maara-en-N'aman. On a few more occasions they were to have sharp engagements with bands of Turks or Saracens. The road to Jerusalem however, was open...

Seated not far from the standard of Bishop Adhemar, Wilton of Mercia looked up at it thoughtfully. He had come through the battle unscathed, a battle which he had thought none of them would survive. And now he would follow that standard on to Jerusalem and when the Holy City had been taken he would return to England. All of that he could see clearly before him. It was the way his life must run.

Behemond joined him and looking up at the standard, said thoughtfully, "It's strange, isn't it, Wilton, how so old and rusty a thing as that lance can change the course of history? With twice as many men as we had, all in good condition, I would have hesitated to attack the Moslems. I even tried to turn our men back but could not stop them. Now nothing can stand in our way."

Wilton smiled. "*Deus vult,*" be murmured.

For a while Behemond was silent, then he said suddenly, "I do not go on, Wilton. I stay here to hold Antioch. I would like to have you with me and I thought, perhaps—"

"Nay, Behemond," Wilton answered. "I must go on. Yet I think that a part of me will always be in Antioch."

"A part of you? I do not understand?"

Wilton closed his eyes and to his mind there came the vision of Shajar's face. He could see her as clearly as though she stood before him. It would not always be thus, he knew. With time that vision would fade, would grow indistinct, but his memory of her would stay forever fresh. Yes, truly, a part of him would never leave Antioch.

Rather annoyed at his continued silence, Behemond got to his feet and said gruffly, "Well, think it over, Wilton. And if you decide to stay—"

Men were gathering around the standard of Bishop Adhemar. Someone had started a song of victory. Wilton stood up, facing resolutely toward Jerusalem. His hand closed on the axe *Bretwalda* and he lifted it, examined it. One of the jewels was missing from the head. He shrugged. That was of little importance. It was a great weapon. He moved the axe to his shoulder and started walking back to the city.

VI

SCOURGE OF THE SEVERN

A new king for England! Its fields lie
untilled, its highways teem with murderers.
Yet there can be no honor in the land while
the Wolf rides toward the throne.

CHAPTER I

OLD SIMON, HEAD caretaker of the Huntingdon Abbey, puttered around the flower garden near the chapel door. Now and again he would glance toward the gate in the Abbey wall. Half a dozen of the bishop's soldiers stood there on guard and the sight of them brought a scowl to his face. Somehow he couldn't get used to the notion that armed men were needed to guard the Abbey against the marauding bands which were abroad in the land. Nor could he understand why William, Bishop of Stafford, should have an army. It didn't seem in keeping with the clergy.

A footstep sounded on the path near the flower garden and a quiet voice said, "Good morning, Simon. Is it not a beautiful day?"

Simon turned, glanced up into the face of the Mother Superior and took off his cap. He said, "Aye, it is a beautiful day." But his voice showed no enthusiasm.

The Mother Superior was quite old. Her face was pleasantly wrinkled. Simon often wondered if she ever frowned. In all the years that he had been at the Abbey he had never seen her look troubled. That was another thing he couldn't understand. Certainly, from all the people who had taken refuge here, she should have heard enough of sorrow to disturb her tranquillity.

"Do you not feel well, Simon?" she asked him.

Simon rubbed his bald head. "I feel well enough. It is of my son I am thinking."

"You have not heard from him?"

"No."

The Mother Superior smiled. "I would not worry, Simon. He is a strong man, and good."

"And so was Sir Richard Wilton a strong man and good." Simon answered. "Yet look what happened to him. He has lost his manor, his lands. His father was slain before his very eyes, his sister was cast from the donjon tower. He has been branded an outlaw by Sir Belan of Gloucester and men hunt him through the forests of Stafford as they would hunt a wild boar."

"But did not Sir Richard have dealings with Henry the Plantagenet who desires the throne of England?"

"Aye. And what if he did? These have been evil times in England. Since Stephen was crowned king in 1135 there has been no honor in the land. Each year conditions have grown worse. In the towns people are starving. Fields lie unplowed, the highways are thronged with murderers. Only by the might of his arms can a man be safe."

The Mother Superior smiled. She put a hand on Simon's arm and said, "I know but little of politics. I know only to care for those who are here and those who come to our gates for refuge. There is someone now."

OUT at the gate there was a sudden confusion. Simon glanced that way. The guarding soldiers were standing stiffly erect. One of them had opened the iron gate and through it, now, there came more men-at-arms clad in glistening plate armor and bearing long spears. Swords were fastened to their sides and shields to their backs.

The men-at-arms were followed by a youth who bore a gold and blue standard. Simon scowled. He recognized that standard as the standard of William, Bishop of Stafford, and a moment later the bishop himself appeared followed by a retinue of nobles.

There in the Abbey garden Wilton swung the great axe, and the bishop's men fell back.

William, Bishop of Stafford, was a short, heavy-set man with a round, red face. He was clad in rich, ornamental vestures and he waddled a little as he came forward. Simon had no liking for him. He knew that he should feel very awed and respectful at the sight of the cleric, but he didn't, and he stood in his flower garden and listened quite shamelessly as the bishop and the Mother Superior talked.

"A fine day," said the bishop after he had greeted her. "A fine day for a wedding?

"A wedding?" repeated the Mother Superior, looking surprised.

The bishop laughed. "Surely. And have you any objections to letting us use the Abbey chapel for the ceremony?"

The Mother Superior, Simon noticed, seemed no more awed of the bishop than he did. She shook her head, bowed and said that Huntingdon Abbey would be honored.

"You must also," said the bishop, "supply the bride."

The Mother Superior's eyes widened. "You speak in riddles, Bishop William."

"Nay," replied the bishop. "Is not the Lady Margaret of Worcester at the Abbey?"

"But the Lady Margaret has said nothing of—"

Again the Bishop laughed. "Bring her here," he commanded. "She will be well pleased, I am sure."

The Mother Superior hesitated and for a moment, Simon held his breath, conscious of a strange, bewildering excitement. The notion came to him that the Mother Superior was going to refuse to do as the bishop had requested. But just as that thought flashed across his mind, the Mother Superior bowed and turned and walked away.

After she had gone, one of the nobles who had been standing near the bishop moved forward and started talking to him in a low voice. At the sight of him, Simon's scowl deepened. The man was tall and slender and dark. A red silk cloak, fur bordered, hung from his shoulders. It was fastened there by two jeweled clasps. The man's helmet was plumed. He removed it as he was speaking, revealing a mass of very black hair. His eyes were black, too, and to Simon they seemed little and mean. His nose was sharp, his lips were thin and colorless. Simon had seen the man only once before but he immediately recognized him as Sir Belan of Gloucester.

The sight of Sir Belan reminded Simon of his talk with the Mother Superior, and his eyes moved over to the high wall which surrounded the Abbey grounds. Beyond the wall he could see the tops of the trees of Stafford Forest. Somewhere out there, he knew, Sir Richard Wilton lay hidden, or perhaps by now he was already dead, another victim to the ambition of Sir Belan of Gloucester, Wolf of the Severn Valley. Old Simon muttered under his breath. Unlike the Mother Superior, he was interested in politics, and he thought he knew what Sir Belan wanted. Nominally he was the representative of King Stephen in this district, but day by day he was growing stronger. Men whispered that royal blood ran in his veins and that he was much more entitled to the throne of England than Henry the Plantagenet.

THE MEN-AT-ARMS had been whispering among themselves, but of a sudden they grew quiet, and turning to look along the path which led past the chapel. Simon saw that the Mother Superior was returning, accompanied by one of the young women who had recently taken refuge in the Abbey. Simon hadn't noticed the young woman before, but now he examined her closely. She was tall, and very fair. Her hair was almost golden, and it hung in two long braids which reached far below her waist. She wore a white gown and a girdle of scarlet and gold. Her lace was thin, with a high forehead, a straight nose and a delicately moulded chin. She made Simon think of his lilies, for she was slender and beautiful, just as they; and yet in her bearing there was a pride and strength.

"You sent for me, Bishop William?" said the woman.

The bishop chuckled. "Aye, Lady Margaret, though really it is Sir Belan who should have sent for you."

Lady Margaret glanced at Sir Belan, and Simon could not interpret the look on her face. "What was it you wished?" she asked quietly.

Sir Belan drew the Lady Margaret aside and began speaking to her in a low tone. Simon couldn't catch any of his words, but he saw an expression of horror and then of fear come into Lady Margaret's eyes. Her breast rose and fell swiftly, and she didn't seem to be able to look away from Sin Belan's face.

The Mother Superior moved over to her side, laid a hand on her arm. "Bishop William tells me," she said slowly, "that it is your wish to marry this man. Is he speaking for your heart, Lady Margaret?"

Once again, then, old Simon knew a thrill of excitement and this time he felt with it a deep pride in the courage of the Mother Superior, who dared to ask such a question in the presence of the bishop. He hoped that the woman would shake her head, that she would say that she didn't want to marry Sir Belan. But her shoulders had slumped forward and her head was bowed. "It is as I wish." Simon heard her say. "Thank you, Mother."

William, Bishop of Stafford, rubbed his hands together. "A fine day for a wedding." He grinned. "A fine day for a wedding. Shall we all go into the chapel?"

A loud, shrill, defiant cry sounded across the Abbey grounds and while its echoes were still in the air, old Simon caught sight of a figure atop the Abbey wall. It was a man, tall, broad shouldered, clothed in a leather jerkin and leather trousers. An old helmet, battered and scarred, covered his head but did not entirely imprison his light, curly hair. Belted to his side there was a sword and he was leaning on what seemed to be a long shaft.

FOR AN INSTANT, Simon looked on the man in wonder, for the wall was tall and there were no convenient trees which could have aided him in climbing it. Then as the man shifted his position Simon saw that it was no shaft that he was leaning on, but rather the handle of an axe. He guessed, then, who the man was, for the axe on which he was leaning was great and cumbersome and in all the Severn Valley there was none other like it. It was wrought entirely of steel, Simon had heard, and in the head there were seven blood-red jewels set above the name *Bretwalda*.

"Sir Richard Wilton!" he gasped breathlessly.

But he might as well have spoken the name aloud, for there were others there before the chapel who had recognized the man on the wall. "Size him!" Sir Belan was shouting. "Seize that man! Whatever reward you name to the one who takes him."

The men-at-arms ran toward the wall, yelling at one another. And then again that shrill, defiant cry sounded across the Abbey grounds. It was a strange, thrilling cry, and it stirred old Simon's blood. He saw the man cast his great axe into the garden below him and drop lightly beside it, pick it up and face the on-rushing soldiers. Then, suddenly, another man appeared atop the wall and leaped down to join the first. A third followed. A fourth. A fifth. A sixth. They were clambering over the wall like monkeys, and each one as he came into sight, voiced the same, shrill cry.

In the garden steel clashed against steel and sharp screams arose above the sounds of the battle. Old Simon pressed forward, his eyes wide. He had picked up a hoe from the flower bed and he was holding it as he might have held a spear, but he wasn't even aware that he had it. Watching Sir Richard Wilton, he caught flashes of the great axe *Bretwalda* as it slashed from side to side and as men fell back before it. From his own son, Simon had heard that the axe was so heavy that no man could lift it, yet in Sir Richard's hands it seemed to move so swiftly that the eye could hardly follow it.

A man stumbled past the place where old Simon was standing and another came after him, running for the gate. More men turned from the battle and fled. Simon heard Sir Belan shouting, cursing them, and then Sir Belan's voice was suddenly stilled. Out of the corner of his eye, Simon saw him slipping through the chapel door, the bishop following him. The Mother Superior and Lady Margaret were still in the path near the place where Simon had been working.

AS ABRUPTLY as it had started the battle was over and Sir Richard Wilton came striding forward, his great axe resting on his shoulder. The men who had followed him over the wall came after him, and a strange band they were. Some were mere heardless youths; some were old men, wrinkled and gray, yet fierce-eyed and clearly exultant over what had happened. Most of them wore old leather jerkins and under them coats of chain mail. A few had bows slung across their shoulders. Some carried swords, some had axes, some, spears. They numbered less than a score and they could not be experienced fighters, Simon knew. Yet he had just seen them vanquish a force twice theirs in number.

Pausing before the Mother Superior and Lady Margaret, Sir Richard bowed and dotted his helmet. "I am very sorry for what has just happened," he said to the Mother Superior, "but I could think of no other way than this to stop the marriage."

Old Simon was standing where he could see Sir Richard's face. It was a thin face, deeply tanned, and it was set in stern, hard lines. His blue eyes were as cold as steel and his lips were a straight line above a blunt, uncompromising, stubborn jaw.

"And why should the marriage have been stopped?" asked the Mother Superior.

Sir Richard shrugged. "Ask the Lady Margaret. A union with Sir Belan would not have been of her choosing."

Lady Margaret straightened. "But it was," she answered clearly. "By what right do you interfere? Who are you?"

The answer seemed to surprise Sir Richard. He blinked at the woman, then suddenly laughed. "Let us say, then," he suggested, "that it was not of my choosing."

Lady Margaret flushed but what answer she made, Old Simon didn't hear. A hand had tugged at his arm and a voice said into his ear, "What think you of him, Father? Did you see the fight?"

Simon swung around. There, facing him, but looking at Sir Richard, stood his son, the son about whom he had been worried.

"Thomas," he cried. "Thomas!"

The young man looked at him and grinned. There was a jagged cut on his cheek, but he seemed to be unaware of it.

"You—you came with him, Thomas," whispered the old man.

"Aye, Father. We heaped a great pile of rocks against the wall. It was easy."

"But what do you with Sir Richard? Do you not know that every man's hand is raised against him? He has been declared an outlaw, and those who aid him face the penalty of death."

Thomas laughed. "Not every man's hand has been raised against him, Father, but though that were true I would rather die at his side than live under the yoke of the Wolf of Severn."

"But what—"

"Look," the youth interrupted. "The Lady objects. See what Richard is doing."

Simon looked around. He saw Sir Richard bend forward and lift the Lady Margaret in his arms, heard his rich laugh ring out and watched him turn toward the gate, carrying her easily despite her struggles.

"I must go now, Father." Thomas said hurriedly.

Old Simon made no immediate answer. He knew not what reason Sir Richard might have for carrying away the Lady Margaret, but he felt an almost irresistible impulse to follow after him. At the gate, Thomas turned and waved, and lifting his voice, old Simon called. "God go with you, my son."

After that, tears filmed his eyes so that for a while he could hardly see.

CHAPTER II

THE LADY MARGARET ceased her struggling as Sir Richard passed through the Abbey gate. "If I must go with you," she said icily, "I prefer to walk. Will you please set me down?"

Sir Richard made no answer. One of his men who had been left behind with the horses was bringing them forward and Sir Richard turned to Michael Godwin.

"After I have mounted, lift her up to me," he ordered.

Michael Godwin was a short, stocky youth with flaming red hair and a round, freckled face. He took the woman in his arms, and after Sir Richard had mounted his horse, lifted her up so that Sir Richard could take her again.

"You will ride into the forest and then separate," Sir Richard commanded. "We will meet again tonight when the moon is an hour high. The place is the mill on the bank of the Severn just below Stafford. The blow you have struck this morning is one which the Wolf of the Severn will feel deeply. I need not warn you to be careful. Hubert, come with me."

Several of the men gave an involuntary cheer. All of them were grinning, even those who had been wounded. Sir Richard waved his hand and turned his horse down the road toward Stafford. He rode slowly, one arm encircling the waist of the Lady Margaret.

The road from the Abbey twisted its uneven way through the heavy foliage of Stafford Forest. Birds sang from the trees and the air was sweet with the scent of wild flowers. Several leagues from the Abbey, Sir Richard turned from the road and directed his horse along a faintly marked trail.

Lady Margaret stirred uneasily. "Where are you taking me?" she demanded.

"To a place where you will be safe," Sir Richard answered.

"Safe from whom?"

Sir Richard made no reply. He thought bitterly that no more was there safety for anyone, anywhere in the land.

They came suddenly to a clearing deep within the forest. At one side of it was a crude log structure with a thatched roof. An old man stood near it, bow and arrow ready in his hand.

" 'Tis just me, Adam," Sir Richard called.

The old man lowered his bow and as Sir Richard came up he muttered, "Aye, master, but in these days a man can never be sure whether it is a friend or a foe who is approaching."

Sir Richard lowered the woman to the ground and dismounted from his horse. Hubert de Clare, who had followed him, rode up and said, "Do we go on or shall I take the horses farther into the woods?"

A tall, thin man was Hubert de Clare. He was about Sir Richards age. His face was pale and there was a strained, intent look about it. His eyes were sharp and dark.

"Take the horses on farther, hide them and then return," Sir Richard suggested.

Hubert de Clare nodded, reached for the reins of the other horse and then rode on.

SIR RICHARD moved over to a fallen log and sat down. He removed the great axe, *Bretwalda*, from the sling by which it had hung from his shoulder, glanced at it thoughtfully and then laid it aside.

"You would have something to eat, master?" asked the old man.

Sir Richard shook his head. He glanced at Lady Margaret. She was standing not far away, holding herself proudly erect. Her eyes were fixed on his face and there was a stormy look in them. Sir Richard blinked. At the Abbey and on the way here he had paid little attention to the woman's appearance, but now he suddenly realized that the Lady Margaret was both young and beautiful.

"What do you intend to do with me?" she asked abruptly.

Sir Richard stood up. "I told you that I was bringing you to a place where you would be safe," he answered. "And I have done just that. Here you need have no fear."

"But why have you brought me here? Why did you—stop the wedding?"

Sir Richards face tightened. He said between his clenched teeth, "The Wolf of the Severn needed only to wed with the daughter of the slain Earl of Worcester, in order to gain control of another five thousand men-at-arms, in order to spread his domination to the north. He is already too powerful."

Lady Margaret took a step forward. "He holds my brother prisoner."

"Aye. That I know. And should you have wed him, your brother would never have left the dungeons of Stafford Castle. Perhaps even now he is dead."

The woman's face paled. "No," she whispered, "no. It can't be. Sir Belan told me— "

Sir Richard moved forward. He said, "Lady Margaret, tonight we go to free your brother. If we are successful I will see that you are returned to Worcester. There, if you wish, you may wed the Wolf of the Severn, for if your brother is alive, Sir Belan will not gain control of that country through his marriage to you. It will fall to your brother and I know how he will feel."

Lady Margaret turned away. She walked over to the wood-cutters house and sat down on a bench near the door. Sir Richard stared after her. He felt that he had been too harsh and he wished that he could recall his words. Then his thoughts turned to Sir Belan and he forgot all about Lady Margaret.

Sir Belan, of Gloucester, the Wolf of the Severn, was not much older than he, but half a dozen years before, on the death of his father, he had inherited his father's estates. Shortly after that he had made a trip to Winchester where he had seen King Stephen and he had returned to this part of the country with an appointment as the king's justiciar. Such an appointment had given him the right to preside for the king at trials, to mete out justice, and he had quickly taken advantage of it. Adding to the men-at-arms under his command, he had set about confiscating estates in the name of the king. Gradually he had come to dominate the entire Severn Valley from Gloucester to Stafford, and finally, only a month before, he had reached out and settled an old score with Sir Henry Wilton.

SO LONG as he lived, Sir Richard knew that he would never forget the day when Sir Belan's men had come to Wilton Hall. There had been no evidence of any hostility on their part as they had approached and his father had admitted them to the hall without question, for the doors of his house were always open, His father had even fed them in the great banquet room and had provided entertainment after the meal.

Then, with a bewildering suddenness, the Wolf of the Severn had struck. A score of his men had turned on Sir Richard's father as he sat at this head of the table. Sir Henry had had no chance at all. The great axe *Bretwalda* which had been in the family for generations had been hanging on the wall behind him. He had not even been able to reach it.

Sir Richard recalled little of the fight which followed. A blow had struck him down as he had sought to gain his father's side. His life he owed to Michael Godwin who had dragged his body from the hall as Sir Belan's men started their looting. Michael had also secured *Bretwalda* for him and later Michael had told him of his sister's death. Pursued by Sir Belan, she had thrown herself from a window.

All of that was now like a horrible dream which stored up in him a deep bitterness. That he was branded as an outlaw mattered not at all.

Hubert de Clare came striding back across the clearing and joined him. "What do you plan tonight?" he asked bluntly.

Sir Richard told him and de Clare scowled. "Stafford Castle! A thousand men could not take it."

"Perhaps not, if they stormed the walls. But there is a more convenient entrance."

Hubert de Clare rubbed his hands together. He said slowly, "I care not what happens if I can only corner Sir Belan with a sword in my hand. He was at the Abbey, I know, and he must have been among the first to flee for as we broke through the men at the wall I did not see him."

"Nor did I," answered Sir Richard.

Hubert de Clare glanced over toward Lady Margaret. "What of her?"

"She will stay here."

Hubert de Clare sprawled out on the ground and Sir Richard looked down at him thoughtfully. He had known Hubert de Clare since the days of his boyhood and there had always been a close bond between them. But there was a stronger tie now, for Hubert had loved his sister and it seemed that her death had drawn them even closer together. Each could understand the others bitterness. Each could appreciate the hatred which colored every thought and action.

Unmindful of Sir Richard's statement a few moments before, Adam Dean brought out a plate of food and set it on the ground near them. He returned to the house and came back with a flagon of mead. Hubert thanked him and Sir Richard, looking over toward Lady Margaret, said, "Hungry?"

The woman shook her head but after a moment she got up

and came over to where they were sitting. "How will you rescue my brother?" she demanded.

Sir Richard shrugged. "We may not rescue him. I said that we would try."

"He is in Stafford Castle."

"Aye."

Lady Margaret stared down at him and from the expression in her face Sir Richard couldn't guess what she might be thinking. Again he offered her food but again she refused it. She walked back to the bench.

Sir Richard called to Adam Dean and when the old man came out of the house, he said. "Care for the Lady Margaret, Adam. See that she has food and drink when she requires it. Also that she has a bed for the night."

The woodcutter nodded and Sir Richard pillowed his head on his arm and slept.

IN THE shadows of the old mill on the banks of the Severn, just below the town of Stafford, Sir Richard Wilton awaited the gathering of his men. They came in groups of twos and threes, just as they had come to him when he had fled deep into the forest to escape from Sir Belan's men. Many of them, he knew, were outlaws by deed as well as by name and might cheerfully cut his own throat if the price offered were high enough and if they could be sure of the chance of living to collect it. Others, however, were men like himself, men who had been driven to the forest through Sir Belan's oppression. A few had been servants in his father's household.

It was a strange company and none knew it better than he. No bond other than that of collective security held them together. If cornered he knew that fully half of them would turn and fight for their own freedom, or might even turn on him. Yet in them he had found the help he needed. Thus far they had not failed him. He prayed they would not fail him now.

As the moon began to reach high into the sky, outlining the

embattled towers of Stafford Castle on the hill above the old mill, Sir Richard summoned the men around him.

"Not far from here," he told them, "lies the entrance to the underground passage into the castle. It will not be guarded for its location is a secret. Nor will there be many men in the castle tonight, for most of Sir Belan's men have been riding far and wide, searching for our hiding place. We should have little trouble in taking the castle."

A deep silence followed that announcement of Sir Richard's. Men turned and stared up at the castle. It had stood there for a long time. It looked grim and formidable. A year before these same men might have laughed at Sir Richard's suggestion, yet each one of them knew that Sir Belan had taken the castle from its former owner through trickery and each wondered if another trick might not serve to take it from him.

Other thoughts, too must have passed through their minds. Some of them were thinking, perhaps, of the loot which might be gained. Some were thinking of the satisfaction of revenge. A few, possibly, of the thrill of such an undertaking.

"Well?" Sir Richard asked.

A deep laugh sounded from the throat of one of the men. He lifted his fist and shook it at the castle. "Show us the way in, Sir Richard," he growled. "I'd like to get my hands on the stuff the Wolf of the Severn has stored away in there."

Other men nodded.

Sir Richard glanced over at Hubert de Clare. De Clare was facing the castle and in the pale light of the moon his face seemed drawn and haggard. "Come on," he said sharply. "Where is the passage?"

Sir Richard led the way across a field toward a great outcropping of rocks. He laid hold of one of them and a dozen hands helped him to roll it aside. Below yawned a great hole. Many years before, when but at lad, Sir Richard had learned of this passage into Stafford Castle. He had seen a man escape this way, had thought that the man had come up from the ground.

The next day he had heard that one of the prisoners had mysteriously disappeared.

"Let me go first," whispered Hubert de Clare.

Sir Richard shook his head. He lowered his body through the hole, reached for a torch he had brought with him and lit it. Ahead of him stretched a long, winding passageway.

CHAPTER III

THE PASSAGEWAY SEEMED endless. In places it was muddy and a green slime covered the walls. The air was foul and the smoke from Sir Richard's torch made it no better. Twice did they come to stairways which led to higher levels and at last they found their way blocked by a heavy iron door.

Sir Richard guessed that they were now under the donjon. He tried the door and found that it opened toward him, but a stone wall lay beyond. He pushed his body against the stones. They were loose, had merely been piled into place in order to hide the door. He pushed against them once more and they fell outward.

The room beyond was small and was almost as damp as the passage had been. Sir Richard moved across it toward a stairway, climbed the stairs and opened another door. It gave into a long corridor, lighted at either end by torches fixed in iron brackets projecting from the walls. From the right came the sound of music, the indistinct murmur of voices. Sir Richard turned that way and his men crowded after him. He cast his torch aside, reached for the axe which hung at his shoulder.

A door at the end of the corridor was suddenly opened and a man started to come out of the room beyond. He caught sight of them, stopped and gaped in surprise, swung around and yelled a warning.

Sir Richard charged for the door. Three guards, called up by the warning shout, tried to block his way, but with his great axe he smashed them aside. Hubert de Clare was just behind him and others were following fast. Like an avalanche they swept through that room. A score of men had been seated at the banquet table when they appeared. A few managed to get out another door, a few put up a futile resistance.

Into the next room and into the room beyond swept the outlaws. One group, under the leadership of Michael Godwin, made for the walls and the watch towers, the others turned to the courtyard. There the defenders had gathered, had drawn up in battle order, but it was an order not long maintained. The outlaws charged them recklessly. They were greatly outnumbered, but they did not seem to realize it. Nor did the defenders, for confusion and terror spread throughout their ranks.

Sir Richard could sense that and his shout rang out high above the sound of the battle. He began to feel the deep exultation of victory. The Wolf of the Severn was not here, he knew, for Sir Belan's voice had not been heard, yet the taking of this castle would not be barren of results. If the Lady Margaret's brother was still held here, he would be freed and Sir Belan's designs on the north country would be ended. Fully as important, or so it seemed then, the taking of this castle would be a blow to Sir Belan's pride from which he could not easily recover.

A sword slashed at Sir Richard's head, broke against the steel handle of his axe, and the man who had swung it staggered back, turned and fled. Sir Richard lowered the axe to his shoulder. He saw other men fleeing toward the drawbridge which had been lowered over the moat. Off to his left, Hubert de Clare was engaging two soldiers and even as he looked that way, one of the soldiers reeled away from the fight, both hands clutching his stomach. The other dropped his sword and ran. De Clare started after him, stopped, came back to where Sir Richard was standing.

"Sir Belan?" he croaked hoarsely. "Have you seen him?"

"Nay. Hubert," Sir Richard answered. "I doubt if he was here."

Hubert de Clare wiped a hand across his brow. There was a thin, red cut on his cheek. He fingered it tenderly. "Of course he would not be here," he said slowly. "He will always escape me, Richard. I will never catch up with him."

More of the outlaws were gathering around Sir Richard, and calling one of them by name, Sir Richard ordered him to raise the drawbridge. To the others, he said, "Scatter throughout the castle, take and bind what men of Sir Belan's are still within the walls, care for those who have been wounded and then come to the banquet hall."

In groups of twos and threes the outlaws scattered to carry out his order, and with Hubert de Clare at his side, Sir Richard moved back toward the donjon. He walked swiftly, as though the strain of the fight had not tired him at all. "I must find Sir Oliver Lacey," he said to Hubert. "It is for that purpose that we came here. Oliver Lacey is the brother of the Lady Margaret, heir to the earldom of Worcester."

Hubert de Clare made no answer. His head was bowed. He did not seem at all interested.

AN HOUR had passed since the taking of the castle, but Oliver Lacey had not been found. The prisoners in the dungeons had been liberated and brought to the banquet hall. Some were so feeble they had had to be carried; all bore the marks of horrible torture, lacerated faces and bodies, gouged eyes, split tongues, broken limbs. Their bodies were alive with vermin.

Sir Richard had taken upon himself the task of questioning those who were able to speak coherently, but from them he had learned nothing, and new he turned to a bench near the long table and sat down, suddenly aware that he was very weary. Michael Godwin came rushing into the room and told him that the outlaws had found Sir Belan's treasure vaults and were fighting over the loot. Sir Richard shrugged. "What of it? Did you expect anything else?"

Another man came hurrying into the hall. "There is a great body of men at the gate," he cried. "They are demanding that we lower the drawbridge."

Sir Richard straightened. "Is the Wolf of the Severn with them?"

"Nay. Who their leader is I do not know."

"Call all our men to this room," Sir Richard commanded.

Gradually the outlaws assembled. Some were lugging heavy chests, others had made sacks of their cloaks and carried them slung over their shoulders. They looked at one another jealously and they eyed Sir Richard with an ill-concealed suspicion. Only a few of the number were without some kind of booty, for even those who had been motivated to join Sir Richard because of their hatred for the Wolf of the Severn considered a part of the spoils of the castle was rightfully theirs.

Sir Richard stood up. "There is a body of men at the castle gate," he announced. "We can stay here, hold them off for many days, or we can leave by the passage through which we came. What do you want to do?"

The men glanced at one another, whispered among themselves. "I am for leaving," announced one. "Let me get to the forest of Stafford and all the men in England could not take me."

"Aye. Let us go," shouted another.

Sir Richard nodded, glanced over toward the men who had been in the dungeons. Most of those men, he decided, would be better off outside the castle than if they were left here. Some undoubtedly had friends who could care for them.

"Let each one of you," he said to the outlaws, "be responsible for helping out one of these men whom we freed from the dungeons."

There was some grumbling at that order, but it was not disputed. Each of the outlaws selected the man whom he would help through the passageway. A few, who were near to death, Sir Richard agreed should be left behind. He looked around for Hubert de Clare, called to Michael Godwin and asked him where de Clare had gone. Godwin didn't know.

Sir Richard moved out into the courtyard, shouted de Clare's name. An answer came to him from the stables and hurrying that way he found de Clare bending over a man's body.

AS HE CAME up, de Clare got to his feet and said. "Sir Belan's gone to Worcester. He took a company of his men and Oliver Lacey, too. This man just told me and I think he spoke the truth."

There was a knife in de Clare's hand and the point was bloody. His eyes were cold and hard and his bitterness sounded in his voice.

Sir Richard put his hand on de Clare's shoulder. He said quietly, "Come on, Hubert. The men are leaving. Soon, those who are outside will be scaling the walls."

"Did you hear what I said?" de Clare said hoarsely. "Sir Belan's gone to Worcester. Young Lacey went with him."

"Lacey would never do as Sir Belan ordered. I know the boy."

Hubert de Clare drew a deep breath. He said grimly, "All right, Richard, here is the rest of the story. Today, just after noon, a messenger arrived from the south. He brought Sir Belan word that Henry the Plantagenet has crossed the channel from France and has landed on English soil with four thousand men."

Sir Richard straightened. This was the word for which he had been waiting, for which, he thought, all England had been waiting. King Stephen was growing old, could not live much longer. His son Eustace was wholly unfitted for the throne, would not be accepted by any of the barons of England. Henry the Plantagenet, a direct descendant of William the Conqueror, was the logical heir.

"So the day has at last come," Sir Richard breathed.

Hubert de Clare laughed harshly. "You forget, Richard, that Sir Belan also claims that the blood of the Conqueror runs in his veins. You forget that for six years he has been strengthening his position here in the west of England."

Sir Richard shook his head. "No one would take his claim seriously."

"But did you not hear me when I said that Henry the Plantagenet had only four thousand men with him and that Sir Belan had left for Worcester with Oliver Lacey? In Gloucester, Sir Belan has an army of five thousand men. The army of the earl of Worcester numbers another five thousand. With ten thousand men, Sir Belan could march south and drive Henry the Plantagenet into the sea."

"Oliver Lacey, heir to the earldom of Worcester, would never fall in with such a plan."

"You have never seen Murtogh, Sir Belan's torturer, at work. Oliver Lacey is but a lad. He need only issue the orders that his army march with Sir Belan. Sir Belan will look after the rest."

Sir Richards lips tightened. He nodded his head. All hat Hubert de Clare had said could be true and he knew it. The Earl of Worcester had been murdered and shortly afterward his son had been secretly arrested by Sir Belan. Lady Margaret had fled to the Huntingdon Abbey for safety. When he found out where she was, Sir Belan had tried to marry her; and if he had succeeded, as her husband and with Oliver Lacey out of the way he could have taken over command of the men of Worcester. That plan had been foiled. What Sir Belan might have tried next, Sir Richard didn't know, hut apparently the arrival of Henry the Plantagenet had forced his hand. It was quite reasonable to suspect that he had done just as Hubert de Care had guessed.

"What can we do, Richard?" de Clare asked. "You know what it will mean to England if Sir Belan succeeds."

Sir Richard nodded. He knew what it would mean. The reign of the Wolf of the Severn would be more terrible than the nineteen years England had passed under King Stephen. There was a chance, he knew, that the barons would rally to the support of Henry the Plantagenet. But their rallying would be slow and Sir Belan would strike swiftly. He said to de Clare, "Come, we must get out of here before it is too late. The others have already gone."

BACK to the donjon and through the passageway the two men hurried, On the way they met Michael Godwin and three others who were returning.

"I thought you had gone," said Michael Godwin "When I learned that you had not—"

"Where are the others?"

"They have fled with their loot," said Michael bitterly. "They thought only of themselves and of the loot they carried."

Sir Richard shrugged. He did not mind he fact that the men had gone. For what they had done they had been well paid and as things had developed, he could use them no more. Events had moved too rapidly for him. The Wolf of the Severn had gone to gather his army and there seemed no way to stop him.

Standing once more in the meadow near the outcropping rocks which marked the exit from the passageway, Sir Richard's eyes turned from Hubert de Clare to Michael Godwin and then to the other two men who had come back with Godwin. One of those other men, he saw, was the son of the caretaker at the Huntingdon Abbey. The fourth man had been his father's steward. From the expressions on their faces he knew that there was nothing that he could ask of them that they wouldn't do, and he knew a deep feeling of gratitude for their loyalty.

"What now, master?" asked Michael Godwin.

Sir Richard smiled. "You have done well, all of you," he said slowly. "The Wolf of the Severn will not forget this night's work. But we have only started. Meet me tomorrow at dawn at the gates of the Abbey."

Michael Godwin's eyes sparkled and he nodded. Hubert de Clare frowned. He started to say something, but Sir Richard interrupted him. "Tell non of the others. What I have in mind requires only a few."

He swung around, then, and moved off forward the fringing trees of the forest where he had left his horse. When he reached it he looked back. The four men were still standing where he had left them.

A faint smile touched Sir Richard's lips. He had little doubt but that those men would do as he had ordered. They would be at the Abbey gates at dawn and they would wait for him with a growing impatience. For he had lied to them. He would not meet them there, he had no plan which involved them.

Sir Richard mounted his horse, waved his hand at the men and turned into the forest.

CHAPTER IV

AT THE EDGE of the clearing near the woodcutters' shack Sir Richard dismounted. He put his fingers to his mouth and gave a peculiar whistle, then moved forward.

Adam Dean stepped out of the shadows and came to meet him, swinging his longbow, which Sir Richard knew had been strung with an arrow only a moment before.

"The woman is still here?" Sir Richard asked.

"Aye," nodded the old man. "And awake. She thought that you would return."

"Go tell her to dress" Sir Richard ordered, "find her some clothing which will be suitable for a long ride and say that her brother is alive and that I will take her to him.'"

"You took the castle, then?"

"We took it."

The old man sighed. "I should have liked to have been with you."

Sir Richard turned away. He returned to the place where he had left his horse and led the animal to a nearby stable. There he switched his saddle to a fresh horse and chose and saddled another. He brought them back to the clearing.

Lady Margaret did not keep him waiting long, but when she came toward him he hardly knew her. She had on baggy, woolen trousers which were turned up at the ankle, a hip length woolen coat. On her head she wore a skin cap and her hair was coiled beneath it. She looked like a tall, thin boy who had climbed, by mistake, into his father's clothing

"Those were my sons clothes," the old woodcutter said from the doorway. "He will not need them again."

Adam Dean's only sort had died six months before at the hands of one of Sir Belan's soldiers.

"Thank you, Adam," Sir Richard said softly.

Lady Margaret's eyes were fixed on his face. She moved up to his side. "Tell me about Oliver."

"He is well," Sir Richard lied. "As soon as he was released he hurried toward Worcester. I told him that I would bring you."

"He is really well? He hadn't been hurt?"

"Nay."

Lady Margaret drew a deep breath and smiled. "Then let us go," she cried. "Perhaps we can overtake him."

Sir Richard moved to help Lady Margaret into the saddle, but she needed no help. She swung easily, gracefully to the horse's back. Sir Richard mounted, turned and said to her, "We do not dare to follow the highway along the Severn River. Follow me. I will show you roads you never saw before."

THE HOURS which followed were hours which Sir Richard knew he would never forget. Sometimes he and Lady Margaret walked their horses through the crowding undergrowth of shadowy woodlands; again, they raced madly across meadows and fields, and Lady Margaret's laugh sounded clear and free; and there were times when they paused to rest their mounts and held brief conversations. Overhead the moon climbed steadily higher into a star-filled sky, bathing the world in its dim radiance.

Once, when they stopped. Lady Margaret wanted to talk about her brother and from the things she said, Sir Richard knew that she and Oliver had always been very close to each other. On another occasion she said. "You knew my father, didn't you? I have heard him speak of the Wiltons and of Wilton Hall."

Sir Richard nodded. "I knew him."

Lady Margaret's eyes rested on his face. "Your father, too, is dead."

"Aye."

Their horses were standing close together and Lady Margaret reached out and laid a hand on his arm. "Here I have been burdening you with my own troubles when your own are so much greater," she said softly.

Sir Richard laughed. It was beginning to grow light in the eastern sky. Soon would be dawn and already they were drawing close to Worcester. "Come," he said. "Let us ride on."

They stopped once more in a leafy grove on the banks of the Severn River from where they could see the towers of the Worcester Castle. Sir Richard's horse has started to limp. He dismounted and examined the injured hoof.

"It is but a little distance more," Lady Margaret suggested.

Sir Richard nodded. He stared toward the castle towers sharply outlined against the golden tinted clouds. The time has come, he knew, when he must tell Lady Margaret the truth, and he did not relish the task.

"Of what are you thinking?" asked the woman.

A faint smile touched Sir Richard's lips. "I am thinking," he said, turning to face her, "that this morning the world seems to be a very peaceful place, a very beautiful place. I am trying not to remember that last night I killed and saw men killed. I am trying, for a few minutes, not to look ahead."

The girl dismounted, tied her horse reins to the branch of a tree and then sank down on the ground. She removed the cap which had covered her hair, loosened her braids. "You are a strange man, Sir Richard," she said at last. "Right now you are not at all like the man who took me from the Abbey."

"I had little time, then, to be pleasant."

"You were thinking only of preventing Sir Belan from gaining control of the army at Worcester?"

"Aye."

"And so you freed my brother from Stafford Castle."

Sir Richard made no answer.

"There might have been an easier way for you to have accomplished what you wanted," said Lady Margaret. "I am surprised that it did not occur to you."

"What easier way?" Sir Richard asked.

Lady Margaret looked up at him. "You might have forced me to marry you."

Sir Richards face turned scarlet. "I would win my lady, not take her by force.'"

The woman smiled. "You might have done even that, Sir Richard."

FOR THE SPACE of several breaths, Sir Richard did not move. His blood was hammering through his veins, and his face was hot. Lady Margaret's head was tilted back so that he could see the long, white column of her throat. She was still smiling and the look in her eyes was warm and inviting.

"Am I over bold?" he heard her whisper.

Sir Richard took a step forward, dropped to his knees. Then suddenly he remembered what it was that had brought him here, and the lie he had told to this woman. His body went rigid and his arms which had been outstretched, dropped to his side. He looked away and said bluntly. "I did not tell you the truth about your brother, Lady Margaret. We did not rescue him. When we took the castle he was not there."

"Not there!"

"Nay. Sir Belan had left with him—for Worcester."

" 'Then—then why have you brought me here?'"

Sir Richard looked back at the woman. Some of the tension had gone from his body and as his mind came to grips with the problem which lay ahead, he could feel his excitement slipping away.

"I brought you here," to said frankly, "because I thought that you would be known to the castle guards, because I thought that you could get me inside."

By the expression in Lady Margaret's eyes, Sir Richard knew

that she didn't understand what he meant and he explained swiftly, telling of the message which had come to Sir Belan and of his fears that Sir Belan would force her brother to furnish him with the armed men held at Worcester.

When he had finished, Lady Margaret was silent and her head was bowed so that he could not see her face. Sir Richard stood up. He could appreciate the blow that he had dealt her and he knew now that it had been a mean thing for him to bring her up here. Yet there could have been no other way.

"So I am to get you into the castle," Lady Margaret said finally, her voice low and thick.

"Aye."

"And to what purpose? What can you hope to accomplish, one man against hundreds?"

"The odds are not so great as that. Within the donjon of the castle itself, there will not be so many men. At your side I should get that far."

LADY MARGARET lifted her head. "Yet if all that you have said is true, you will never return. You know that, don't you?"

"I know only what it will mean to England if the Wolf of the Severn is not stopped from marching south with his army."

The woman got stiffly to her feet. She shook her head. "I will not take you through the gates."

"Then," said Sir Richard, "I must go alone."

"You dare not."

Sir Richard laughed and there was in his laughter all his bitterness and all the recklessness which had driven him through the past few weeks as an outlaw. He turned to his horse, reached for the bridle.

"Stop!"

It was the woman's voice and it was high and shrill and somehow desperate.

Sir Richard looked back at her and the expression on his face softened. "I am sorry, Margaret," he said slowly. "Perhaps what I would try is foolish, but I can see nothing else to do."

Lady Margaret hurried up to his side. She was breathing heavily and her face was wholly without color. "Is there nothing I can say to make you stay here?" she whispered. "Is there no way I can stop you?"

Sir Richard smiled. "You are forgetting your brother, Margaret."

"How can your death serve him?"

Acting on a sudden impulse, Sir Richard leaned forward and kissed the woman on the forehead. Then he pulled himself up into the saddle, lifted the reins. "Goodbye, Margaret," he said quietly.

The woman made no answer, and for a moment Sir Richard sat there on his horse looking down at her and wondering what kind of a life he and this woman might have had together, were it not for Sir Belan. Then once more he said. "Goodbye, Margaret," and shaking out the reins of his horse he headed for Worcester.

The sun was just creeping up over the hills when he reached the highway, and as he came to the broad meadows below the castle the slanting rays struck glittering sparks of light from the stacked lances of the men-at-arms encamped nearby. Here and there gaily colored banners waved gently in an idle breeze, and the smoke of the morning fires spiraled upward from a hundred places.

Sir Richard glanced casually from left to right. There were no men on the road and for that he was thankful. Then he suddenly heard the drumming hoofbeats of a horse behind him. He turned in the saddle, reached for his axe, then lowered his hand and stared at the approaching rider in surprise. It was the Lady Margaret.

She came up even with him, reined in at his side. Her face was flushed and there was a strange, sparkling light in her eyes.

"Margaret," Sir Richard cried, "what—"

But the woman gave him no time to finish his question. "I am going with you," she announced, her voice clear and strung.

"When we get to the drawbridge, say nothing. Let me do the talking."

CHAPTER V

AND SO IT was side by side that Sir Richard Wilton and the Lady Margaret of Worcester rode up the highway to the castle. As they drew nearer to it, Sir Richard saw that her fingers were loosening her braided hair. He saw, too, that in the light of the early morning sun, it looked like fine-spun gold.

Lady Margaret noticed him watching her and she said, "By my hair will they know me. Otherwise, in these clothes, the guards might not know who I was."

Sir Richard smiled. "It is beautiful hair. I do not see why you ever braid it."

Tears came suddenly to Lady Margaret's eyes. She blinked them away, biting her lips.

They were now close to the moat and Sir Richard stared up at the towers on either side of the suspended drawbridge. He could see men's figures there, could see that they were looking down at him and his companion. Lady Margaret lifted her voice and called, "Dermott! Dermott!"

"It is Lady Margaret," cried a voice from the castle wall. "Lower the bridge!"

With a great creaking noise, the drawbridge began to tilt away from the wall. Sir Richard drew a deep breath. He glanced behind him and saw a small group of riders galloping up the road, the churning feet of their horses kicking up great clouds of dust

"It is not yet too late to turn back," whispered the woman.

Sir Richard shook his head. "Ride with me across the courtyard to the donjon," he said swiftly. "But do not go inside. Surely among these men there are some who will protect you."

"Aye, Richard."

The drawbridge touched the ground and beyond it, at he

open gate, Sir Richard could see a group of soldiers. Lady Margaret urged her horse forward and Sir Richard rode at her side. As they drew near to the soldiers, Lady Margaret called, "Is my brother here, Dermott?"

A tall, wide-shouldered man, with a short, brown beard and a deeply tanned face, nodded his head. "He arrived yesterday with Sir Belan, My Lady."

"They are in the donjon?"

Dermott looked troubled. He again nodded his head and his sharp, dark eyes turned on Sir Richard.

Lady Margaret glanced over her shoulder. The horsemen approaching the castle were much nearer now, but Sir Richard knew that he need not trouble about them. A word from the Lady Margaret would clear his way through this gate and to the donjon. Then he needed only to get to Sir Belan.

Even as that thought occurred to him, Lady Margaret gave such word. "Ride on to the donjon, Sir Richard," she said clearly. "Find Sir Belan and my brother and tell them that I am here."

It was as simple as that. The men at the gate fell back when Sir Richard urged his horse forward and as he rode toward the great, square, stone building across the courtyard, no one made any effort to stop him. He had been passed by the guards at the gate and that was enough for such other men as happened to notice him.

THE ENTRANCE to the donjon was by means of a long incline which led up to the doorway on the second floor. That incline worked on the same principle as the drawbridge. In times of danger it could be raised against the donjon wall, but normally it was left down and it was down this morning. Sir Richard rode up close to it, dismounted and hurried toward the door. Two guards stood at top of the incline and as he drew near to them they blocked his way.

"A message for Sir Belan," he snapped at them. "Take me to him, at once."

His voice was imperious commanding, and perhaps he

looked a good deal like a messenger, for he seemed tired and his face was streaked with dust and his eyes are sunken and bloodshot.

The guards hesitated only momentarily, then one of them said. "Come with me," and led the way through the door and down a long corridor.

Once inside the door, Sir Richard took the axe *Bretwalda* from the sling at his shoulder, and the very feel of it in his hands seemed to bring him a new strength.

A brief smile touched his lips as he recalled suddenly his fathers story of this axe.

It had been in the Wilton family for generations, had been handed down from father to son, just as in other families, territorial possessions were handed down.

Yet his father, he knew, had prized *Bretwalda* above everything he had owned, and now he was beginning to understand the reason. No common axe was this.

Forged entirely of steel, set with seven blood-red jewels, and so heavy that most men could not swing it, in his hands as in the hands of other Wiltons before him, it was a weapon before which no enemy could stand. "Fear not its weight," his father had once said to him, "for the strength to wield *Bretwalda* comes not from your arms but from the axe itself."

For a long time Sir Richard had not understood that statement but he understood it now. As his own body grew more weary in the strain of a long fight, the axe seemed to become lighter, seemed to pour into his arms some of its own good steel, seemed to strengthen him.

The guard who was marching ahead of him suddenly stopped, pushed open a door and called, "A messenger, Sir Belan. Will you receive him?"

"Aye, bring him in."

Sir Richard stepped through the door, slammed it shut. His eyes went swiftly around the room. It was a broad, wide room and it was lighted from apertures on two sides. Streaks of sunlight made bars across the floor from the openings to the east, and on two of the walls hung long, rich tapestries.

There were almost a score of men in the room as Sir Richard came in. They were seated at a table piled high with steaming food. Sir Richard caught a glimpse of Sir Belan's thin, dark face gaping at him in wide-eyed astonishment. He saw the thick, bulky figure of Murtogh sitting next to Oliver Lacey. Oliver Lacey was pale and thin and there was a glazed, frightened expression in his eyes. Perspiration stood out on his forehead and around his colorless lips.

ALL THAT Sir Richard caught in a glance. As he started forward he saw Sir Belan leap to his feet and clutch at his sword, saw other men spring up. He heard the Wolf of the Severn shout his name and heard Murtoghs deep growl as the torturer recognized him.

Then he had reached the table and *Bretwalda* was slashing out at those men, cutting through armor, sending them reeling away from him, screaming, yelling, calling for the guards. The table crashed to the floor, carrying Oliver Lacey with it. Murtogh's axe broke against the steel of *Bretwalda* and the torturer died with a swifter mercy than he had ever showed to any of his victims.

Sir Belan escaped the first fury of that fight, springing out of the way of the flailing axe with the agility of a young man. His shouts urged the others on, and the noise of the battle brought a score of men pouring through the door. They hemmed Sir Richard in on every side. Sword points slashed his leather jerkin to shreds and cut him on leg and arm where his coat-of-mail offered no protection. He tried desperately to reach Sir Belan, but as the fight surged across the room. Sir Belan moved out of the way, his cold, dark eyes ever watchful.

Then in the doorway another fight started, and, cutting his way into the room, came Hubert de Clare, followed by Michael Godwin, the youth Thomas, and the old man who had once been Sir Henry Wilton's steward. Sir Richard blinked at them in surprise. How they could have come here he didn't know. He called, "Hubert, Michael, Thomas."

Hubert de Clare laughed. "Did you think that we would let you try this alone, Richard?" he called. "You were never a good liar. We almost overtook you on the road. We were just behind you when you entered the castle."

Out of the corner of his eye Sir Richard saw Oliver Lacey get to his feet, wipe a hand over his face, stagger toward one of the apertures in the wall, and then he heard Lacey's voice shouting, "Men of Worcester! Henry the Plantagenet, rightful heir to the throne of England, has crossed the channel, but Sir Belan would have used you to drive him into the sea and make himself king. Lower the drawbridge. Drive the men of the Wolf of the Severn from the castle!"

A cry of anger came from Sir Belan's throat. He lifted his sword, ran toward Oliver Lacey. Sir Richard shouted a warning, but Oliver Lacey did not heed it. He still stood at the aperture, calling to the men in the courtyard. Then, even as Sir Richard tried desperately to break through the group which surrounded him, Hubert de Clare cut his way across the room and with uplifted sword, caught the blow which might have felled Lacey

"Ah, Sir Belan," he cried, "for a long time I have looked forward to this hour."

A coward Sir Belan might have been as Sir Richard had long suspected. Yet cornered, he would fight; he turned on de Clare and slashed at him with his sword.

De Clare caught the blow, turned it aside, whipped his own point across Sir Belan's face, leaving there a long, red gash. "That," he said grimly, "is just the beginning. And now—"

De Clare had been moving forward when his foot suddenly slipped and he fell to his knees, lowering the point of his sword. That was the opportunity needed by the Wolf of the Severn. With a loud cry he cut down at de Clare's unprotected head.

Sir Richard saw the blow. He saw de Clare's body tilt sideways, sprawl to the floor. And in that moment a rage more bitter than he had ever known swept over him and *Bretwalda* became as a live thing in his hands. It bowled men out of the way as if they had been paper images; it slashed a path across the room to the place where Sir Belan was standing.

At that moment. Sir Richard saw no one but the Wolf of the Severn. He did not see young Thomas strike down a man who might have slain him; did not know that Michael Godwin rushed across the room to defend his back or that Oliver Lacey had picked up a sword from the door and had joined Godwin.

Sir Belan slashed at his head, but *Bretwalda* turned the blow aside and Sir Richard, lifting the great axe high into the air, struck downward. Gleaming and new and of the finest steel was that helmet which covered the head of the Wolf of the Severn. Yet it might as well have been cloth for all the protection it offered against that blow. Midway to Sir Belan's waist did *Bretwalda* shear its way, and the soul of the Wolf of the Severn had fled from his body before it had dropped to the floor.

SIR RICHARD turned away, glanced around the room. Four of Sir Belan's men who were still standing, had cast down their arms and were pleading for mercy, and on every side bodies littered the floor. Young Thomas, blood streaming from his side, staggered against the wall but held himself grimly erect. Oliver Lacey was on his hands and knees. Michael Godwin wiped a hand across his brow; leaned against the man who had once been the Wilton steward. Godwin's breath was coming in heavy, labored gasps, and a red froth showed at his lips.

"You are hurt, Michael?" Sir Richard said unsteadily.

"Nay, master. It is nothing."

Sir Richard moved over to where Hubert de Clare was lying. He knelt down beside him, looked sadly at the pale, wan face, so quiet now in death. "I would not have had this happen to you, Hubert, for all the lands in England," he said heavily. "Nay, not for all the lands in the world."

He folded Hubert de Clare's hands across his chest, stood up, moved over to the window from which Oliver Lacey had shouted to the men in the courtyard. There was still fighting near the gate-house but the men of Worcester were slowly pushing Sir Belan's men over the drawbridge.

Sounds from within the room caused him to turn around and he saw that Lady Margaret had come in and was kneeling at her brother's side. A group of soldiers, too, had entered and under the direction of Dermott were removing the dead and caring for the wounded.

After a moment Lady Margaret stood up and came over to where he leaned against the wall. Her eyes were brilliant and all of the strain and worry had gone out of her face.

"He is not hurt badly," she said, and Sir Richard knew that she was speaking of her brother. "After a little rest he will be well and strong. And the thing you feared will never come to pass. Sir Belan is dead. When the men of Worcester ride south it will be to join Henry the Plantagenet, not to fight him."

Sir Richard nodded. He did not know it then, but not only would the men of Worcester ride south to join Henry the Plantagenet. From all over England the barons would hasten to meet him. And on November 6th of 1153, only a few months away, a treaty was to be signed at Winchester between King Stephen and Henry the Plantagenet, a treaty naming Henry as the heir to the English throne.

"Will you stay here with us until my brother can lead his men south?" asked the Lady Margaret.

Sir Richard stared into her face and something in her eyes or perhaps in the tone of her voice reminded him of a moment in that grove far down the road from the castle. He glanced down at the axe *Bretwalda*, smiled and said abruptly, "Some day, Margaret, I would tell you the legend of this axe of the Wiltons, but a part of the story I must tell you now. It is said that to him who holds *Bretwalda* will come a great victory and a great defeat, a great sorrow and a great joy. I have known all but the last."

The woman's hands reached out and rested on his shoulders, crept about his neck. "All but the last?" she whispered. "Then you will stay, Richard. You will stay forever."

VII

TRIBUTE TO NONE

Beware, King John! The load that England bears is crushing, and no man's soul's his own—but a hero bears Bretwalda.

CHAPTER I

SIR HENRY DE CRESSY was in a vile temper. In the tournament, that afternoon, an unidentified knight had unseated him, and the humiliation rankled bitterly. "By the teeth of Judas," he muttered, for the hundredth time, "I will have his heart's blood. It was not a fair tilt. His lance was longer than mine."

Earl Robert of Compton, at whose castle de Cressy was stopping and who was now seated beside him in the banquet hall, nodded his head and with his knife speared a roasted fowl from the platter which a servant brought him.

" 'Tis strange you do not know his name," de Cressy continued. " 'Tis more strange how he disappeared."

A brief frown crossed the earl's face and his glance circled the banquet table which had been set up there in the great hall of his castle at Compton. It was round in shape and at it were gathered more than two score of the nobles from the surrounding country as well as the retinue brought with him by de Cressy, the King's Justiciar. Meat, taken in the hunt the day before, and bread and wine were being served to them by the castle servants, but the usual hilarity attendant upon such a feast seemed to be lacking.

Earl Robert thought that he knew the reason. It was not a wise thing to offend the King's Justiciar, especially considering the mission which had brought him north, and most of these people would hold their emotions in check until Henry de

Cressy downed enough wine to forget what had happened that afternoon.

There were a dozen or more figures sprawled on the reeds in the open space within the wide enclosure made by the table. To one side a troupe of ragged jongleurs fought over scraps tossed to them from those at the table, snarling, kicking and tearing at one another much as a pack of dogs might have done. Later, at the earl's command, they would put on an exhibition of vaulting, tumbling and sleight of hand which might be amazing, or which might be very poor.

Not far from them was a company of actors, and directly in front of the earl's seat were two troubadours who had come to the castle only the day before.

The earl's glance rested for a moment on the two troubadours. They were strange men, he thought, to be following such a profession. Both were young and broad of shoulder with well muscled bodies which even their ragged cloaks couldn't hide. The taller of the two had a thin, gaunt face and was sharp of eye. His hair was long and tangled and almost yellow in color. His companion was darker and had thick, heavy features and a black beard, which in spots was rather thin. Both of them, Earl Robert now noticed, ignored the fragments of food cast from the table. The taller man was plucking softly on the strings of his harp. His lips were moving as though he were singing to himself.

"By the teeth of Judas," de Cressy roared. "I want that knight. Do you hear me, sir?"

The earl nodded and sighed. These were hard times. He would probably be forced to pay a fine if he could not discover the identity of the unknown knight. The king's courts assessed fines on every provocation.

Earl Robert could easily understand why King John had to have more money. Long ago the king had lost his revenues from Avignon and in order to pay the large army he maintained, he was always in need of more funds. Last year, in 1214, he had

To the king's men gathered there he sang
the song of Caedmon's axe.

increased the scutage required of the nobles who had refused
to join him in his campaign against France, and this year, despite
objections on every hand, he had levied new and heavier taxes.

The earl glanced at Henry de Cressy. It was de Cressy's
mission, he knew, to see that those taxes were paid and he didn't
envy the man his job. Rumors had come to him that the northern nobles would refuse to pay and there were even some whispers of a rebellion.

Henry de Cressy called for more wine, and then leaning
forward said sharply, "You must find that knight before morning,
for on the morrow I leave for Northampton."

"I will find him, Lord," the earl answered. And as he spoke
he again noticed the taller of the two troubadours. The man's
lips were still moving as though in practice for his song. Earl
Robert wondered what the man was singing.

THE TALLER of the two troubadours was named Brian and
he really was no troubadour. And he was not practicing his
song. He was talking to the dark haired man who sat beside
him and who was no more a troubadour than he.

"You heard him, Arthur," he was now saying, "Tomorrow he leaves for Northampton. You had better leave now and ride to Stamford. Tell Fitz-Walter. We have waited long enough for word from the king. It is time that we showed our teeth."

"And you, Brian?" asked the dark haired man.

Brian struck a soft cord on his harp. "It might look strange if we were both to leave now. I will follow as soon as I can."

"Shall I wait for you at the place where we left our horses?"

"Nay, for I must journey west."

The dark-haired man reached out and put a hand on Brian's knee. "It will do you no good, Brian, to again see your father. His loyalty to the king is too much a part of him. It has blinded him to conditions. I wish that you would ride with me."

A worried look came into Brian's eyes and after a moment's pause he said, "Aye, friend. You are right. But there is another purpose which sends me west. My father has always looked on Henry de Cressy as a good friend. I fear that he may go to Northampton to meet him. I would stop that. Did you wonder why I entered the tournament lists this afternoon?"

"So that was it," Arthur whispered.

"Aye, it was my hope to keep de Cressy from continuing north. Unfortunately he was not injured in the fall from his horse. But enough of this talk, Arthur. You had best leave."

The dark-haired man nodded, crawled on his knees under the table and headed for the door. Brian went on plucking at the strings of his harp, now and then glancing up at the fat, bloated face of Henry de Cressy and wondering at his father's friendship for this man who was notorious for his cruelty and injustice. In a thousand ways, Brian thought, de Cressy had proven that he could be loyal to no one but himself. Even his service to the king had been a service which looked first to his own desires.

"Ho, troubadour," Earl Robert called suddenly. "Give us a song."

Brian got slowly to his feet. "A song, Lord? What song would you like?"

Earl Robert glanced at de Cressy and then said judiciously, "A song in honor of our great king."

"Our king, Lord?"

A faint smile touched Brian's lips. There were a dozen songs which the troubadours sang to the glory of King John, but Brian liked none of them. He plucked three times at the heavier strings of his harp; then, as a brief moment of silence followed that cord, he said clearly, "I will sing you a song taught to me by Snorri Sturluson, the great scald of Norway. It is the song of Balder's death. I dedicate it to King John."

THEN again his fingers plucked at the strings of his harp and in a deep, rich voice, he sang:

> *Brothers slay brothers*
> *Sisters' children shed each other's blood.*
> *Hard grows the world.*
> *Sensual sins wax huge.*
> *There are sword-ages, axe-ages,*
> *Shields are cleft in twain,*
> *Storm-ages, murder-ages,*
> *Till the world falls dead.*
> *And men no longer spare*
> *Or pity one another.*

Brian paused and struck several cords, glancing around the room. There were barbs in that song and he wondered if they were striking home.

Henry de Cressy was scowling at him, and as he was about to continue, de Cressy jumped to his feet and said sharply:

"Enough of that, troubadour. If you would sing, give us a song of England."

Brian shrugged. "I will give you, then, the song of the axe of Caedmon."

Again his fingers plucked a cord, a lighter cord this time, and his voice rang out triumphantly as he sang!

> *I am the axe of Caedmon,*
> *Forged in Saxon fires.*
> *True is my steel, sharp my edge,*
> *Alive are my desires—*
> *To know the strife of a battle,*
> *To slash against the foe,*
> *But only a Wilton shall hold me,*
> *And only a Wilton—*

A hoarse cry interrupted Brian's song. Henry de Cressy was again on his feet and his face was livid with rage.

"Stop!" he shouted. "Stop! By the teeth of Judas, you are that man!"

Brian did not have to ask what de Cressy meant. He lowered his harp and a mocking expression came into his eyes.

"Did you not like my singing, Lord?" he murmured.

With a rasping oath, de Cressy swung his body over the table. He was a large man, heavy, and almost as tall as Brian. His hair was dark and shaggy and his eyes were almost hidden below thick, bushy brows. One of his hands reached for the sword fastened at his side and as he drew it he said grimly, "Aye, you are the man. Come here."

Brian had moved away from de Cressy and he was standing, now, near to the troup of jongleurs who had crowded against the table. He stooped over, grasped a blade from one of them, straightened up, removed the wood block from its tip and faced de Cressy. He was not smiling now. His eyes had narrowed and his lips made a thin, straight line across his face. A jongleur's foil, he knew, was no match for the heavy blade de Cressy carried, but it was the only weapon handy.

A hoarse laugh came from de Cressy's throat. He started forward, slowly, and then with a sudden rush, his sword jerking up into the air, starting down.

THE ACTION which followed was almost too swift for the eye to note. Only slightly did Brian's foil touch de Cressy's sword, yet it turned it enough so that, with a sideward twist of his body, Brian evaded the blow. Once, then, did his own blade flick out in a sweeping motion which brought the point across de Cressy's forehead.

De Cressy screamed and staggered away. Blood, spurting from that cut, ran down into his eyes and blinded him. His sword dropped to the floor and he raised his hands to his forehead.

A score of the men in the Justiciar's retinue had leaped to their feet as they saw what had happened to their leader. Swords scraped from their scabbards, and two men, quicker than their fellows, swung over the table and rushed at Brian. But Brian was no longer armed only with a jongleur's foil. He had picked up de Cressy's sword. One slash of its blade stopped the first man to reach him and sent him stumbling against his companion so heavily that both of them fell to the floor.

Loud cries and shouted commands now rang in the great hall. More men started clambering over the table. Brian glanced from side to side. He could see that the castle guard was blocking the door which led outside. Only one other course was open to him. He whirled around and rushed toward the far end of the table, threw the weight of his body against it. The table crashed to the floor. Brian stepped over it. His sword, slashing from side to side, cleared a quick path to a doorway which led deeper into the castle, and in another moment Brian had gained that door and was racing up a long corridor.

Behind him he heard Earl Robert's voice shouting, "He is trapped. Hubert! Hubert, come here!"

Brian tried a couple of doors on either side of the corridor. He found them locked. Ahead lay a stairway which led to the floor above. He could understand, then, what the earl's shout had meant. There was no other door on this floor through which he could escape. Like most castles, this one had but one entrance and that lay behind him.

For a moment Brian hesitated; then he dashed to the stairway and hurried up it to the floor above.

The corridor above was lighted by several torches fixed in sconces on the wall. Brian started down it but he had gone hardly any distance at all when a door was suddenly opened and a girl's voice said swiftly, "In here. Close and lock the door."

The voice had a friendly sound and without an instant's delay Brian stepped into the room.

CHAPTER 11

JUST AS THE hallway, the room was lighted by torches and in the dim, yellow radiance of the smoking flame Brian could see that the girl who had admitted him was young and slender. The top of her head came barely to his shoulder. Her hair was long and hung in braids. It seemed very dark against the white sheen of her gown.

"Close and bolt the door," whispered the girl again. "Quickly. Before others come."

Brian turned and slid a heavy bolt across the door. Then he swung around to survey the room—the wide wooden bed at one side with the usual chest for clothing at its foot; the thick carpet on the floor; the table with its flagon of water and the two chairs which stood near it. Over the shuttered windows there were long, heavy tapestries of a rich, red color.

Brian's eyes went to the girl's strained face.

"Who are you?" he asked abruptly.

"I am Lady Eleanor, daughter of the earl."

Brian's eyes widened with surprise. He had heard mention of Lady Eleanor, daughter of Earl Robert, but he had imagined her a much older woman.

"They are coming," Lady Eleanor whispered.

Brian sucked in a deep breath. He heard footsteps clamoring

down the hallway, heard a heavy rapping on the door. The girl moved past him. "Who is it?" she called. "What do you want?"

"It is Hubert, my lady," answered a rough voice. "Will you open the door?"

"But I am ready for bed, Hubert."

"It is your father's orders that I search the castle."

"And my orders, Hubert, are that you go away and leave me alone. I am tired and have gone to bed."

A sound of mumbling voices came from beyond the door and after a moment the men moved on.

Lady Eleanor turned around, looked at Brian. Her eyes seemed very bright.

"They will search the rest of the castle," she whispered. "Then, perchance, they will come to believe that you jumped into the moat. I do not think they will come back here."

Brian was scowling. He was not so sure that they would be let alone and he had no wish to be found in her room. "Why have you called me in here?" he asked suddenly. "Why did you send them away?"

The girl bit her lips. "I saw what happened in the banquet hall. I had slipped down to the door. I heard your songs and when I heard the last one I knew who you were. Your name is Wilton, Brian Wilton. And you are one of the men who have aroused the people of Northumbria against the king."

"But still—"

The girl took a step forward. "You count my father an enemy, a man loyal to the king, don't you? And I can't blame you for it, for when the summons came to him to join the other nobles at Stamford he did not go. But do you know why he didn't go? He didn't go because he was kept here by Sir Henry de Cressy, the King's Justiciar. He and his entire household are virtual prisoners. On the hunt, de Cressy's men ride with him and de Cressy's guards man the walls of the castle. My father tries to fool himself into the belief that this is not so, or that it is only temporary, but he knows that it is the truth. Now do you understand why I wanted to help you?"

The girl's voice had been very earnest.

Her eyes looked steadily into his.

Brian nodded. "I did not guess that the Justiciar would be so bold, yet as he gets farther north he will not find things so easy."

"The nobles will really rise against the king?"

"Not against the king but against the king's injustice, against his excessive taxation, against his attitude toward the church which he would harness and use to his own ends."

Brian paused, scowling. He realized, suddenly, that he had used almost those same words in explaining his attitude when he had last talked to his father. But his father hadn't listened.

"Are they ready now?" whispered the girl.

"Aye," Brian answered. "Last Christmas a group of the barons presented their demands to the king. He asked until Easter to consider what he would do. Easter has come and gone and he has done nothing more than to levy higher taxes and to try to cause trouble between us. That last, as much as anything else, is what has brought de Cressy north. He was ever a good trouble maker."

Again footsteps sounded in the hall outside but they passed the door without stopping.

LADY ELEANOR turned toward the window, lifted a hand to the tapestries. "Help me pull these down," she whispered to Brian. "This window overlooks the moat. The tapestries can be cut and tied into a rope."

Brian hurried to the girl's side. He jerked down the tapestries and with his sword started cutting them. The girl opened the shuttered windows, leaned out.

"Men are searching along the banks of the moat," she reported, drawing back into the room. "But they will soon give it up, and if you can swim—"

"I can swim." Brian grinned. "And in the woods I have a horse."

The girl smiled and inspected the rope Brian had made from the tapestries. She looked up and said suddenly, "Tell me, were you not the knight who unseated Henry de Cressy in the tilting this afternoon?"

Brian's grin widened. "Was it not a shameful thing to do?"

"A rash thing."

"And pleasant."

A serious expression came into the girl's face. She again turned to the window and looked outside.

Brian made the tapestry rope fast inside the room and then moved to her side. He was suddenly thankful that de Cressy was planning to leave this castle on the morrow. If Earl Robert had played well his game of loyalty to the king, he decided, the chances were that de Cressy would move on and leave him and his daughter unmolested.

"Are the men still there?" he asked.

"Nay. They have gone away."

Brian leaned out of the window. The shadows below were quiet and still.

"I can try it now," he muttered.

The girl said nothing but watched silently as he lowered the rope. Brian put one leg over the window, turned back to look at her.

"Words are of little use at a time like this, Lady Eleanor," he said to her. "But for you de Cressy would now have his revenge for what happened to him this afternoon."

"And but for you, Brian Wilton, and but for men like you," the girl answered, "England would no longer be England. Go now, quickly. I hear someone in the hall. It may be my father and if Henry de Cressy is with him—"

Brian swung through the window. He lowered his body down the swaying rope and came finally to its end with his feet almost touching the dark waters below. He released his hold on the tapestry, dropped into the moat. The water was swift and cold and it drove the air from his lungs. He kicked his way to the surface, struck out for the opposite bank, made it and pulled himself up into the grass near a clump of bushes.

After a moment be stood up and looked back. The window from which he had escaped was dark but the shutters were still open and Brian thought that he could make out a slender white figure. He waved his arm, turned and set out toward the forest.

IT WAS almost noon of the following day before Brian drew near to Wilton Hall. The morning had been clear and bright and fragrant with the promise of an early summer, but it had given no lift to Brian's spirits, and as he drew rein at the edge of the broad meadow surrounding the plowed fields nearer the hall, his face bore a worried frown.

The scene which lay before him was a beautiful one, a peaceful one. Here and there men and women were at work in the fields, tending crops which had already pushed through the rich, dark earth. Browsing cattle roamed the meadows and the surrounding forest was pleasantly green. In the distance Brian could make out the blue waters of the river Avon and near to its bank was the village with its crooked and friendly streets, its spired church and its wide market place.

Wilton Hall was some distance nearer. It was built of gray stone with four corner towers rising above its two stories. No castle with wall or moat, it still had an appearance of rugged strength. An azure banner fluttered from a staff above one of the towers and on it was the black figure of a raven which carried in its claws a great axe. Such was the coat-of-arms of the Wiltons.

The axe, Brian knew, represented *Bretwalda*, the axe of Caedmon, whose story he had started to sing the night before. It had long been the treasured possession of the head of the Wilton family. The origin of the raven was more obscure, but his father had told him that it had come down from some ancestor who had been sold into captivity and who had sailed the seas with the Vikings of old.

There were sudden signs of activity from beyond the hall and Brian made out a company of horsemen starting for the road which led east and north along the river Avon. One of the horsemen carried a standard similar to the banner which floated above the castle. Brian's scowl deepened and he suddenly urged his horse forward, taking a course which would intercept the horsemen. .

He waited for them in the road, and just as he had guessed, one of the horsemen, recognizing him, ordered the others to wait and came on alone.

Tall, heavy and broad of shoulder was the man who came on to meet him, and though thicker, his features were the same as Brian's. Both had the same high forehead, the same clear blue eyes, the same stubborn jaw. Anyone who had chanced to see them together would have guessed at once that they were father and son.

"Well, Brian?" said the older man abruptly.

Brian shrugged. "Where are you going, Father?"

The older man looked at his son narrowly. "And I might ask you where you had been?" he countered.

Brian made no reply to that and there was a long silence.

It was Brian's father, Sir Aubrey, who broke that silence. "A messenger came to the hall this morning with word from Sir Henry de Cressy, the King's Justiciar. I am going to Northampton to meet him."

The horses of the two men were close and Brian lifted his hand toward his father as though to take his arm, then lowered it again. "Sire, do not go to Northampton," he said earnestly. "Or if you must go, wait a few days. Do not go now."

"Why, Brian?" asked the older man bluntly.

Again Brian was silent and again it was his father who spoke first. "Northampton," he said slowly, "is a strong castle, son. It could not easily be taken, even by men who are inspired as only you can inspire them."

"Do not go to Northampton, sire," Brian cried again. "Why would you have dealings with a man like de Cressy?"

"He is the King's Justiciar."

"Aye," said Brian bitterly, "and a murderer unhung, a thief uncaught, a scoundrel with a heart blacker than the Judas by whose teeth he swears."

"But still the King's Justiciar."

Brian drew a ragged breath. No logic which he could command would serve to stand against his father's loyalty to the king and unreasonable though that loyalty was, Brian could not help but admire it. His father leaned forward and said quietly, "Brian, I know what you have been doing. I know how hot and impatient is the blood of youth. In a way I can understand it. But when the final test comes, I charge you to remember this. No Wilton was ever disloyal to his king. This standard I bear has never been dirtied. Its azure field must stay clear as the sky."

A sudden tremor shook the younger man. Tears which he could not hold back came into his eyes.

"Come, Brian," said his father. "Ride with me."

But Brian made no answer, and after one of the longest moments he had ever known he heard his father sigh. Then Sir Aubrey turned and called to his men and they rode on.

Brian's eyes followed the men as long as they were in sight.

CHAPTER III

AS THE AFTERNOON waned and as the shadows of the coming night stretched out from the forest, Brian paced restlessly back and forth across the great hall in his father's house, his mind torn by indecision, his thoughts rambling and confused. Over near the door stood the tall and stalwart John Tuck, peer of all yeomen in the north country. He could knock a sparrow from the top branch of the highest tree with an arrow shot from his longbow and he could move through the forest as silently as though he were a part of it.

"Tell me, Lord? Shall I send the word?" John Tuck asked quietly.

Brian frowned. John Tuck had asked him that question many times during the past few hours but he had not yet given any answer. He stopped, now, and stared at Tuck. At a word from him he knew that Tuck would hurry away and that within a few minutes a dozen men would be riding to the north and east, carrying with them a call which would assemble at any point he might designate hundreds of yeomen and burghers from the towns and villages, all of them ready to do his bidding.

What trick of fate had given him a leadership over such people, Brian didn't know. Later he was to realize that it had grown up gradually through his attendance at county fairs, through the sympathetic way in which he had listened to the people's complaints.

When he had realized that the common people of the north country would follow him in a revolt against the king's injustice, he had felt all the thrill of a great power.

And Fitz-Walter and William Marshall, and Cardinal Langton, the leaders of the nobles, had been as pleased as he. But that had been six months before. Right now he wished that he had never grown interested in the political problems which England faced.

John Tuck stepped forward and said earnestly, "These new taxes, Lord, are more than we can endure. It cost me a hundred shillings to share in the land left me by my father. The men of Worcester have had to pay a hundred shillings for the right to buy and sell dyed cloth, and the men of Burgh were taxed for the right to hold a market. We are being stripped of money, and in the courts decisions are always given to the man who bids the highest. You know all that."

Brian nodded. "Aye, conditions are even worse than you have told me."

"Then let me send word to those who are awaiting it. They have been ready for a long time."

"To turn against their king?"

"Nay, but to fight for justice if it can be had in no other way."

Brian wiped a hand across his brow. In just such a way had he argued with others and even now, he knew, the nobles who had assembled at Stamford must be riding toward Northampton, for when the king had made no answer to their demands on Easter, it had been decided to await the coming of his Justiciar, and then to show their teeth.

He straightened, nodded to John Tuck and said briefly, "Send the word. Northampton. At once."

John Tuck drew a deep breath. "Northampton, at once," he repeated. And turning, he hurried from the room.

S O I T happened that by the afternoon of the next day a strange and motley army gathered in the meadows around the embattled walls of Northampton Castle. From Stamford, where they had gathered to receive word from the king, came the nobles from the north country who rebelled against paying more scutage to finance the king's wars against France. A few retainers had come with them. Yeomen from the forest countries and burghers from city and town, many of the latter poorly armed, made up the rest of the army. In all it numbered less than two thousand, but the call to assemble had been hurried and more men would arrive with each succeeding day.

In a tent set up by William Marshall, son of the Earl of Norwich, a group of the leaders had gathered and it was to that tent that Brian made his way. Arthur Pinel, who had carried word of de Cressy's plans to come to Northampton was there; Fitz-Walter, Cardinal Langton, Sir James Wycliffe and a score of others whom Brian knew. They had all been talking together rather loudly, but as Brian came in the tent grew quiet.

Brian nodded to the men and turning to Fitz-Walter, he said, "There is still no word from the king?"

"There is still no word," Fitz-Walter answered. He was a tall, rugged man, fiery of temper, bitter toward the king. "There is still no word and the king means to send no word. He does not think we would dare to rebel against him."

"What said de Cressy? Have you talked to him?"

"He appeared on the walls of the castle. He asked us, in the king's name to disband. He promised safety to all who would throw down their arms and go home."

Brian laughed harshly. "De Cressy's promises are worth nothing," he said bluntly.

Others agreed, and Cardinal Langton started speaking of the man. Arthur Pinel got up, drew Brian aside. "Your father is in the castle," he said quietly.

Brian nodded. He looked blankly at his friend and said, "What of it, Arthur?"

"I thought you might not know."

Another man stepped up and touched Brian on the shoulder. He was a stocky, heavy-set fellow with a red beard and a leathery face. "My name is Hubert Mandeville," said the man. "Until last night I was captain of the castle guard at Compton."

"At Compton?" Brian repeated.

The man nodded. "It was I who was charged with finding you after you fled from the banquet hall. I searched all but one room."

Brian scowled. "What do you want?"

"Only to tell you this," the man replied. "So angry was de Cressy when you were not found that he ordered the earl and his daughter to accompany him to Northampton. I thought you would want to know that."

There was a shrewd expression in the man's eyes. Brian stared at him and then looked over toward the castle. Anger rose in him slowly. His mind called up a picture of the Lady Eleanor, slender, fair, her eyes brilliant. And now he was remembering the evil stories of women who had suffered cruelly at de Cressy's hands.

"I thought you would want to know that," repeated the man.

Brian's lips smothered an oath. He whirled back to face those in conference in the tent and there was a great urgency in his voice as he cried, "Why do we waste time here in talking? Why do we not act? Why do we not go ahead, take this castle move on to Bedford and then on to London where we can see the king?"

"Storm Northampton? Without catapults? Without towers?" someone cried.

"Aye," Brian answered. "The drawbridge is lowered now for several wagons to pass across it. More are coming down the road and it will be lowered again. By a ruse we can take it. Are you with me?"

There was a catching enthusiasm in Brian's voice. William Marshall sprang to his feet. "Aye, Brian! We are with you." And while his shout still echoed, others took up the cry.

A harsh sound came from Brian's throat. His hand dropped to his sword and he stared toward the castle and tried desperately not to think of his father.

THOSE men on the castle walls and those who were responsible for guarding the gate and the bridge across the moat, could have seen little to make them suspicious of the ragged group of men trudging up the road ahead of several wagons which were coming in from the fields. The men were moving slowly as though very tired, They had the look of villains, men bound to the soil. No glittering armor covered their bodies and they seemed to be carrying no weapons. When they passed groups of soldiers who stood a safe bow-shot distant from the castle walls and when the soldiers mocked them, the ragged group did not even have the spirit to answer.

It was natural that the drawbridge should be lowered to them and to the following wagons, for those who surrounded the castle were still a safe distance away, and every additional man admitted meant another warrior in defense, in case of trouble.

The great bridge dropped slowly over the moat and the ragged group started across it. Suddenly, then, two of them turned back to the wagons, seized hidden axes and started chopping at the heavy chains which had lowered the bridge.

A shout of warning went up from the bridge tower and soldiers poured through the gates with leveled lances and bared swords. However those others now produced weapons which had been hidden under their clothing and within a moment the drawbridge was the scene of a desperate battle.

At the same time a body of mounted men came charging from the camp of the rebels and those who did not have mounts came running after them, shouting and waving their weapons. Nearer to the castle a few of those running men stopped and, fitting arrows to their bows, began picking off the guards on the castle walls.

The mounted men, led by Fitz-Walter, William Marshall, Brian, Wycliffe, and Arthur Pinel, crossed the drawbridge before their mounts were slain, and now others, charging after them, pressed against the castle gates, forced them open, battled their way on through. Outside, the archers had moved closer and under John Tuck's direction were keeping the walls clear of men. That chain on the drawbridge had been severed and so now the way into the castle was blocked only by the defenders who jammed around the open gate and tried to hold the rebels back.

After the first fury of the charge, after his first taste of the battle, Brian staggered aside and leaned on his sword. He felt a grim satisfaction in the success of his ruse to gain entrance. It had worked better than he had thought it might. All that remained now was for them to overcome this resistance at the gate and the castle would be theirs. He wiped a hand across his face, straightened, and then plunged back into the battle, his sword slashing.

"A Wilton!" shouted a voice. "A Wilton!"

A cold chill swept over Brian's body. His hands grew weak and under the heavy blow of a sword, his own blade was twisted from his grasp. Someone reached out from behind him, pulled him out of the way and took his place. The rebels had been surging forward, gaining ground foot by foot, but now they stopped advancing and again Brian heard that cry:

"A Wilton! A Wilton!"

BRIAN saw him then as the mass of men to one side of him gave way, and it was a sight that he would never forget. In the forefront of the defenders stood his father and with both hands he was wielding the axe *Bretwalda*.

There was a light in his father's face which Brian had never seen before. Memory of that was to stay with him, too, and later he was to understand that it was the light which always comes to the face of a man who delights in battle, who loves to pit his strength against the strength of others. But in the moment Brian saw his father as a stranger; and he stood motionless, stricken of his own will to fight. He heard his father's cry ring out again and then he saw that behind his father the defenders were moving forward.

Men fell back against Brian, carrying him with them; but the rebels rallied and drove forward again toward the gate. For several minutes, then, the tide of battle wavered back and forth. Brian had lost sight of his father but he could still hear his cry, still see, occasionally, the slashing movement of the axe *Bretwalda*. Then around that place where his father stood there was a sudden press of men, a more furious clashing of steel on steel.

"A Wilton! A Wil—"

The shout broke off suddenly and Brian seemed to feel the blow which had choked off his father's cry. With a wild shout he threw himself forward. Of how he reached his father's side he had no memory. He only knew that in some way he reached the place where his father had fallen. On all sides of him the battle still raged, but of it he was hardly conscious. He stooped over, called his father's name but there was no response from the silent figure which lay sprawled over the bodies of those he had slain.

Brian's eyes then fell on his father's axe, the axe *Bretwalda*. How long it had been in the Wilton family he didn't know, all of its story he didn't know. He had never swung it, had been afraid to try, for he had seen other men, more powerful than he, who could not handle the weight of the great axe forged long ago by Caedmon. Now, however, his hands went out to it, and he lifted it as easily as though it had no weight at all. And then, still standing over his father's body, he slashed from side to side, hurling men away. Ringing back any from either group who sought to pass by him.

What might have happened had not Arthur Pinel stooped down and taken his father's legs and pulled him away and then lifted him in his arms, Brian never knew. Some were to whisper later that had not Brian taken his stand over his father's body, the assault would have been successful, and that may have been the truth. But whatever the case, Brian fought no more after he saw Arthur Pinel back away, carrying his father. He lowered the axe to the ground and stared after him, his shoulders bowed.

Behind him there arose a great shout from the defenders and they surged forward. And fighting bitterly every step of the way, those who had made the assault on the castle retreated through the gate and then across the bridge.

Brian didn't see that. Still dragging the axe *Bretwalda*, he followed Arthur Pinel to his tent.

Pinel lowered Sir Aubrey Wilton to the ground, knelt at his side, looked down at him for a moment and then arose.

"He is dead," Brian muttered hoarsely.

Arthur Pinel shook his head. "Nay, Brian, but he has a grievous wound between the shoulder and neck where a plate of his armor broke away and someone's sword cut him deeply."

"But he will not live," said Brian.

Arthur Pinel looked away. "There is a chance for him," he said slowly. "There is a chance."

His words, however, were flat and Brian knew that he did not mean them.

"Leave me alone with him," he said to Arthur. And Arthur walked out of the tent and left him.

CHAPTER IV

AFTER IT HAD grown dark, William Marshall brought two lamps to the tent in which Sir Aubrey Wilton was lying and one of these was placed on either side of the pallet. Wycliffe had bound up his wounds, but the one in the shoulder continued to bleed and could not be stopped.

Brian sat on the floor near him and waited for the end. He knew what the result of the assault had been just as a man is often unconsciously aware of the weather. It made no impression on his mind. Outside the tent he heard two of the nobles talking in lowered voices.

"We have started now," said one of them. "Aye," commented the other. "And there can be no turning back."

Sir James Wycliffe, who was waiting in the tent with Brian, touched him suddenly on the shoulder and said, "Look, he is opening his eyes. He is conscious."

Brian's head turned and he stared at his father. Sir Aubrey's eyes were open and they were fastened on his face.

"Father," Brian whispered. "Father—"

Sir Aubrey's lips moved but no sound came from them. His eyes didn't leave Brian's face.

Wycliffe lifted his head and helped the wounded man to take a draft of wine. Having lowered him again he said to Brian, "He seems stronger. I can't understand it. An ordinary man would long ago have been dead of such a wound."

Brian tore his eyes away from his fathers face. He couldn't bear the quiet, impersonal look of the older man. Over to one side lay the axe *Bretwalda* and Brian recalled now that a part of the legend of the axe lay in an old prophesy that to those who held *Bretwalda* would come a great victory, a great defeat, a great sorrow and a great joy. He thought of how he had lifted that axe and stood with it over his father's body. He had held it and had known defeat and sorrow, such a sorrow that he felt that he would rather have known death.

Arthur Pinel came to the tent opening and motioned to him. Brian got up, looked at his father and then walked over to join Arthur.

"How is he?" Arthur Pinel asked.

"He looks at me," Brian answered flatly. "He just lies there and looks at me."

"He is too weak to speak," Pinel guessed.

"I would almost like to believe that."

Arthur Pinel took Brian's arm. "Brian," he said slowly, "we have taken a step this afternoon from which there can be no turning back. Though Northampton has not fallen, we will yet take it. A guard has been thrown around the walls, and not long ago a patrol captured a woman who said that she had escaped from the castle. She has asked to speak to you."

"Why?" Brian asked gruffly. "What care I to speak with any woman from Northampton?"

"The woman is Lady Eleanor of Compton."

Brian stared at his friend. He said, "Lady Eleanor?" And from his tone the name did not seem to mean anything to him at all.

Arthur Pinel lifted his hand and motioned to a group of soldiers standing a little to one side. One of them came forward leading a slender, dark-cloaked figure.

LADY ELEANOR stopped a pace from where Brian was standing and looked up into his face. It seemed to him that there were tears in the girl's eyes, but the sight of them did not seem important. Lady Eleanor was not important to him now. He blinked at the girl and said flatly, "What do you want?"

"I saw the fight at the gate," Lady Eleanor said slowly. "I saw your friend carry your father away. How is he?"

"He is dying," Brian answered. "What do you want?"

The girl's figure was very straight and she did not flinch under his gruff reception.

"When Henry de Cressy left Compton," she said, "he insisted that my father and I go with him and my father did not dare refuse. He brought us to Northampton. I was in the castle when your father came to see the Justiciar. I want you to know what happened."

"Well, what was it?" Brian asked.

"Henry de Cressy told your father that because he had failed in loyalty to the king his lands were to be forfeited."

"My father was ever loyal to the king," Brian said sharply.

"So he told Henry de Cressy, but de Cressy only laughed and said that informers had told him a different story."

"Lies!"

"Aye, but has not justice under King John's rule always been something that could be bought or sold?"

Brian looked around toward the tent in which his father was lying. He stared back at the girl and asked, "What else said de Cressy or my father?"

"Your father said that he would appeal directly to the king and de Cressy asked him why he did not join the rebels who were even then gathering outside the castle gates."

"And my father?"

"He repeated that he had always been loyal to the king, that he would still be loyal, that he still believed that it he saw the king he could get justice."

Brian turned away and looked out across the camp. Here and there were fires and all about were moving figures, but he saw none of them. Once more he was trying to understand the deep loyalty which had characterized his father's life, trying to understand how he could still have faith in a king who had done all that King John had done, how he could still fight for such a king in the face of what de Cressy had done. Such loyalty passed his understanding but it gave him a deep and enduring pride in the man who was his father.

"How did you escape from the castle?" Brian asked finally.

"Tapestries may still be cut and made .a rope," Lady Eleanor replied.

"And de Cressy, does he still think that this rebellion is a thing to laugh at?"

"Aye. That is why I have come to you. Henry de Cressy is sure that you can never take Northampton. While you are wasting your time here he plans to escape through some passageway, hurry back to the king. He will raise an army in the south; brand all rebels as traitors to their king, you and my father among them."

"You know where this passageway is?"

The girl shook her head.

Brian rubbed his hands together. He called to Arthur Pinel and said, "Find me John Tuck. Bring him here."

From the doorway of the tent Brian again stared at his father. Sir Aubrey's eyes were open; seemed fixed on his face. Brian drew a deep breath. "I was with those, Sire, who made the assault on the castle," he said slowly.

Sir Aubrey's lips did not move, but his eyes never turned from his son.

Brian moved away. He could no longer stand there under his father's gaze. John Tuck came up to him and Brian said, "Get me my father's axe there in the tent."

John Tuck entered the tent, came back with the axe *Bretwalda* and handed it to Brian.

Brian stared at it and his lips tightened. "There is a passageway from Northampton Castle," he said abruptly. "Where does it lead?"

John Tuck frowned. "Such a passage would be well guarded on the inside. You could never gain entrance that way."

"Where does the passage lead?"

"I do not know but there is a man with us who was once on the castle guard. Perhaps he—"

"Let us find him," said Brian sharply.

AN HOUR had passed and at a spot near the bank of the Nene River Brian and three companions waited silently. Brian's eyes were fixed on a point some score of paces away and every now and then he would twist the great axe in his hands and draw a long, shuddering breath.

"You are sure that is the place?" asked John Tuck of one of the other two men.

"Aye, that is the place where the passage opens," came the answer. "But why have we come here?"

"Be silent," Brian ordered sharply.

The minutes dragged slowly by and piled up into another hour, and then at last there was a faint movement at the spot which Brian was watching. A stone slab was pushed aside.

"They are coming," Tuck whispered.

Brian said nothing. He waited while an armored soldier appeared from the passage-way back of the slab, looked around and then called to his companions. He waited while another half-score men came out and while the slab was being replaced.

"Where will we find the horses?" asked the gruff voice of Henry de Cressy.

"This way," someone answered, and started moving off to the right.

Brian stood up. He gave no warning of his intentions, gave no orders to the men who had come with him. His charge was sudden and unexpected and the slashing blows of his axe were so heavy that none could stand against it. Screams rent the air and hoarse shouts echoed throughout the night. All of those men who had come through the passageway had carried bared weapons with them and some of them made an effort to defend themselves. But their swords might as well have been of wood.

Four men rallied around de Cressy, and seeing only Brian and John Tuck, de Cressy called to those who had fled, ordering them to return.

Brian laughed. "We meet still once more, de Cressy," he shouted. "And this time to finish what was started in the tournament at Compton."

"You!" grated de Cressy.

Again Brian laughed. The slashing blows of *Bretwalda* had sent two of the men sprawling to the ground. Now the third man staggered back, blood pouring through a gash in his coat-of-mail where *Bretwalda's* edge had struck.

Henry de Cressy screamed now, screamed in terror. He struck viciously at Brian, but the great axe of Caedmon, smashing down at him, sheared off his arm at the shoulder and cut deep into his body.

Brian watched him fall. He heard men running toward him from the camp, heard John Tuck saying something about those who had escaped. He lowered the axe to the ground, bit his lips. In this victory he could feel little triumph. He turned away and started walking slowly toward the blinking fires of the camp.

CHAPTER V

FITZ-WALTER, WILLIAM MARSHALL and a few of the other leaders of the rebellion were standing in front of Arthur Pinel's tent when Brian reached it. Fitz-Walter said bluntly, "In half an hour, Brian, we are riding toward Bedford Castle. We have received word that it will not resist us. We will take that castle and then move on to London. Word has come from London that all the merchants there will join us. When we have taken London the king will have to listen to our demands."

"Aye." William Marshall nodded. "But we shall leave enough men here to keep up the siege of Northampton. Until the King's Justiciar—"

"Henry de Cressy is dead," Brian interrupted. "What matters Northampton Castle now?"

"The Justiciar dead? Then Northampton matters not at all."

Fitz-Walter's eyes were gleaming. "We ride for Bedford!" he shouted.

"And London!" called another voice.

Brian moved past them, stopped in the entrance to the tent. The lamps were still burning on either side of his father's body but Sir Aubrey's eyes were now closed and the stiffness of death had settled over his features.

"Brian?" said a quiet voice. "Brian?"

He turned his head. Lady Eleanor was standing over at one side, looking at him earnestly. Her face seemed very pale in the flickering, uncertain light from the lamps.

"You here?" he said quietly.

"I came in just after you left," the girl replied. "You should not have gone, Brian. Your father—asked for you just before he died."

"He asked for me?" Brian repeated.

The girl nodded. "Some man asked me to give him more wine. I did, and for a while it seemed to strengthen him."

A sudden trembling came over Brian.

"What—what did he say?" he asked unsteadily.

The girl looked down at Sir Aubrey's body. She said slowly, "He asked for you, Brian, and I told him that you would be here in just a moment. Then he said, 'Tell Brian this. Tell him that every man has to stand on his own two feet. Tell him that every man has to be true to what he believes. Tell him that loyalty to himself is more important than any other loyalty.'"

It seemed to Brian that a tight cord was choking his throat. His breath was coming fast and he was still trembling. "My father said that?" he heard himself whispering.

"Yes, Brian. Your father said that."

"That is the truth? Those were his words?"

"Those were his words."

IT SEEMED to Brian, in that moment, that a heavy weight had suddenly been lifted from his soul. He moved over and stared down at his father and he was conscious of the fact that Lady Eleanor had come with him and was still at his side.

"You must do as he would want you to do," he heard her whispering. "The men here are riding on to Bedford and then to London. They will want you with them. You want to be with them. Your father would want you to go. I have spoken with Hubert. He will see that Sir Aubrey is taken back to Wilton Hall."

Brian turned away. From the entrance to the tent he could see signs of great activity. Men were kicking out their fires, folding their canvases. A good many were already mounted and were ready to depart. Orders were being shouted and here and there men were singing.

He could sense a new spirit in the men. When he had arrived here they had been grimly silent, almost desperate. After the assault on the castle they had been sullen and a little shaken. But now they were exultant. Word of the message from Bedford and London had passed from mouth to mouth and already they could taste the victory which was to be theirs.

John Tuck came up with his horse and said, "Ready, Lord? We ride to see the king."

Brian nodded. Ahead of him and of the others lay the ride to Bedford, which was to fall without a blow; a ride on to London and a session with the king. And after that a meeting on June 15th between Staines and Windsor in a meadow which was called Runnymeade. On that day at Runnymeade, King John was to attach his seal to the document which in later years was to be known as the Magna Carta and which was to become the bulwark of the English Constitution.

All that lay ahead of him, and in the days to come was to mean a great deal; but just then Brian was not thinking of this ride to Bedford and to London. He was thinking of the man who lay there in the tent behind him and of that man's words as told to him by the girl.

"Come, Lord," said John Tuck. "They are ready to leave."

Brian swung around once more, looked down at the silent figure of his father and then up at Lady Eleanor. "I will expect you, too, to be at Wilton Hall," he said abruptly.

The girl made no answer but the trace of a smile showed for a moment on her lips and Brian felt a sudden assurance that she would be there and that it would not be so hard to return to Wilton Hall if he knew that she was waiting for him.

He lifted *Bretwalda* to his shoulder, and turning away, mounted his horse.

VIII

THE VALIANT ARM

Somewhere in the woods near the Scottish border is reason for darkest treachery, to king and to friend. And Bretwalda, mighty axe of the Wiltons, gives strength against traitors.

CHAPTER I

ROGER WILTON PACED angrily back and forth across the narrow room in the tower of the castle at Windsor. Now and again he would pause at the open window and stare out at the broad, green meadows below.

Encamped there were the first few thousand men of the army King Edward was gathering for his campaign against Scotland and against William Wallace, the Scot rebel, who eight months before, in September of 1297, had cut to pieces an English army at Stirling Bridge.

The warm, soft smell of early summer was in the air but Roger was unaware of it. The bitterness which churned through his veins had clouded his mind and had whipped his thoughts into a vicious circle from which he couldn't seem to get away.

"Lies," he blurted out suddenly, "Lies. But to what end, Tuck? That I cannot understand."

The tall, thin man leaning against the wall just inside the door, shook his head. "Nor can I, Sir Roger. What think you that King Edward will do?"

Roger shrugged. He was a taller man than John Tuck and there was a look of great strength in the well knit lines of his body. His hair was light in color and was worn long in the fashion of the day, reaching almost to the gray tunic which fell loosely from his broad shoulders and which was gathered at the waist by a wide leather belt. There were marks of a stubborn nature in the set of his jaw; and despite the turmoil which

Roger looked squarely at the king; the flush on his
face rose not from shame, but from anger.

seethed within him, his blue eyes were clear and steady. He was
still young but there was a maturity in his expression which
belied his years.

"There is little doubt in my mind what King Edward will
do," he said slowly. "The king is loyal to his friends and no one
is closer to him than Sir Thomas Seagrave."

"It was Sir Thomas' word against yours."

"And he will believe Sir Thomas."

John Tuck scowled. "Tell me again what happened in the
battle at Stirling Bridge."

Roger Wilton's mind turned back to his memories of that
fight. Many stories had been told of it, some conflicting, some
in agreement. Speaking rather slowly, he said, "Wallace and his
men were on the north of the Forth River, the English on the
south. Across the river was a narrow bridge. Sir Hugh Cressingham, who commanded the English, ordered us to advance
over it. I was among the first to cross over and when half of the
English were across, the Scots made their attack. So furious
was it that it swept us away from the bridge; and having taken

the bridge, the Scots prevented any more of the English from crossing. They then set about cutting down those of us who were already over, and they did good work of it, for scarcely any of us escaped. My head was laid open by a sword which made me lose consciousness. When I awoke it was dark and the scavengers were robbing the dead, I got up, managed to get away. It is Sir Thomas' story that I turned my horse and fled at the first charge of the Scots."

"Some of those who were left on the English side of the Forth must have seen that you did not flee."

"Perhaps, but the Scots crossed that bridge and the remaining half of our army could not stand against them. For days the Scots pursued the English through Torwood Forest, killing them as they overtook them. As you say, some must have seen that I didn't flee. Yet I know not where to turn to find such witnesses and you, Tuck, have been unable to find any."

"Aye," John Tuck answered soberly. "Or perhaps I should say that no man I have found has a liking to name Sir Thomas as a liar. The man is too powerful, too close to the king."

"I thought him a friend," said Roger bitterly.

"You have had no trouble with him?"

"None. I talked with him on the eve of the battle, talked with him for a long time. He was very friendly."

THERE was a sharp knocking at the door. When Roger opened it, a man in the uniform of the King's Guard said bluntly, "The King would like to see you at once in his council chambers."

Roger's lips tightened. He stepped out into the corridor and other guardsmen formed a double line on each side of him: thus was he marched down from the tower and into the broad council chambers. The thought came to him, as he approached the king, that in just such a way were ordinary felons or murderers brought into this room to hear the pronouncement of their fate.

Roger knelt before the king; then standing, looked squarely into his face. There was little of humility in his attitude.

King Edward was a large man, ruddy of cheek and light of hair. He had been a wise and able ruler and it was well known that it had long been his ambition to make of England and Scotland a united kingdom. Almost ten years before, arrangements had been made for his son to marry the Maid of Norway, heir to the Scottish throne, and word of her death in Orkney in 1290 had been a severe blow to him. Yet because of the pledge of that marriage he had assumed an overlordship of Scotland; and in spite of the objections of men like William Wallace, he meant to maintain it.

There was a deep scowl on the king's face. For a long moment he stared at Roger Wilton; then, speaking in a clear, distinct voice, he said, "Sir Roger Wilton, I have considered your case long and earnestly. Cowardice I can never stomach, but you were more than a coward. Had you not fled, Stirling Bridge might not have been lost, hundreds of men slain by the Scots might still have been living, Scotland might now have been a part of England. I have sent men to their death for less than you have done. Yet because of the memory of the service of your father, my judgment is not death. Instead, your estates are confiscated to the crown and I banish you forevermore from English soil."

A deep silence followed the king's statement. Roger knew that a flush lay over his face but it was a flush of anger, not of shame. He clenched his hands at his sides and fought desperately to maintain his self control. There were a score of men standing on either side of the throne, men with whom Roger had fought, men he had counted as his friends. His glance turned from side to side. Cold, chilling expressions or looks of indifference were on every face. Near the king he saw Sir Thomas Seagrave. Sir Thomas was a thick shouldered, heavy man, well past his youth. His dark eyes stared flatly at Roger out of a dark skinned face.

"Out of my sight," said the king bluntly, "You sicken me."

Roger knelt again. He stood up, backed for several paces, then turned and strode toward the door. The deep silence still lay over the room and the soft leather of his deer-skin boots made little noise. The guards did not march with him now for he was no longer a prisoner. Judgment had been pronounced. He was free to go, so long as his going carried him out of the country of his birth.

BACK in the tower room which had served as prison while he had awaited the king's word, John Tuck met him; and when Roger repeated the king's judgment, a relieved expression came into the older man's eyes.

"It might have been worse, Sir Roger," he muttered.

Roger laughed harshly. "Could death have been worse?"

Tuck said nothing and Roger crossed over to the window and stared out across the meadow. For a long while he was not conscious of any process of thought; then he found himself considering all that he knew about Sir Thomas Seagrave, the man whom he had felt was a friend, and who for no apparent reason had lied to the king about him.

Sir Thomas, he knew, had long been close to the king. Twice during the past few years the king had sent him to Rome, as a special emissary to the Pope. Eight years before he had been chosen with Bishop Antony Bek to go to Orkney, for the purpose of bringing the Maid of Norway on to England. In a score of very personal missions, Sir Thomas had played a large part.

The man's estates were in the North, on the border of Scotland. His castle, Dundale, was not far from Stirling Castle and was in a wild and rugged country. Roger remembered it well. Six years before when he was but a tall, gangling youth and when his father was still alive, he and his father had been guests at Dundale.

They had gone there for a hunt. Roger remembered that hunt specially because he had become separated from the others and had been lost. A woodsman's daughter, a thin, shy, bird-like creature of about twelve, had found him and had taught him build a shelter. The night before the battle at Stirling Bridge,

Roger recalled, he had mentioned that incident to Sir Thomas and they had laughed over it. In fact, they had even discussed it for some time, Roger asking about the girl and her father and threatening lightly to hunt her up after the battle on the morrow.

Roger's mind fastened on that conversation with Sir Thomas, not because he could read anything into it but because it was the last talk he had had with the man. He recalled that Sir Thomas hadn't been any too well pleased with his threat to seek out the girl; and when he had referred to the girl as Margaret, Sir Thomas had said bluntly that her name was Marion. Aside from that they had had no differences of opinion.

Clouds were sweeping in from the West, bringing with them the thickening shadows of an early dusk. Roger sighed, turned from the window. He looked over at John Tuck, the third man of that name to serve the Wiltons. Gaunt, thin, almost ugly in feature was John Tuck. To most he might seem a surly, uncouth, awkward man. Yet between him and Roger there was the close bond of long association and of mutual liking. Roger had never been John Tuck's equal in the ways of a man in the forest or in the use of a longbow.

"Where will we be going, Sir Roger?" Tuck asked.

"You will be going back to Stafford Forest," Roger replied slowly. "As for me, I do not know."

"I have no wish to return to Stafford Forest."

"Yet you will return. I command it."

A brief smile touched the dry, crooked lips of the woodsman. "If the king confiscated your estate, where I held land at your pleasure, you are no longer my master, Sir Roger, and you cannot command me. The road I will take when we leave here is the road you take."

A thickening of the cords in his throat choked back whatever answer Roger might have made. He knew that it would do no good, to argue with Tuck. He reached out his hand and felt Tuck's firm clasp, than turning to the wall he took down a coat of chain mail and donned it. Over his shoulders he threw a strap. *Bretwalda*, the great axe which had been his father's and which he had used in the battle at Stirling Bridge, stood in the corner of the room. Roger lifted it, feeling as he always did when he touched the axe, the pride of a man in a good weapon.

Bretwalda was made entirely of steel, was long of handle and broad of head. So great was its weight that men marveled that he could swing it, knowing not that the axe itself gave strength into the arms of its owner.

Roger slipped the axe into the strap over his shoulder, suddenly thankful that he had been treated with the courtesy due a knight under trial, thankful that his armor and weapons had not been taken from him. He buckled on his sword, reached for his helmet and said to John Tuck, "Ready?"

Tuck nodded, and the two of them left the tower room and started for the stables.

THE SHADOWS had thickened by the time they reached the courtyard and most of the men-at-arms seemed to have gone. Roger heard some man mention that the king had departed for London and he guessed that most of the nobles who had been here had gone with him, taking their retinues with them. He and Tuck walked on to the stables, opened the door.

There was no warning before the attack. It came suddenly. Too suddenly, perhaps, for one of the men lying in wait for them within the darkened stable rushed forward, thrusting with his sword while they were still in the entrance. Roger saw only the blurred shadow of that man's figure as he charged at them, and how he managed to escape that first sword thrust he didn't ever know. Yet escape it he did and with a blow from his hand he hurled that man aside and reached for his axe.

"He is the man!" shouted a voice from within the stable. "He is the man!"

More figures were now rushing forward but with a sudden loud shout, Roger met them. He did not understand this attack, was not to understand it for a long time, yet here in this struggle was a chance for him to vent some of the anger and bitterness which he had been storing up in his body for days. *Bretwalda* slashed from side to side, cutting men down, hurling them back. Screams and yells and the slapping sound of steel on steel made the night hideous with noise. Several horses which had been quartered within the stable tore loose and ran blindly for the door, adding to the confusion.

"Catch us mounts, Tuck!" Roger shouted, "Catch us mounts!"

More horses churned toward the door and some of those inside were struck down by their thudding hoofs. Tuck was shouting that he had caught two of the horses. Whirling away from the door, Roger saw that men were hurrying toward the stables from all over the courtyard. He raced toward the place where Tuck held the rearing, frightened horses, threw himself into the saddle of one of them and turned it toward the gate. No one had thought to lower the portcullis or to raise the drawbridge, and with Tuck just behind him he thundered through the gate and galloped down the road.

A scant league from the castle he drew rein and Tuck rode up to his side.

"Know you who they were, Sir Roger?"

Roger frowned thoughtfully. It had seemed to him that he had heard a familiar voice from the stables just at the onset of the attack—the voice of Sir Thomas Seagrave. Yet he could not be sure. He admitted as much to John Tuck; then, still frowning, he said, "I have not thought until now where I would go. Have you wondered, Tuck?"

"Nay, Sir Roger."

"You have guessed, then, that there is only one place for me to go."

"Aye. To Scotland. For it is to Scotland that the king marches and Sir Thomas with him."

Roger Wilton nodded. He turned his horse to the north and said softly, "To Scotland, to Dundale, and to another meeting with Sir Thomas."

CHAPTER II

WILD AND RUGGED was Glyncoe Forest. Within its boundaries lay a veritable paradise for the huntsman or for the man who would try angling for trout in its deep, clear streams. To the north was the frowning height of Balmoral and in its shadow lay Loch Elinoe, where sapphire blue waters caught and pictured the changing moods of the sky. Here and there were wide glens, deep grown with tussock grass and heather. Narrow pony-tracks twisted through the folds in the hills, leading near to some of the more favored watering places for the deer.

Deep within the forest on the towering craigs of a hill was built the castle Dundale.

A well marked road led up to the castle and then twisting through the forest made its way on to another road which ran east to Edinburgh or west to Falkirk and Glasgow. There was not much travel on that road which led past the castle; for highwaymen preyed on those who would travel that road, and most people going north preferred to go by some safer way.

Deep within Glyncoe Forest and above Loch Elinoe there is a place where a cold spring of water bursts from a crack in a high, granite cliff; and to that place, early in July, came Roger Wilton and John Tuck. They had been in Glyncoe Forest for almost a month, seeing a score of woodsmen, but seen by no one. To Tuck alone did Roger give credit for that fact. In the sections of the birds or animals, or sometimes, it seemed to Roger, almost in the very smell of the air, John Tuck could sense the approach of any who came near to them; and thus warned, they had always hidden.

John Tuck stooped to drink from the pool of water made by the spring, then straightened and faced to the east, frowning. "Men are camped near here," he said suddenly. "I can smell the wood of their fire."

Roger sniffed the air but was unable to note the smell of

burning wood. He listened intently but could hear nothing save the twittering of the birds and the rustling of the wind.

"I think that this is near to the place where I was lost during the hunt, six years ago," he said quietly.

A faint smile touched Tuck's lips. "You have thought that before of other places in this forest."

"I suppose I was not an observing lad," Roger grinned. "Yet this time I think I am right."

Tuck sighed. "'Tis not likely that we will ever find the girl you seek. She would be of age to marry and by this time some woodsman would have claimed her for his bride."

"Perhaps."

"Or she and her father may have gone away. I cannot think that Sir Thomas would be a good man to serve."

Roger scowled, plucked at the string of the bow John Tuck had made for him. He said slowly, "It is perhaps a waste of time to try and find her, yet I can think of nothing else to do. I never had trouble with Sir Thomas, nor had my father during his lifetime, Our talk before the battle of Stirling Bridge was entirely friendly save when I threatened to hunt up this girl."

"You are young. Sir Roger. She might have looked on you with favor. Perhaps Sir Thomas wanted her for himself."

"Would he marry a huntsman's daughter?"

"I did not say that he wanted to marry her."

"Aye. The other would be like him."

John Tuck lifted his hand. "Listen!"

Again Roger strained his ears but he could hear nothing unusual. "What is it?" he whispered.

"A fiddle!"

"A fiddle! Here in Glyncoe!"

"Aye. Come, let us see who is playing."

Tuck led the way down along the stream which ran from the spring and then over the fold of a hill and across a narrow glen. When they topped the hill Roger had been able to catch the faint strains of a fiddle and as they drew nearer he could make out the tune, though he did not recognize it. The glen closed in and he and Tuck made their way more cautiously now through a wild tangle of thick bushes until they came at last to the place where they could see the fiddler.

HE WAS apparently a young man, his body large-framed, his shoulders broad, his hair curly and brown. A wide bandage covered his eyes, but his nose, jaw and forehead were well proportioned. He wore a tunic of deer-skin and a leather hat in which there was a green feather. Near him a thin, awkward appearing young fellow was sprawled on the ground. This one held a sword and was turning it over and over, scowling at it.

As the fiddler came to the end of the tune he had been playing, the scowling fellow sat up and said, glumly, "I think this is a fool's errand. I have no liking for it."

"Be quiet, Donel," ordered the fiddler. "Here is a new song of the Campbells. What think you of it?"

The air which the fiddler now played was bright and lilting and he hummed to himself as he drew his bow across the strings. Roger listened to the tune and liked it. He turned his head to glance at John Tuck and saw that Tuck was staring off to the right and that a look of surprise was on the man's face.

Roger's glance followed Tuck's and of a sudden he caught his breath and felt a sharp tremor of excitement run over his body. Across the little clearing but still hidden from the fiddler by a clump of bushes stood the tall, slender figure of a girl. She wore the rough clothing of a woodsman but the morning sunlight glinted against the mass of golden hair which fell over her shoulders. In one hand she carried a bow and under her arm Roger could see the end of a feathered shaft, ready for instant use should she need it. As he watched, the girl took a step forward and he noted how lightly she moved.

The fiddler suddenly stopped playing and in an easy, friendly voice said, "You like the song. Come. Sit down. I will play you another."

The abrupt stopping of the tune and the sound of the man's voice seemed to startle the girl. She drew back, turned as if to run away, stopped, and then as the fiddler again began to play, moved forward into the clearing.

Roger grasped Tuck's arm, nodded his head at the men. This, he was sure, was the girl for whom he had been seeking. The same shyness was in her face and her hair had not changed, though the years had made her a woman.

"Like it?" asked the fiddler, lowering his bow.

The girl nodded and in a tone so low that Roger hardly caught her words, she asked, "How knew you that I was near?"

"I heard you, my child," said the fiddler, "even though your step is as light as a deer's. To those who are blind is given a good hearing. Tell me your name."

"Marion."

"And your father?"

"Angus, the woodsman, deer-warden for Sir Thomas Seagrave."

The fiddler nodded. "And you have lived here for long?"

"Aye, for long. Will you play some more?"

A sudden crackling of branches sounded through the woods around the clearing and half a score of men burst on the scene. They were led by a huge, brawny figure clad in a rough skin jerkin and carrying a heavy club. A sword was belted at that man's waist and over his shoulder was slung a bow. His face was ruddy and was heavily bearded and he was dark of skin and hair.

The others, like their leader, wore the garb of woodsmen but also carried swords. Some of them Roger and Tuck had seen before as they lay hidden near some clearing just as they were hidden now.

The girl had started away as the men broke through into the open but she stopped not far from where Roger and Tuck crouched. The fiddler had jerked erect and the youth had come to his feet and had stepped in front of him and was swinging his sword from side to side.

"Who are you?" demanded the leader of the woodsmen, facing the fiddler. "And what do you in this forest?"

"I am known as Blind David," answered the fiddler. "I am a singer of songs. And with my companion Donel I am on my way to Glasgow and then to Ayr."

A deep scowl came to the woodsman's face. "You are far out of your way. It is in my mind to teach you to stay to the main roads."

"We—we meant no harm," stammered Donel. "We—"

The woodsman struck out with his club and such was his reach that he struck the young man's arm and knocked the sword from his hand. A sharp cry of pain burst from Donel's throat. He stooped over to reach for the sword with the other hand but the fiddler pushed him out of the way. He had dropped his fiddle and bow and now, very swiftly, he reached up and jerked the bandage from his eyes, grabbed the sword and stood erect.

"So you are not blind after all," shouted the woodsman, "I know then what to do."

THE WOODSMAN dropped his club and drew his own sword. With a sharp cry to his companions to follow him he rushed at the fiddler.

There followed, then, one of the prettiest exhibitions of sword play which Roger had ever seen. Under the onslaught of the woodsmen, the fiddler had backed up against the shelter of a heavy bush and his sword, moving from one side to another, now up and now down, fended off his attackers and drew from several of them sharp cries of pain.

Roger had lifted himself to his knees. He saw the girl run forward, saw her grasp the leader of the woodsmen by the arm, heard her crying to him to leave the fiddler alone. The big man laughed at her, shoved her aside so violently that she fell. "Kill him," he shouted hoarsely. "Those were our orders." It was this that Sir Thomas feared.

The fiddler, who apparently had other accomplishments, laughed loudly at that order and there was a mocking note in the sound. "Come then and finish it," he taunted. "Come then and taste my steel."

One of the woodsmen drew back and picked up a long stick. With it he jabbed at the fiddler's body and though the fiddler's sword broke the stick, it had thrown him a little off balance.

Encouraged by that success, two other woodsmen backed out off the fight and reached for long sticks with which to prod the man. Roger stood up. He reached to his shoulder and seized the axe *Bretwalda*. "It is time that we took part in this," he said to John Tuck. "I have no liking for murder,"

A loud shout tore from Roger's lips as he sprang across the clearing, Several of the woodsmen turned to face him. Swords flashed into the air but were no protection or defense against the heavy, slashing strokes of the great axe.

"A friend, fiddler," Roger called. "Let us end this struggle."

"Aye, let us end it," the fiddler answered.

And end it they did. The fiddler's sword seemed to become as a streak of lightning. It stabbed through the shoulder of one man, through the stomach of another; it crashed against the head of a third. Of those who had turned to face Roger and were still standing, a few hacked into the blade in the hands of the fiddler, others swung around and fled.

The fiddler lowered his blade, looked at Roger's axe. "A handy weapon, that," he said slowly. "I hope that few of the English are so armored."

"You are then a Scot?"

"Aye."

Roger shrugged. "You did well with the sword yourself—Blind David."

A brief smile came to the fiddler's face. "I am blind only on occasion." He moved over to the side of his companion. The fellow he had called Donel was sitting up, holding his arm. It looked to Roger as if the arm was broken. He glanced around for John Tuck but didn't see him. Nor did he see the girl.

The fiddler jerked Donel's arm so that it was straight, then found sticks and with the cord from a bow tied them around the arm. Roger moved among the men who had been slain. He found two whose wounds were only slight and these he fixed up with crude bandages. The leader of the woodsmen seemed to have escaped.

While he was working over the last of the two men the fiddler came up to him and said, "I must take my companion Donel to where my friends await, but before I go I would thank you for your help."

Roger shrugged. "'Tis a little matter."

"You are English, I know by your speech. And your name?"

"Roger Wilton."

"A friend of Sir Thomas?"

"Nay. Hardly."

"Yet this is his land."

"Perhaps, like Blind David, I was but passing through it,"

The fiddler frowned. "I have a feeling," he said slowly, "that we will meet again." Then without explaining what he meant he turned and joined the youth and at his side, moved off through the forest.

CHAPTER III

ROGER WAITED WHERE he was. Where John Tuck had gone he did not know but he was not greatly alarmed at his absence. John Tuck was a man well able to take care of himself. The notion came to him that perhaps Tuck had gone after the girl, for Tuck knew that he wanted to find her.

While he waited, Roger paced back and forth across the clearing. The two men who were not badly wounded got to their feet and stumbled away and he made no effort to stop them. All that had happened here was very confusing to him. It seemed obvious that the fiddler had been no mere fiddler; but who he was or why he had been here, Roger couldn't guess. He wondered whether the woodsmen had known him and why they had tried to kill Donel.

Roger scowled. His thoughts turned toward the girl. She must have been attracted to this spot by the sound of the fiddle, even as he and John Tuck. And the thought came to him that it might have been to see her that the fiddler had come. If so, who was this girl and what was the mystery surrounding her, and why did Sir Thomas have her hidden away here, deep in the forest?

Quite suddenly, and without any previous warning of their presence, John Tuck and the girl appeared at the edge of the clearing. Tuck was grinning. He held the girl by one wrist.

Roger Wilton hurried forward to meet them. He heard Tuck saying something about how the girl had run away but he was hardly conscious of the man's words for his eyes were resting on the girl. A light tan lay over the smooth skin of her face and below it her cheeks were flushed. Leaves and twigs were caught in her hair. Her eyes were as blue and as clear as the sky above them.

Roger stopped in front of the girl. He said slowly, "Come six years ago, during a hunt in this forest, a tall, thin boy who looked on himself as a man became separated from the others and was lost. A girl, the daughter of one of the woodsmen, found him. She taught him how to build a shelter, for they were far from any *bothy* and the night looked stormy."

As Roger was speaking the girl's eyes widened and when he paused she said swiftly, "You were that boy."

Roger laughed. "So you remember, Margaret."

A momentary frown showed on the girl's face. "Did I tell you my name was Margaret?"

"Aye, and is it not?"

" 'Tis Marion, or at least—"

John Tuck had released the girl and now he touched Roger on the arm and said bluntly, "The maid led me to a place almost two leagues from here where there is a *bothy*. She turned back from it or I would not have caught her. I was close enough, however, to see that there was a company of men at the *bothy* and to see that one of them was Sir Thomas."

Roger sucked in his breath, "Then the man has come north."

"Aye, Sir Roger. And with him at the *bothy* were several woodsmen and a score of men-at-arms. There were also three brindled hounds. I am thinking that he will soon hear from the men who escaped from you that you are nearby, and with the hounds—"

Roger glanced over at the girl. "Why did you turn back from the *bothy*? Was it there that you lived?"

The girl nodded.

"Then why did you turn back? Was it because Sir Thomas was there?"

"I—I do not know. I—it was because of Sir Thomas."

"We cannot stay here," John Tuck interrupted.

Roger was looking at the girl. "I have no desire to meet Sir Thomas right now," he said slowly. "And it seems that neither have you. Will you go with John Tuck and me?"

"Go where?"

"Beyond Loch Elinoe," said John Tuck, "the hills are wild and rough and heavily wooded. I thought that we might journey down to a wide stream, that you might wade up it for a distance and then make your way to that part of the forest. As for me, I will leave you at the stream and make a trail for the hounds to follow, a trail on out to the Glasgow road. After that I will come back."

"Well, Margaret?" Roger asked.

"I should not, but—"

Roger took her arm. "Let us go."

AT A STREAM a half league distant, John Tuck left them

and struck off through the forest at an easy run which Roger knew that he could keep up for hours, Roger and the girl waded into the stream and moved up it for a long way; then climbing out over some rocks, started down toward Loch Elinoe and the rugged country beyond it. They talked but little, for Roger was anxious to get the girl to a place where she would be safe from Sir Thomas. It was very clear that she feared him. He could read that fear in the expression which came over her face when he mentioned the man's name.

The sun crawled across the heavens and started down in the West and in the late afternoon a sharp, chilly wind came up. "It will rain tonight," said the girl, during one of the times when they stopped to rest.

"You are sure of that?" asked Roger.

"I am sure."

"And can you still build a shelter, Margaret?"

The girl frowned. "Why do you call me Margaret when I have said that my name was Marion?"

"You said six years ago that it was Margaret, Do you not like the name Margaret?"

"Aye, but—"

"Then I shall call you Margaret."

The girl shrugged. She did not seem tired. Though the pace Roger had set had been a fast one she had always been right at his heels.

They skirted the edge of Loch Elinoe and made toward the huge, towering heights of Balmoral. Their way was slower, now, for tangled undergrowth often barred their path and the trees grew close together. After the sun had gone down and when the shadows of the coming night began to close down over them they came to a narrow canyon and in one of its rock-walled sides Roger found a cave. He knew that by night it would be safe to build a fire within that cave for the light of the fire could not reach very far. Also, it seemed to him, this would be a good place to wait for Tuck and at the same time be out of sight.

Roger was never to forget the next two days, for it was not until the morning of the third day that Tuck found them. The waiting time was made forever memorable by his strange companionship with this forest-reared girl whom he called Margaret but who insisted that her name was Marion. She was a quiet girl, given to long periods of moody silence. At times she would talk with him willingly enough and he learned much about her life in the forest and about her father Patrick Angus; but she did not like to discuss Sir Thomas, nor would she tell him why she feared the man.

Though they had built a shelter near the cave they spent most of each of those two days high on the rocks on one side of the canyon. From there they could see over most of the forest. Below them Loch Elinoe lay like a jewel in a setting of green and far away they could barely made out the towers of the castle Dundale.

It was there on the second day that Roger told the girl of Wilton Hall and Stafford Forest, of the battle of Stirling Bridge and the charges made against him, of his trial before the king and his banishment from England.

"Then you are on your way to Scotland?" asked the girl.

"Nay, I am here because the forest of Glyncoe belongs to Sir Thomas Seagrave, who made the charges against me; because I felt that he would come here, because I have not finished with him, and finally, because he did not want me to see you."

The girl frowned but did not speak.

"Tell me," said Roger, leaning toward her, "why is it that you fear Sir Thomas? What made you flee with me?"

The frown on the girl's face deepened and after a moment's hesitation, she said slowly, "As I neared that *bothy* I saw that a priest had come along with Sir Thomas. For years, now, my father has said to me that I was to marry Sir Thomas and I was afraid—"

"Marry him?" Roger gasped.

The girl drew herself up proudly. "Think you that the daughter of a huntsman is not good enough for that beast whom men call Sir Thomas?"

"Nay, 'tis not that," Roger answered. "Yet knowing the man I wonder. Two years ago he might have married Catherine of Savoy, and through her could have controlled a rich and wealthy province. The man is ambitious, I cannot help but be surprised that he would marry even a girl so fair as you, could that marriage not benefit him in some material way."

"Yet I have spoken the truth."

The girl stood up, moved out to the edge of the cliff. And as she stood there but a pace or two from where he lay, Roger stared up at her, at the long, slim length of her body crowned by her golden hair. She was a girl, yet a woman; a creature half wild, yet with a gentle, almost cultured cadence in the tone of her voice. He got to his knees, stood up. And at that moment a fissure opened in the earth between him and the girl; a tree which was growing at the cliff's edge began to slant out over the canyon.

A COLD chill swept over Roger's body. He leaned forward, grasped the soft skin of the girl's tunic, and jerked her toward him. A sharp cry escaped from her lips but was drowned in a louder noise as the edge of the cliff dropped away.

Roger lifted the girl, carried her several paces back, and then lowered her to the ground. He could feel her body trembling. He left his arms around her and began telling her, quite foolishly, that she was all right. After a moment the girl pushed her body away from his, looked up into his face and then looked away, quickly, and something in that glance made Roger remember a guess of John Tuck's.

"Back in England before we came up here," Roger said slowly, "John Tuck told me that Sir Thomas did not want me to come and see you because he was afraid I might take you away from him. I—I think I would like to do just that."

"You have," said the girl without looking up.

"I mean forever."

"You mean—that you would marry a woodsman's daughter?"

"Aye."

"Can you be sure? Are there not ladies more fair in the great towns of England?"

"None, Margaret," said Roger. And then he laughed softly and reached his arms once more toward the girl.

CHAPTER IV

IT WAS THE next morning that John Tuck found them. For a long time he stood in the shadows of the trees a little distance from where they sat and watched them talking and laughing together, acting perhaps more like children than like a grown man and woman, still a little shy with each other but loving that shyness.

"I knew where you were while yet far away," said John Tuck, suddenly moving forward. "Think you that there are no other ears in the forest?"

Roger and Margaret got to their feet; and Roger, thinking of the long and dangerous race which Tuck must have endured for them, felt suddenly very guilty and abashed.

"Tuck," he said slowly, "I had not thought—"

"It is no matter," Tuck answered. "By this time Sir Thomas must think that you are far away. Yet his men are still searching for the girl."

"You had no trouble, Tuck?"

"Not a great deal. And I learned something, Sir Roger. In fact I learned several things."

"What things?"

John Tuck sat down cross-legged on the ground and Roger sat beside him. After a moment's hesitation, Margaret, too, dropped to the ground.

"Near the Glasgow road," said John Tuck, "I came near to a

camp of soldiers. This was the night before last. In the darkness
I crept quite close to the camp. The soldiers were Scots. From
what I heard them say I learned that the English have been in
Scotland for almost a month. Edward has taken Edinburgh.
He marched on as far as Kirkliston which is eight or nine miles
west of Edinburgh; then, but a few days ago, marched back.
From what the soldiers said I gathered that the Scots had driven
all the cattle into the hills and have moved all supplies away."

"King Edward was never a man to overlook the importance
of supplies. He will have supplies coming up from England."

"Aye, but he must wait until they arrive. In the meantime,
the army of William Wallace is gathering in the forest near
Falkirk."

"So close as that?"

"Aye."

"Then a battle is not far off."

John Tuck nodded. He was silent for a moment and Roger
glanced over at Margaret. The girl was watching Tuck closely.
She seemed vitally interested in what he had been saying.

"Last night," John Tuck continued, "I came past the castle
of Dundale. And near it I learned another thing from the gossip
of two of Sir Thomas' men."

"What was it?"

The older man scowled. He said slowly, "Sir Thomas is at the
castle. He is there awaiting a visit from William Wallace."

"Wallace?" Roger gasped.

"Aye, the Scot firebrand himself."

Roger's hands opened and closed and his body was rigid. For
a moment his thoughts turned back to the days preceding the
battle at Stirling Bridge. For almost a week before that battle,
Sir Thomas had been away from the English camp and when
he came back he had said that he had been to Dundale. Roger
wondered whether or not Sir Thomas might have met Wallace
on that occasion.

"You are sure that it is William Wallace whom Sir Thomas expects?"

"I am sure. From what I overheard I cannot doubt it."

Roger stood up, and speaking almost to himself, he said slowly, "Some of us wondered who it was who persuaded Cressingham to attempt to cross that bridge at Stirling. It might have been Sir Thomas. But even if it were not I wonder what it means that Sir Thomas, close friend of the English king, should have a secret meeting with William Wallace, leader of the Scots?"

"It could have nothing to do with you or his lies about you," said John Tuck.

"Aye, but it might have much to do with King Edward and his army. No man is closer to Edward. Did Sir Thomas advise him to advance, Edward would advance. If Sir Thomas is a traitor he could very easily lead the king into a trap."

"A king who has banished you."

"Aye," said Roger proudly, "but still my king. John Tuck, tonight I am going to Dundale castle."

"To Dundale castle! It is madness."

"Not so, for who would think to look for me there?"

"How would you get in?"

"By the vines which grow up the north wall. Remember how we marked them long ago."

A hand fell on Rogers arm and Margaret's voice whispered in his ear, "Nay, Roger. Do not go. You would have no chance at all."

Roger looked around at the girl. There was an imploring look in her eyes and all color had drained from her face.

Roger turned to John Tuck. He said sharply, "Tuck, I want you to stay with Margaret and to guard her well. She means more to me than Wilton Hall or all that I have lost. I will return as soon as I can."

"But Sir Roger—"

Roger broke free from the girl's grasp. He started hurrying down the narrow canyon and though he heard John Tuck and Margaret calling after him, he did not stop nor look back.

DARK, heavy clouds scudded across the sky late that afternoon and night came early. Through its moist shadows, Roger Wilton could make out camp fires in the meadow below Dundale castle. He passed by them and made his way to the north side of the *craigs* on which the castle was built; climbed slowly and cautiously to the castle wall. He was thankful, now, for that day which he and John Tuck had spent in studying this castle and planning how they might enter it should the occasion ever arise which made it necessary; for they had even mapped their path up the *craigs* and noticed where the vines grew heaviest.

At the foot of the wall Roger Wilton hesitated. What dangers he faced should he enter this castle he knew full well, for the hand of every man in it would be raised against him. Yet he could see nothing else to do. To go to Edinburgh and report to the king that Sir Thomas was a traitor would gain him nothing. Again it would be his word against the word of Sir Thomas; and again as in England, the king would believe the man he thought his friend, Only through a complete knowledge of what Sir Thomas and William Wallace planned could he hope to thwart them. And only through completely revealing Sir Thomas as a traitor could he hope to clear the Wilton name.

There seemed to be no guards on the wall of the castle. Grasping at the vines, Roger drew himself up. Then, lying flat on his stomach on the top of the wall, he studied the courtyard.

Torch light showed through the windows of the gate-house and of the donjon and near the gate-house there was a group of men. The donjon, that building which served as the living quarters for those in the castle, was set over near the east wall. It was not so large as he had thought it would be. At the top of the incline which led to the doorway he could make out the figure of a single guard. As he watched him, a man came up that incline, spoke to the guard for a moment, and then went on into the donjon.

Roger crawled along the wall to a stairway which led down into the courtyard. Near it he paused, and looked again toward the gate-house. The men there seemed busy in some discussion. Roger stood up, moved down the stairs and started boldly toward the incline which led up to the door of the donjon. If Wallace and Sir Thomas were to meet here tonight, it would be in the donjon that they would meet. And it was there he had to go.

Every sense in Roger's body was acutely alert as he moved across that courtyard. He heard a burst of laughter from the gate-house, felt his muscles bunch and a cold perspiration break out on his face. From the foot of that stairway to the incline seemed one of the longest distances he had ever traveled, Yet he made it at last, and grimly forced himself to walk slowly as he started toward the guard, though every impulse in his body made him want to run.

The guard was leaning against the wall, a long spear in his hands. He glanced casually at Roger, straightened as Roger drew near, scowled, and suddenly demanded, "Who are you? What do you want here?"

Roger mumbled something about having a message for Sir Thomas. He swayed, staggered, seemed about to fall. The guard moved forward, staring at him with wide open eyes. With a seeming effort, Roger forced himself erect and at the same time his hands shot out and closed around the guard's throat.

A half-choked cry escaped from the man and his spear slipped from his grasp. Hands clawed at Roger's face and the man's knee kicked him in the groin. Roger held the fellow close against him, moved over into the shadows to one side of the door. His fingers tightened and after a moment he could feel the man's muscles relaxing and in spite of the shadows could see a mottled color spreading over his face.

When he felt it safe, when he was sure that the man had lost consciousness, Roger loosened his grip and lifted the man into his arms. The spear which the guard had dropped he kicked off the platform at the top of the incline. Looking once more at the gate, he saw several men coming toward the donjon.

Still holding the guard, Roger turned inside. The hallway beyond the door was lighted by torches and to each side there was a door. Roger turned through one of those doors, looking around for a place to dispose of the guard's body. This guard must not be found by others, who would become immediately curious as to what had happened to him.

The room Roger had entered was a court room, At the far end was an elevated chair with a velvet canopy above it. A carpet stretched down the middle of the room and benches lined the walls. This room, like the hall, was lighted with torches, and the black smoke from them pressed up against the ceiling. Here a visiting monarch might sometimes hold court, and as a rule the lord of the estate acted as a judge in trial cases and disputes among those who were vassal to him. To one side of the room was a door which Roger guessed might open into a small closet where arms were sometimes stored. He turned that way, opened the door and discovered that he was right.

SUDDEN voices from the outer hall stiffened him. Roger lowered the guards body to the floor inside the closet, jerked around, and stared across the room.

"You say there is no word of him," came the heavy voice of Sir Thomas Seagrave.

"No word," some man answered.

Sir Thomas muttered something, then said clearly, "Keep a close watch at the gate. As soon as he arrives send me word and have him brought to the court room."

Roger drew a deep breath. He heard Sir Thomas and the others move away and for a long time, then, there was silence within the donjon. The guard at his feet showed signs of regaining consciousness. Roger tapped him on the head with the side of the axe *Bretwalda*; then, with a piece of cloth torn from his tunic, he bound his mouth.

How long he waited there within that closet with the door

pulled almost shut, Roger never knew. His nerves grew raw with the strain of it. Then suddenly voices again came to him from the hallway and after a moment a body of men stepped through the door. They were half a score in number and most of them were clothed as woodsmen; yet through rents in their tunics Roger could make out the glitter of chain mail and all of them, he saw, wore swords.

The apparent leader was a tall man and there was something familiar about him. Roger scowled through the crack in the door, "I like this not at all," said one of the men bluntly. "I think—"

"Patience, John," answered the tall man "I would hear what he has to offer."

As he spoke, that man turned so that the light from one of the torches fell on his face. Roger's eyes widened. That tall man was the man he had known as Blind David, the fiddler!

More voices came from the hall, and glancing that way Roger saw Sir Thomas Seagrave move into the room. There was a broad, friendly smile on Sir Thomas face. He stepped directly up to the tall man, held out his hand, and said in a deep voice, "Welcome to Dundale, Sir William Wallace."

A SHARP thrill of excitement ran over Roger's body and he stared again at the man he had known as Blind David but whose real name was William Wallace. And thinking back to that fight in the forest he suddenly understood how Wallace had been able to fire the Scots to a point of rebellion. The personal bravery and daring of the man as shown there had captured the imagination of his people. Roger had been inclined to doubt some of the feats attributed to Wallace, but the feeling came to him now that he had been wrong.

"Why did you wish to see me, Sir Thomas?" Wallace asked bluntly.

Sir Thomas shrugged. "Edward is in Scotland. His army is twice the size of yours."

"Suppose that it is," Wallace answered. "In a month he has accomplished little."

"He is in need of supplies. When they arrive it will be a different story—perhaps."

"What do you mean?"

Sir Thomas took Wallace's arm. "Let us go over here where we can talk more privately."

He led Wallace across the room, away from the closet in which Roger was hiding, Roger strained his ears but he could not catch a word of what they were saying. He saw that Sir Thomas was talking earnestly, that Wallace was now and then nodding his head, and he knew the deep bitterness of seeing success almost within his grasp, yet of feeling it slip away.

After a while the two men moved back into the center of the room and in a voice which Roger could hear, Sir Thomas said, "You like it then? You will do it?"

"Aye," said Wallace. " 'Twill save a lot of trouble—if it works."

"It will work," boasted Sir Thomas. "Did I not promise you that I would persuade Cressingham to try to cross Stirling Bridge?"

Wallace nodded. "We should start tonight."

Roger's eyes narrowed. Whatever plan those two had discussed must necessarily, he knew, involve the cooperation of Sir Thomas. And though he did not know what the plan was, he realized suddenly that there was yet another way to block the success of the plan. Sir Thomas stood only a few paces from the closet door, with no men between. Roger's fingers closed around the handle of the axe *Bretwalda*. He shouldered open the door, stepped out into the room.

Immediately he was seen. A stiffening in the attitudes of those men who stood beyond Sir Thomas and William Wallace told him that. Hands jerked toward sword hilts, and the scraping of steel against scabbard sounded through the room. Wallace turned around to face him; and almost at the same time Sir Thomas swung his way.

The puzzled frown on Sir Thomas' face twisted into a look of startled surprise and froze there as he stared at Roger. His lips moved stiffly and in a tone scarcely louder than a whisper, he gasped, "Wilton—you!"

Roger Wilton nodded and there was a mocking light in the depths of his cold, blue eyes.

"Ay, Sir Thomas," he answered. "Though you might have named me *death*!"

He lifted *Bretwalda*.

Sir Thomas drew his sword. It was a long sword and was beautifully ornamented. It had been presented to him, Roger recalled, by King Edward. The blade was of fine Damascus steel. It whipped up into the air like a flash of light, slashed at Roger's head but was turned aside by the handle of the axe.

"Hugh!" Sir Thomas shouted. "Cuthbert! James!"

At that cry several of Sir Thomas' men came running into the room and toward the place where Sir Thomas was standing. Roger saw them and he saw, too, that Wallace and the Scots had drawn back, puzzled perhaps at his sudden appearance, uncertain just what to do. A sound which was half a laugh and half a shout of triumph came from his lips. Again Sir Thomas struck at him with his long sword, struck heavily, desperately; but as before, *Bretwalda* turned the blow aside and the great axe, crashing on down, bit through the armor which covered Sir Thomas' shoulder as easily as if that armor had been made of paper.

A scream, high and shrill, rang through the court room. Sir Thomas staggered back, half turned, fell to the floor; and by the way he fell, Roger knew that he was dead and that whatever evil the man had contemplated was ended. The fight, however, was not ended; for those men to whom Sir Thomas had called, and more men, charging through the door, slashed at him with their swords and drove him back to the door of the closet where he had hidden.

THERE Roger Wilton made his stand. His last stand, he

thought, as he faced those men; for there were so many of them that he knew his time had come. Swords cut at him from right and left. Some broke against the axe *Bretwalda*, some reached him and left a mark of blood where they cut through the skin of his tunic.

A mocking laugh came from his throat and the great axe in his hand moved from side to side with the swiftness of a light blade. None could stand against it.

"John," shouted a ringing voice. "Take the door. You others follow me."

And then of a sudden William Wallace and the Scots moved into the fight; and under that unexpected charge, Sir Thomas' men gave way. Some threw down their arms and flew for the windows. Others cast themselves to the floor. In a scant minute's time, those who had pressed around Roger were gone and in their place stood William Wallace and the group which had come with him.

Roger lowered his axe, stared at the tall, heavy leader of the Scots. There was a glint of admiration in Wallace's eyes, but to Roger they looked stern and sharp.

"We meet under reversed circumstances, Roger Wilton," said Wallace slowly. "My help was tardy, but I trust no more unwelcome than yours the other day."

Roger blinked, astonished at those words.

Wallace was frowning. "Wilton," he said, "I know you for an Englishman, and that under the circumstances you should have slain Sir Thomas is not surprising. But will you tell me what brought you to the forest of Glyncoe?"

" 'Tis a confusing story."

"But I would hear it."

Roger shrugged his shoulders. He told Wallace of Sir Thomas' charges against him, of the king's order.

"With Sir Thomas dead, what will you do?" asked Wallace. "How can you clear your name?"

A deep scowl came to Roger's face. "I thought not of that. I knew only that I must stop him from what he planned to do."

A strange look came into the Scot's eyes. "We could do with more loyalty such as yours in Scotland," he said slowly, and almost to himself. Then in a louder voice he added, "It was Sir Thomas' thought that we might kidnap Edward and the adventure appealed to me. Yet I do not fear a test of arms between our countries."

"And for that service, what did Sir Thomas ask?"

"Only that after our victory I publicly acknowledge his help. I think I know why. 'Twas a strange thing he planned on doing after the defeat of the English."

The man whom Wallace had called John and whom Roger now guessed was John the Graham, close companion and friend to William Wallace, stepped forward and whispered a sentence in the Scot's ears. Wallace nodded, He glanced at Roger and said, "Perhaps we had best leave. I will see you safely from the castle. Our accounts then, I think, will be even,"

Roger leaned forward. "First, what was this thing Sir Thomas planned to do?"

Wallace shrugged. "He planned to announce that the Maid of Norway, the rightful heir to the throne of Scotland, was still alive. He planned to bring out of hiding a girl trained to play that part. 'Twas to see that girl that I played the part of Blind David. You must have seen the girl, too. Remember her?"

THREE hours after the rising of the sun the next morning, Roger Wilton came again to the narrow canyon where he had left John Tuck and Margaret. His wounds had been bound up and none of them were serious.

Ignoring Tuck who rose to greet him as he came up to the shelter near the cave, he turned to face Margaret, and in a voice which was almost harsh, he said, "Tell me, Margaret, where lived you and your father before you came to this forest?"

The girl bit her lips. "I—I do not know."

"Think," Roger commanded. "Do you recall the sea—a ship

on the sea—a man with hair as light as yours who held you in his arms when you became sick?"

A sudden pallor showed below the sun-painted tan on the girl's cheeks. "It is the dream I have had," she said in a whisper, "The dream which—"

Roger Wilton drew a long, shuddering breath. "Six years ago when I came to this forest on a hunt," he said slowly, "you called yourself Margaret. That was once your name, wasn't it?"

"My father changed my name to Marion, long ago. It was after—after I was sick. But—but what difference does all this make? Why are you asking me these questions?"

Roger turned away. He stared out across the canyon with eyes which saw nothing.

"What is it, Roger?" asked John Tuck.

"She is the one," Roger answered. "Sir Thomas was more clever than any of us thought. Everything is now clear. This girl is no mere woodsman's daughter. She is Margaret, the Maid of Norway, heir to the throne of Scotland."

John Tuck caught his breath. "Impossible. The Maid of Norway died in Orkney, eight or nine years ago."

"Nay, Tuck," Roger answered. "She lives. Do you forget that Sir Thomas was one of the men sent to Orkney by the king to meet the Maid of Norway? Well, he did meet her, a little girl sick from an ocean voyage. It would be easy for a man of his parts to substitute the body of another little girl for the Maid, for him to bring her here and keep her here until it suited his purpose to use her."

Both men turned to stare at the girl. There was a puzzled, bewildered, almost frightened look in her eyes.

"Sir Thomas was annoyed when I mentioned to him before the battle of Stirling Bridge that I remembered this girl, and especially when I called her Margaret. He did not want me to see her and talk to her for fear of what I might learn. That is why he lied about me, hoping that the king would keep me imprisoned or perhaps order my death. That is why his men attacked me when we left the king's castle. He brought about the defeat of the English at Stirling Bridge, would have betrayed the king in Edinburgh. With Edward a prisoner or slain, with the English army defeated, he could then have married the Maid of Norway and produced proof as to who she was. Through her he would have become the real ruler of Scotland, for the people of Scotland loved the Maid of Norway, granddaughter of their great king Alexander."

Margaret kept shaking her head as Roger was speaking. When he had finished she reached a hand to his arm and said, "Nay, Roger. None of that is true."

"Look at me, Margaret," Roger insisted.

The girl lifted her head, stared into his eyes. But she could not meet them for long and suddenly she turned her head away and said in a choked voice, "What does any of this matter? Why can I not just go on being Marion, the daughter of Patrick Angus?"

Roger turned to John Tuck. "We must find horses," he said bluntly. "We are riding to Edinburgh. The Maid of Norway can stop a useless war."

John Tuck drew Roger aside. "You have no proof of all this," he objected.

"Yet proof can be found."

"The Maid was pledged to marry Prince Edward of Wales."

"Aye."

" 'Twas my thought that you loved her."

Roger's hands were clenched together at his side. "I do, Tuck," he said slowly. "And I would to God that she were but a woodsman's daughter. Yet the unity of Scotland and England rests in her hands. 'Tis a destiny I cannot alter. Come."

CHAPTER V

IN A SMALL room outside King Edward's quarters in Edinburgh, Roger Wilton was kept waiting for several minutes

while his presence was announced to the king. Margaret and
John Tuck were with him. Theirs had been a silent ride to
Edinburgh. Now and then Roger had heard Margaret and John
Tuck whispering together, but of what he didn't know. And the
girl had had no words for him at all.

She sat now at his side, looking quietly at the floor, but in
her carriage there was the pride of a queen. Roger looked at
her and then looked away. His heart was as a stone and there
was a sickness in his stomach which sent throbbing pains to
his head. Those two days which he had spent with Margaret
deep in Glyncoe forest now seemed very vague and far away.

A guard came to the door and summoned him; and as he
rose and started for the door, Margaret didn't even look up.

There was a smile on King Edward's face as Roger Wilton
came into the room. At the sight of it Wilton halted, for he
had expected no such welcome. Then recovering himself he
moved forward, bowed, and said, "I bring you, Sire, a strange
story and a strange visitor. I beg that you—"

King Edward lifted his hand. "One moment, Sir Roger. May
I tell the story in acknowledgment of a mistake I made?"

"A mistake?" Roger gasped.

The king nodded gravely and then while Roger listened,
amazed, he told of the arrival of messengers from Wallace only
that morning, of prisoners that they brought with them from
the castle Dundale, and of papers which Wallace had sent label-
ing Sir Thomas Seagrave as a traitor.

"I have been very unjust to you," the king added at the end
of his story. "Your banishment have I ended, your estates have
I restored, and to them I have added castle Dundale and the
Glyncoe forest."

Roger Wilton stared at the king and was only dimly conscious of the full meaning of his words. He thought of William
Wallace and wondered what strange impulse had prompted the
man to make such a gesture; then he realized that it was such

impulses which had made the man great and which had endeared him to the heart of Scotland.

"That is all, Sir Roger," said the king.

Roger Wilton shook his head. "There is but one thing more, Sire. The Maid of Norway lives."

As he spoke those words a startled silence fell over the room. King Edward straightened, lifted a hand to his forehead. Others in the room stared at him.

"Impossible," said the king finally. "She died in Orkney."

"Nay, Sire. She did not die in Orkney."

The king moistened his lips. "If this be true, Wilton, our war with Scotland is at an end. She will marry the prince and when he becomes king, all this land will become one united kingdom. Where is this person you call the Maid of Norway?"

"She came with me," Roger answered. "She awaits in the outer room."

"Bring her in."

Roger turned to the door but others were ahead of him. He stood back and waited, and could not look at the door. There was a murmur of excited whispering in the room, then a sudden hush.

Roger looked up, stared toward the door. A woman had just come into the room. She wore the clothing which Margaret had worn, yet this woman looked like no one he had ever seen. Her hair was dark and there was a thick, sticky look about it. Her face was dirty and its features were screwed into a haggard, vacant expression.

"What foolishness is this?" roared the king. "Sir Roger, explain this joke!"

Roger strode toward the woman. Until he was close to her he would not believe that this was Margaret, yet he saw suddenly that it was. Into her hair had been pressed a sticky substance which hid its golden color and dirt soiled her face. But the twisted features and the vacant stare were of her own making.

"Margaret!" he said sharply.

THE GIRL looked at him and laughed coarsely. She lifted a hand to her head, scratched it vigorously, scratched her side, stooped over and scratched her knee.

Somewhere a man started laughing. Another began to laugh and then another and presently the room was filled with roars of mirth. Roger glanced at the king. Edward, he saw, was laughing with the rest.

"The Maid of Norway!" he gasped. "The Maid of Norway! And what a maid! Sir Roger, I deserved this. I blame you not. But please take her from my sight before I forget how funny she looks. Were the prince here I fear he would not see the joke."

With a mixture of emotions which he could not analyze, Roger took the girl's arm and led her from the room. Sounds of the laughter followed him out of the building and down the cobbled street. John Tuck joined them and there was a deep twinkle in the old woodsman's eyes.

After they had gone a ways a quiet voice at his side said, "Roger, are you awfully angry at me?"

Roger made no answer.

"I did not wish to be the Maid of Norway," continued the quiet voice. "And I think now that you will never be able to resurrect me again. People will laugh at the thought."

Roger bit his lips, knowing that the girl spoke the truth. Rumors that the Maid of Norway still lived, however, were to continue for a long time in Scotland.

"What did you do to your hair?" Roger asked bluntly.

"Tuck found some berries to dye it. We fixed it up when you went in to see the king."

Roger stopped, faced the girl. "Margaret," he said earnestly, "have I been wrong? Are you but the daughter of a woodsman?"

"And if I were?"

Swiftly he said:

"Still would I love you, only in that case—"

Margaret smiled. She said, "Come, Roger. Over by yonder house men are staring at us."

And so they moved on, Roger, Tuck and the girl, and as they made their way down the street Roger suddenly realized that Margaret hadn't given him a direct answer to his question, He wondered whether he would ever know for sure just whether or not she was the Maid of Norway. A little farther on he decided that it made no difference. He had offered her a kingdom. She had turned it down. But there was still another kingdom he could offer her—Wilton Hall and Dundale.

His shoulders straightened and a smile came to his lips.

"We can find quarters here," said John Tuck suddenly.

Roger Wilton nodded. "And water to wash Margaret's hair. I like not dark haired women."

IX

THE LONG JOURNEY

In that terrible year of the Black Death another Wilton returns to find his home despoiled. And to him comes this knowledge: The man who wields Bretwalda shall see great victory... and great defeat.

CHAPTER I

THE HUGE BULK of a merchant vessel loomed up suddenly through the thick fog of the early morning. Tattered canvas dangled from its three masts. At its wheel was no helmsman, on its decks no visible figures.

The captain of the ship from Le Havre gave a warning shout, then bawled an order to his crew; and so abruptly was the course of the ship from Le Havre changed, that Sir Hubert Wilton was thrown to his knees. He scrambled at once to his feet, made his way to the rail and stared at the derelict vessel.

It wallowed past in a choppy sea and a moment later was blanketed by the fog.

"Another ship of the dead," said a voice at Sir Hubert's shoulder. "That makes three which we have sighted,"

Sir Hubert looked around. Near him stood the tall, cowled figure of the Franciscan monk who had begged passage on this ship which he had chartered. The monk was thin, stern of face; yet there was a look of compassion in his eyes.

"Aye, that makes three," Sir Hubert nodded. "When think you that the great pestilence will end?"

"When God wills it," said the monk quietly.

Sir Hubert drew a ragged breath. There was no comfort for him in the monk's words.

It was now the early spring of 1349. Three years before in the battle of Cressy, more than thirty thousand men had been killed; yet for one who had died in that battle, a hundred had

*The mighty weapon swung from side to side, making a wall
of steel around him; and none could stand against it.*

been claimed by the great pestilence which had swept across
France from Italy; where, it was said, fully half of the population
lay dead.

In places, entire towns and villages had been wiped out
within only a few weeks. To what extent the great pestilence
had touched England, Sir Hubert did not know; but the fears
which he had built up in his mind caused him more torture
than the wound which had held him in France after most of
King Edward's army had returned home.

"Land ahead!" called the helmsman.

Sir Hubert Wilton turned away from the rail. He was a tall,
broad-shouldered man of about thirty.

The plate armor which he usually wore had been laid aside
in favor of a lighter coat-of-mail; such a change being neces-
sitated by the wound which had almost taken his life.

His face was thin, sharp-featured, with high cheek bones

and wide spaced blue eyes. Blond hair, almost golden in color, fell to his shoulders. At his side he wore a long sword and strapped to his back was a heavy axe.

The ship from Le Havre moved slowly into a port which was almost deserted and from the deck of the vessel Sir Hubert stared into the empty streets of the town. The fog had lifted a little and beyond the town he could make out the green hills of England.

For three years, now, he had been looking forward to such a sight, and on many an evening before and after the battle of Cressy and during the long siege of Calais he had dreamed of the delight he would know in returning home. Yet as the ship was made fast to one of the docks, cold, icy fingers gripped his heart.

He did not have to be told, now, that the great pestilence had reached England. He could see that in the silence of the harbor and in the quiet of the town. For this was Malcombe Regis, one of the greatest ports of England, always in the past a place teeming with activity, its waterfront lined with ships, its streets crowded with people.

SIR HUBERT paid to the captain the sum agreed upon for the journey, then, swinging over the rail, he dropped down to the dock. The Franciscan followed him, stared up at the town and said slowly, "It was through this port that the great pestilence reached England, brought here on a ship from the East."

Sir Hubert bit his lips. He started up toward the town and as he moved through its deserted streets the feeling came to him that he was in a strange country, that this couldn't be England.

His eyes, jerking from side to side, caught the vision of a face beyond the pane of a window in one of the houses; and turning abruptly that way, he knocked on the door.

"Away!" cried a voice from within the house. "Away! Away!"

"Where can I find a horse?" Sir Hubert shouted.

"There be no horses in Malcombe Regis," came the answer.

On up ahead a door banged open and from it staggered a man. He was grasping a swollen throat with his hands and horrible noises were struggling from his lips.

The skin of his face was flushed and in several places there were black spots. The man stumbled, sprawled to the ground, rolled over, got to his knees. A froth of blood showed at his lips.

Sir Hubert shuddered. He wiped a hand across his face and the hand came away moist with perspiration. The Franciscan monk hurried past him, stopped at the kneeling man's side, bent over. In three swift strides, Sir Hubert reached the monk. He grasped the Franciscan by the shoulder, jerked him away.

"You fool!" he said harshly. "There is nothing you can do for him. If you touch him, you too will be stricken by the pestilence."

The Franciscan looked steadily at Sir Hubert. "The man needs me," he said quietly. "Wait here."

Sir Hubert dropped his hand. He watched the Franciscan bend over the victim of the dreaded pestilence, lift him into his arms, and carry him back into the house from which he had fled.

Sir Hubert waited, frowning, and when the monk reappeared he instinctively backed away; for all men knew that to touch a victim of the pestilence, or even to catch the breath of an afflicted person, meant death.

The Franciscan, however, did not seem to notice his fear. "Come," he said, turning up the street. "We will find our horses waiting in a pasture behind yonder house."

Sir Hubert stared at the monk curiously. He followed him on up the street and around a house with shuttered windows. Tied in a pasture back of the place were two saddled horses.

They were large and strong looking and seemed to have been well cared for.

"Whose are they?" Sir Hubert demanded.

"Ours," said the Franciscan. "Did I not tell you?"

Sir Hubert mounted one of the horses and turned north out

of the town. He was not surprised, on looking back, to see that the Franciscan was following him; but staring again to the north he soon forgot all about the man.

There were but few travelers on the road. Now and then Sir Hubert passed a heavy, lumbering cart, piled high with the provisions of some family which hoped to escape the pestilence by moving. He rode through several deserted villages and toward evening skirted a large, walled town. Outside the walls of that town a number of men were digging a wide, deep trench. Sir Hubert stopped to rest his horse and stared at the diggers soberly.

"Tonight," said the Franciscan, riding up to his side, "they will bring out the bodies of the dead and bury them there."

Sir Hubert nodded. He had viewed similar scenes in France.

"We can stop for the night in yonder forest," the monk continued.

"You can stop," said Sir Hubert bluntly. "I will ride on."

"But your wound."

SIR HUBERT frowned. He could not recall having mentioned his wound to the monk. "I will ride on," he repeated. And then when the monk said nothing, he added, "For three years I have been in France. I left behind me at Wilton Hall my bride of scarcely a year. Shortly after I left a son was born to her. I have never seen my son, never held him in my arms. In view of what we have seen, in view of what those men are doing over there, can you not understand my impatience to hurry on?"

"I can understand it, Sir Hubert," said the monk; "but—"

His voice broke off and into his eyes came the same compassionate expression which Sir Hubert had seen there as the man had stared after the derelict ship. A sudden stab of fear knifed through him.

"But what, man?" he shouted hoarsely. "But what?"

The Franciscan looked away. "One day, more or less, can make little difference."

Sir Hubert forgot that the Franciscan had touched a man

stricken with the pestilence. He grasped the monk's arm. "Tell me what you know," he grated. "Tell me what you know!"

The Franciscan did not reply for a moment. When he did it was to say, "Come on, then. We will find fresh horses waiting for us at the edge of the forest."

All throughout that night did Sir Hubert and his companion ride north toward Stafford Forest and Wilton Hall and by noon of the next day they came to the edge of a broad clearing which sloped gently down to the river Avon.

There on the banks of the river Sir Hubert could see the spire of the church in which he had been christened and knighted. A village was clustered about it, a village of narrow, crooked streets and of low, thatch-roofed houses.

To the left, across wide fields, stood Wilton Hall, his ancestral home. It was a low structure of grey stone with four square towers, one at each corner. No wall or moat surrounded the hall but there was a look of strength about the building.

Sir Hubert stared at it for a breathless moment, and all the apprehension which had been growing within him for months suddenly concentrated itself into a sharp, agonizing fear. He leaned abruptly forward in his saddle and urged his horse to a gallop.

As he neared the hall he saw the great wide doors swing open; but no Lady Marian came running out to greet him. Instead, a mass of armed churls appeared in the entrance, some of them partially armored, some bearing swords, some spears, a few with axes. At the sight of them a cold chill swept over Sir Hubert's body. He stopped his horse near the door to the hall, swung stiffly to the ground and turned to face those men.

One of them, a huge, wide-shouldered fellow with a shock of red hair and a tangled beard, stepped forward and ordered bluntly, "Stay back. You come from the south. We can take no more in here."

"Who are you?" Sir Hubert demanded hoarsely. "By what right are you here?"

The red-headed man laughed coarsely.

"We be men of Bristol," he boasted. "Free men! If you would challenge our right to be here, come ahead."

Sir Hubert made no answer. At that moment he was incapable of clear thought. A vision of Lady Marian, his wife, appeared before his eyes and a black rage swept over him. He lifted one hand to the axe strapped to his shoulder, loosened it, swung it free.

It was a heavy axe, for both head and handle were of steel, and its blade was a full six hands broad. Many there were who wondered that anyone could swing it. Above the cutting edge was engraven the name *Bretwalda* and four blood-red jewels were set above that name. They glistened dully in the light of the midday sun.

"He shows fight," muttered the man with the red hair.

There was a general forward movement from those who stood in the doorway. A few brandished their weapons threateningly.

CHAPTER II

SIR HUBERT WILTON spoke not a word. He swung the axe *Bretwalda* above his head, charged toward the door slashing from left to right. The sword in the hands of the red-headed man was snapped off as if it had been made of wood; and *Bretwalda* bit deep into his shoulder, jerked away, and cut down another man who had come rushing forward.

Angered shouts came from those in the doorway and several of them came at him desperately. With a hoarse cry, Sir Hubert sprang to meet them, smashing out with *Bretwalda* from one side to another. He pushed on, unaware of the press of men, hardly conscious of their screams as they fought now to get out of his way, to escape the heavy blows of his great axe.

Through that door he went and on into the wide hall which lay beyond it. Half a score of the men, as yet unharmed, broke under his attack and fled for the windows, sprawled through them to the outside. Sir Hubert let them go.

He lowered *Bretwalda* to the floor, scarcely noting the wreckage which had been done to this place which had been his home. Only one thing was on his mind.

"Marian!" he called "Marian! Marian!"

The high walls threw back the echo of his voice but there was no other answer.

"Marian!" he called again. "Marian!"

There was still no reply.

Sir Hubert glanced around. In the doorway he saw the Franciscan monk bending over one of the men who had been wounded in the fight.

As he stared at him the Franciscan looked up and said quietly, "She is not here, Sir Hubert. She has been gone—for a long time."

Sir Hubert sucked in a ragged breath. His hands tightened on the axe *Bretwalda*. "If you know so much," he said grimly, "tell me where she is. Tell me what has happened to her, to my son."

The monk shook his head sadly. "That I cannot do."

Sir Hubert turned away, hesitated, then swung back to face the Franciscan. "Who are you?" he demanded. "What is your name?"

"I have no name," said the monk slowly. "Call me—Friend."

"Friend?"

"Aye, Sir Hubert...."

After a quick search of Wilton Hall, Sir Hubert turned to the village on the bank of the river Avon, and there almost the first person that he saw was old Richard Tuck.

A tall, gaunt man was Richard Tuck, with long, matted gray hair and sharp, dark eyes. He came of a family which had served the Wiltons for generations and which had served them well.

Sir Hubert, however, forgot that when he saw the old man,

and rushing up to him he grasped him by the shoulders. He heard Richard Tuck cry out his name and there was a sound of pleasure in the old man's voice; yet that too, escaped him.

"The Lady Marian?" he demanded gruffly. "Where is she? What has happened to her and to my son? Answer me, Tuck. Answer me."

The old man blinked at him in some surprise. "But—but did you not meet her? Did she not come to you, Sir Hubert?"

"Come to me?" Sir Hubert gasped.

"Aye," nodded Richard Tuck. "Your messenger reached the Hall more than three weeks ago. Lady Marian left at once. She would not even wait until the next day."

Sir Hubert moistened his lips. "I sent no messenger, Tuck."

"You sent no messenger?"

"Nay. Who was the man? What was the message?"

Old Richard Tuck scowled. He said slowly, "I was not at the Hall when it came but I heard of it from Alan, my son. The word was that you had arrived at Hastings, but that you were too sorely wounded to come on to Wilton Hall."

"And the man who brought that message?"

"Alan called him Sir Guy de Froissart."

A SLAP in the face by the hand of Richard Tuck could not have been any more surprising to Sir Hubert. He dropped his hands from the old man's shoulders, stepped back, repeated that name under his breath.

"You did not send him?" asked Richard Tuck.

"Nay, never such a one as him," Sir Hubert breathed.

He lifted his hand to the wound in his shoulder, the wound which had delayed his return to England, and his mind went back to a certain night in the streets of Calais, when, alone and unattended, he had been attacked by a half score of men-at-arms.

In spite of the darkness he had recognized them and had recognized their leader, Sir Mortimer Balsham. Sir Mortimer had died in the fight which had followed—or so he had thought until just now.

"Sir Guy de Froissart," he said slowly, "was the friend and boon companion of Sir Mortimer Balsham, the man to whom I owe the wound which delayed my return. He did not know Lady Marian, but Sir Mortimer did. In this crazy world where the living are dead, even the dead might come back to life."

Richard Tuck laid a hand on his arm. "My son Alan and those who went with the Lady Marian would have protected her, Sir Hubert, as long as they could draw at breath."

"Aye, Tuck."

"And when she thought you wounded, nothing that I might say would have kept her here."

Sir Hubert nodded.

"When those men came and took possession of Wilton Hall," the old man continued, "there were not enough men left in the village to put them out."

"Which way did the Lady Marian go?"

"To the south."

"And you have not heard from Alan since they left?"

"Nay."

Sir Hubert nodded. He turned around and started back toward the Hall; but before he had covered more than half of the distance, Richard Tuck and four others overtook him.

All were armed, Sir Hubert noted, and three of the men carried packs on their backs.

"We would go with you, Sir Hubert," Tuck stated simply.

"Go with me? Where?"

"In your search for Lady Marian."

Sir Hubert shook his head. "My way lies to the south, through a region made desolate by the great pestilence. Here you are free of it. Perhaps it will never reach this far."

"Yet we will go," said Tuck.

The other four men all nodded and as he looked into their

faces Sir Hubert was aware of a thickness of the throat. What help they might be he did not know; certainly all of them were too old to be of much help in case of a fight with men of the type de Froissart would have around him.

Yet he knew that he could not send them back. These men had loved Lady Marian for kindnesses too many to be counted.

"Come, then," he said gruffly. "We will start at once."

In the stables near the Hall, Sir Hubert found six horses already saddled and waiting to be mounted; and at the time his mind was so clouded with other thoughts that such a fact did not occur to him as strange. He selected one of the horses, swung into the saddle, and turned back to the south.

THEY camped that night in the depths of Stafford Forest, near a clear, bubbling spring; and while some of the men prepared food and others cut boughs to make beds, Sir Hubert sat close to the spring and thought back to the last time he had been here.

Marian had been with him, then, and they had made a camp here, together. Over to one side of the spring was a pile of rocks which he had built up and over which he had arranged a bower. He had laughingly called the place her throne and had named her Queen.

In the early dawn, he recalled, Marian had awakened first and in a pool a little way down from the spring, she had been bathing her feet when he found her.

Sir Hubert glanced that way now, stiffened. The sound of splashing water came to him. He got abruptly to his feet, strode toward the pool, stretched out his hand and pushed aside the bushes which screened it; then stared amazed at the sight which met his eyes.

Standing in the pool, entirely naked, was the man who had named himself Friend, the Franciscan monk. In the pale light from the stars his body seemed a silvery white. Now and then he would stoop over and scoop up handsful of water which he poured on his chest and arms.

After a while he stepped out of the pool and dried his body with a square of cloth which he took from a pack nearby. That finished, he donned clean linen and then his cowled robe; and while Sir Hubert still stared at him in some amazement, the monk washed the clothing which he had removed from his body before the bath and spread it out over the bushes to dry.

Sir Hubert stepped suddenly forward. "How came you here?" he demanded abruptly.

The Franciscan looked up. "I rode with you."

"I saw you not," said Sir Hubert.

"You did not once look around."

Sir Hubert scowled. He felt uncomfortable and was not sure of the reason.

"Where are you going?" he demanded.

"For a while," said the Franciscan, "my path follows yours. After that, I know not."

Richard Tuck joined them and Sir Hubert noted that the old man did not seem surprised at the presence of the Franciscan. "The food is ready," he stated bluntly.

They all moved over to the place where the camp had been made and Sir Hubert saw that seven beds had been prepared.

He called Tuck aside. "You know this monk?" he asked frowning.

"Friend? Aye, Sir Hubert."

"Where did you meet him?"

"He joined us just as we left the Hall. From the way he spoke of you, I know that he came with you from France; yet I knew him before that."

"When, Tuck?"

The old man looked puzzled. "I—I am not just sure. Perhaps it was long ago in my youth."

Sir Hubert glanced over at Friend. The Franciscan was seated near two of the other men, was eating slowly. He had hardly touched his meat but seemed to be making his meal mostly of herbs he must have found in the forest.

He looked up at Sir Hubert and smiled and Sir Hubert noticed that when he smiled all of the sternness seemed to be gone from his face.

"We must be away before dawn," Sir Hubert said to Tuck. "Come. Let us eat."

CHAPTER III

THE WEEKS WHICH followed were like a nightmare to Sir Hubert Wilton. He and those with him journeyed to the south coast of England, to Hastings, Brighton, Portsmouth, Southampton and Bournemouth. They passed through Salisbury, Winchester, Aldershot, and London.

At times they made their camp at the side of the road, at times in forests, at other times in some deserted house in one of the towns. And from any to whom they could get close enough to speak they asked information as to Sir Guy de Froissart or the Lady Marian.

This England, which Sir Hubert saw on that journey, was an England such as he had never dreamed might exist.

The green hills and the broad forests were as he had known them in his youth, but all else was changed. Many towns and villages were totally deserted, save for the decaying bodies of the dead. Fields and cattle were untended. Serfs, who had been bound to the soil, were bound to it no longer. Fear had loosened the chains which held them.

Some had thronged to seaport towns, hoping to escape the great pestilence by boarding some ship. Others had fled north toward Scotland. Still others roved the country in marauding bands.

Here and there Wilton and his men came across groups of people who called themselves Penitents, who wore somber garments marked with a red cross, and who marched through the streets of the cities, singing a mournful dirge and calling upon the Lord for forgiveness. Such people took vows of poverty and turned over all their possessions to the charity of their order.

London he found a house of death, a city of fear-stricken, bewildered people. Bodies lay untended on the streets sometimes for many days and all pretense of law and order had been forgotten.

Outside the walls of the town, a new graveyard of thirteen acres had been provided near Charterhouse, and there in great trenches the dead were buried, as fast as men could get to them.

In Bristol, the dead exceeded the living. In the meadow near London which was called Runnymede and where the Magna Carta had been signed more than a hundred years before, Sir Hubert and his men made their camp after leaving London. And there, that night, Friend called him aside and leading him to the bank of the Thames, sank down on the grass and looked back toward London.

"What think you, Sir Hubert, of all you have seen?" asked the Franciscan.

Sir Hubert drew a deep breath. "I am wondering if this is not the end of the world, if any shall survive."

" 'Tis not the end of the world, Sir Hubert, but rather the end of an era," said the monk.

"What mean you, Friend?"

"I mean that no more will men be bound to the soil, made to work for a lord and master. All of the petty kingdoms which have been built up here in England are at an end, this system of life which you have known will be changed. There will be a greater equality among people, a better life for all."

There was a deeply serious note to the Franciscans voice. Sir Hubert stared at him thoughtfully.

This monk still puzzled him. Hardly a day had passed but that he had stopped somewhere to care for one of the afflicted; yet though he handled their bodies, he himself had been untouched by the great pestilence.

Sir Hubert leaned forward. "Let me see your palms, Friend," he commanded.

THE FRANCISCAN held out his hands. They were long and bony. Sir Hubert stared at them but did not see the marks for which he was looking, the scars which might have been made by nails.

"In what way think you that I am different from others?" asked the monk.

"You have no fear of the pestilence."

The Franciscan shrugged. "For that matter, a man can die but once. Nay, in what other ways am I different?"

Sir Hubert frowned. "You eat but little, and rarely ever of meat which is our main item of food."

"And how else?"

"You bathe your body each day, continually wash your clothing. You drink only from the flask which you always carry. What is in that flask?"

"Water, Sir Hubert."

"Water?"

"Aye, water which has been boiled and so is pure."

Sir Hubert shook his head. He couldn't believe that things so simple were of any importance.

"After the great pestilence has passed," Friend continued, "men will learn the importance of keeping themselves clean, of keeping clean the houses and cities in which they live, of burying their garbage rather than throwing it outside the town walls or into a stream from which others drink."

Sir Hubert shrugged. Thoughts of Marian and of the son he had never seen still tortured his mind. He could not long keep his attention on anything else.

Only the day before he had stood at the side of an open trench near the wall of London, near where laborers were covering the bodies of the dead. In that trench he had seen the figure of a youth about three years old, a golden haired youth who might have been his son. Had not Friend's hand restrained him he might have thrown himself into that trench, more closely to examine the boy's face. The memory still was with him.

"Where shall I turn, Friend?" he asked abruptly. "Where will I find Marian and the boy?"

"In the north, Sir Hubert."

"In the north! Why did you not tell me before?"

The Franciscan smiled. "Would you have listened to me?"

Sir Hubert knew that he would not have listened. He doubted now that it was wise to turn to the north; yet at the same time he knew that he would do it.

"Each of us," said Friend slowly, "has some task to fulfill in the world, yet each of us must do his task in his own way, and not as another would have it done. I have gone with you, Sir Hubert, almost as far as I can. In a little time I must be gone."

Sir Hubert hardly heard the words of the Franciscan. He was standing erect, staring to the north. The passing of the weeks had taken their toll in his strength but he was unaware of it. His face had grown gaunt and haggard and there were deep circles under his eyes.

He said under his breath, "Marian, Marian, I am coming." And it seemed to him that wind whispered an answer.

He knew the spirit of Marian, knew that she would never let herself live to suffer indignities at the hands of men like Guy de Froissart or Sir Mortimer, had he escaped death.

He knew, too, that had she managed to flee from her captors, there was but little chance that she and the boy might have escaped the pestilence.

Yet that night for the first time in many weeks he slept soundly, untroubled by any dreams. And he awoke the next morning, miraculously refreshed and ready for the long journey north.

CHAPTER IV

FAR TO THE NORTH was Newcastle-upon-Tyne, a sprawling village stretched out along the banks of a narrow, deep river. There, many centuries before, the Romans had built a fort to guard the eastern end of the wall which Hadrian had built across Briton.

Robert of Normandy, son of William the Conqueror, had chosen this town as the site of one of his castles; and a hundred years later, Henry II had erected still another, a massive structure with walls eighteen feet thick and with turrets which reached more than a hundred feet into the air.

Just what month it was when Sir Hubert Wilton and his companions reached Newcastle, he didn't know. He had lost all track of time.

The road north had been crowded with many travelers, trudging Penitents, bands of serfs, companies of mounted soldiers, all of them fleeing from the great pestilence. Many of them were fleeing in vain for it had already spread into Scotland; yet they couldn't have known that.

Newcastle had been almost deserted by the people who had once lived there, yet those traveling to the north had repopulated it. Those staying there now kept for the most part to their houses.

Only the Penitents thronged the streets, marching back and forth with their eyes fixed on the ground, singing their mournful dirge.

Sir Hubert and his companions made their camp near the town and at midday turned to wander the streets just as they had in many another place, searching the faces of those they saw for a glimpse of the features of one of the men who had accompanied Lady Marian from Wilton Hall, stopping to question any who would talk to them concerning a man who called himself Sir Guy de Froissart.

Sir Hubert felt no different on this day from the way he had

felt on any other. There was nothing to warn him that this day
would be different from the rest. At the end of two weary hours,
he and his companions came to the market place, an almost
deserted square in the center of the town. To one side of it there
was a marching group of the Penitents. Sir Hubert turned that
way, stared at them as they passed.

Behind him sounded the clatter of hoofbeats as a group of
mounted men rode across the square. They were heading toward
a street whose entrance was blocked by the marchers; and of
necessity they stopped.

"Out of the way, fools!" commanded a deep, heavy voice.
"Out of the way!"

The Penitents seemed unaware of the command. They
marched on unmindful of it. Sir Hubert turned around to stare
at the mounted men. There were about a score of them, all well
armored and heavily armed.

The man who seemed to be the leader wore black armor
similar to the armor worn by the Black Prince. He was of huge
stature and his helmet was closed so that Sir Hubert couldn't
see his face. Near him, however, was a knight with opened visor.
That man's head was turned toward Sir Hubert. His face was
thin and dark-skinned and a scar was visible on his forehead.

As Sir Hubert glimpsed that face a chill of excitement ran
over his body and his lips formed the words, "Guy de Froissart!
At last! At last!"

He reached up to his shoulder, loosened the axe *Bretwalda*,
stepped toward the body of mounted men, and then with a
loud shout he was among them, swinging *Bretwalda* from side
to side, cutting at the horses, disabling them so that the men
would have to dismount or be thrown.

The screams of the wounded animals rose above the surprised
shouts of the men. Several of the horses started rearing and
plunging and unseated their riders, other horses fell to the
ground more seriously hurt, two of them pinning their riders
beneath them.

The churning hoofs had stirred up a thick cloud of dust and through it Sir Hubert caught sight of Guy de Froissart. The man had drawn his sword and was staring from side to side, bewildered.

"Here, de Froissart!" Sir Hubert yelled. "Have you no memory of me?"

Guy de Froissart stared at him and Sir Hubert saw a look of recognition come into his eyes. "Wilton!" he gasped. "Hubert Wilton!"

Sir Hubert moved forward. "Where did you take Lady Marian, de Froissart?" he demanded. "What have you done with her?"

The dark-faced man laughed harshly. "She is dead, Wilton. As dead as you are going to be in another minute."

Others of the men who had been unseated from their horses or who had dismounted now joined Guy de Froissart, their swords bared and ready.

Out of the corner of his eyes Sir Hubert saw Richard Tuck and his other companions running forward.

Like him, they wore only chain mail, and none of them, he knew, were adept in the art of fighting, They were foresters, plowmen. And they were all of them well past middle age.

"Back, Tuck! Back!" he shouted.

HE HAD no time to say more. With angry shouts, de Froissart and those with him rushed forward. He jerked up the axe *Bretwalda*, slashed out from left to right. Sharp, heavy, death-dealing blows were those which met that attack. Back of them was all the stored-up bitterness of weeks of fruitless searching.

The men of Guy de Froissart could not stand up against him. Those who did not go down backed quickly away, turned to flee. But they could not escape that way, either, for by now Tuck and the others had come up.

Sir Hubert heard Tuck's deep, shouting voice, heard the high, pitched cries of Gilbert Cuxham, one of his other companions.

He saw Guy de Froissart swing away and rush at Richard Tuck and he sprang after the man.

"Turn, de Froissart," he shouted wildly. "You have an appointment with death!"

Guy de Froissart jerked around. He swung his sword at Sir Hubert's head but the axe *Bretwalda* was in the way, turned it aside, and then cut on down through the man's helmet to a point midway between his shoulders.

As abruptly as it had started, the fight was over. Sir Hubert wiped off the blade of his axe, stared down at the body of de Froissart and then around at the other silent figures which lay on the ground. He saw with some surprise that none of his companions had been hurt.

Friend stood a little to one side, not far from Richard Tuck. The Franciscan's hands were clasped in front of him and Sir Hubert had never before seen so stern a look as was now on his face.

Sir Hubert glanced once more at the figures on the ground. None of them wore black armor. The man in the black armor must have escaped; and though he had not seen his face, Sir Hubert had the sudden feeling that the real leader of these men had been Sir Mortimer Balsham.

Ever since he had learned that it was Guy de Froissart who had taken Lady Marian from Wilton Hall he had been of the opinion that Sir Mortimer must still be living and must be the man who had planned the abduction.

Friend had walked over to two of the slain horses and from a pack tied to one of them he had taken several massive books. Sir Hubert joined Tuck. "Where was Friend while we fought these men?" he demanded abruptly.

"Why, right at my side," Tuck answered.

"Nay," said Gilbert Cuxham, joining them. "He fought with me."

"And what did he use as a weapon?" asked Sir Hubert.

"A long-bladed sword which flashed like silver."

"He has no sword."

"Yet he had one during the fight," said Tuck. "Had it not been for that blade of his, I would not be here."

"Nor I," Cuxham nodded.

Sir Hubert drew a deep breath. He stared again at Friend. The Franciscan was studying the books he had found. He seemed to be completely absorbed in the task.

"One of these men still lives," said Tuck suddenly.

Sir Hubert turned toward the old man, saw him bending over one of the figures on the ground. He moved that way, stooped over the man. "He in the black armor! Who was he?" Sir Hubert demanded.

"Sir Mortimer—Balsham," came the weak answer.

"And where will I find him?"

A cunning look came into the man's eyes. "At Straleigh Castle—to the north."

Sir Hubert bent lower. "Have you ever heard of the Lady Marian?"

The man attempted some answer but what it was Sir Hubert couldn't hear; for a sudden flow of blood choked the man's throat.

"He is dead now," said Tuck.

Sir Hubert straightened. He recalled that Guy de Froissart had boasted that Lady Marian was no longer alive; but he had a feeling that the man had lied. Now that he knew that Sir Mortimer Balsham lived and that he could be found at Straleigh Castle, he had the conviction that his long search was about at an end.

"We ride on north," he said grimly. "Have you ever heard of Straleigh Castle, Tuck?"

"Nay, Sir Hubert."

"I can show you the way," said the voice of the Franciscan.

"Show me then," Sir Hubert answered. And then frowning, he asked, "Where is your sword, Friend?"

The Franciscan did not seem to have heard him. He had turned away and had started back toward the camp where they had left their horses.

Clouds swept over the sky in the late afternoon and with the coming of night a heavy rain started falling. It was accompanied by a sharp, chilling wind and by jagged streaks of lightning. With his chin sunk against his chest and his head lowered against the storm, Sir Hubert pushed on. Friend rode beside him and the others followed.

After several hours of such travel, Friend pulled up his horse and called to Sir Hubert, "We must stop here until morning."

Sir Hubert tried to probe the darkness with his eyes, but could see nothing. He had no idea where they were save that it was north of Newcastle.

"Why stop?" he shouted back. "Could we get more wet than we are?"

Friend made no answer but turned from the road, and after a moment's hesitation Sir Hubert followed him. In but a little way they came to a low-roofed house. Friend dismounted and called to Sir Hubert and the others to do likewise and when they had done so, a man came out of the house and took charge of their horses.

CHAPTER V

THERE WAS A warm fire burning on the hearth inside and its light brightened the whole room. Sir Hubert and his companions gathered around it. The man who had taken charge of their horses came back and brought them food and blankets; and the men took off their wet clothing and wrapped in blankets, sat near to the fire and ate a belated supper.

It occurred to Sir Hubert to wonder how Friend had found this place in the darkness, how he had come to it so unerringly, who the man was who had cared for their horses and for them without asking any questions.

Then because the search for Marian overshadowed every other thing in his mind, he wondered how much farther they had to travel before they would reach Straleigh Castle, and turning to Friend, he asked him.

"It lies just ahead," said the Franciscan.

"Why then did we stop?" Sir Hubert demanded. "Tonight would have been a good night to surprise the guards."

"You will not need to surprise the guards. Any who come can enter Straleigh Castle. It is leaving it which may be difficult."

Sir Hubert scowled. "What know you of the place?"

"You saw me examining those books in the market place at Newcastle?" asked Friend.

"Aye. What were they?"

"Books of manorial records, with many a new entry recording the transfer of lands."

"But what of it?"

The stern expression was back on Friend's face. "Sir Hubert," he said slowly, "do you recall the story of the Knight Templars?"

Sir Hubert nodded. "I have heard of the order."

"The organization," Friend continued quietly, "was founded in the Holy Land after the First Crusade, in which marched one of your forefathers, by name, Sir Henry Wilton. It was founded by nine men who were tired of the bloody, pointless fighting in the Holy Land, of the struggle for loot, of the degeneration of the cause.

"They pooled their wealth, meaning to use it for charity, and they took vows to lead simple, chaste lives. With the passing of time the organization spread and grew strong. More and more men joined it, turning their wealth and possessions into a common fund.

"And at last the order known as the Knight Templars was so strong that no king in Europe dared make war without consulting them. They owned the very thrones on which the kings sat, the men the kings commanded. Such a condition continued until fifty years ago when the Knight Templars were overthrown by a general uprising of the people."

"What has all this to do with Sir Mortimer Balsham?"

"Those records of the manorial courts which I examined would give you that answer. Sir Mortimer is striving to emulate the Templars."

"How?"

"He is the man named as the chosen head of the Order of the Penitents. All those who have been frightened into joining that order have been made to give away all worldly possessions, assigning land and property to the order. It is so registered in those manorial records. Out of the suffering of a deluded people, Sir Mortimer is building himself a great kingdom."

"How like the man," Sir Hubert growled.

"This great pestilence will pass," Friend continued, staring into the fire, "and a new order of things will follow. The Penitents will disappear unless some man who controls all the wealth which was once theirs steps forth to keep the order alive. It is because Sir Mortimer is such a man that you must go to Straleigh Castle."

Sir Hubert shook his head. "I go to Straleigh Castle for another reason—my wife and son."

For several moments the Franciscan was silent; then glancing over at Sir Hubert, he said quietly, "Our time together, Sir Hubert, has almost run out. After I am gone, forget not the things I have told you."

Sir Hubert was hardly aware of the man's words. He sat looking into the fire, thinking of the morrow, fearing, yet impatient for what it might bring.

SEVERAL leagues north from the cottage where they had spent the night the road came suddenly to a wide meadow, and across that meadow, in the shadow of the towering hills which lay beyond, was Straleigh Castle, a massive structure of gray rock and stone.

The sun was three hours high when Sir Hubert first sighted it. He drew rein and stared at the place thoughtfully. A winding road led across the meadow and up to the drawbridge which was lowered over the moat.

Sunlight shimmered against the armor of the men there on guard. How many men there would be Sir Hubert didn't know; but considering the story Friend had told him, he was sure that Straleigh Castle would be well manned.

"You say we will have no trouble entering the place," he said to Friend.

The Franciscan shrugged. "Would a man who plans to rob all of England hesitate to strip the casual stranger who stopped at his gate?"

"Nay. Perhaps not."

"We will be graciously welcomed," Friend predicted. "What will follow, rests in the hands of God."

For a long time Sir Hubert Wilton sat quietly on his horse, staring ahead toward the castle. He had no delusions as to what awaited them there should they enter the place boldly. Sir Mortimer would not be long in recognizing him, in guessing why he had come.

It might be better, he knew, to study the castle for several days, to try to enter it by stealth, or to wait, perhaps, until Sir Mortimer left before approaching it.

But a savage impatience ruled out any such plans. He had already been too long in getting here, already he might be too late to find Marian and the boy alive.

Sir Hubert glanced around at Tuck and the others. All of them were watching him soberly and by the expressions on their faces he knew that they understood what lay ahead.

"I will go on alone," he said bluntly.

Tuck shook his head. "Not so. I will go with you."

"And I," said Richard Cuxham.

The others nodded.

Sir Hubert drew a deep breath. "You may never return. I do not ask this of you, I do not—"

Richard Tuck shook out the reins of his horse. He said gruffly, "Come, we are delaying too long. I would see the inside of yonder castle."

Again Sir Hubert's glance moved from one face to another and from what he could read of their expressions he knew that no arguments of his would serve to turn these men back. Old they might be and poorly versed in the art of fighting, yet within them there was a deep strain of loyalty which not even the fear of death could break. A sudden emotion choked him. He wished that he could command the words to tell these men how he felt; and without knowing it, he did tell them when he said thickly, "Come on, then. We will all ride on together."

Across the meadow and up to the castle gate they rode. There a guard of soldiers stopped them and a tall, bearded fellow asked bluntly what they wished.

Before Sir Hubert could answer, Friend spoke up in a quiet, almost musical voice. "Peace, Sir Knight. We be but a company of men who have come a long way. Our horses are weary. Perhaps we could exchange them here for fresh mounts, were we willing to pay in gold whatever sum is fair in the exchange."

A greedy look came into the guards eyes. "In gold did ye say?"

"Aye, or precious stones."

The guard moistened his lips with the tip of his tongue. "Ye are welcome to Straleigh Castle," he said thickly. "Our lord, Sir Mortimer Balsham, will be glad that you have come."

At an order from him the guards withdrew from the gate and Sir Hubert and his companions rode into the courtyard and over to the stables where they dismounted. Attendants came up to care for their horses and the guard who had met them at the gate joined them and led them to the donjon and into a small courtroom with bench lined walls.

At one end of the courtroom there was a high seat where

the lord of the castle customarily sat in judgment on cases brought before him by those who lived on his manor lands. The courtroom was well lighted by high, narrow windows, but the air in the place was stuffy and damp.

CHAPTER VI

A GOOD MANY of the soldiers, Sir Hubert noticed, had followed them into the courtroom and now stood around the wall, trying to act unconcerned, but easily betraying their tension. They were coarse-faced, bearded men, not too clean. They kept their hands nervously close to their sword hilts.

Sir Hubert's eyes dropped down to the reed covered floor. Here and there through the reeds he could see deep, red stains; stains such as could only have been made by blood. Had he not guessed before why the guards were under such a tension he would have guessed it now.

Other travelers had doubtless been brought to this courtroom and the manner of their reception was told by the stains. No courtroom was this, but rather an execution chamber.

During the few moments that they were kept waiting for the arrival of the lord of the castle, Sir Hubert's thoughts turned to Marian and his son. Though he had not seen Marian for three years he could picture her in his mind with such startling clearness that at times he almost sensed her presence at his side.

Yet this morning the sense of her nearness evaded him and he was suddenly reminded of de Froissart's boast that Marian was dead. A cold chill ran over his body and he lifted his eyes to the door through which Sir Mortimer must come. The low murmur of Tuck's voice reached his ears and he heard Friend's calm answer.

A clatter of noise came from the corridor and a moment later Sir Mortimer Balsham stepped into the room, followed by several more armored figures. A tall, heavy man was Sir Mortimer. He was clad in black armor but carried his helmet in his arms. There was a wide smile on his thick, ruddy face as he came forward and in a deep, booming voice called out, "Welcome to Straleigh Castle, strangers. I am told that ye have horses which ye—"

His voice broke off suddenly as his eyes fell on Sir Hubert and he came to an abrupt stop, some of the color running out of his cheeks.

Sir Hubert felt very calm at that moment. He was unaware of the drama. He could see that Sir Mortimer had recognized him and that the recognition had shocked the man. He could sense a sudden stiffening in the attitudes of the soldiers around the wall and he heard a rasping sound as several of them drew their blades.

Yet all of that meant nothing to him. He took a step forward and said quietly, "Where is she, Balsham? What have you done with my wife and son?"

The heavy sound of Sir Mortimer's breathing was clearly audible in the room. His dark, deep set eyes were wide and staring. He backed a step away from Sir Hubert, backed away another step.

"What have you done with my wife and son?" Sir Hubert asked again. And this time his voice was not so quiet. It was sharp and was edged with steel and each word was like a blow.

"Hugh! Walter! Giles!" Sir Mortimer cried suddenly. "These men are no mere travelers! Slay them! Slay them!"

Sir Hubert's hand reached up to his shoulder, loosened the axe *Bretwalda* from its fastening. He saw Sir Mortimer jerk around and start toward the door, then saw him recoil from that door and fumble for his sword. The door was closed and against it leaned the figure of the Franciscan monk.

Sir Hubert blinked his eyes. How Friend had reached that door he didn't know. He couldn't remember having seen the man cross the room; yet there he was, and though he held no sword, he seemed absolutely unafraid.

"Back, Sir Mortimer," Friend said sternly. "None may leave the room by this door."

For several moments, then, the rushing attack of the soldiers occupied all of Sir Hubert's attention. They came at him and his companions from all sides, slashing at them with long swords, stabbing with spears.

"Back to the door!" Sir Hubert called. "Back to the door!"

TUCK and Cuxham and the others heard him. They fought their way to the door, and with it at their backs they turned to face the soldiers. Sir Hubert looked around for Friend but didn't see him. Halfway across the courtroom, Sir Mortimer was donning his helmet and in a loud voice was urging his men on.

Nor were they unwilling to attack. In a half-circle they hemmed Sir Hubert and his men against the door and wall. Some bore shields and from the way they handled them and their swords, Sir Hubert knew that they were fighting men of wide experience.

Now and again they would lunge forward desperately, hacking at the blades of his companions and at the sweeping strokes of his great axe. Now and again they would withdraw a little in an effort to entice Sir Hubert and his companions from the wall. The din of steel clashing against steel, the shouts of the fighters and the screams of those who had been wounded, filled the room with noise.

Sir Hubert's eyes jerked from side to side. Not one of his companions was down! He couldn't understand it. No great fighters were they, yet they were still standing under strain of an attack which should already have vanquished them.

Near him on one side was Richard Tuck. The sword in the old man's hand was stained a deep red. He swung it clumsily, as a man unfamiliar with the feel of it in his hands; yet in spite of that he was still able to turn aside the blows of those attacking him and to deal sharp, heavy strokes in return. And so was it with Cuxham and the others.

Increased shouts came from across the room, and glancing up Sir Hubert saw more men come running through a small doorway near the high seat. He caught sight of Sir Mortimer, still standing back and urging the others on.

The press of the fighting grew heavier and over to the left there was a loud shout. He risked a glance that way and saw that Cuxham was down; and even as he looked, another of his men stumbled forward and reeled to the floor.

After that the fight lost all reality for Sir Hubert Wilton. The great axe *Bretwalda* cut from side to side, making a wall of steel around him, tumbling the bodies of those who sought to reach him into an ever growing battlement of human flesh.

Twice did his feet slip in the blood which ran over the floor. The first time he jumped up almost at once; the second time it seemed to him that someone helped him up and he had the confused impression that it was Friend, the Franciscan.

And it seemed, too, that a silver-streaked sword was in the monk's hand and that he was fending back the blows which might otherwise have killed him.

But that, he knew, couldn't have been true, for when he blinked his eyes and looked around for Friend he couldn't see him. Nor could he see Tuck or any of the others who had come into this room with him. Of them all, he was the only one left.

Sir Mortimer's voice, harsh and rasping, again came to his ears and through the men ahead of him he caught sight of the man's black armor. With a sudden, desperate fury he charged forward.

Bretwalda was like a live thing in his hands. Increasing strength seemed to flow through its handle and into his arms. It cut a swift pathway across the room and to the place where Sir Mortimer Balsham was standing.

A blow from the back struck Sir Hubert across the head, half stunning him. He reeled to his knees, pushed himself erect. Sir Mortimer's sword was drawn back for a swift thrust and he knew that he could not avoid it. He saw the sword start forward, tensed the muscles of his body.

And then suddenly the figure of Friend was between him

and Sir Mortimer, and the sword thrust meant for him pierced Friend's side.

SIR HUBERT jerked *Bretwalda* into the air and smashed it down at Sir Mortimer's head as Friend fell against him. He saw the black helmet split open under the stroke of the axe, saw the black knight fall.

A man who had raised his sword to cut at him suddenly drew back and with a scream of terror fled toward the door. Others followed him, several of them looking back over their shoulders toward the place where Sir Hubert stood holding Friend's body. The faces of those men were filled with fear.

Sir Hubert had dropped his axe and now he lowered Friend's body to the floor and stared down into his face. Friend's eyes were closed and there was a faint shadow of a smile on his lips. Sir Hubert wiped a hand over his brow. He wondered what those men could have seen in Friend's face which had caused them to flee and then he wondered why Friend had stepped in front of him and taken that blow meant for him.

He dropped to his knees beside the Franciscan's body, cut open his clothing and studied the wound in his side. It seemed to him that he could see there near it the faint scar of another wound and a sudden trembling seized him. He closed his eyes, murmured a prayer.

"You have done well, Sir Hubert," said a quiet voice. "Burn first the records in the room above this, then hasten to Calderkenneth Abbey."

Sir Hubert's eyes blinked open. He stared down at Friend. That had been Friend's voice he had heard, he was sure, yet he could see that Friend was dead. He looked around the room, but there was no other living person in it save himself.

"Calderkenneth Abbey?" he repeated.

There was no reply. Sir Hubert stood up. He walked over to where the body of Richard Tuck was lying, stared from it to the faces of the others who had come here with him. And on each face, it seemed to him, there was a look of infinite peace, as if those men had died possessed of a happiness of which he was unaware.

He turned away at last and went to the room above. There he found a chest of records, many of them pages from manorial court books. He made a pile of them and burned them, not thinking of the fact that in later years historians would be puzzled at the absence of such records, covering land and property transfers during the years of the epidemic which was to become known as the Black Death.

With that task finished he returned to the courtroom. Friend's body was gone. For a moment Sir Hubert stared at the place where it had lain. He was not greatly surprised. Some men still about the castle might have removed it, he knew, but he didn't think that anything like that had happened.

He crossed over to where *Bretwalda* was lying, picked up the axe and turned back to the door. In the courtyard he mounted a horse. No one made any effort to stop him as he rode from the castle.

CHAPTER VII

CALDERKENNETH ABBEY WAS deep in the forest which flanked the south bank of the river Tyne; yet the great pestilence had reached even here. As Sir Hubert rode up to the gate he could see the symbol which had been placed there as a warning to travelers. Sight of that marking struck a sudden fear into his heart. He swung to the ground, rang the bell at the gate, then in his impatience, tried to force the gate open.

"Just a moment, Sir Hubert," called a voice.

Sir Hubert straightened, stared through the gate. A short, stocky, cowled figure was hurrying forward. The figure came up to the gate, unlocked and opened it.

"Come in, Sir Hubert," he invited. "I have been expecting you."

"You knew I was coming?" Sir Hubert gasped.

The abbot nodded. He was a round-faced man, ruddy of complexion, and with startlingly clear blue eyes.

"My wife and child?"

"They are here."

The figure of a small boy came toddling up the walk, saw the two men near the gate and came to a sudden stop. Sir Hubert stared at the boy, dropped to his knees. The boy's hair was a light, golden color and his eyes were blue. His face was thin but was marked with the stubborn Wilton chin. It was a very expressive face.

"Edward," said Sir Hubert huskily.

The boy looked up at the abbot then came forward a little hesitantly. He said something in a childish tongue which Sir Hubert couldn't understand.

"Yes, he's your father," said the abbot.

Sir Hubert's arms reached for the boy. He lifted him a little clumsily, stood up and stared into the boy's face. He said again, "Edward. Edward."

"That's me," said the boy.

Sid Hubert laughed. It was a nervous, high-strung laugh. He said, "Yes, that's you. Edward Wilton." And then looking over at the abbot he asked, "Where is the boy's mother?"

The abbot was looking down at the ground. He made no reply. Sir Hubert set the boy down. He seized one of the abbot's arms. "Where is the lad's mother?" he asked again.

"She is here," said the abbot slowly, "but before you can see her I must warn you that—" His voice trailed off and he drew a long, shuddering breath.

"You mean—the pestilence?" Sir Hubert asked hoarsely.

The abbot nodded. Still without looking at Sir Hubert he said slowly, "Late yesterday afternoon some people came to the gate seeking shelter for the night. One of them was a woman who was ill. Lady Marian cared for her. This morning—"

Sir Hubert heard no more. His heart, which but a moment

before had been almost bursting with joy, now felt as a dead thing in his chest. He looked at his son Edward but was not conscious of seeing him. A numbness crept over his mind.

"Where is she?" he heard himself demanding. "Take me to her."

The abbot led him on up the path and around the corner of a building, through a doorway and down a long corridor. Near its end he stopped.

"She is in the last room," he said quietly. "As yet she is not very ill. She complained of pains in the stomach and head this morning and her throat is a little swollen. By tomorrow or the next day the symptoms will be more pronounced. Those who stopped here last night have gone on. There are none others here. We were waiting only for you."

Sir Hubert walked on to the last door in the corridor. He knocked on it and called, "Marian! Marian!"

"Hubert!" came the answer. "Hubert!" And then swiftly, "Do not come in. Have you not heard—"

Sir Hubert opened the door. The room beyond it was small and was furnished only with a straw pallet, a crude chair and a table. In the far wall was a window and near it Marian was standing.

She seemed thin, terribly thin; but the light from the window falling across her face touched up the features which had been constantly in Sir Hubert's mind—the soft, oval curve of her cheek; the steady smile of her lips; her deep, clear blue eyes. Golden hair fell over her shoulders almost to her waist.

There was so much that Sir Hubert wanted to say and so little time in which to say it that for a moment he was silent, wondering where to begin, how to start.

"I KNEW that you would come, Hubert," Marian said slowly. "I wish that it might have been sooner; but since it could not be, I am glad that you have come today."

"You have been here long?" Sir Hubert asked.

"Since I escaped from those men who were to have taken me to you. I could not get back to Wilton Hall. I had no conveyance, no money. Those men of ours were all slain. I would have sent word to you where I was but I could find no messenger who would risk going south. All were fleeing north from the pestilence."

Sir Hubert nodded. His thoughts turned to Edward and he smiled suddenly and said, "He is a fine lad, Marian, this boy of yours."

A flush of pleasure showed in Marian's cheeks. "He is much like you, Hubert. He is so tall for his age that I know he will grow up to be fully your height. And he is strong, straight of back. You will some day be very proud of him. I have that feeling. I know that I am right."

Tears blinded Sir Hubert's eyes. He turned away, left the room and moved back up the corridor to the place at which the abbot and his son were waiting. Long and earnestly did he look into the abbot's eyes; then, as if satisfied with what he saw there, he said simply, "You will look after the lad, I know. He will be safe in your hands."

The abbot did not seem surprised at Sir Hubert's request. "I will care for him," he answered.

Sir Hubert studied him again for a moment, accepting the abbot's answer and yet wondering how he could have known. At length Sir Hubert said:

"You knew that I would ask this?"

"Aye."

"How did you know?'

The abbot shrugged. "I cannot answer that. Some things we—just seem to know."

"Are you acquainted with a monk named Friend?" Sir Hubert asked suddenly.

"Friend?"

"Aye. A tall, thin man with features like—like the Christ."

The abbot stood in silence a while, and he seemed almost to have forgotten Sir Hubert. Then he answered:

"There is a Franciscan monk by that name whom I met long ago, a man very stern of face, yet very compassionate."

"Who is that Franciscan monk?"

"You just named him—Friend."

"And he is only a monk?"

"Except as there is something divine in all of us."

SIR HUBERT lifted a hand to his shoulder. He loosened the axe *Bretwalda*, lowered it to the floor, stared down at it. There were now but three jewels set in the head above the name. When it had come to him from his father there had been four. Once, so the legend went, there had been twelve. That thought flitted across his mind as well as memory of the meaning of the inscription on the handle, that to whoever should wield *Bretwalda* would come great victory and great defeat, great sorrow and great joy.

He remembered now, staring down at the great axe, that for centuries the Wiltons had met this same destiny—the destiny prescribed by *Bretwalda*. This his father had told him long ago.

For a moment he hesitated; then passing the axe over to the abbot, he said abruptly, "For the boy. It is a part of his heritage. Take him and the axe and go. I will stay here with his mother."

"You know what that means?"

Sir Hubert laughed. "Would you think to frighten me with death?"

The abbot made no reply but turned away and started down the hall. Sir Hubert glanced at his son, then looked quickly away, He swung around and walked back to the door of Marian's room, stepped inside. Marian was still standing near the window but as he entered her body swayed unsteadily.

Sir Hubert crossed swiftly to her side, ignoring her cries that he keep away. He caught her as she might have fallen, lowered her to the floor and sat down beside her. Marian's face was flushed with fever. He placed his hand on her forehead, smoothed back her hair. "The abbot will care for our boy, Marian," he whispered. "Have no fears for him."

"You—you should not have touched me," the woman moaned. "The pestilence—"

She broke off and looked up into his face. Her eyes were wide with fear now, and her lips were trembling, But she did not attempt to draw away from him.

Sir Hubert smiled. He said, "Hush, Marian. Do you know that even while we were apart I always felt very close to you? Sometimes at night—"

"You felt that way too?" Marian whispered.

Sir Hubert reached for the woman's hands. "All around us," he said slowly, "a new world is being born through the agony which we have called the great pestilence. Let me tell you what Friend told me about it."

"Friend?" said Marian. "Who is Friend?"

Sir Hubert Wilton shook his head. "I do not know. Perhaps he was but a Franciscan monk, yet sometimes I think—"

Golden rays from the lowering sun reached through the window and touched Marian's hair. Outside the room, birds were singing. Something which Friend had once said came Jack to Sir Hubert's mind and he repeated it slowly, "Each of us has some task to fulfill in the world, yet each of us must do his task in his own way, and not as another would have it done."

"What did you say?" asked Marian.

"I was thinking of Friend," Sir Hubert replied. "Let me tell you about him."

X

ENGLAND, FAREWELL

That mystic, invincible axe Bretwalda, *maker and breaker of kings, makes her last magnificent fight in the land which generations of Wiltons have honored.*

CHAPTER I

ALL DAY THE cannonading had continued and toward dusk a small breach appeared in the south wall of the fortifications surrounding Drogheda. Young David Wilton and John Arundel who stood on the bank of the Boyne tidewater, south of the town, heard a shout go up form Cromwell's camp and soon noticed the breach.

"Another day will do it," said Wilton slowly. "Tomorrow we can make our assault."

Arundel nodded. "Tomorrow, David. September the eleventh, 1649. It will be a date which will go down in history."

"Oliver Cromwell has marked many a date for history."

"There was never a man like him, David."

Wilton frowned. He was a tall young man, broad of shoulder and long-armed. His face was thin but square-jawed and stubborn. There was usually a commanding sharpness to his glance but the look now in his eyes was troubled.

"Aye, John," he admitted. "You know full well how I feel about Oliver, but—"

"But what, David?"

Wilton lifted his arm and pointed toward the camp. "You heard that shout which went up a moment ago when the breach was made in the walls. There was a savagery in it which I have never before marked in Cromwell's men. It was like the shouting of hungry wolves."

"We will have to be wolves tomorrow, David. Drogheda will not fall easily."

"True enough."

"And of all men I know, none is more savage in a battle than you. I recall how men laughed at you for carrying that old battle-axe of yours into the fight at Marston Moor. Yet there were none who laughed at you after the fight was over. With that axe in any press of battle, you are the equal of a score of men. That is not my praise. 'Tis Oliver's."

Wilton shrugged. "Yet after the fight at Marston Moor and more particularly at Naseby, I did not participate in the slaughter that followed. I am no killer of women or of camp followers."

"You are thinking now of Colonel Brand."

"Aye, and of how men in the rage of battle can gorge themselves with a lust to kill. I am thinking of the women and children in Drogheda and of the tone of that shout we just heard."

John Arundel touched Wilton's arm. "Look! Yonder is Oliver."

At a little distance from the camp but quite near to where they stood was a short, stocky figure with thick brown hair and massive shoulders. The man's hands were clasped behind him and he was staring up at the fortifications of the town.

"The Irish leader, Ormonde," Arundel whispered, "boasted that Drogheda could withstand a siege for a month; yet Oliver Cromwell will take the place in two days."

Wilton nodded, staring at the man so loved by many and so hated by as many more.

He wondered whether the world would ever know Cromwell as he knew him—would ever understand the man who had changed almost overnight from a gentleman farmer to an outstanding military genius, who in less than five years time had overthrown a king and had made of England a Commonwealth governed by a committee of the people.

Puritanical in his beliefs, rigid in his code of justice, the man still had a very human side which but few people had been privileged to see.

"Oliver summoned the town yesterday," Arundel muttered. "He will offer the defenders no quarter tomorrow."

DAVID WILTON drew a deep breath. He tried to throw off the heavy feeling of depression which had settled over him. Cromwell had turned back to the camp and the sun was down back of the green hills to the west.

He touched Arundel on the shoulder. "Come. We are summoned to a meeting tonight at Oliver's tent. Had you forgotten?"

"Nay, David."

"And forget what I just said. Perhaps I am growing a little tired of wars."

John Arundel laughed. He was of slighter build than Wilton, of a darker complexion. His mouth was wide and generous, his eyes large. "Agreed," he answered. "And now a wager."

"What wager?"

"My sword against yours that I am in Drogheda before you."

"Done," said Wilton. "I have a fancy to that blade you wear."

A score of the troop leaders gathered that night in the space before Oliver Cromwell's tent; and as they awaited their leader, Wilton could sense an undercurrent of excitement in the group.

Here and there a few of them talked of the Irish rebellion a few years before and of the atrocities of that period. They had little regard for the Irish, these men of Cromwell's. In general, they thought of the Irish as a savage, backward race. That much was clear by their talk.

And they had even less respect for the English loyalists who had taken refuge with them.

A great fire burned in the open space before Cromwell's tent and the men who had come to meet with him had gathered around it. Most of them wore steel-brimmed helmets, light steel armor under long cloaks, and boots of soft leather which reached above the knees. Swords were belted to their waists and many of them carried braces of pistols.

They were both old and young; but without exception all were seasoned campaigners. And Wilton, staring from side to side, could read in the faces of these men one measurement for Cromwell's success. They were a grim and stubborn group.

To one side of the circle there was a sudden excitement, the sound of shouting voices, a heavy trample of feet.

"Bring him into the firelight," ordered a sharp, heavy voice. "He is a man I would question."

In common with the others, David Wilton turned that way. Four soldiers dragging the limp figure of a man had come into view. They pulled the man near to the fire, released him and stepped away.

"Whom have you there, Colonel Brand?" called a voice.

"A loyalist caught trying to escape from Drogheda through swimming down the Boyne tidewater," was the answer.

Wilton's eyes jerked toward the man who had made that reply.

Tall and slender was Colonel Brand. His skin was olive-tinted and coarse. A Latin, Wilton thought him, though the man insisted that he was not. His features were heavy and irregular and a mocking sneer was always close to his lips. It broke through to the surface now as he stared down at the crumpled figure near the tire.

"What is this, Brand?" said the sharp voice of Oliver Cromwell.

MEN who had crowded near to the figure backed away to make room for Cromwell. Colonel Brand bowed. He indicated the figure near the fire. "My men caught this loyalist trying to escape from Drogheda. I brought him here for questioning."

"To what purpose, Brand? We know the defenses of Drogheda."

Colonel Brand shrugged. "I was not thinking of that, I was thinking of another matter. A year ago a certain loyalist escaped from gaol. I thought that this man, who is his son, might be able to tell us how the escape was accomplished."

And as he spoke, Colonel Brand's eyes, passing from face to face, came finally to rest on David Wilton.

But Wilton was unaware of that look. He edged forward, stared down at the figure on the ground. He could not see the face; but he was suddenly sure that this man was Roger Huntley, son of Sir George Huntley and brother of Barbara.

A strangely cold feeling ran over his body and his thoughts turned back to the days before Marston Moor and Parliament's break with the king, back to the days when he and Roger Huntley and Barbara had played at childhood games along the river Avon.

A hand clutched at his arm and he heard John Arundel's voice whispering, "Steady, David! Steady."

"You speak in riddles, Brand. What do you mean?" Cromwell demanded.

Colonel Brand leaned forward. "I mean just this. Sir George Huntley could never have escaped from gaol had he not help from some traitor. I think we can pry the traitor's name from this man's lips."

David Wilton lifted his head. He stared at Brand and into his eyes there came all the loathing and disgust he had felt for the man for many a month.

"Have him speak, then," Cromwell ordered.

Colonel Brand drew his sword, bent over the figure on the ground; but at the same moment David Wilton stepped forward, caught his arm, and jerked him away. A cold anger was churning through Wilton's veins at that moment. It showed in the tension of his body, sounded in his voice as he addressed Cromwell.

"It is Colonel Brand's hope," Wilton said bluntly, "that Roger Huntley will give you my name. Brand knew of my interest in the Huntleys. He knew that I went to this man and his sister a year ago and offered to help them. They refused my help. How Sir George escaped I do not know."

Oliver Cromwell's face tightened, "Have the prisoner speak," he said again.

The men around that fire were staring at Wilton with puzzled or antagonistic looks but he gave scarcely a thought to them. Swinging around he bent over the young man lying near the fire. "Come, Roger," he said steadily. "Can you stand?"

With his help, the young man got slowly to his feet. There was a dazed expression in his eyes. His face was pale excepting where blood from a cut in his head trickled across his cheek.

"Your name is Roger Huntley?" Cromwell demanded. "Your father is Sir George Huntley?"

At the sound of that voice, Wilton could feel Roger's body stiffen. He saw the young man's head come up, saw him staring at Cromwell. And then, drawing on some hidden strength, Roger Huntley pushed him aside and cried proudly, "Aye, Roger Huntley is my name, and a good tame, too."

Cromwell's scowl deepened and the glow of the fire made his cheeks seem more ruddy.

"Know you this man, David Wilton?" Cromwell asked.

Young Huntley's eyes turned toward Wilton but no sign of

recognition came into them. "A Roundhead," he said bitterly. "Had I ever known him I would be ashamed to admit it."

"He lies," Colonel Brand whispered.

Roger Huntley's eyes moved from side to side and in the stern faces of those who stood around him he could easily have read what fate lay in store for him. Yet that seemed to bother him not at all; for his eyes were steady when they turned back to Cromwell. He lifted one arm, pointed at the leader; and as Cromwell was about to speak, Huntley's voice interrupted him.

"You are Cromwell," he cried. "Oliver Cromwell, the betrayer of England, the murderer of your king! As God is my judge the day will come when all people will hate you, when none will dare breathe your name above a whisper. Take care, Cromwell, for the Stuarts are not dead nor is—"

A SWORD blade flashed through the air and its edge struck against young Huntley's neck, just above the shoulder. Blood choked his voice. He slumped over, sprawled out on the ground. For a moment one of his hands twitched, then it was still.

David Wilton glanced up from the young man's body. He saw Colonel Brand wiping off the blade of his sword, heard him making some apology to Cromwell for what the young man had said.

Cromwell nodded but his eyes were not on Brand. They were watching David Wilton. And others in that group, Wilton suddenly realized, were watching him too. Especially Brand who had not put away his sword.

Wilton glanced at Brand, moved around to face him. He felt very calm and very sure of himself in that moment; and in his voice, as he spoke, there was no trace of any emotion.

"Colonel Brand," he said clearly, "this afternoon my thoughts went back to the battle of Naseby. There was one man of our troop who hung back in that fight, who stayed always well to the rear, where he was safe.

"Yet when the enemy had been routed, that same man charged forward and with loud shouts led an attack on the camp followers and women who were behind the king's lines. That afternoon he gorged himself on blood—not enemies' blood, but the blood of women and of half grown youths. You were that man!"

Brand's face had paled. He took a step backwards, looked uncertainly from side to side.

Wilton laughed and his laugh had a grating sound.

"I hold not the death of Roger Huntley against you," he continued. "Death would have been his lot, whatever the circumstances. Yet I do hold against you the cowardly blow with which you took his life; for if any man be taken as you took him, it is his right to a trial.

"And I promise you this, Brand, because I am proud of the name of the Ironsides. I promise you this in the name of those men who have fallen in honest battle. If you live through the assault on Drogheda tomorrow, I will kill you with my bare hands."

Not a word was spoken in answer to that challenge of Wilton's. He swung about, faced Cromwell, said bluntly, "I will be in my quarters if you wish to see me, Oliver." And then looking neither to right nor to left, he marched away.

CHAPTER II

FROM IN FRONT of his tent, David Wilton could hear the drone of Cromwell's voice as he addressed the leaders of his army and he could easily imagine what was happening.

Oliver Cromwell had talked to his men before Marston Moor, before Newbury, before Naseby, before every important engagement in which they had taken part. The man's genius for leadership was not limited to military strategy. He had the power of firing those under him with a zeal and an enthusiasm which was unquenchable.

Cromwell's Ironsides went into a battle, not as an army of

men but as crusaders with a God-given mission. Therein lay much of the secret of his success.

A shadow fell across the space in front of Wilton and glancing up he saw John Arundel standing near him. There was a tight, worried frown on Arundel's face.

"Well, John?" Wilton asked.

Arundel sank down on the ground. "You need not have said what you did about having wanted to help Sir George Huntley to escape," he remarked slowly. "Men will not understand that, David."

"What matters it?" Wilton shrugged. "Will my loyalty to Oliver be questioned because I sought to help the man who was one of my father's closest friends?"

Arundel's fingers drew a pattern in the dust. He said after a while, "Oliver will not question your loyalty but others may. And as for Brand, you were over-rash. The man has a following of sorts."

Wilton laughed. "A following of cowards. I am not worried by Colonel Brand. It is something else which bothers me now."

"What, David?"

"Roger Huntley was caught making an effort to escape from Drogheda. I wonder if that means that his father and sister are within the town?"

Arundel shot him a quick look. "And if it should?"

Loud cheers and shouting from the center of the camp told Wilton that Cromwell's speech was over. He listened to the sounds for a moment, then glanced over at Arundel and smiled. "I have a feeling that Oliver will come to see me."

Arundel stood up. "If Sir George is in Drogheda, nothing you can do would save him, David. Oliver is more bitter toward the English who have taken refuge here than toward the Irish."

"I know that, John."

For a moment Arundel's troubled eyes rested on Wilton's face; then shrugging his shoulders the young man turned away.

Hardly had he gone before Oliver Cromwell appeared. Cromwell was unattended. He looked tired and the half-light from the stars deepened the wrinkles on his face. David Wilton stood up. He said quietly, "I expected you, Oliver." And there he stood there waiting for Cromwell's answer.

When it cane it surprised him for it was not at all what he had expected.

"David," said Oliver Cromwell, "I would like to see the axe you carry into battle."

Wilton turned into his tent and a moment later came back out with the axe. It was a long-handled weapon made entirely of steel. Curious engravings marked the handle and above the curved, cutting edge of the axe were deep letters spelling the name *Bretwalda*. Three blood-red jewels were set above that name.

"*Bretwalda*," Cromwell muttered. "You told me, I think, that the meaning of that name was *Ruler of Britain*."

"Aye, such is the meaning."

"The weapon has been in your family for a long time?"

"Since the days of King Alfred."

OLIVER CROMWELL stretched out his hand for the axe but he made no attempt to lift it. Clasping the handle he stared into Wilton's face. "I am thinking, right now, David," he said slowly, "of a day in Cambridge when a young student came to me and said that he had heard that I considered raising a troop of cavalry. You recall that day, don't you?"

Wilton nodded.

"From that time on," Oliver Cromwell continued, "you have been with me, David. Men call me a great general, yet at Marston Moor when the day seemed lost and I gave the order to wheel and ride to the east, you were in the vanguard of the men when we struck Goring's horse and Newcastle's White-coats. There and in every other battle you have always found your way to the place where the fighting was the thickest. In your hands this old axe has well earned its name, *Ruler of Britain.*"

Wilton shrugged. "I but followed you, Oliver."

"And tomorrow?"

"Tomorrow as always."

Cromwell nodded. A faint smile touched his lips and he said abruptly, "I knew of your interest in Sir George Huntley, or perhaps I should say in his daughter. I knew that you did not help him to escape from gaol. I asked his son to speak tonight, knowing what his answer would be, but also wanting to seem to be dealing justly in the matter of Brand's accusation.

"After Drogheda is taken, David, I want to talk to both you and Colonel Brand. Until such time I charge you to remember that we have the Irish to deal with."

Wilton's lips tightened. "The trouble between Colonel Brand and me is of long standing, Oliver. It is a trouble which cannot be settled by words."

"You have heard my order, David."

David Wilton made no answer and after a moment Oliver Cromwell passed the handle of the axe back to him, turned and stared toward the walls of Drogheda.

"The breach should be widened enough by tomorrow noon for an assault," he muttered. "I cannot spend much time on this Irish campaign. I must get back to England."

He looked around at Wilton. "They had their chance to surrender. We will offer them no quarter tomorrow. Here in Drogheda we can break the backbone of the rebellion."

AFTER Cromwell had gone, David Wilton sat for a long time before his tent, staring now and then toward Drogheda. The thoughts which ran through his mind were a curious mixture of childhood memories, of recollections of his life with Cromwell, and of vague and troublesome anticipations of what might lie ahead.

He could realize how important it was to the Commonwealth of England to crush this rebellion in Ireland; yet that order of "No quarter" kept running through his mind. It was not an order which applied to the townspeople or to the women and children who might be with the defenders of Drogheda. He knew that.

Yet after Naseby, even the women and children who had followed the king's march had been slain. And from the temper of the men here in camp, he had the feeling that they would not be too particular tomorrow.

About Sir George Huntley he did not concern himself. If Sir George was with the defenders of Drogheda he had elected to cast his lot with them. But if Barbara were there—

Wilton got to his feet. He crossed over to a blanket-wrapped figure which lay near his tent; knelt at the man's side and woke him. The man sat up, rubbed the sleep from his eyes, stared at Wilton and then asked quickly, "What is it, sire?"

This man was Benjamin Mays. He was past middle age; was short, stooped, almost entirely bald. He had long served the Wiltons and David knew that he could trust him with his life.

"Lady Barbara Huntley is in Drogheda," Wilton stated. "Just where, I do not know. Yet I have the feeling that she is there."

Mays blinked. "What would you have me do, sire?"

Wilton stared toward the town. Men would be busy there, he guessed, throwing up an embankment behind the opening breach in the walls. If that were true, they might not gain the town through their first assault. There would be a desperate battle beyond the breach.

Looking back at Mays, Wilton said slowly, "Tomorrow, Benjamin, I want you to find Aaron Whitlock and Thomas Blake. Tell them what I have told you. These are my orders. The three of you are to stay in camp until after the first assault, until after the second. If you think that the third may succeed, join in it.

"And after you have gained the town, try to find Lady Barbara. Where she will be I do not know. Perhaps near her father—any of the English loyalists there might know. If you find her send word to me and guard her until I come. You will speak of this to no other men than those I have mentioned. Is that understood?"

Benjamin Mays nodded. "Aye, sire. We will find her."

David Wilton clasped the man's hand.

"You can do me no greater service, Benjamin. And now sleep well. You will have need of your strength tomorrow."

THE CANNONADING of Drogheda was started again at dawn and slowly the breach in the wall was widened. Noon came and the sun passed overhead and started down the western sky.

Now and then puffs of dust from the wall told of a direct hit and each hit brought a cheer from Cromwell's soldiers. Most of them had donned their light armor and had made ready their muskets and pistols. They could not use their horses in this attack, but Wilton could sense a deep confidence in the men.

The wall proved stubborn; yet by late afternoon Wilton felt that the breach was deep enough to risk an assault. Others must have thought that, too, for a quiet fell over the soldiers and here and there a few of the more devout dropped to their knees for a moment of prayer. John Arundel, whose company was near to Wilton's, joined him for a while.

"You have not forgotten our wager," he challenged.

"Nay, I have not forgotten it," Wilton answered grimly. His hand reached up to his shoulder. There, in a leather halter, swung the axe *Bretwalda*. Pistols and muskets, in an affair like this, were good for only one discharge. After that, men had to depend on pike and sword.

A sudden, wild shout went up from the men; and staring over to one side, Wilton caught a glimpse of Oliver Cromwell. He did not hear the order for the assault but he saw Cromwell's arm pointing toward the town and the men back of him surged forward.

The attack had begun.

He started running over the ground toward the breach. Little puffs of smoke from the guns of the defending musketeers stabbed out at them and here and there a man went down. But those in the assault did not fire in answer. They had been well trained not to fire until they were almost close enough to the enemy to touch them.

Then quite suddenly they were at the wall and clambering through the breach. A volley of pistol shots flung back the defenders and through that breach came the Ironsides, pike and sword ready.

Wilton reached a hand to his shoulder and freed the axe *Bretwalda*. He threw himself forward, slashing from side to side; yet so great was the pressure of the defenders that their progress was stopped and they were forced back to the breach and through it.

Screams, hoarse shouts, the slashing of steel on steel and the rattle of musketry told of another wave in the assault; but this time, just as at first, the Ironsides were beaten back.

CHAPTER III

IT WAS CROMWELL himself who led the third assault. Wilton heard his voice while he, John Arundel and a score of others still battled at the breach in the walls. He had lost all count of time.

Before him and outside of the wall, bodies were piled high. Out of the corner of his eye he caught a glimpse of John Arundel. Blood streamed across Arundel's face from a cut in his scalp. He had a sword in one hand, a broken pike in the other. He was shouting but Wilton couldn't catch his words.

A huge figure loomed up in front of Wilton but *Bretwalda* smashed the man aside. How many had fallen before that axe Wilton couldn't guess. Behind him there was suddenly the pressure of those charging to the third assault.

Pistol shots mowed down a line of the defenders and Wilton felt himself carried forward. They reached the barricades beyond the breach, were over them and beyond them; and as the defenders fell back David realized that the town had been taken.

No charge could now stop Cromwell's men. They were pouring through the wall, turning to left and right up the narrow streets, rushing ahead toward the bridge across the tideway which stretched through the town.

For a moment, then, Wilton lowered his axe to the ground. He drew a ragged breath, stared from side to side. Not far distant be saw four Irish soldiers who had thrown down their arms and crowded back in a corner made by two houses. They were holding their hands over their heads, crying for mercy. One of them was just a boy.

A group of Cromwell's soldiers ran that way; swords flashed in the air and the four Irish were cut down. Similar scenes were being enacted everywhere. At some points the Irish had elected to fight; and a good many of them, Wilton could see, had fled across the bridge toward the north part of the town.

He thought suddenly of Barbara Huntley and he started running for the bridge. Where he might find her, how he might find her, he did not know; yet from the way the slaughter had started he knew that unless he found her before someone else came across her, he might be too late.

He was unaware that he called Barbara's name as he ran through the streets of Drogheda. Everywhere, it seemed, there lay bodies of the dead. Most of them were the bodies of soldiers; but here and there were the crumpled figures of townspeople, of women and of children.

A hand grasped his arm and jerking around he saw Benjamin Mays. "This way, sire," Mays shouted. "Thomas has found her."

"Barbara! Barbara Huntley!"

Mays was drawing him toward one of the thatch-roofed houses which lined the narrow street. "Thomas saw Sir George," Mays was saying. "He followed him here. At the door, Sir George was struck down. Lady Barbara dragged his body inside."

Wilton jerked open the door. On the bare, earthen floor inside sprawled a man's figure, Lady Barbara crouched at its side. She wore a light gown, gathered at the waist by a red girdle. Her long brown hair had been loosened and fell over her shoulders.

At Wilton's entrance she looked up, then stood suddenly to her feet, straight and slim and pale of face. Her dark brown eyes stared at him with no trace of recognition; her lips were pressed tight against her teeth.

"Barbara!" Wilton cried. "Barbara! Thank God you're safe!"

The girl seemed not to hear him. "Go ahead," she said huskily. "Finish your work, murderer!"

Wilton glanced at Mays. "Fasten the back door," he ordered. "Then see how badly Sir George is hurt."

He moved out the front door, closed it and leaned against it. Save for dead bodies the street was almost deserted. Toward the north there was the sound of battle. There was a hillock that was known as Mill Mount and there many of the defenders were making a last stand. Near St. Peter's Church the fighting had stopped.

"It will soon be over," Wilton muttered.

But he was wrong. The fighting was soon to be over but not the slaughter. Those who had taken refuge on Mill Mount were to be killed to the last man. Eighty persons who had thought to find safety in the tower of St. Peter's church perished in the flames as its steeple was fired.

All night long and throughout the next day the killing was to be continued as people were dragged from their hiding-places and put to the sword. In all, fewer than thirty persons were to escape alive, and they only to be sold into slavery.

Such was the story of the taking of Drogheda.

IT WAS dark and cloudy the next morning. The sharp tang of fall was in the air and rain fell intermittently. From the doorway of the house in which he had found Barbara and her father, David Wilton stared out into the street.

A score of times during the night his sharp command had ordered looting or searching parties to pass on and skip this house. It was here, he had sent word to his command, that he would make his headquarters. If any of the men thought it strange, no such comments came to him.

Mays had gone off and secured food and water; Blake and Whitlock had reported to him and were inside. Whitlock, who was a doctor of sorts, had done what he could for Barbara's father. With the girl, Wilton had had no further word.

A body of horsemen coming up the street attracted Wilton's attention and a deep scowl came to his face as he recognized that the leader of this group was Colonel Brand. He had not seen Colonel Brand during the assault on the town, had almost forgotten him; but the sight of him now stirred a slow, heavy anger in his veins. Brand, he could guess, must have spent a very busy night. Searching out those who had sought to hide and putting them to the sword was a task in which the man specialized.

Colonel Brand's eyes, shifting from side to side, suddenly marked where he was standing and as the man rode closer Wilton could see that the muscles of his face had tightened and that one hand rested on his sword. He reined up his horse, asked a question of one of the men who was with him. That fellow looked curiously at the house before which Wilton stood, shrugged his shoulders and made some answer.

Wilton stepped out from the door. He said bluntly, "I made you a certain promise, Colonel Brand. I have not forgotten it."

A twisted smile touched Brand's lips.

"Nor I," he answered. Then without saying more he touched his horse with his spurs and rode on.

Wilton frowned, moved back to the door. He had thought that by his stepping out that way and reminding Brand of their trouble, it might not occur to the man to wonder why he had selected this particular house. Yet he liked not the memory of the way Brand had looked at the house nor his whispered question to one of those who rode with him.

An hour later a soldier rode up with a summons from Oliver Cromwell. Wilton acknowledged it. Such a summons he knew he dared not ignore. He turned into the house, called Mays aside. "I must go to Oliver," he told him, "but I will not be gone long."

Mays nodded, "I will watch the door. None shall enter, sire."

"Sir George?"

Mays shrugged. "He is badly injured. I know not what chance he has."

David Wilton felt a deep rush of gratitude for Mays and for Aaron Whitlock and Thomas Blake. They all knew Sir George for a loyalist and none of them could have had any particular interest in the man. They all knew of Cromwell's order that no quarter be given and what it would mean to them if what they were doing was discovered. Yet without any question at all, they had obeyed his commands.

Wilton said, "Thanks, Benjamin."

HE TURNED to the door, stepped outside and hurriedly sought Cromwell's headquarters. A man at the bridge directed him back to the north part of the town. Wilton turned, and in a few moments came again to the street which he had watched all night.

Up in front of the house in which Barbara and her father had been found there was a crowd of soldiers. They were pressing forward, shouting, yelling. Bared swords flashed in the air and steel grated against steel.

David Wilton ran swiftly up the street, drawing his own sword. He struck that group without any warning at all, struck it with the fury of a man gone mad. His blade, cutting from left to right, mowed a pathway through those men and to the side of Benjamin Mays whose figure swayed unsteadily from side to side and who could now scarcely stand.

Wilton jerked around, parried a blow which was aimed at his head, and ran the man through the throat. "What is the meaning of this?" he demanded. "By whose orders do you attack the residence of one of Cromwell's men?"

He was hoarse with anger.

Several of the soldiers backed away, started running up the street. The others stood a little way off for a while and then one of them answered, "We are but a searching party. We were given orders to miss no house."

"Who gave you those orders?" Wilton harked.

The man hesitated, then said, "Oliver Cromwell."

Wilton was sure that the man was lying. He had a sudden conviction that the summons from Cromwell had been false, that it had been sent by Colonel Brand as an excuse to get him away from this house, that these men had been sent here by Colonel Brand.

"I will answer for those in this house," he said sharply. "Tell Cromwell that."

The man laughed, said something under his breath to the others, and they all moved away.

Benjamin Mays fell heavily against Wilton's shoulder and dropping his sword, Wilton caught the man in his arms. He carried him inside, lowered him to a straw pallet. There was a deep gash in the man's shoulder, another wound in his chest. A red froth showed on his lips.

"I should never have left, Benjamin," Wilton said slowly. "I should have guessed it was but a trick."

"They did not get inside," Mays whispered. "I told you that I would watch the door."

Whitlock came across the room and knelt at Mays' side. A young man was Aaron Whitlock, tall and thin and sharp-featured. He made a swift examination of Mays' wounds, looked up at Wilton and shook his head.

Wilton turned away. There was a mist in his eyes which made it difficult for him to see. Someone stepped up to his side and he heard Barbara's voice saying, "He did that for us, David? Why?"

"Because I asked him to," Wilton answered.

He felt the girl's hand on his arm but did not look at her. Almost roughly he moved on across the room. There was a sag in his shoulders, bitterness in the tight way that his lips pressed against his teeth. He glanced over at Sir George Huntley. The man lay as one dead. There was no possible chance that he could escape. He was not fit to travel. And if Brand had not guessed it before, he could be sure, now, who was hidden here.

Wilton jerked around. He said to Whitlock, "There is nothing you can do for him?"

"Nay, sire. He is dead."

Wilton drew a ragged breath. "Then you and Blake get out of here. Find a place with others of our men. I ask only this. Say nothing about what has happened here."

Whitlock glanced at Blake, shook his head. "I would stay here, sire."

"And I," Blake said gruffly.

FOR A MOMENT a soft smile rested on Wilton's lips and his shoulders straightened, Every line of his body showed the pride that he took in those answers. "You are good soldiers," he said quietly. "I have never known better. Yet what I said to you was an order. Obey it."

"But sire—"

Wilton pointed to the door. "Go—before it is too late."

The two men hesitated for a moment, then turned to the door. Wilton followed them, stood there staring after them. Behind him he could hear Barbara moving about in the room, could hear Sir George's heavy breathing. It began to rain and it seemed that the day had grown darker though it was not yet noon.

He closed the door, turned around and looked across the room at Barbara Huntley. He noticed things about her now that he hadn't seen before. He had thought of her as a girl but she had become a woman. The lines of her mouth had strengthened and there was a fullness in the depth of her breast. She was bending over her father, bathing his head.

As suddenly aware of his regard she looked up and for a moment her eyes met his squarely.

"Why do you not follow them?" she asked suddenly. And then when he did not answer, "What can you think to accomplish by staying here?"

Wilton shrugged. He had no answer ready. Oliver Cromwell, he knew, thought a great deal of him. But Cromwell would never condone his protection of a loyalist. Those who had fled to Ireland, who had been taken here among the defenders of Drogheda, had been marked for death. Sir George Huntley would be made no exception.

Wilton leaned back against the door. "Why did you come here, Barbara? Why did you not flee to France or to the new world across the sea?"

The girl stood up; and as she spoke Wilton could sense the same pride in her voice that had been in the voice of her brother the night before, when he had faced Cromwell at the campfire.

"You forget, David, that we are Huntleys. It is not in us to run away."

"Your brother—"

"Last night he escaped from the town to carry a message to Ormonde. Cromwell has not conquered Ireland and his commonwealth will last only so long as his army of murderers is undefeated."

David Wilton frowned. He could see no point in telling Barbara what had happened to her brother. It was better, he decided, to let her think that he had escaped.

"I heard those men of yours talking together," the girl continued, "but I had already guessed what had happened in this town. Do you think the world will ever forget Drogheda?"

Wilton made no reply. He sought in his mind for some answer to the girl, for words which would picture to her the Cromwell he knew; a Cromwell who loved England and the

English people, who sought for them a full measure of justice, who dreamed of a nation ruled by the people for the benefit of the people, and who worked to that end.

Yet he knew that he could never make Barbara see that man. This was an old argument between them. They each saw the man from a different side and neither of them, he knew, would ever accept the judgment of the other.

"Go. Follow your men," said the girl sharply. "Let others, if you will not do it, finish the work here."

Wilton shook his head. "I cannot go, Barbara."

"It is too late to change sides."

"I have not changed sides."

A strangely puzzled look came into the girl's eyes. He was aware of the way that her eyes followed him as he crossed the room to drink from the pail of water and as he then walked toward the back of the house to make sure that the rear entrance was blocked. When he came back she was again bending over her father and Wilton moved on to the front door without speaking.

CHAPTER IV

JOHN ARUNDEL CAME riding up the street that afternoon, swung from the saddle of his horse and joined Wilton in the doorway. He wore a thick bandage around his head, no helmet. And though he tried to make his greeting very casual, Wilton could sense a vague uneasiness in his friend.

"Our men have finally cleared out the towers in the wall," he said to Wilton. "Those who were not slain, about thirty, are being shipped to the Barbadoes. Brand and others like him have searched every corner of the town for refugees. You were right in what you guessed might happen, David. It was worse than after Naseby."

"When do we march on?" Wilton asked.

"Tomorrow, perhaps, though a garrison will be left here."

Wilton stared out across the street. The rain had stopped for a while but it was still damp and cold and here and there were puddles of water.

"A little while ago," said Arundel, "I was talking to a man named Whitlock. He mentioned the fact that he had discovered a small skiff tied up to the shore of the tideway. It is just at the foot of this street."

Wilton shot a swift glance at the man standing beside him. Arundel was not looking his way. His eyes were fixed on the ground.

"Quite a nice little skiff, to hear Whitlock talk about it," he murmured. "And as it happened I ran across Colonel Brand. He's been quite concerned that because among the dead they have not found the body of a certain loyalist, Sir George Huntley. He's talked quite a bit about this Sir George. It seems that he thinks the man is still alive and in hiding somewhere in the town."

"Here, perhaps," Wilton suggested bluntly.

Arundel looked around at him. "Aye, Wilton. I think that he has mentioned this house as one place which hasn't been searched. He has also hinted that it is strange that you have withdrawn so from the others. I heard him speak of that to Oliver."

Wilton scowled. He said slowly, "Thanks, John. And now hadn't you better be getting back to your men?"

"You have not asked me why I came to see you. Have you forgotten our wager? My blade against yours that I would be first into Drogheda?"

Wilton unbuckled his sword belt. "Here, John."

"Nay. You were before me. 'Tis my blade you have won, yet I cannot undo the buckle of my belt. I am afraid, David, that you must accept me as well as my sword."

Arundel's words were light but the meaning behind them brought a thickness to Wilton's throat. He lifted a hand to John

Arundel's shoulder. "Nay, good friend. There are some dark roads which a man must travel alone."

"I have a liking for dark roads."

"But John—"

"And I am a very stubborn man, David."

THE CLATTER of hoofbeats came to them from up the street. Wilton jerked around, looked that way. A company of men was riding toward them; and leading those men was Oliver Cromwell. Wilton's hand dropped to his sword, fell away. He watched in silence as the men drew nearer and then stopped, and though his glance took in others of the company he was aware only of Cromwell.

There was a weary, almost a strained expression on Cromwell's face and his usually dark eyes were webbed with red lines.

"I have not seen you since the assault, David," Cromwell said slowly. "I had thought surely to find you at my side last night."

Wilton's lips tightened. He had never lied to this man now facing him and deception came hard. "It was a confusing night, Oliver."

Cromwell's eyes went to the door beyond Wilton. He frowned, rubbed his hands together. Others in that group were also looking at the closed door and Wilton had the sudden conviction that every one of them had guessed what lay beyond it. That scene in the camp the night before the assault and Brand's clever innuendoes had made them all suspicious.

"I have a mission for you, David," Cromwell said abruptly. "I would like to have you report to me within an hour."

"Within an hour?" Wilton repeated.

Cromwell nodded. For a moment his eyes rested fairly on Wilton's face and in his look there was nothing soft or forgiving. All of the sternness of the man was there for Wilton to read.

"Within an hour," said Cromwell again. And then lifting the reins of his horse he rode on and the others followed him.

"He has guessed," Wilton muttered, staring after Oliver Cromwell.

"Aye, David. He was never a dull man."

"Yet he made no attempt to force his way into the house. He did not order me to stand aside."

Arundel nodded. "He has done for you what I doubt that he would do for any other man. He has given you a chance to return to him. David, if you go to Oliver Cromwell within the hour he will greet you with a smile, drop his arm around your shoulder, and never will this incident be mentioned between you."

"But those in this house?"

Arundel did not seem to have heard him. "David," he said quietly, "there are none of us who have served with Oliver who stand higher in his regard than you, on whom he counts more than you, who is closer to him than you. Here in Drogheda he has broken the backbone of the rebellion in Ireland. He will return to England as a conquering hero. The Commonwealth is well established and no man is more powerful than he. There is no limit to what lies ahead of you at Cromwell's side."

"But those in this house?" said Wilton again.

Arundel shrugged his shoulders and fell silent.

"I told you, John," Wilton said quietly, "that it was a dark road that I followed. Oliver's task is well clone. He has more need now for diplomats at his side than he has for soldiers."

"Men such as Colonel Brand?"

For a moment the old anger stirred in Wilton's veins but he held it in check. "Men such as Brand run a short course."

Arundel glanced up at the sky. The clouds had thickened, giving promise of an early dusk. "It will be dark within an hour," he muttered.

"Aye, and you must be gone."

"You are forgetting the blade you won and my liking for dark roads. Besides, David, I am a sailor of sorts."

"But John—"

Arundel laughed and there was an easy naturalness to the sound. He dropped an arm around Wilton's shoulder and said, "Come on, I would meet the lady. Surely you will not deny me that."

BARBARA was standing just inside the door and as they entered her eyes went from one man to the other. Wilton caught the impression that she had heard all that hey had said. He mentioned Arundel's name and then stood watching the girl, wondering what she thought.

John Arundel bowed in as courtly a manner as if he were meeting Barbara at some hall. He cast Wilton a swift glance and said, smiling. "Now I can understand you better."

Barbara's face was a frozen mask. It gave no indication of her feelings, and when Wilton spoke of the boat her eyes looked steadily at his. They were cool and unblinking.

"I will carry Sir George," he told her. "It is swiftly growing dark. With luck we should reach the boat without any trouble."

Barbara shook her head. "No, David. Leave us here. My father cannot be moved."

Wilton shrugged. "'Tis a risk we must take."

"No."

Wilton looked over at Arundel and Arundel said, "Whitlock and one other man will be at the boat. We should not delay too long. When Brand hears Cromwell's order he may hope that you will try something like this."

The axe *Bretwalda* stood against the wall. Wilton moved that way. He lifted it and placed it in the sling over his shoulder, moved out to the back door and opened it. A narrow passage-way ran along the rear of the house and to a cross-street below. From there it was not far to the Boyne tideway.

He returned to the room, crossed to the side of Sir George. Blood-soaked bandages across the man's chest told of the seriousness of his condition. His face was flushed with fever.

Barbara touched him on the arm. "No, David. Please." There was a catch in her voice; for the first time, it seemed to him, the girl's iron reserve had broken. He looked around at her and what he saw in her eyes made him feel that all of the past five years had been wiped away and that nothing stood between them any longer.

That swift impression gave a sudden rift to his spirits. It was as if the warmth of the sun had made its way through the clouds. Something of that feeling sounded in his voice as he looked over at John Arundel and called, "Ready, John. We'll go the back way."

"Ready, David," said Arundel.

David Wilton slipped his arms under the wounded man's body. He lifted him easily, stood up, turned to the back of the house; and glancing over his shoulder he saw that John Arundel and Barbara were following him.

Though the shadows had thickened it was not yet dark, Wilton could see easily to the end of the passageway as he started down it. He moved swiftly, almost running; came to the side street and turned up it to the crossing. Arundel caught him there, grasped his shoulder and held him back.

"Look," he whispered huskily, pointing straight ahead.

CHAPTER V

OUT OF THE THICK, gray, fog-like shadows came a marching column of men. They were not in orderly file and no leader preceded them. Some carried bared swords, a few had pikes. They seemed in a hurry.

"Around the corner," Arundel said sharply. "The skiff is at the jetty at the end of this street."

"There they are!" shouted a voice. "Take them!"

A chorus of loud cries echoed that command and the men started running forward. Wilton jerked around the corner, raced down the street. He heard Barbara and John Arundel following him; heard the pounding footsteps of the soldiers. They were close, terribly close.

A flung pike grazed his shoulder. He was beginning now to feel the weight of the man he carried. Just ahead lay the jetty, a narrow structure of stone and wood stretching out into the tideway; and near the end of it he could make out the skiff. Someone was raising its sail and the figure of another man stood beside it leaning forward and watching the chase.

Close they were, yet they would not make the skiff. Wilton realized that as his feet touched the jetty. Those who followed them were too close. Before he and those with him could get aboard and cast off, they would be overtaken. Even now the muscles of his back had stiffened against the shock of a blow. Then, sharp and clear, John Arundel's voice came to him.

"Hurry, David! Hurry! I will entertain these men for a while."

The sudden clashing of steel, a loud, piercing scream of agony, and Arundel's mocking laughter followed that cry. Wilton didn't stop though he knew what must have happened. Arundel, even as he, had realized how narrow their chance; and he had taken the one opportunity that there was to improve it. At the point where the jetty reached out into the tideway, he had stopped and was holding back those who would have followed.

It was Whitlock who stood beside the skiff. Coming up to him, David Wilton called, "Here, take Sir George. Carry him aboard and cast off."

He forced the wounded man's body into Whitlock's arms, turned and caught Barbara's wrist. "Into the skiff," he said almost roughly. "You may trust these men."

Thomas Blake was the man who had raised the sail and now Blake reached out and helped Barbara into the skiff.

"Look after them, Thomas," Wilton ordered. "And you, Whitlock. Lose no time in getting away."

"David!"

The cry was Barbara's. She was standing amidships looking back at him. One hand was raised to her breast. Only a glance did Wilton have at her face; but he could see the fear that was written there, the shocked and numb surprise.

"Cast off," he said sharply to Whitlock; then lifting a hand to his shoulder he grasped the axe *Bretwalda*, turned and started running back along the jetty toward the place where John Arundel still held their pursuers at bay.

The jetty was wide enough so that three men might stand abreast on it and still have room for the movements of their sword arms as they thrust and jabbed at the one who blocked their progress.

As he ran toward Arundel, David Wilton again heard the man's mocking laughter and caught the flash of his sword as it jerked from side to side, now engaging the blade of one man, now the blade of another. He knew something of Arundel's skill with a sword but never had he seen him fight as he was fighting now—grimly, desperately, and yet with a recklessness that surpassed all reason.

He was still a dozen paces away when some man back of those in the front rank suddenly pushed the center man forward. He could see clearly what happened. Arundel's blade whipped over to stop that man, pierced his body—and before Arundel could draw it clear the two men on each side struck swiftly with their swords.

Yet even then, John Arundel did not fall. Staggering back he drew his blade free, slashed to the right and then to the left.

"Back, John! Back!" Wilton shouted. But whether or not John Arundel heard those words, Wilton did not know. The man stumbled to his knees at the edge of the jetty, rolled over and then slid swiftly into the waters of the tideway.

THE CRY which passed David Wilton's lips at that moment was a cry such as he had never uttered before. It carried in its tones all of the rage and anger and all of the bitterness and sorrow he felt.

He was unaware of the shock of combat when he came up

to the place where John Arundel had stood and slashed his way into those men crowded along the jetty.

Bretwalda had never felt lighter in his hands, had never moved so swiftly or with deadlier force.

Here and there he saw, momentarily, faces which were familiar to him. These men were not the comrades with whom he had campaigned for five years. These were the followers of Colonel Brand, scavengers in the guise of soldiers.

As Arundel had guessed, Brand had suspected that he might try to escape and had gathered these men to come and watch the house.

Here and there men jumped from the jetty to escape the flailing blows of his axe. Suddenly, just before him, he caught sight of Colonel Brand. The man was trying to back away but the pressure of those who were behind prevented it, for more men had been drawn to the jetty by the sounds of the struggle.

"Remember my promise, Brand," Wilton shouted. "I have not time to use my bare hands on you but *Bretwalda* will do as well."

A hoarse scream tore from Brand's throat. He jerked his sword into the air, trying still to back away. For an instant longer David Wilton could see the man's fear-twisted face, then as *Bretwalda* smashed down it disappeared from his view.

A stabbing sword caught Wilton in the side and a pike-point lanced through his shoulder. Hardly aware of it, he began giving ground, backing up step by step.

A buzzing sound gathered in his ears and the thickening shadows seemed to be pressing against his eyeballs. He wondered whether Benjamin Mays had felt this way as he stood in the door of the house, holding back those who had tried to break in; whether John Arundel had known this feeling in the last few moments of his life.

Yet strangely enough, his arms were not weary; and *Bretwalda*, almost of itself, held back those who would have rushed him. An ancient legend of the axe as told to him by his father flashed across his mind. The strength to wield *Bretwalda*, so ran the story, came not from a man's arms and shoulders but from the axe itself. He had felt that before, but never as clearly as he felt it now.

From the corner of his eyes, Wilton suddenly made out the skiff. It was still fast to the jetty, and the sight of it there was like a sudden, stunning blow. He tried at first to make himself believe that it was some other skiff; but even in that moment he knew that it was not. Barbara was standing at the mast, slim, erect, her dark hair tumbled around her shoulders.

A slamming blow on the head drove Wilton to his knees. He tried to get up but could not. A sharp voice rang out, ordering, "Back! Everyone! Stand back!"

And though Wilton could not see the man who gave that command he recognized the voice as Oliver Cromwell's.

While thick shadows crowded around him he heard Cromwell's voice asking questions, the murmured replies of soldiers on the jetty. Then he felt hands turning him over and he looked up into the face of Oliver Cromwell. Cold and stern was the expression in those dark eyes which stared down at him; yet there was a softness in the man's voice when he spoke.

"A great soldier was David Wilton and much do we owe him. One last thing can I do. It was his wish to be buried at sea."

Cromwell removed his helmet and stooping over, lifted David Wilton in his arms. He stepped into the skiff, lowered his body to a blanket, and then straightening up, said bluntly, "I will trust you men to see that it is done."

David Walton had no doubt that he was dying. He felt a moment's gratitude toward Oliver Cromwell and after that he felt nothing for a long time.

WHEN he woke to consciousness the sun was shining brightly and he lay wrapped in blankets on the deck of a boat much larger than the skiff. For a while he tried to puzzle out where he was; then, turning his head, he saw Barbara at his side. There was a calm and peaceful expression on her face and her eyes seemed fixed on a point far in the distance.

"Barbara?" Wilton whispered.

The girl looked down at him and smiled. "We are going to the new world, David. You and I and Thomas Blake and Aaron Whitlock. Three days out of Drogheda this ship picked us up."

Wilton considered that for a moment, then asked, "Your father?"

A look of pain crossed the girl's face. She shook her head. "He died the second day out in spite of all that Aaron could do for him."

Again Wilton was silent for a while. He knew little of this new world across the sea, had little desire to go there; yet it was obviously impossible for him to return to England after what had happened at Drogheda. And thinking of that his mind turned to Oliver Cromwell and a vague memory of that scene in the skiff at the jetty's edge.

"Barbara," he said slowly, "I never in my life told Cromwell that I wanted to be buried at sea. He knew that I wasn't dead, that I wouldn't die. Yet by all his standards, he himself should have finished me."

The girl frowned. "Let us not talk of Cromwell, David."

"Then tell me this," Wilton asked. "Why did you not cast off while John Arundel and I held back those men?"

Barbara's hand closed over his. "Had you really thought, David, that I would go away and leave you?"

Wilton stared up at the sky. Far overhead a white gull was circling. He watched it for a time and suddenly he was aware again of Barbara's voice.

"There is a loyalty, David, more important than loyalty to any king or any cause. It is the loyalty of one soul to another."

"You are thinking of John Arundel."

"Of John Arundel and Benjamin Mays and Thomas Blake and Aaron Whitlock—and—even Oliver Cromwell. I know that he knew you were not dead by the way he looked at you and by the fact that he had your axe put into the boat. I should not have asked you to keep silent about him,"

David Wilton smiled. "We have left him behind us, Barbara. Ahead is a new world and a new life."

A second gull joined the one in the sky and together they circled the ship. David Wilton watched them for a while and after a time he slept.

COURSE OF EMPIRE

A Wilton for America! On that September morning in '59, when Wolfe met Montcalm on the Plains of Abraham, the tide of battle was determined by a silent warrior—Bretwalda!

CHAPTER I

THEY HAD ABOUT five minutes together in the early dawn of that second September morning in 1759. It was a bright, clear morning and the sharpness of the winter was in the air.

Rose-tinted clouds hovered on the horizon. Captain Andrew Wilton stared at them and the thought came to him that never again, so long as he lived, would he be able to face another dawn without thinking back to this moment.

"Don't hold it against General Wolfe," said the tall, thin man standing at his side. "Wolfe would have saved me if he could; but the evidence against me was too damning."

"A framework of lies," Wilton answered between his teeth. "Every word against you a lie,"

"Nay, Andrew," said his brother, "It was no lie that French gold was found buried under my tent; that the dispatches I was carrying the other night had been opened and tampered with; that I have slipped away on several occasions to visit someone within the French lines."

"Lucie de Cournal," Wilton said bitterly.

"But not the Lucie de Cournal who was described at the court martial. The girl I went to see was no siren, no adventuress."

Andrew Wilton's hands were tightly clenched and there was a sharp tension in every line of his body. He and his brother had been over this same ground many times before. There was nothing to be gained now through a review of the case.

How John could take it all so calmly he couldn't understand. Why he couldn't see the part the woman had played in the game, he didn't know. The dying words of a French spy, whispered to Colonel Stanhope, had definitely implicated her; and advices from English spies within Quebec had verified her part in the plot.

"Who buried the gold in my tent I do not know," his brother continued, "but I am not concerned with that now, Andrew. Innocent men have died before for the sins of others. It is one of the tricks life sometimes plays on a man. I should have liked to live long enough to see Wolfe take Quebec; for I have a feeling that he will."

Andrew Wilton couldn't look at his brother. He kept his eyes fixed on those rose-tinted clouds on the horizon. The rose was turning to a golden color and soon, he knew, the sun would be up. With the coming of the sun…

"ANDREW," John Wilton continued, "I want you to listen carefully to me for a minute. I want you to listen to every word that I say. You are impetuous, hot-tempered. What has happened to me is going to leave your nerves on edge, is going to fill you with thoughts of revenge. I can sense that in you now. I can see the bitterness you feel in the lines around your mouth. It won't do. You've got to get over it."

"Get over it?" Wilton said huskily.

The taller man nodded. "You are a soldier, Andrew, a soldier in a British army. There is a long tradition back of the Wiltons. They have always placed their country before themselves. I want you to do something for me. Will you?"

"Anything, John."

"It is this. For two months, now, Wolfe has laid siege to Quebec without any apparent result. Abroad, France and England are engaged in a bitter war and this struggle here is but a part of it, yet to my mind the most important part.

"Here on the St. Lawrence river the question as to whether the New World is to be French or English will be decided. So

*With a sudden wrist movement, Wilton sprayed wine into
their faces. Angry cries rose; swords leaped from scabbards.*

long as the French hold Quebec they hold the upper hand. It
is a city built on a rock with natural fortifications greater than
men could build and its garrison outnumbers our army, four to
one.

"Yet despite those odds, it must be taken. The task which
Wolfe faces is well nigh impossible. Many of his officers are
discouraged. There is talk that he is about to give up; but the
man will not give up, Andrew. I have felt that all along."

Andrew Wilton scuffed his feet impatiently. "What do you
want me to do, John?"

"I want you to forget all thought of revenge. I want you to
bear all the insults you will have to face as the brother of a
traitor. I want you to stay by James Wolfe until the English flag
waves over the citadel in Quebec."

The two men were standing in front of the prison tent at the
edge of Wolfe's camp at Montmorency, several miles above
Quebec; and now a detail of men appeared suddenly from one
side and came marching forward. At the sight of them a steel
hand seemed to close tightly on Andrew Wilton's heart and
his breath began coming faster.

"Will you promise me that, Andrew?" John asked.

Wilton looked at his brother, unashamed of the mist that filmed his eyes. There was a faint smile on John's lips, a calm serenity in his face.

"Don't think that it isn't hard for me to take this," John was saying, "but the harder task is yours. Death solves all problems for those who die, by passing those problems on to the living. I am waiting for your promise, Andrew."

Wilton put out his hand and clasped the hand of his brother. "Until our flag is over the citadel," he said huskily.

The detail halted a few paces away and the officer in charge presented an order to the captain of the guard who had been watching the brothers closely.

"Do not come with me, Andrew," John said slowly. "This is something I would rather face alone."

"I will come with you."

"No."

"John Wilton!" called the officer of the detail.

John Wilton's hand rested for a moment on Andrew's shoulder and Andrew felt the pressure of his fingers. Then quite suddenly that hand was removed and the prisoner turned around and walked over to where the detail waited.

Andrew blinked the tears from his eyes. The thickness in his throat almost choked him. He was aware of a violent, hammering ache in his head. He heard a mumbled order, saw the detail wheel around and start away, saw John raise an arm in a gesture of farewell.

He tried, or it seemed to him that he tried, to move after that detail; but he didn't move a step from where he was standing. The top of the morning sun reached up over the trees on the horizon and its glaring brilliance struck him in the eyes.

A bugle call woke the camp to life. Then, just as its last notes were echoing across the camp, there came a sudden, sharp rattle of musketry from the direction of the forest, the direction which the detail had taken.

ANDREW WILTON straightened. He was a tall young man, slender and thin of face. He had blond hair and blue eyes, wide lips which could twist into an easy smile. But there was no smile on them now and the expression in his eyes was cold and hard.

Someone stepped up to him and a voice said, "Come on, Andrew. Morning drill as usual. Your men will he waiting for you."

Without even recognizing the speaker, Andrew Wilton turned around and started marching back toward his quarters.

Captain Andrew Wilton moved through the details of his work that morning with no conscious realization of what he was doing. For three hours he drilled his command, moving them back and forth across the parade ground as had been the custom each day.

And if there were curious or sullen looks in the eyes of any of his men or in the glances of any of the other officers, he was unaware of it.

He did not know, either, that there was a new sharpness to his voice as he barked commands, that there was a whip of steel in every tone.

The drill finished he returned to his tent, washed and shaved, then in uniform once more he moved outside and walked over to where he could see the St. Lawrence river.

English batteries, from a point on the other side, were again shelling Quebec. They had been at it, now, almost since the day of Wolfe's arrival, but to little effect. Here and there were ships on the river, all of them English ships.

Between this camp and Quebec lay Beauport. Wolfe had tried an assault on that little town; but the French defenders there were heavily entrenched, and had driven the English back.

"Until our flag is on the citadel," Wilton muttered, staring toward the French stronghold. "Until our flag is on the citadel."

"What's that, Andrew?" asked a voice.

Wilton whirled around. At his shoulder stood Captain Henry Page, short, heavy, round faced. Like Andrew and his brother, Page was from Virginia. There were a good many Americans or Colonials in this English army, for the British colonies had suffered greatly at the hands of the French and their Indian allies.

A brief smile, gone almost at once, touched Wilton's lips. "I said only that I was looking forward to the time when we would take Quebec," he answered.

Page scowled. "Wolfe is sick again. What keeps him alive I do not know. There is more talk that he will turn back."

"Not Wolfe. He has never turned back. John told me—" Wilton stopped speaking.

"Maybe I shouldn't say this right now," Page muttered, "but those of us who knew your brother know that he wasn't a traitor, Andrew. It was Wolfe's damnable discipline that was responsible for what happened to him. That, and the English officers who made up the court which tried him."

Wilton didn't answer and after a moment Page said, "Wolfe is running this discipline of his into the ground. He insists that we drill our men until they are almost ready to drop. He holds to the rules he sets down as if they were given to him by God. His punishment for the disobedience of an order is so severe that I do not see why men put up with it."

"Yet the men love him," Wilton answered slowly.

THE TWO MEN turned and started back toward the Camp. It was just after the noon hour and this was a time of rest. Here and there men were lounging about their tents or had gathered in groups for casual conversation or at games of cards.

Near General Wolfe's headquarters were a good many officers. Shade trees were there, sheltering benches; and custom had made of this spot a gathering place for the leaders of the army.

Wilton headed that way but Page grasped his arm and said, "Come to my tent, Andrew. I have a letter from home you would like to read."

Wilton shook his head. "Later."

"Now, Andrew."

They had stopped not far from a group of officers. While they hesitated Wilton heard someone say clearly, "Montcalm has always known every move we made. Maybe now that the traitor is dead we can accomplish something."

A sharp wave of anger swept over Wilton's body. He said again to Page, "Later," and then he moved on forward so that he stood very close to that group of officers.

"Shut up, you fool," one of them hissed.

The man who had spoken first looked around and caught sight of Andrew Wilton. He was a young British officer, pink-cheeked, clear of eye. His name was Thomas Brandt and he was a major in Lascelles' regiment.

Near him stood Colonel Stanhope, one of Wolfe's aides, and Captain Hardy of the Royal American regiment. Stanhope was a thin-faced, elderly man with a close-clipped white mustache and iron gray hair. Hardy was large, wide-shouldered, dark-skinned.

"Why should I shut up?" Brandt said sharply. "He was a traitor and he has died a traitor's death. And it seems to me that I smell a foul odor in the air."

"Stop it, you fool," Stanhope ordered. Wilton's lips were pressed tightly together. It was situations such as this, he realized, to which his brother had referred that morning. It was this that John had asked him to bear, insults to his brothers memory, insults to his own name.

A MOCKING sneer was on Brandt's lips and there was a bright glitter to his eye. "Do you not hear me?" he asked. "I said that I smelled a foul odor, such an odor as comes only through contamination with the French."

He was looking directly at Wilton as he spoke and over the officers near him and all those around Wolfe's tent there was a sharp, strained silence.

Wilton was rigid. Every impulse that he knew called upon

him to step forward and ram those words down the young officer's throat; but a steel will held him.

"Must I make my words more pointed?" Brandt asked scornfully. "What would you say to this?"

He stepped forward then, lifted his hand and slapped Wilton lightly across the face.

Andrew Wilton lifted a hand to his cheek and a seething anger made the hand unsteady. He stared from side to side. Nowhere did his eyes meet a friendly look. Under his breath he said, "John, you wouldn't have asked this. You wouldn't have asked me to take this."

"Cowardice runs in the family," Brandt laughed. "Does anyone have a whip?"

Wilton took a step toward the man, stopped as a sharp voice called his name, whirled around toward Wolfe's tent. The flap had been thrown back and General James Wolfe stood in the entrance. His was not an imposing figure. He was slight of build, pale-faced. His flaming red hair was all awry and there were deep shadows under his eyes.

"Captain Wilton," said Wolfe bluntly, "you will go at once to your quarters and confine yourself to your tent until further orders."

Wilton saluted. He said flatly, "Yes, General."

"That is all," Wolfe answered.

The general stepped back inside the tent and the flap fell into place. Wilton again stared from side to side. Stanhope was frowning and so was Hardy. The sneer was still on Brandt's lips. Somewhere a man muttered, "He's finished."

Without a word, Andrew Wilton swung around and started away. He ran into some man who pushed him roughly aside but he didn't notice who it was. The derisive sound of mocking laughter followed him.

CHAPTER 11

THE AFTERNOON DRAGGED by slowly. Outside on the parade ground, men marched back and forth in the endless drill. Dust kicked up by hundreds of feet sifted into the tent and sharp orders rang out through the camp.

Along toward dusk a colored servant who had followed the Wiltons north brought Wilton some food and tried to talk to him; but Wilton had nothing to say, had no stomach for the food.

It grew dark and the camp quieted down. Then suddenly, without any warning at all, the tent flap was lifted and a short slender figure moved through the entrance.

There was no light within the tent and Wilton could not see who had entered.

He jerked to his feet and said gruffly, "Who are you and what do you want?"

"I wanted to talk with you, Captain Wilton," came the answer.

"General Wolfe!" Wilton gasped.

He reached for a candle, struck a light, stared wide-eyed at his visitor. There were deep lines in Wolfe's face, made more prominent by the shadows of the night, by the flickering of the candle.

Wolfe stood very straight. Though he could not hide the marks on his face, no hint of his suffering showed in his eyes.

That the man was dying of an incurable disease, that he was in constant agony, was an open secret in the camp; yet each time he faced his men there was a calmness in his expression which only a stubborn courage could have forced.

"You do not think your brother was a traitor, do you?" Wolfe said abruptly.

"I know that he wasn't," Wilton answered.

"Yet in the face of the evidence there was nothing else the court could do."

Andrew Wilton drew a ragged breath. "He was no traitor."

"Men have often criticized me," Wolfe continued, "for keeping such close counsel. I could number on the fingers of my hands the men who have been in my confidence.

"Your brother was one, for I respected his judgment. Another is Colonel Stanhope who has been with me for years. A third is Captain Hardy and a fourth, William Brandt—both young men, yet trustworthy and level-headed.

"Admiral Saunders, General Monckton, and Colonel Howe are three more. All are loyal, yet things which only those men knew were learned by Montcalm."

Wolfe's voice lowered. "Your brother's interest in this Lucie de Cournal was definitely established; and it is known that after a visit from her, Montcalm was prepared for our attack on Beauport. The French gold in your brothers tent and the fact that the dispatches with which he had been entrusted had been tampered with, were other facts against him. But you know all that."

"I know all that," Wilton agreed. "But I knew John, too."

"The ordinary spies, the deserters who move from one force to another, would not bother me. With them, one always has to contend."

Wilton said nothing. He wondered what purpose was behind this visit of Wolfe's, why Wolfe had reviewed the case against his brother.

GENERAL WOLFE moved over to the door, threw back the flap of the tent and stared across the darkened camp toward Quebec. "They have given me four thousand men to take that city," he said under his breath.

"Montcalm has many times that number. He is a clever leader. It will not be easy to surprise him. Yet I am going to take that city, and if I cannot get in the front way I will try the back."

"A few hundred men could defend the cliffs beyond Quebec," Wilton muttered.

Wolfe jerked around. "I hope to God you are wrong about your brother. I hope he was the traitor who was dealing with the French. If it was not he—"

Wolfe did not finish his sentence. He lowered the tent flap.

"If it wasn't John," Wilton breathed, "the traitor still lives. Montcalm will still learn your plans. And he will. That will be the proof that my brother—"

"Captain Wilton," Wolfe interrupted, "it is only natural that the other officers should resent your presence after what happened this morning. I have no choice but to keep you confined to your tent."

The general's words were cold and distant. There was a sharp, hard look in his eye.

"Perhaps it would be to the best of the service if you would resign your command," he added. "Consider all that I have said. I will expect to hear your decision in the morning."

That statement was like a slap in the face. A moment before General Wolfe had been almost friendly. Andrew Wilton stiffened. He said flatly, "You will have it, General."

The smaller man nodded, turned on his heel and left the tent. Wilton moved after him to the entrance, stared out across the deserted parade grounds. The night was dark and still and heavy clouds hid the stars from sight. There was a cold, sharp wind blowing from the north.

Wilton felt suddenly very weary; yet he knew that he would not be able to sleep. His nerves were too tight for that.

He thought again of all that Wolfe had said and he muttered under his breath, "The traitor still lives. It wasn't John who betrayed Wolfe's plans. It was another—Saunders, Howe, Monckton, Stanhope, Brandt or Hardy. I wonder why Wolfe mentioned those names. I wonder—"

A figure moving up through the darkness called, "I've brought you John's things, Andrew. I thought perhaps you might want them."

Wilton backed into the tent. "Come on in, Page."

Henry Page entered with a blanket-wrapped pack. He lowered it to the ground and Wilton unwrapped it.

There was not much in the bundle—shirts and sox, an extra pair of boots, two pistols and a saber, a watch which was still running, an old leather wallet, a knife, a bundle of letters.

Wilton's lips quivered as he stared down at those things. He closed his eyes on hot, salty tears.

"Thanks, Page."

"There was little else that was personal," Henry Page told him.

"Wasn't the old axe there? The one Bacchus, my father's servant, brought with him when he followed us up here?"

"You mean that old battle-axe that your brother sometimes carried with him?"

"Yes. It was an axe my grandfather used when he fought with Oliver Cromwell. He brought it with him to this country. It has been long in the family."

Page shook his head. "It wasn't in the tent."

"It's no matter," Wilton shrugged. "The axe had only a sentimental value, and sentiment took a death blow this morning."

PAGE shifted uncomfortably on his feet but Wilton had nothing more to say. The silence between them grew strained. Page rubbed a hand over his chin.

"What about Brandt?" he asked suddenly. "There are many who do not label you as they label your brother. If you were to meet him in a duel—"

Wilton shook his head. A curious train of thought had come to him. John had insisted that he stay with Wolfe and bear all insults until Quebec had fallen—that he forego any thought of revenge.

But Wolfe, himself, had made that course impossible, unless Wolfe's visit had been for the deliberate purpose of asking him to undertake the task of discovering the identity of the traitor.

And that was essential now. How could he better serve Wolfe

than through uncovering the man among his trusted allies who was responsible for sending the French word of Wolfe's plans?

"What will you do, Andrew?" Page asked.

Wilton looked up. He said slowly, "When you see Wolfe tomorrow tell him that I will give him his answer in Quebec."

"In Quebec?" Page repeated. "What answer? What do you mean?"

A tight, grim laugh came from Wilton's throat. "Just tell him that, Page. And now leave me alone. I'm—rather tired."

As soon as Page had gone Andrew Wilton turned to a box in the corner and from it he took the leather trousers and leather coat of a woodsman.

It was in such a uniform as this that he had served as a scout with Braddock, several years before. A skin hat and moccasins completed the outfit. Wilton laid that apparel aside, wrapped it in a blanket.

He took what money he had and a few personal articles and added them to those Henry Page had brought. Page, he was sure, would look after these things when it was discovered that he had gone. His pistols he left, too; for it would be fatal, he knew, to carry an English pistol where he was going. His sword followed the pistols into the discard but his knife he kept. It was long-bladed, similar to the knives carried by many woodsmen.

With the bundle of clothing under his arm, Wilton snuffed out the candle and moved to the tent's entrance. For a moment, then, he hesitated.

Once he had embarked on this crazy scheme which had come into his mind, there could be no turning back. He knew that as definitely as he had ever in his life known anything.

His brother, once, in a burst of confidence, had told him of the location of the manor house where he had met Lucie de Cournal. It was on the plains west of Quebec near the Sillery road.

He could reach that place, Wilton thought, within a few

hours, by circling far to the rear of the French camps. And the lore he had picked up as a scout under General Braddock and Colonel Washington, his knowledge of the country to the west and his fair command of French—which he had learned at an academy near Boston—might enable him to pass as a French *coureur de bois.*

With a little luck he might be able to reach this woman, Lucie de Cournal; and through her, he might be able to discover the identity of the traitor.

His plan was no more formed than that. What he would do when he found Lucie de Cournal, he didn't know. He would have to let those problems take care of themselves. It was a foolhardy plan, he knew. The plan of a desperate man. But there was no other course open to him.

CHAPTER III

HE TURNED SWIFTLY away from the tent, crossed to the far edge of the camp, keeping well in the shadows. He was thankful, now, that the night was cold and dark. Except for the sentries, hardly any others were abroad; and from the shelter of the last tent in a long line, he watched the shadows of those on guard.

It was not difficult for him to slip past the first line of sentries or to make his way past the outposts beyond the camp and at the edge of the forest. Long years before he had learned to move cautiously, silently through the night; and the skill had not left him.

Half an hour after he had left his tent he melted into the shadows of the forest. In a little clearing some distance beyond, he paused to change his clothing. That job done he wrapped his uniform in the blanket he had brought with him and looked around for a place to hide it.

"Wilton!" cried a sharp voice from the shadows behind him.

Andrew Wilton jerked around, every muscle taut, one hand

slipping to the knife in his belt. The vague figure of a man moved into the clearing. There was a pistol in the man's hand.

"I thought that you might run away," the voice continued. "I watched and followed you. When I noticed that you brought no blade I secured another as we passed my tent."

"Brandt!" Wilton gasped.

The man laughed, threw off his cloak and then tossed a rapier at Wilton's feet.

"Pick it up," he ordered. "England's cause would be better off if I shot you; but I have heard rumors of your skill and I would like to see how a coward can acquire such a reputation."

Wilton stooped over and picked up the rapier. Had it been a mere accident, he wondered, that Brandt had been watching his tent and had followed him—or had Brandt guessed at his mission? That question slapped across his mind but found no answer.

Brandt tossed the pistol aside, jerked out his own blade. In the half-light from the sky his face was set in harsh, grim lines.

"On guard, Wilton!" he cried sharply. "Let me see how you like English steel!"

THERE was none to see that duel in the narrow clearing of the forest a little above Wolfe's camp on the Montmorency; none save such wild creatures as might have been disturbed by the clashing of steel or by the sounds of the two men's labored breathing.

They pressed back and forth across the grass, slashing out with their blades, trying first straight sword-play and after that such tricks as had been taught them through long hours of practice.

In the first few minutes of that fight. Andrew Wilton knew that he was pitted against a master. He could sense the strength of Brandt's wrist, the quickness of the man's thought. He gave ground slowly, testing his opponent by every method that he knew.

Then quite suddenly he moved to the attack; but for every trick he tried Brandt had a foil.

Back and forth across the grass they moved, sometimes engaged in a furious exchange, sometimes with wrist locked against wrist in a test of strength. Wilton's body grew warm and perspiration broke out on his face.

Brandt, too, was suffering from the strain of the fight; and that realization gave Wilton a new courage. He sprang back, seemed to trip, threw his sword arm up as if to regain his balance.

The opening for Brandt looked perfect. Perhaps by day or with better light he would have seen that Wilton hadn't really tripped; but the fact escaped him. His rapier stabbed out and its point caught in the leather of Wilton's jacket as his body twisted away from that thrust.

A searing pain burned across Wilton's chest but he only laughed, His own blade, twisting suddenly downward, stabbed through Brandt's shoulder.

With a hoarse cry, William Brandt reeled backwards, half stumbling, his rapier dropping from his hand. Wilton lowered his point. He was breathing heavily and perspiration stung his eyes. This fight had been a close call for him, he knew.

"It's not far to camp, Brandt," he heard himself saying. "You must make it alone. I am going the other way."

Brandt straightened, holding one hand against his wounded shoulder. His face was pale; anger blazed in his eyes. "We will meet again, Wilton," he said thickly.

Andrew Wilton shrugged. He tossed the rapier aside, turned and started on through the forest. Far up the Montmorency he stopped and bathed the wound on his side. It was only a scratch. The bleeding had stopped.

He crossed the river and turned west, came to a trail and followed it at a steady lope. It occurred to him that perhaps John, his brother, had come this way on the nights when he had slipped off to meet Lucie de Cournal; and he wondered why John had ever become interested in such a woman.

His knowledge of his brother gave him an answer. John had ever been a dreamer, a sentimentalist. To fall in love with a French woman, to slip off to meet her, would have appealed to his imagination in the same way as did that old battle-axe which Bacchus had brought north with him.

John had liked to carry that axe about because it bore the name *Bretwalda*, which his father had translated as meaning *Ruler of Britain*. And because many a Wilton in years gone by had carried that axe to victory.

A grim smile came to Andrew Wilton's lips. He forgot Brandt and the fight that was just over, forgot General Wolfe and the strangeness of the man's visit.

"You'll find me a different Wilton, Lucie de Cournal," he said half aloud, "One not so easily tricked."

THE MANOR house was wide and long and of two stories. It was set far back from the road and within a sheltering circle of trees. A score of saddled horses were tied to the picket fence which ran in front of it and here and there were carriages.

Music and the sound of shouting and laughter came from the crowd inside; and as he drew near the place Andrew Wilton recalled several tales he had heard of the manor house of the Seigneur de Cournal. The revelries and the carousals held here were said to rival the drinking bouts held in the Intendency in Quebec.

But De Cournal's place was supposed to be open to every-one—soldiers or townspeople, cavaliers or *coureurs de bois*. This, Wilton decided, was a point in his favor. And the lateness of the hour was another point. Minds befuddled by liquor were not quick at thought.

He staggered up to the door, very much as if he had already had too much to drink; pushed it open and wandered inside.

There were almost half a hundred people in the great dining hall, some of them gathered at the long table which was loaded with food, others at smaller tables where they were playing at cards or throwing dice. The room was warm and the air was heavy with the scent of perfume mingled with tobacco smoke.

At the far end of the place three violinists were playing a lilting air and some woman was dancing. Wilton noticed several men who were clothed in an outfit very similar to his; but most of the men there were French officers in neat blue uniforms.

Several women in gaudy silks moved through the crowd, their faces flushed, their laughter high and shrill.

All that, Andrew Wilton saw in one swift glance as he staggered forward and dropped into a chair at the table. For several moments he ate ravenously of the food within his reach; then, as no one seemed to be paying any attention to him, he began to study the crowd.

One of the serving girls stopped at his shoulder and set a flagon of wine on the table near him. She started to go on, stopped. Wilton could feel her eyes on him.

"You are new," he heard her say, her voice low and swift. "I have never seen you here before."

"I just got to Quebec," Wilton answered thickly. "I—"

The girl moved back to his side, leaned over the table and said in a whisper, "Why have you come here? Get out! Quickly! Before you are noticed."

There was a sharp urgency in the girl's tones. Wilton glanced at her. She was slender and young, fair-skinned and very dark of hair. Her breath was coming very fast and there was a tight, almost frightened expression on her face. How she had so quickly penetrated his disguise, Wilton didn't know, but the fact that she had and that she hadn't given him away was at least encouraging.

Wilton leaned toward her. "I must see Lucie de Cournal," he said under his breath.

The girl bit her lips. "What do you want of her?"

"I have a message for her," Wilton lied.

"What is the message? I will take it to her."

Wilton glanced from side to side. No one seemed interested in him or the girl. He shook his head. "Where is she? Point her out to me."

The girl's eyes moved around the room and Wilton followed her glance. He suddenly caught his breath. Leaning against the wall not far away was a tall, broad-shouldered figure in a French uniform. But the man wearing that uniform was no Frenchman, He had broad, dark features, thick bushy hair.

"Hardy," Wilton muttered. "Captain George Hardy."

"I will find Lucie, send her out back," the girl whispered. "Hurry outside before you are discovered."

AS SHE spoke the girl straightened and then moved away. Andrew Wilton did not budge. George Hardy was one of the men in Wolfe's confidence; yet here he was at the manor house of the Seigneur de Cournal in a French uniform—and apparently very much at home.

A woman in a long blue gown moved up to Hardy's side and the American flashed her a smile. They started whispering together. The woman wore a powdered wig and her gown was cut very low. Her shoulders looked smooth and soft.

Hardy laughed at something that she said and turned and glanced around the room. His look passed Wilton, came back again.

By the expression on his face Wilton knew that the man had recognized him. Two French officers joined the woman at Hardy's side and Hardy said something to them. One of the officers moved away, started circling the room.

Wilton glanced over at the door. A moment before it had been empty; but now several officers were standing there, staring at him. He looked over his shoulder and saw that several others were regarding him suspiciously. The officer who had been talking to Hardy was with them.

It had happened as quickly as that. A moment before no one had seemed aware of his presence. Now the door was guarded and the men behind him were moving forward.

A surging excitement swept through Wilton's veins. He shot a quick look at Hardy. The woman to whom he had been talking had moved off and a Frenchman now stood on either side of Hardy. As Wilton looked that way, Hardy and the two men with him started across the room, arm in arm. Hardy looked around and there was a curious strained expression on his face.

A hand tapped Wilton on the shoulder and a man's heavy voice demanded.

"What is your name, *m'sieu?*"

Wilton got to his feet, turned clumsily around. There were six or seven officers in the group which had come up behind him. Several of the men had their hands on their swords and all of them were watching him closely.

Far across the room Wilton saw Captain Hardy and several others leaving by a back door. Out of the corner of his eye he caught a glimpse of the woman who had been talking to Hardy. She was now talking to another man and the sound of her high-pitched laughter came to Wilton's ears.

A sudden, sharp anger boiled through his veins. His glance turned to the man who stood at his side.

"My name, *m'sieu*, is Père Tache," he answered.

"And where are you from?"

"From far beyond the great lakes."

"What do you think, Iberville?" asked the man of one of the others.

A tall, thin, pale-faced Frenchman shook his head. "He is clean shaven. No *coureur de bois* ever bothered to cut his beard."

The man's tones were cold and incisive. His eyes were very sharp. Wilton leaned back against the table. He knew that he had little time. In another moment these men would grasp him, lead him outside. Perhaps he would be dragged into Quebec or perhaps they wouldn't even bother with that formality.

His hand fumbled on the table behind him, grasped a glass of wine. He half turned, started to lift it to his lips.

"You will come with us, Père Tache," said Iberville. "There is a little matter—"

CHAPTER IV

WITH A SUDDEN, deliberate movement of the wrist, Wilton sprayed the contents of the wineglass into the faces of those who were standing around him. Startled and angry cries rose from that group, swords flashed from their scabbards.

Wilton threw himself forward, stabbing out with both fists. This was his only chance and he knew it. A swift and desperate bid for freedom, for an opportunity at that door and for the comparative security of the darkness outside.

A sword slashed across his shoulder and another caught him in the upper arm. From some man's hand he twisted a blade and with it he slashed out from left to right.

A stabbing pain lanced through his back and he stumbled forward. The men who had been guarding the door had left it and were rushing toward him.

Wilton's sword caught one of those men in the throat. He drew it back and cut at the other, raced for the door. Again he felt a stab of pain in his back.

His vision blurred and there was a hammering noise pounding in his ears. Above it he could hear men yelling and shouting to one another and the trample of feet behind him. Then suddenly he was outside and was stumbling around the house and toward the shelter of the trees.

Something tripped him and he went down. He tried to get up but couldn't.

"Over that way," it seemed to him that someone was shouting. "He's gone over that way."

Again Andrew Wilton tried to get up but there was no strength or feeling in his legs.

"Keep perfectly still," said a quiet voice in his ears. "Don't move."

The darkness grew thicker and the voices of those searching for him faded away....

THE SUN striking against Andrew Wilton's face woke him. He stared up at the ceiling of the room in which he lay, and for several minutes could not orient his thoughts.

Then as he tried to shift his body and as sharp twinges of pain shot through him he recalled all that had happened; his brother's execution, his trip to the manor house of the Seigneur de Cournal, the fight which had followed and his attempted escape.

He turned his head and stared from side to side, puzzled. This, surely, was no prison cell. The bed in which he was lying was large and soft and the room was big. There were curtains at the windows instead of bars and there was a carpet on the floor. To one side there was a high cabinet and near it a low table and an oval mirror.

A sound at the door attracted his attention; he looked that way. A tall, slender girl had entered the room. She wore a long, white cotton dress, the sleeves were rolled up above her elbows. In her hands she carried a basin, and over her shoulder was a towel.

Wilton recognized her at once. This was the girl who had come to the table at the Seigneur de Cournal's manor house, who had warned him to leave, who had promised to find Lucie de Cournal for him and have her meet him outside.

She looked younger in this morning light than she had the night before and there was a freshness about her face which even her somber look couldn't hide.

"You are awake this morning," she said quietly, crossing over to the table.

Wilton followed the girl with his eyes. He watched her set down the basin, turn around and move back to the bed. Her hand was cool against his forehead.

"Where am I?" he asked her, and his voice was strangely weak.

"This is my room in the manor house," the girl answered. "I brought you here three nights ago after the trouble downstairs."

"Three nights ago?" Wilton gasped.

The girl nodded. She folded down the covers, bent over and studied the bandage around Wilton's chest. "I think we won't disturb this," she said after a moment. "Your fever seems to have gone down. Perhaps—"

"Who are you?" Wilton demanded.

"Marie Gamache. I work here for the *seigneur*."

"Does he know—"

The girl shook her head. "When you fled from the hall downstairs you stumbled and fell near the corner of the house, in the shadow of a clump of bushes. All of those who followed you thought you had got much farther. I pulled you around back and up the back stairs. You—you were very heavy and you didn't help me much."

"You knew that I was not French," Wilton said. "How did you guess? Why did you bring me here?"

THE GIRL bit her lips. She turned away from the bed, crossed over to the window. After a moment's silence, Wilton heard her saying, "You looked very much like another man who used to come here. At first I thought you were that other."

"That other man was my brother," Wilton said in a low voice.

The girl didn't turn. She made no answer.

"He came here," Wilton went on, "to see this Lucie de Cournal."

"And you came to see her. Why?"

Wilton stared up at the ceiling. "I came to find out from her what man it is who has been betraying Wolfe's plans to the French. My brother was arrested, was tried and was executed as a traitor."

The girl swung around. Her face seemed very pale. "Your brother was—executed. You mean—"

"John was no traitor," Wilton said slowly. "I saw the man

who betrayed Wolfe in that hall downstairs. I saw him talking to this Lucie de Cournal. He saw me there, pointed me out to others and then went outside thinking that I would be taken. I must get back to the English camp. I must warn—"

He tried to lift himself up from the bed but again, as he moved, those sharp pains shot through him and a film came over his eyes. As if from a great distance away he heard the girl's soothing voice and then he felt her hands on his shoulders holding him down.

He must have lost consciousness, then; for when he next opened his eyes it was dark and from below he could hear the murmur of voices and the vague noise of laughter and an occasional muffled shout.

For a long time he lay there in the bed listening to the sounds of merriment from below. He could think more clearly now. This girl—Marie Gamache she had said her name was—had recognized him because of his likeness to his brother. Through some whim she had saved him from being taken by the French.

But she herself was French and how far he could trust her he did not know. In some way or other he had to get word to Wolfe, word of Hardy's visit here; and the surest way was to carry that word himself. In spite of the pain in his chest he forced himself up in bed. A wave of dizziness swept over him and he dropped back.

He couldn't make it tonight, but tomorrow night—

The door of the room opened softly and Marie came inside. She crossed to the bed, stared down at him, let her hand rest for a moment on his forehead; then moving back to the door, she locked it.

From the far comer of the room he heard the rustle of her clothing; and when a moment later she moved through the faint light from the window, Wilton saw that she had on a nightgown.

Again she came up to the bed and looked down at him; then stooping over she drew several folded blankets from beneath it, spread them out on the floor and lay down. After a while he heard the even sound of her breathing and knew that she had gone to sleep.

CHAPTER V

ON SEPTEMBER THIRD, General Wolfe abandoned the camp at Montmorency, loaded his men on Admiral Saunders' transports and sailed across the river to Point Levy.

After several days there the men were again loaded on the transports and some of the ships sailed up the St. Lawrence past Quebec to a place across from Cap Rouge. Other ships sailed downriver or around the Isle of Orleans.

The French knew at once of the abandonment of the camp at Montmorency. They guessed that it was predicated on one of two things. Wolfe was either about to make an attack or he was getting ready to withdraw. Most of the French soldiers and most of the people in Quebec were inclined to the latter point of view.

Word of what was happening was brought to Andrew Wilton by Marie Gamache one evening just at dusk. "They are leaving," she said to him positively. "Quebec could never be taken by as few men as Wolfe has with him. He has realized that at last."

Wilton shook his head. "How little you know of Wolfe. He is not leaving."

"Why do you think that?"

"I know the man," Wilton answered.

Marie shrugged her shoulders. "You will see. Now eat your supper."

The girl had brought him bread and meat rolled up in a cloth and in another cloth she had brought a bottle of wine. Wilton was much stronger. His wounds had healed over but he knew that too great a strain would start them bleeding again. He began to eat slowly, now and then glancing over toward the girl who stood at the window.

The past ten days had been as strange as any he had ever known. He had seen no one but Marie and a close companionship had grown up between them. Twice a day she had brought him food and each night she had slept there on the blankets at the side of his bed.

To his insistence that she take the bed and he the blankets, she had only smiled and shaken her head. When he had asked her what would happen to her should his presence be discovered, she had shrugged her shoulders and answered, "That won't happen. No one ever comes to my room."

Three days before he had asked her about Hardy, had described the man, had said. "He was the large, dark-faced man in the French uniform leaning against the wall and talking to Lucie Cournal at the time you stood at the table with me."

"Oh, that man," said Marie.

"Has he been back?"

"No. He hasn't been back."

"Will you tell me if he does come back, Marie?"

"I will tell you," Marie had promised.

And now, thinking of Hardy and of what the girl had said about the English army, Wilton asked about the man.

"He hasn't been here," Marie answered. "Why are you interested in him?"

Wilton threw back the covers of the bed. He sat up, swung his feet to the floor. "Marie," he said abruptly, "I am leaving here tonight."

The girl caught her breath. "No! You can't. You are not able to leave."

"Today while you were gone I walked back and forth across the room a score of times. I can make it, Marie."

The girl shook her head. She was biting her lips and her hands were clenched at her sides.

"I have to go, Marie," Wilton said simply. "But I didn't want to run away without telling you that I was going without thanking you for what you have done for me."

MARIE came slowly forward. In the quickly gathering dusk her features were a white blur. "You can't go, Andrew." Her voice was very low and husky. "The English are all across the St. Lawrence. There is no way you could reach them."

"But I must try."

"You will be killed."

Something in the girl's voice sent a sudden thrill of excitement racing through Wilton's veins. "Does it mean so much to you, Marie, if another of Wolfe's men should die?"

The girl's answer was low, so low that Wilton hardly caught it. "If that man is you, Andrew."

"Marie," he cried.

The girl came forward, dropped to her knees at his side. Her head and shoulders fell across his lap and he could feel the warmth of her breast against his legs. He lifted a hand to her head, smoothed it over her hair and for a moment there was a thickness in his throat which kept him from uttering a single word.

"You mustn't leave, Andrew," he heard her whispering. "You are safe here—safe."

Wilton lifted the girl's head. He could feel the moisture of tears on her face. "I guess this had to happen," he said slowly. "From that first morning when I awoke and saw you, Marie, from that instant when you put your hand on my head, I have wanted to hold you in my arms."

"A servant girl—in a place like this?"

"A girl who risked her life to save my own, who has risked it ever minute for more than a week."

"But still a servant girl."

A deep laugh came from Wilton's throat, "A servant girl worth a thousand of such trollops as Lucie de Cournal. Why did we wait so long, Marie? Why did we wait until the night when I must leave?"

"But you can't leave now."

"I must."

Marie tore herself away from him, stood up. "I—I have to go, Andrew. You will not leave until—until later. Until after I have come back."

Wilton stretched out his hands. "No, Marie. Not until later."

The girl took his hands, pressed them against her face. Then she turned and hurried across the room. "I will get away as early as I can," he heard her whisper from the doorway.

After she had gone, Andrew Wilton got to his feet and crossed unsteadily to the window. He stared for a long time out into the night, now and then laughing softly as he thought of Marie, now and then growing serious of face as his mind turned to a consideration of what might possibly lie ahead.

General Wolfe would never turn back, he knew. His abandonment of the camp at Montmorency and his movement of the men up and down the river could only mean one thing. He was determined upon an attack and was maneuvering to get his forces aligned so that the attack would come as a surprise. Only in such an event could he hope for victory.

A carriage drew up below and the sound of voices reached up to where Wilton was standing. In the banquet hall below the violinists started playing. More people arrived and now and then Wilton could make out an angry shout or a loud peal of laughter.

When he thought of Marie working down there a wave of disgust swept over him. This was no place for a girl such as she. He would be glad when he could get her out of it.

Wilton crossed back to the bed. He drew on his clothing, leaned back and smiled in the darkness. After a while he got up and stomping over, reached under the bed to pull out the blankets Marie had used, which after tonight she wouldn't need.

THE BLANKETS had been pushed far back. He lay down on his stomach and his fingers, reaching for them, touched against something hard and cold.

It seemed to be a piece of iron. Wilton drew it out, stared at it, caught his breath. A cold chill ran over him. This was no mere piece of iron which he had found under Marie's bed. It was an ancient battle-axe with a wide, curved head.

Andrew Wilton stood up. He lifted the axe to the bed, felt of the head. There above the cutting surface he could feel the letters which he had known would be there, and above these letters the raised points of two jewels.

This was the axe *Bretwalda*, the axe which had been in his family for so long; which Bacchus had brought north with him when he had come to Wolfe's camp, which his brother John had sometimes carried around with him; which had been missing from John's things when Page had searched his brother's tent.

But how had it come here? What was it doing under Marie's bed?

Wilton carried the axe across the room and stood it against he wall. It was heavier than he remembered it and he wondered how those ancient ancestors of his had managed to swing it as lustily as the legends said that they did. Leaving it there he moved back to the bed and lay down to wait.

The thoughts that kept him company were not pleasant ones.

The sounds from the room below thinned out. Carriages moved away and farewell greetings floated on the air. There was at last a noise at the door and in another moment Marie had entered the room.

She stood for a moment just inside the doorway and Wilton could imagine her smiling. He sat up and called her name. She came forward and once again dropped to her knees at his side.

"I couldn't come any sooner, Andrew," she whispered.

"They are all gone."

"All but a few who are still throwing dice."

"Why does De Cournal run a place like this?"

Marie hesitated a moment, then shrugged her shoulders. "Perhaps he loves to gamble. Perhaps he loves crowds of people. Noise. Excitement, Perhaps—and I think this is the real reason—he does not like François Bigot, the intendent, and he gives entertainment here to rival that at the Intendency."

Wilton got to his feet. He crossed the room to where he had left the axe *Bretwalda*, lifted it and returned to the side of the bed. "Where did you get this?" he asked bluntly.

He could hear the swift sound of Marie's breath. "I—your brother left it here. He brought it to show it to Lucie de Cournal. She had no liking for it and gave it to me."

THERE was a sudden, sharp knock on the door and from the hallway the sound of a man's voice calling, "Lucie! Lucie! He is here again. You must come at once."

Marie jerked to her feet. "It is the Seigneur de Cournal," she whispered. "He must think his daughter is here. I will have to go and find her."

Again that knocking sounded on the door. Marie hurried that way, opened it. From where he stood near the bed, Andrew Wilton could hear the man and Marie whispering together. In another moment Marie had stepped out into the hall and had closed the door after her.

For the space of several seconds, Andrew Wilton didn't move. He told himself, desperately, that the suspicions in the back of his mind had no reality. But even as he fought to believe that he had to recognize that this room was finer than any servants room he had ever seen; that here he had found the axe *Bret-walda*; that the man at the door had called for Lucie and that he had referred to some one who had come again.

A cold chill ran over Wilton's body and bitterness choked him. His grip tightened on the handle of the axe. This was an old and an out-moded weapon; yet he had no other, and in times past it had served his family well. He lifted it suddenly to his shoulder and was unaware of its great weight. Stepping swiftly to the door, he opened it.

The hall was silent and dark. Wilton strained his ears for some sound but could hear nothing. He stepped from the room, moved along the hallway to the right and came to a flight of stairs leading to the floor below.

He turned down them, came to the wide dining hall, and toward the rear of the room he saw a crack of light showing under a doorway. As he approached that door he could hear the murmur of voices; and then, loud and distinct and in English, he heard someone speaking.

"But he has not turned back. Most of his men are now on transports moving down the river from Cap Rouge. He plans to land them at the Anse du Foulon, to ascend the cliff. Unless Montcalm moves swiftly, by dawn the English army will be out there on the Plains of Abraham."

"Impossible," came an answer. "Bougainville guards the cliff."

"With but a handful of men. I know what I am talking about. The English are coming."

"We have had word that an attack is to be made tonight below the city."

"That will be but a feint," said the English voice. "It is to fool Montcalm. The main English army plans to scale the cliff by the path from the Anse du Foulon. Have I ever been wrong? Was I not right in warning you of the attack on Beauport?"

Andrew Wilton moistened his lips. He needed to hear no more. Such a plan had all the markings of the genius of the English leader. He didn't doubt that the traitor beyond the doorway had spoken the truth. He stepped quietly forward, twisted the knob of the door, pulled it open and moved into the room.

CHAPTER VI

IT WAS A small room which he had entered, one which

might customarily have been used for private games of chance. In the middle of the room was a table and around it were several chairs. A candelabrum hung over the table and its lighted tapers flickered in the draft made by the opening of the door.

There were six people in the room—five men and the girl Marie. One of the men was quite old, red of face, gray-bearded; Wilton guessed at once that he was the Seigneur de Cournal. Three of the others were young French officers.

The fifth man's back was to Wilton and he didn't at once turn around.

Andrew Wilton kicked the door shut behind him. He saw Marie's eyes go to his face, saw all the color drain from her cheeks. The old man stiffened, looked swiftly at the girl and then looked at him. The three French officers dropped their hands to their swords, one of them half drawing his blade from its scabbard.

"So far as you in this room are concerned," Wilton said bluntly, "the English are already here. Turn around, Hardy. We have a score to settle."

The man whose back was to Wilton swung suddenly around and Wilton caught his breath. The informer was not Captain Hardy. There, facing him, a tight, strained expression on his face, was Colonel Stanhope.

"You!" Wilton gasped.

Stanhope looked from side to side. The assurance of aid must have given him courage, for a taint smile showed at his lips. "Yes, Wilton," he answered.

"But I saw Hardy here—in French uniform. He—"

"He had perhaps the same thought that you did," Stanhope answered. "He came here for information but was taken by the French and was executed."

Wilton remembered, then, the strange look Hardy had thrown at him over his shoulder as those French officers had accompanied him toward the back door. At that moment he must have guessed that his disguise had been penetrated; yet he had made no signal for help.

And Wilton recalled another thing. It was Stanhope's statement with regard to the word of a dying French spy which had done as much as anything else to convict John Wilton of treason. This man's work and his lies were responsible for the death of his brother.

Stanhope moved back a pace, pushing the table behind him. His hand dropped to his sword at his side. "We are too many for you, Wilton. Move away from that door."

Wilton shook his head but made no other answer. The three Frenchmen drew their blades, moved up to Stanhope's side. The Seigneur de Cournal backed across the room, biting his lips nervously.

"Andrew," Wilton heard the girl whispering, "Andrew—no. They will kill you."

Wilton looked at the girl and a bitter, mocking smile came to his lips. "And would you not like that, Mademoiselle Lucie de Cournal?" he asked flatly.

The girl twisted her hands together. "It is true that I am Lucie de Cournal, Andrew, but I—"

"It was to see you that my brother came here. Had it not been for that he would be alive today."

"I did not want him to come."

"You say that when your main business here is to serve as a station for spies, to learn what you can and carry word of it to Montcalm?"

The girl straightened and a hint of pride showed in her face. "After all, I am a French woman, Andrew Wilton. I serve my country even as you serve yours. And tonight I will ride again to General Montcalm's camp with word of Wolfe's plan. You cannot stop me."

WILTON swung the axe from his shoulder. The two red jewels in its head caught light from the flame of the candles. Again a brief smile came to Wilton's lips. The axe had a familiar feeling to his hands though he had never swung it before. It didn't seem so heavy as he had thought it.

"Away from that door," shouted one of the Frenchmen, rushing forward.

The axe in Wilton's hand swung up to parry the stabbing sword, caught it and turned it away, slashed down and caught the Frenchman in the side. The man screamed and staggered away, his hands clutching at the wound.

And now the other two officers and Colonel Stanhope surged forward, and back of them came the Seigneur de Cournal. Their blades whipped in and out like streaks of light as they feinted, lunged, slashed and then jerked away.

There was a grim, tight expression on Andrew Wilton's face. He met that attack stubbornly, desperately, swinging the great axe from side to side.

He had no hope during the first moment of that fight that he could stand against four others with so clumsy a weapon as an ancient battle-axe. Yet in that early attack not a sword reached him; and it seemed, suddenly, as if *Bretwalda* were as light and as easily handled as a rapier.

A strength, equal to its weight, had come into his arms. That was in line with one of the old legends of the axe he now recalled. The strength to swing *Bretwalda*, so the story went, came not from a man's muscles but from the axe itself.

Such a notion was absurd, Wilton knew; yet absurd or not it seemed true. The axe whipped up and blocked a slashing cut from one of the Frenchmen; it jerked down and turned aside the blade of Colonel Stanhope.

And then quite abruptly, with a shout which rose involuntarily to his lips—perhaps an echo of a shout uttered by one of his armored ancestors, centuries before—Andrew Wilton rushed to an attack.

The great axe sweeping out from one side to another sheared

through the arm of one of the French officers and deep into his chest. It smashed against the head of another.

A chair whirling through the air from the hands of the Seigneur de Cournal sent Wilton to his knees, clouded his mind. He felt a stabbing pain in his shoulder, saw Stanhope jerking back his sword for another thrust.

He lunged to his feet. *Bretwalda* rose in the air above Stanhope, then crushed through the man's skull as the traitor's last, despairing cry rang through the room.

And then again a chair flung by De Cournal tumbled Wilton to the floor. He got to his knees, leaned forward and cut at the man with the axe. De Cournal went down.

AS SWIFTLY as that was the fight over. Still on his knees, Wilton leaned against the axe. He lifted one hand to his face, wiped it across his eyes. Over against the wall, the girl was staring at him.

He said, "Marie—Marie—" And then he remembered that that wasn't her name, that the girl was Lucie de Cournal. He saw her turn toward the door, reach for the knob.

"Where are you going?" he heard himself asking, and his voice sounded so strange that he hardly recognized it as his own.

Lucie de Cournal turned to face him. "I'm going to General Montcalm. I'm going to tell him that the English are coming. What did you expect?"

Wilton tried to get up but there was no strength left in his legs. He shouted, "No, Marie! No! Get away from that door!"

The girl twisted the knob, pulled the door open. "I am going, Andrew Wilton, but first I want to repeat this. I had nothing to do with what happened to your brother. I want you to believe that."

Wilton stared at the girl. Within a few hours, he knew, Wolfe's soldiers would be landing at the Anse du Foulon, would be starting up the cliff.

If Montcalm knew that such was Wolfe's plan he could move his men to the head of the path up the cliff. A single regiment there could hold off the entire English army.

If this girl left here, reached Montcalm, the English cause was lost, the fight in this room would count for nothing.

"Wait, Marie! Wait!" he called desperately.

The girl shook her head. She was standing now in the doorway. "I am a French woman, Andrew," she said proudly. "Though you stood here with your axe I would still try to pass."

Wilton's grip tightened on the handle of the axe. He made one more effort to get to his feet, thinking that he might catch her, that he might be able to stop her that way. But he still could not get up.

The girl turned, started away. Wilton lifted the axe. He drew one long, shuddering breath, and then he hurled it at the girl. Candle light glistened on *Bretwalda*'s steel as the axe whirled through the air.

It struck the girl in the shoulder. Wilton heard her piteous cry. He saw her fall and then he leaned forward and buried his face in his hands.

WITH the turning of the tide at two o'clock in the morning of September thirteenth, 1759, the English transport ships started down the St. Lawrence river from a point across from Cap Rouge.

Twice did sentinels on the cliffs challenge them; but the night was dark and a convoy of food was expected, and clever answers lulled the guards' suspicions.

At the Anse du Foulon, some day to be called Wolfe's Cove, the ships put in to the shore. An advance party hurried over the path up the cliff, surprised the small detail stationed at its head, and opened the way for others.

Ship after ship discharged its men and throughout the early hours of the morning Wolfe's army assembled on the Plains of Abraham, a high plateau west of the wallet city.

Word of their coming reached Montcalm, the French general, first as a rumor. He couldn't believe it possible. In the early dawn he left his camp at Beauport and rode toward the city.

From the bridge across the St. Charles he could see them, a long scarlet line atop the plain. It is said of him that he rubbed his eyes and still didn't believe it possible that all of that scarlet represented the English army.

But whatever he thought he was not long in determining a plan of action and messengers were sent at once to bring up the French army from Beauport.

From the window of Marie's room, or rather of Lucie de Cournal's room, Andrew Wilton watched the gathering of the two opposing forces. Now and then he glanced at the bed where the girl lay.

She still lived, but by what miracle he did not know. The crude bandage which he had fixed to her shoulder had finally stopped the bleeding of her wound; but it had bled for so long that he knew she could pot have much strength left.

He had little memory of how he had brought her here, of the struggle up the stairs. All that had gone before was hopelessly confused in his thinking.

This manor house of the Seigneur de Cournal's was located at the north of the broad plain on which the two armies were forming. A little to the right were the English in their scarlet coats. To the left were the French, uniformed in blue, reinforced by a company of *coureurs de bois* and a good many Indian allies.

Here and there along the English line Wilton could make out regimental banners. He saw his own and wished that he had the strength to join those men he had drilled for so long. He saw Ashurts' banner, Monckton's, the banner of the Royal American regiment.

And opposed to them were famous regiments from France— the La Sarre, Languedoc, Royal Rousillon and Berne.

AND NOW, suddenly, the French line started forward. As they moved nearer to the English it seemed to Wilton that there were at least three blue-coated figures for every man in scarlet. They came on steadily to the sound of rumbling drums.

"It's started, Marie. It's started," Wilton called. There was a tightness in his throat and he was breathing faster with an excitement he couldn't control.

No answer, no sign came from the figure in the bed. Wilton glanced toward her and then again looked out of the window.

The French suddenly started firing but there was no response from the English line. The English soldiers stood rigid, motionless, their muskets shouldered as if they were on parade. The French fire increased; and here and there the English soldiers in the front rank fell to the ground. Others from the rear quietly stepped forward to take the places of those who had dropped.

Nearer and nearer drew the French, shouting now as they came, tumbling to reload their guns, firing them again. Up and down the English line moved the officers, giving no word of command, seemingly unmindful of the rain of shot. With them was General Wolfe, his wrist already shattered by a ball, his face very pale, his eyes calm.

Wilton's hands were gripped so tightly that his fingernails dug into his palms.

Never, he thought, had there been such a test of courage as this. Never before had men stood so boldly in the face of death and awaited word to strike back.

But back of that stubborn courage lay all of the hours and days of drill and all of the discipline so strictly enforced by General Wolfe. It counted now. It held that English line steady.

Not more than thirty yards now separated the two forces. Suddenly above the rattle of the French guns came an English command. Those shouldered muskets came down, were leveled. Another command rang out and a sheet of flame burst from the scarlet-clad line.

The French wavered, were hurled back. Never before in the history of gunpowder had a more devastating or a more effective volley been fired.

Again an English command rang out. Muskets were re-loaded, primed, leveled once more. Another order and a second volley tore into the wavering line of Frenchmen, a volley almost as deadly as the first. And now the English started to advance with the same orderly precision as if going through maneuvers on the parade grounds.

It was too much for that shattered remnant of an army which had charged forth so confidently. They broke and fled.

And on the battlefield, the slender, pale-faced English general who had accomplished the impossible, who at the head of his men had been shot through the chest and groin, leaned back in the arms of one of his men, and assured of victory, whispered, "God be praised. I now die in peace."

ANDREW WILTON had seen the rout of the French army from the window. He saw the English set out in pursuit. For a time he watched them as they advanced on the city; then finally he turned away and moved back to the bed.

"Is it all over?" asked a voice.

Wilton stiffened, lifted his glance to the girl's face. Her eyes were open and a flush of fever had come into her cheeks.

"Marie," he whispered. "Marie."

"Is it all over?" asked the girl again.

"It is all over," he answered.

"Wolfe has—taken the city?"

"The way is open."

The girl's eyes closed and a faint sigh escaped from her lips.

"Marie," Wilton said again. "Marie." And then remembering, "Lucie. Lucie—"

"Yes—Andrew."

"I—I didn't mean—that is—I had to do what I did. I would much rather it had been me."

"You had to do what you did—and I—I had to do what I did. There was no other path for either of us."

The girl's voice was very low. He could hardly distinguish her words. But dropping to his knees at the side of the bed he reached for her hand and said quietly. "That is all ended now, Lucie. We will work things out together."

It seemed to him that there was an answering pressure from the girls hand and his mind raced ahead to the future.

His own status still had to be cleared up but he thought there would be little difficulty about that Colonel Stanhope's body in a French uniform in that room below should serve to clear not only himself but the record of his brother.

And with the fall of Quebec there would be an end to the war here in the new world. Canada as well as the American colonies would become English.

"We'll work things out together," he said again, and he felt very sure of himself.

XII

FOREVER ENGLAND

Through cowardice and treachery and red death he strode, shoulder to shoulder with the great Lawrence of Arabia. And when his final magnificent fight was over, the last of the Wiltons inherited that corner of a foreign field that was—Forever England!

CHAPTER I

SOMETIMES IN THE night, during a long trek across the desert, James Wilton could close his eyes and call back to his mind visions of the green hills of England, of the broad meadows which sloped down toward the tree-bordered river Avon, of the pattern of moonlight across the curving High Street at Oxford.

Sometimes it would seem to him that he could feel the spattering of rain against his face or sense the cool, chilly embrace of an early fog, coming at evening.

And sometimes when he was very tired, his imagination could make those pictures so real that a sudden burst of song from the Bedouin guard would startle him as sharply as a slap in the face.

He usually tried to keep himself from slipping off that way; for always, when he came out of it, his spirits were weighed down by a depression which lingered with him for a long time He couldn't quite understand the reason for it, and he often wondered whether any of the other men out here had the same experience and whether they had been able to analyze it.

Tonight, try as he would, he couldn't keep his thoughts from England.

Weariness, he knew, was partially responsible for it. He had hardly been out of the saddle for sixty hours and the past three days had been almost unbearably hot.

Even Shereef Tabari and the Bedouins were showing the

strain of the long ride. There hadn't been any singing for hours. Wilton closed his eyes, drew a long, slow breath. He tried to shake off the thoughts which were crowding in on him.

"Look, *sidi*, on yonder hill!" Tabari cried suddenly.

James Wilton straightened in the saddle; stared the way Tabari was pointing. Off to the left, perhaps a mile distant, was a body of mounted men. The minute figures were clearly outlined against the gray background of the sky.

"Turks," said Tabari, and the word was almost an epithet.

WILTON nodded. They were nearing the fringe of the desert and he had half expected to run into a Turkish patrol. This region was alive with them.

Their main duty, he knew, was to protect the railroad and the highway bridges on the line between Damascus and Amman, where the main force of the Turkish army was quartered; but anxious to capture Lawrence and to earn the reward offered for his capture by the Germans, they often ventured out into the desert, hoping to cross his trail.

As the last of the figures disappeared over the hill, Tabari leaned forward in his saddle. "They are not many, *sidi*. They did not see us. We could easily overtake them."

There was an eager note in the young *shereef*'s voice. Wilton could understand it. Tabari's hatred of the Turk was like a consuming flame.

He had been with King Hussein at Mecca the year before and had taken part in that first struggle with the Turks. Since then he had ridden with Emir Feisal and with Lawrence on many a raid. He knew not the meaning of fear. Wilton had the feeling that Tabari would not have hesitated to charge that patrol alone.

"We could easily overtake them," Tabari said again.

Wilton shook his head. "The message we bear from Sidi Lawrence is more important than the destruction of a Turkish patrol, Tabari. It may bring about the destruction of the whole Turkish army."

Tabari, scowled, reached up and stroked his beard.

"We ride on," said Wilton.

Tabari shrugged but made no comment, though he looked regretfully to the left.

They continued on toward the west. This was no road or trail they were following, for the ever-shifting desert sand blotted out the marks of their passing just as it obliterated the tracks of any who had gone before them.

More than a hundred and fifty miles behind them lay the oasis of Azarak where Wilton had met Lawrence. Somewhere in the valley ahead was Ramleh where General Allenby's headquarters were now located.

"Another patrol, *sidi!*" cried one of the Bedouins.

Wilton's eyes swept the country ahead and then turned to the rear. This patrol had come up behind them; it was lighter now, and they had been seen. A rifle bullet screamed a warning over his head.

Tabari had swung around and was firing back at the Turks. His dark face glowed with excitement.

"Tabari!" Wilton called. "After me!"

He shook out the reins of his horse, leaned forward over the saddle, looked back. After a momentary hesitation, Tabari and the other Bedouins rode after him, still screaming their defiance.

IT WAS mid-day before James Wilton reached General Allenby's headquarters in Ramleh. When he dismounted from the saddle he was so stiff that he could hardly stand erect.

The sentries near the general's tent looked at him curiously. Wilton wondered if any of them could guess that he was an Englishman. He didn't look like one, he knew. His face had been tanned by the wind and sun until it was almost black; he hadn't shaved for more than a year; and he wore the clothing of an Arabian *shereef*.

A white silk *kuffieh* was held in place on his head by an *agal* of two black, woolen cords. A long camel's-hair robe reached from his broad shoulders to the ground. Around his waist he wore a gold-brocaded belt from which hung a short curved sword.

"I will care for your horse, *sidi*," Tabari offered.

Wilton nodded. "And rest, Tabari, for we must ride at dusk."

The Arab's teeth flashed in a smile. He caught the reins of Wilton's horse and turned away.

General Allenby appeared suddenly in the doorway of his tent. He glanced over at Wilton, called him by name; then asked anxiously, "Did you see him?"

Wilton lifted his arm in a salute: not a very correct salute. His work as a member of the Near East Intelligence Corps had kept him out in the desert almost continually during the past year. He had had little contact with routine army life.

"Yes sir," he answered. "I saw him two nights ago."

Allenby said, "Come on in," and backed into the tent.

Wilton followed him, stood to one side as two staff officers left, and a faint smile came to his lips as he noted the same curious expressions on their faces as he had seen on the faces of the sentries.

General Allenby indicated a camp chair. "Sit down, Captain," he suggested. "You made a quick trip. You must be tired. I'm anxious to know whether Lawrence has heard from the *shereef* of the Ruallas."

"He has not heard from him," Wilton answered. "But he sent me with this message. *With or without the Ruallas, Lawrence will begin operations near Deraa on the sixteenth.*"

Allenby's eyes narrowed. He studied Wilton for a moment, then asked abruptly, "Do you know our plan?"

Wilton nodded. He knew the plan which Lawrence and Allenby had worked out and the daring of it thrilled him. His mind checked over the whole picture of the near-Eastern situation as it had developed since the outbreak of the war.

When Turkey had been pulled into the struggle as an ally of Germany, the Turks had counted on throwing a million armed men into the struggle, fully half of whom would have been Arabs. And Germany had counted on the Turks to whip the Moslem people into the frenzy of a "Holy War."

Things hadn't worked out that way, however. On June ninth, 1916, Grand Shereef Hussein had denounced his masters, the Turks, and had led the tribes of Arabia against Mecca, Jeddah, and Medina, then in Turkish hands.

This revolt, at first successful, had bogged down and might have faded entirely had it not been for a young Briton named Lawrence, who, as a member of the Near East Intelligence Corps, went into Arabia for the express purpose of keeping it alive.

How well Lawrence had succeeded the Turks knew to their sorrow. He had banded together the desert tribes, had raided and taken one town after another.

A British Expeditionary force shortly after the outset of the war had freed Egypt of the Turks and had pushed up into Palestine; and now, in close contact with Lawrence, the nominal head of the Arabs, was driving on toward Syria.

Thus the Turks had been able to furnish few soldiers for he struggle in Europe. Indeed, they were sore pressed to hold the

Ottoman Empire together; and now, in September of 1918, were making a desperate attempt to stop the drive of the British.

IT WAS possible that they might do it, Wilton knew. On the western front, in France, Ludendorff was making another stab at Paris and several divisions of Allenby's men had been called home to bolster up the defense.

Yet in spite of this, Lawrence and Allenby had worked out a plan, which, if successful, might completely break the Turkish grip on Arabia.

"You know that we mean to attack Deraa and Damascus?" Allenby asked.

"I know that," Wilton admitted, "and I know that the Turks are sure that your army is concentrated in the valley of the Jordan and that your objective is Amman. How you have managed to fool them I couldn't say."

Allenby smiled. "I gave them something to look at. We have shifted all our camel-hospitals to the Jordan valley. We have brought up thousands of wornout tents front Egypt and set them up in the meadows. We have placed hundreds of captured cannon around the camp.

"We have thrown ten thousand horse blankets over bushes and have tied them up to look like horse lines. We have painted a picture in the valley of the Jordan, a picture of an army which doesn't exist."

Wilton caught his breath. "You mean—just that?"

"There are a few regiments there."

"But if the Turks guessed—"

"The Turks could do to me what I plan doing to them. They could sweep in around behind me, cut off my lines of communication, my lines of supplies."

Wilton knew that Allenby and Lawrence planned to do just that to the Turks. Lawrence had already left Azarak and was heading for Deera, a railroad junction south of Damascus and between Damascus and Amman where the Turkish army lay watching the picture Allenby had painted for them.

It was Lawrence's part in the plan to cut all lines of communication on between that army and the force in Damascus. Allenby, then, would lead the British toward Damascus.

Once Damascus was in British hands, the Turkish army to the south would be helpless: entirely surrounded, wholly cut off from supplies.

"I had hoped," said Allenby, "that you would bring me word that Lawrence had heard from the Rualla tribe. I know that he counts on them in the engagement ahead."

Wilton straightened. "I bring you word to go ahead. With or without the Ruallas, Lawrence will not fail you."

"Remarkable chap, Lawrence," Allenby nodded. "You were with him before the war, weren't you?"

"I was a member of the same archaeological expedition. That's where I learned what I know of Arabia, its language and customs."

CHAPTER II

THE DRUMMING ROAR of an airplane's motor sounded overhead. Allenby listened for a moment, then said, "One of the new Handley-Page planes. I've been able to get several. You are going back to meet Lawrence?"

"Tonight," Wilton answered.

"Tell him to go ahead as we planned. The railroad lines must be cut. No word of what we are doing must get through to the Turks and if their army starts back toward Damascus, it must be stopped."

Wilton nodded. He saluted Allenby, a little better this time; shook hands with him and declined a proffer of hospitality. "Shereef Tabari and some of the Bedouins came with me," he said to the general. "I will rest with them until night and then leave to join Lawrence."

Allenby walked with him through the doorway of the tent, summoned a staff officer who was waiting outside and then turned back.

Wilton moved down the company street. There did not seem to be many men quartered here in Ramleh. He wondered where the main body of Allenby's force had been sent, whether it could already be heading toward Deraa and Damascus.

A dozen paces from General Allenby's tent, Wilton came upon a group of men gathered around an officer who wore on his cap the insignia of the Royal Air Force. The airman's back was toward Wilton; but something in the way the man stood arrested his attention.

The man was tall and broad of shoulder and there was a strut in every line of his figure. His voice was loud and it carried easily to Wilton's ears.

"There's nothing to it," the aviator was saying. "Let this man Lawrence plant his tulips. I'll take a load of eggs up in that crate I brought in here and in half a day blast away ten times as many bridges."

Several of the men in the group managed a polite laugh— though it seemed to Wilton that their attitudes had perceptibly cooled.

"I guess you didn't get out here soon enough," someone suggested.

James Wilton moved around so that he could see the airman's face. It was a bold handsome face with strong lines. The man's mouth was broad and was smiling. If there had been an insult in that last statement he didn't seem to have recognized it.

"Guess that's right," he nodded. And then, "Say, where'll I find Allenby?"

Wilton moved forward. He said sharply, "Major Scott, I'd like to see you for a minute."

THE AVIATOR whirled around to face him and for a moment there was no recognition in his eyes. Then Wilton could sense the sudden rigidity which swept over him and he saw Scott moisten his lips with his tongue. Those lips formed syllables of Wilton's name but no sound came from his throat.

Wilton took Scott's arm and led him several paces away from the group which had gathered around him. He said, "Yes, I'm James Wilton, Harold's brother."

Scott's breath was coming heavily. There was a note of desperation in his voice as he said, "I—I wanted to explain to you about Harold. I thought he was dead. Honestly I did. I thought—"

"He is dead," Wilton said flatly. "He died in a plane shot down in France more than two years ago. He and another plane in his squadron were separated from the rest of the flight in the fog of an early dawn. They ran into a bunch of German planes. Harold's companion turned and ran and left Harold to face them alone. He got three of the Boches at that before they got him. You were the one who ran, Scott."

Scott's hands were gripped together. He said swiftly, "No, Wilton. No. It wasn't that way at all, I—"

"Harold's plane fell behind the French lines," Wilton said quietly, "A French officer talked to him before he died. I had the story from him. I can understand why you are still alive. *He who fights and run away—*"

There was perspiration on Scott's forehead and a pain which Wilton could almost feel showed in the man's eyes.

A cold rage which had long been bottled up took possession of Wilton. He wanted to smash his fist into the handsome face of this braggart who had fled to safety and who had left his brother to face death alone.

Instead he heard himself saying. "I don't know how you've managed to get by this far, Scott, but if you thought to find the fighting out here any safer than in France, you're wrong. If we didn't need your plane I'd go to Allenby with what I know about you. Instead, I'm going to be still about it—as long as you carry out whatever orders he gives you. Do you understand?"

Scott didn't make any answer but after a moment he turned

and walked away, moving a little unsteadily up the company street.

Wilton watched him for a while, then turned and moved on, looking for the place where Tabari had made his camp.

A HAND, lightly shaking his shoulder, aroused Wilton from a deep slumber and he sat up to hear Tabari saying, "One has come for you, *sidi*, with word that Lord Allenby wishes to see you again."

Wilton got to his feet, stretched. His eyes were tired and the muscles of his back still ached. It had grown dark and nearby there was a fire. Several of the Bedouins were squatting around it and the smell of roast mutton reached to where Wilton was standing.

Tabari moved over to the fire and returned with some of the food, baked desert bread, mutton, and the inevitable dates. Wilton sat crosslegged and ate. He said to Tabari, "We must ride tonight as soon as I have seen Allenby."

"Wilton!" called a voice from the shadows to one side. "Wilton! By Jove! I would never have recognized you."

Wilton got to his feet, stared in the direction from which the voice had come. A short, rather heavy-set British officer was moving forward, one hand outstretched. The man was young and had a round, chubby face and was grinning.

"Cavanaugh!" Wilton gasped.

The young man seized his hand and pumped it up and down. "You and Lawrence," he said enthusiastically. "That's all I've heard about since I got out here. Wilton and Lawrence, the leaders of the Arabs. How did you ever do it, man?"

Wilton shook his head "I didn't do it, Cavanaugh. Lawrence is the man who is responsible for all that has happened; and like a dozen other officers I have only been helping him as I could."

"You are too modest," Cavanaugh claimed. "By Jove, it's good to see you."

Wilton felt a little embarrassed. He was glad to see Cavanaugh but he had never thought very much of the man. For Helen's sake he had tried to be nice to him; but there was a weakness in the girl's brother which kept cropping out.

Cavanaugh was an inveterate gambler, a heavy drinker. Only his fathers high position and influence had kept him from disgrace, time and time again. Wilton guessed that the young man had been sent out here as he had been transferred to other places—to give him a new chance.

"Tell me about Lawrence," Cavanaugh demanded. "Where is he?"

Wilton shrugged his shoulders. "One never knows. He's likely to turn up any place."

"At Damascus?"

Wilton frowned, shrugged his shoulders again.

"I can't figure out what Allenby's got in his mind," Cavanaugh said slowly. "It's been whispered about that he intends to attack at Deraa and Damascus, but he doesn't dare try that for he hasn't enough men to protect Jerusalem if he brings a force north. The Turks could swing around behind him or could march back this way and defeat him in a battle,"

"I've got to go see Allenby," Wilton mentioned. "Let's walk that way. How's your sister, Helen?"

"She's here." Cavanaugh answered.

"Here?" Wilton gasped.

"With a Red Cross unit."

Wilton stared at the man in amazement. He couldn't believe that he had heard him correctly. A thrill of excitement swept over his body and made him feel suddenly very weak.

Cavanaugh laughed. "I thought that would get you. I always had a notion that you and Helen were rather fond of each other. Yes, she's here, Wilton. And the hospital's over that way."

Cavanaugh pointed to the left with his arm. Wilton bit his lips. His breath was coming very fast and he could feel his heart thumping against the walls of his chest.

"Come on," Cavanaugh insisted. "You said you had to see Allenby."

GENERAL ALLENBY was with a staff officer when Wilton reported at his tent. He was saying, "You will arrest him at once. The court martial will be deferred until after this campaign is over."

The staff officer saluted, swung around and marched out of the tent.

Allenby looked up at Wilton. "I have just received definite information indicating which of my staff officers has been acting as a spy for the Turks," he said slowly. "I have ordered his arrest. We knew that there was a leak somewhere. That is why Lawrence and I have been so close about our plans."

Wilton nodded. "You wanted to see me?"

"I did. Lawrence is always asking for more planes. He says that his Arabs feel that they need planes because the Turks have them. We've sent him what planes we could and it has occurred to me that perhaps he could make use of one of the Handley-Pages. A big bomber like that ought to impress the tribes. Besides, it should be useful to Lawrence around Deraa.

"Unfortunately there isn't a pilot here who knows the country up that way. I want you to take the observer's place in the plane and direct the pilot to Lawrence's camp."

Wilton frowned. "What pilot are you sending?"

"A man named Scott who just arrived here today. Know him!"

"Yes, I know him," Wilton answered slowly.

Something in his voice caught Allenby's attention, but Wilton's face was expressionless.

"He will leave at dawn," Allenby continued, "He does not know where he is going. I have told him that he will take his orders from you."

Wilton's lips tightened, He had little liking for this assignment, even though it would bring him to Lawrence's side much sooner than he had anticipated.

Allenby stood up. "I'm counting on you and Lawrence," he said soberly. "I can't possibly impress upon you how important this campaign is. If we are successful, the hold of the Turk on Arabia will be broken and the Kaiser's dream of a *Mittel-Europa* empire will be crushed. If we fail the war may be prolonged for years, may even be lost. I feel that sincerely. The future destiny of the world will ride with you and Lawrence during the next few days."

Something in Allenby's tone of voice stabbed through Wilton's body with the keenness of a knife. He knew the importance of this campaign, how disastrous it would be for the allies if Turkey and Germany controlled Arabia and the east coast of the Mediterranean Sea.

Allenby put out his hand. "My regards to Lawrence. Tell him that I will see him in Damascus."

CHAPTER III

JAMES WILTON TURNED away, stepped from the tent. He had half expected to find Arthur Cavanaugh waiting for him but Cavanaugh was not in sight. Tabari came forward, touched his arm. "The horses are waiting, *sidi.*"

Wilton shook his head. "I cannot ride with you, Tabari. Lord Allenby is sending one of the giant planes to Sidi Lawrence. I must go along to point out the way. It is the will of Allah."

The Arab bowed. "And your servants?"

"You will join me near Deraa, Tabari. The hour for the final blow has come."

Tabari sucked in a long, slow breath. "We are ready," he muttered almost to himself. "We are ready."

James Wilton accompanied Tabari to where the other Bedouins waited. He spoke to them for a moment, then bade them farewell and took his own horse and led it back to the place where their camp had been. There he tied his horse to a date palm; and after that he moved off in the direction of the hospital established by the Red Cross unit.

At his request, an orderly entered the hospital tent to summon Helen Cavanaugh. While he waited, Wilton was conscious of a growing excitement and of an embarrassment which made him feel a little foolish and a little afraid. He touched a hand to his beard and stared down at his strange costume; and he told himself that in the three years which had passed since he had seen Helen, many things could have happened.

Then quite suddenly a tall slender figure in a white nurse's uniform appeared in the hospital door; hesitated a moment and stepped outside.

The faint light from a nearby fire touched the girl's face, giving a sudden reality to the vision which Wilton had carried in his heart for so many years. An impulse came to Wilton to rush forward and take Helen in his arms, but he was powerless to move. He couldn't do a thing but stand there and look at her and try to swallow the choking feeling in his throat.

"Jim," said the girl. "Jim." And then she was hurrying forward, almost stumbling. As she reached him her arms lifted up and went around his shoulders in an embrace as natural as if they had never been apart.

For a long time, then, they just stood there; and the thought came to Wilton that this was the strangest of all strange things that had ever happened to him—and that it was at the same time the most natural thing in the world. It was altogether right that Helen should be so close to him at this moment. She was trembling a little, and his arms tightened instinctively. The deep fragrance of her hair almost shut everything else out of his consciousness.

Almost—not quite, He saw the orderly who had gone after the girl show up at the door, stare at them and back away.

But then Helen pushed her head back and looked up into Wilton's face; and he could see only that there were tears in her eyes.

"I never thought I'd like you—with a beard," she said, a little unsteadily.

Wilton laughed. He bent over and kissed her on the lips. After a moment she drew away from him, but still clung to one arm.

"It's you, isn't it?" she whispered. "It's really you.... I can get away for a while, Jim. Where can we talk?"

WILTON led her away from the circle of light made by the fire and found a place near a grove of palm trees not too far away. They sat on the ground there, close to each other; he took her hand and held it.

"I never thought that this could happen," he said. "That I should meet you here like this—after all the changes that three years have brought, the other changes I was afraid they might bring—Tell me I'm not dreaming."

"It isn't a dream, Jim—and I haven't changed."

His hand closed more tightly about hers. "I know that, now. And it makes everything else seem quite small, unimportant."

Helen touched his arm, "Tell me about yourself. Tell me what you have been doing. I have heard, of course, about you and Lawrence, but—just talk, Jim."

"Tell me first about yourself. How did you happen to come down here?"

"Someone had to come. Besides, father thought that I—that I might be able to help Arthur. Something happened in France. I don't know what it was but father suddenly arranged to have Arthur sent down here. I—I think he's straightened up, Jim. He's not bad at heart. He's just—weak."

Wilton frowned. There had never been any misunderstandings between him and Helen on Arthur's account. They had faced the situation frankly. He pushed away his thoughts of Arthur.

"But what of you? What have you been doing?"

"Serving with the Red Cross. First in France and now here. I don't want to talk about it, Jim. If I let myself talk about it, think about it, I'd go crazy. I want to hear about you."

WILTON began to talk, slowly at first and almost wholly of Lawrence. He told of how Lawrence had been turned down when he had tried to join the army in England, and later had been accepted by the Near East Intelligence Corps, mainly because of his knowledge of Arabia.

And the rest of the story—Lawrence's two-week furlough, from which he had never come back; his alliance with Emir Feisal, and his work in welding the tribal units of Arabia into a marauding army to harass the Turks.

"I am only one of those helping him," Wilton told Helen. "There are dozens of us who, because of our knowledge of Arabia, have been pulled in to do our part."

"You live with the tribes?"

"Live with them, sleep with them, dress as they do, eat their food, almost think as an Arab. The Bedouin tribes, the desert people, on whom Lawrence depends the most, are very primitive. They—you remember that old battle-axe which hung over the mantel at home?"

Helen nodded. "I remember it."

"Well, I have it with me. I carry it when we ride. Most of the Bedouins, in addition to rifles and pistols, carry swords or spears or axes, medieval weapons such as that one. And *Bretwalda* has helped to lift me some in their estimation.

"It's an enormous axe, very heavy—too heavy for others to swing. The thought that I can wield it means something to the Bedouin."

"*Bretwalda?*" Helen repeated.

Wilton nodded.

"That's the name of the old axe. It's cut in the head just above the blade. The word means *Ruler of Britain*. It was the custom in the old days to name weapons."

The girl's cool hand smoothed back Wilton's hair. "Let's talk no more of war," he heard her whisper. "I must go back to the hospital in a minute, I've already been away too long."

Wilton drew a slow breath. He said, "Tell me of England,

Helen. Are the lights on the Thames just the same? Was last spring as early and as beautiful? It seems as if I have been away for a lifetime. Sometimes I wonder—"

"Wonder what, dear?"

Wilton shook his head. "It doesn't matter. All that matters is this interlude in a world that has gone crazy."

From the direction of the camp some man shouted an order and a moment later the clarion call of a bugle shattered the stillness of the night. Wilton closed his ears to those sounds. He looked up into the girl's face, vague and shadowy just above his head.

He thought that she was smiling. She said, "I went up to Oxford the last time I was in England, Jim. I stood on that corner under the great tree where centuries ago we used to meet. Nothing seemed to have changed The old stone house across the street—"

Wilton closed his eyes and listened. By some strange magic Helen's voice was bringing him a feeling of contentment and peace. He had the wish that this night might never end—that its enchantment might stay with him forever.

Then drumming through the walls or his consciousness came the sound of marching feet.

CHAPTER IV

THE HANDLEY-PAGE CIRCLED above the village of Umtaiye, thirteen miles south-cast of Deraa. James Wilton leaned over the edge of the observer's cockpit.

He could make out a great body of horsemen at one side of the village; and near them another troop mounted on racing camels. He was sure that these were Lawrence's men.

Scott swung around, cut the motors

"Is this it?" he shouted. "Where do we land?"

"This is it," Wilton called hack. "Pick out your own landing field."

The plane sank lower and circled the village again. Scott cut in the motors and started to climb. He screamed something at Wilton and though Wilton couldn't catch all of it he thought that the man said, "It's impossible to land here. The grounds too rough."

Wilton drew a pistol from his belt. He loosened the strap around his waist, stood up, leaned against the rushing air and tapped Scott on the shoulder. Scott turned, saw the pistol in his hand.

Wilton motioned to the ground, then swung the pistol so that Scott could see straight down the barrel. What he meant was unmistakable.

Again Scott cut the motor, "We'll crack up," he screamed. "There isn't a chance to land down there, I tell you—"

Wilton hadn't enjoyed this ride with Scott. All the way over here from Ramleh the sight of the man's broad back had reminded him of his brother and of his brother's death.

"I said land," he grated. "And I meant just that. Put this kite on the ground."

Scott turned back to the controls. The plane had started down again. It circled back toward the village. Wilton sat back and re-fastened the strap around his waist. He put away his gun, braced himself against the shock of a landing.

The plane bumped against the earth, bounced up into the air, rocked precariously and then jolted down again. After another series of bumps it came to a stop.

Wilton swung over the side to the ground. He looked up at Scott and said bluntly, "I told you this wasn't like flying in France. We haven't had much time to level off landing fields. Now try pulling yourself together. These men who are riding up are my friends. I'd hate them to see the color of your skin."

Scott had taken off his helmet. He was perspiring and he wouldn't meet Wilton's stare. Wilton turned away from him.

A dozen or more Bedouins were riding toward the plane and with them was one man, shorter than the others, clean-shaven.

His *kuffieh* was of gold-embroidered white silk and his long dark cloak was laced with a pattern in silver thread.

THIS was Lawrence, the man so puny in size that the British army had rejected him, the man who had taken a furlough from another service and stayed away to raise and to head the greatest Arabian army since the time of Saladin.

"I was in a hurry to get back," Wilton said as Lawrence and the Bedouins rode up.

"Allenby?" Lawrence asked.

"He is ready."

Lawrence nodded and stared off toward the valley through which ran the highway and the railroad. "We must get on with our part of the work," Wilton heard him mutter.

Scott clambered from the plane and Wilton introduced him to Lawrence. Lawrence nodded. "German fliers sent down to help the Turks have owned the air around here," he said to Scott. "You'll find plenty to do."

Even as he spoke the throbbing of an airplane's motor could be heard and over the western horizon appeared two dark-winged ships. Scott looked at Lawrence and then at Wilton. He turned back to his plane. "Spin the prop for me, will you, Wilton?" he asked.

Wilton lifted the axe he had brought with him from the plane. He walked around to the prop and at Scott's signal, spun it. The motor caught; he backed away and watched Scott take off.

The Handley-Page circled around and around, fighting for altitude, then finally straightened out and made for the two German planes. The German planes had turned and were scooting away and the Handley-Page followed them over the horizon.

"I'm glad to get that ship," Lawrence remarked. "We need a few more."

Wilton said nothing, wondering whether he would ever see Scott again. He didn't think it likely. After he was out of sight,

Wilton felt, Scott would probably turn south and head out of the danger zone. Landing in some British-controlled city he could blame everything on engine trouble.

One of the Bedouins brought Wilton a horse and gazed admiringly at the great axe in Wilton's hand. He pointed to the single, blood-red jewel in the head of the axe. It had caught the rays of the sun. It sparkled as if it were alive.

Wilton stared down at it. According to the legend of the axe which he had heard from his father, there had once been an even dozen jewels such as that left in the axe *Bretwalda*; but one by one they had been lost.

Another phase of the legend came to his mind. The inscriptions on the long axe handle were supposed to carry a motto which promised to the man who swung the axe *a great joy and a great sorrow, a great victory and a great defeat.*

"We will ride for Deraa," Lawrence said to him. "North of there we will strike our first blow. I have brought along a good supply of tulips."

Several of the Bedouins laughed. A tulip, as all of them knew, was Lawrence's term for a bomb. His tulips had been his most effective weapon in his campaign against the Turks.

Wilton swung into the saddle and at an order from Lawrence the Bedouin army rode north.

THE RAILROAD which reached from Constantinople through Syria and Palestine, and then on down through the Hedjaz country to Medina, was the lifeline of the Turkish army.

That lower part of Arabia they could control no longer, for the Hedjaz tribes had driven them out of all centers excepting Medina. But northern Palestine and Syria were still under Turkish domination. There were Turkish garrisons in every large town and all along the railroads there were outposts to patrol the tracks.

Down that railroad to the Fourth Turkish Army, now located mainly at Amman, went trainloads of supplies and ammunition and new troops as they were needed.

Above Amman, Palestine and Syria belonged to the Turks. And it was above Amman that Lawrence meant to strike. His job it was to cut that Turkish lifeline and to see that it stayed cut while Allenby pushed northward toward Damascus, around the flank of the Turkish army.

At a point several kilos above Deraa, Lawrence and his men came out of the foothills and within sight of the railroad. On up a little way was a bridge over a deep ravine and near it were several huts, marking the quarters of the outpost left to guard the bridge.

"A good place to begin," said Lawrence, waving one hand above his head.

No other order was needed. Wild, screaming yells burst from the throats of the Bedouins as they charged forward—and Wilton found himself screaming with the rest.

A new and strange excitement surged through his veins. This raid, he could feel, was different from the others in which he had taken part. Most of all that had gone before had been in reality an annoying, guerrilla warfare, designed to worry and harass the Turks; but this time there was a sober design in their raid.

On other occasions they had perhaps wiped out an outpost and blown up a bridge and a few miles of track which the Turks had quickly repaired. This time they had to see that the line stayed cut and that the highway, too, was blocked.

So sudden and so unexpected was that attack of Lawrence's men that the Turks, although almost equal to them in number, had no chance. A scattering volley of rifle fire echoed across the valley and here and there a Bedouin horse reared up and screamed in terror.

Then the two forces came together.

Guns were discarded now by the Arabs and glistening swords flashed in the sunlight. The dark and swarthy face of one of the Turks loomed up at Wilton's side.

He twisted his pistol that way, pressed the trigger but did

not feel the gun's recoil. A clubbed rifle swung at his head. He ducked it and threw his pistol directly into the Turk's face. A Bedouin slipped between them and a sword rose and fell. The Turks slid screaming to the ground.

As swiftly as it had started, the fighting was over. Wilton wiped a hand over his brow, stared up the track. There, at the far end of the bridge, Lawrence was already planting his tulips, and nearer at hand several of the Bedouins had dismounted and with long staffs were prying loose the steel rails of the track.

As fast as a rail was loosened, three men would grasp it, carry it to the ravine's edge, and slide it into the chasm below.

Lawrence finished planting his tulips and carrying the detonator box, hurried away from the bridge and to a point of safety. The Bedouins drew aside to watch the explosion. Lawrence pushed in the plunger; and with a roar which was deafening to the ears, the bridge buckled, reared up into the air and then sagged down into the ravine, a broken, useless thing.

"So much for a beginning," Lawrence muttered.

An airplane swooped down from overhead and Wilton saw with some surprise that it was the Handley-Page. Scott waved to them from the cockpit, swung the plane around. Half a mile down the track he started dropping bombs. Several of them scored direct hits.

"Yes, a good beginning," Lawrence nodded. "But only that."

THAT day and the next two were days of almost continual riding, of almost continual fighting. Just above Deraa they ran into a Kurdish patrol and below Deraa they had a brush with another.

Lawrence, Wilton and a few others turned aside to Mezerib where they joined one of the Arab tribes Lawrence had started that way, early in the morning. At Mezerib they succeeded in cutting the telegraph wire which stretched down from Constantinople.

Then, turning back toward Nasib, they were almost captured by a troop of Turkish cavalry out on patrol duty.

Such was the first day and the next two were like it. At a score of places along twenty miles of the track, the Bedouins struck. At a score of places they overpowered the Turkish patrols and tore up the track.

Reënforcements sent down from Damascus and up from Amman to put down what the Turks considered only some local rebellious tribe, found themselves facing an emergency with which they couldn't cope. While they pursued one band of Arabs through the foothills, three other groups would strike the line at widely separated spots.

Soldiers set to work to repair the track fell victim to distant and well hidden snipers, By the third day the lifeline of the Turkish army was so effectively cut that it would have taken a week of constant work to put it into condition.

In the evening of the third day Lawrence drew Wilton aside and led him to an outcropping of rock on Mount Tell Ara, near where his men had made their camp. The sky was clear that night, and the stars seemed so close that Wilton had the feeling he could almost reach up and touch them.

He was tired but hardly aware of it; and Lawrence showed his weariness not at all.

"We have done our part thus far with very little trouble," Lawrence said to him. "The reserves which have been sent up from the south haven't bothered us much but they have greatly weakened the Turk. Tomorrow is the nineteenth, the day Allenby has named to start his march toward Deraa and Damascus. It he moves swiftly enough the Turkish army will be trapped."

"But if they have guessed what he plans—"

Lawrence frowned. "I have been worrying about that. If the Turkish army at Amman should start this way within the next two days we would have to change our plans. I want you to fly to Ramleh tomorrow. I want you to tell Allenby what we have done.

"Tell him to push forward with all possible speed. And on

your way I want you to fly high over Amman and see what you can observe."

Wilton's first inclination was to beg off; but he did not do that. He knew how important it was that Lawrence and Allenby work closely together. Allenby's force had been weakened by the withdrawal of several divisions for service in France; and the main body of the Rualla tribe, on whom Lawrence had counted, still hadn't shown up.

Together, Allenby and Lawrence had but a skeleton army with which to defeat the Turks.

"I'll leave at dawn," he promised.

Lawrence nodded, leaned back against the great rock by which he was standing. And then after a long pause he asked quietly, "I wonder what people are doing in England tonight?"

Wilton could hardly believe that he had heard correctly. He had always thought that Lawrence's only interest was in Arabia.

CHAPTER V

THE HANDLEY-PAGE HAD been grounded for the past two days. The trouble, according to Scott, was with the motor. He had torn it down and had put it back together and then had torn it down again.

The morning after Wilton's talk with Lawrence he was still working on it. It was noon before he announced that it was ready for a trial flight.

Wilton doubted that anything had been wrong with the plane's motor and he told Scott so with a characteristic bluntness.

Though his words brought a touch of pallor to Scott's cheeks, the airman had nothing to say.

They took off just after noon; turned south, following the line of the railroad through Palestine. At an altitude of ten thousand feet they circled Amman.

The camp of the Turkish army could be easily distinguished.

From it a steady stream of soldiers was heading north, some mounted, some on foot. Motor lorries and armored cars were lifting a dust in the road.

The sight of all that activity brought a tight, strained expression to Wilton's face. This was what Lawrence had feared might happen. If only a few reserves were sent back to quell the trouble around Deraa, he could easily handle them; but if all the thousands of men under the command of Djemal Pasha, the Turkish commander-in-chief, were to fall back, Allenby's coup would be ruined.

When Scott looked back at him after circling the place for several times, Wilton waved his arm toward Ramleh and the plane straightened out and thundered off in that direction.

The landing field at Ramleh was near the hospital established by the Red Cross.

As the Handley-Page bumped along the ground Wilton thought that he caught a glimpse of Helen Cavanaugh standing in front of one of the hospital tents, waving at him. The realization that he might see her brought a smile to his lips and for a moment lifted the feeling of depression which had settled over him.

"Gas up the plane," he ordered Scott as he swung to the ground. "We're going back as soon as I've talked to Allenby."

Wilton hurried directly from the landing field to Allenby's headquarters. There was a suppressed excitement around the place. Couriers were dashing up on horseback with reports, were leaving again with new orders. Allenby's push had started. Wilton could sense that as definitely as if the fact had been announced by posters.

HE WAS admitted to the general's presence almost at once. As soon as Allenby saw him the general asked sharply, "What has happened at Deraa?"

"Just what Lawrence promised you would happen," Wilton answered. "The railroad has been cut, the highway blocked. No trains or lorries have moved south of Deraa for four days."

"The telegraph wires?"

"Down."

Allenby nodded, rubbed his hands together. Excitement showed in his usually calm face. "We have started," he said to Wilton. "There has been almost no resistance. By this time Nablus should have fallen and our men should be entering Nazareth."

"I flew here by way of Amman," Wilton interrupted. "From what I could see it looked as if the whole Fourth Turkish Army was starting north toward Deraa."

Allenby stiffened. "What's that?"

Wilton repeated what he had said. He didn't need to explain. By the expression on Allenby's face he knew that the general understood the seriousness of the situation. The general turned to a map, studied it for a moment. He said under his breath, "Lawrence will have to stop them south of Deraa. He will have to hold them for three days."

"He can't," Wilton answered simply. "He has a few armored cars, a few dozen machine guns. The Turks have ten times as many. Lawrence's men are Bedouins. They fight on horseback. They know only how to dash in at an enemy, strike as vicious a blow as they can—then if the odds against them are too great, they can only wheel around and ride away. They haven't the training to make a stand against a modern army."

Allenby clenched his fists. "I know that all you say is true," he admitted. "Still, in spite of that, Lawrence must stop them. If the Fourth Turkish army passes Deraa and reaches Damascus before we can get there, our cause is lost. I tell you, Lawrence must stop them."

Wilton's lips tightened. He nodded his head.

"Tell Lawrence," said Allenby, "that my army will drive forward faster than any other advance was ever made in all history. Tell him if he holds those Turks back for two days it will he enough. Tell him England demands it. We can make no variation in our plan to meet this emergency."

Again Wilton nodded. He said, and it seemed as if someone else were speaking the words for him, "Lawrence will stop them, General."

WILTON left Allenby's headquarters in a strange sort of mental trance. He had a feeling that the promise he had made in Lawrence's name would be kept—but he did not know how. He knew only that it had to he kept.

He walked back to the landing field, out toward the plane; and then at the sudden memory of Helen Cavanaugh, turned in the direction of the hospital.

Helen must have seen him coming. She was waiting for him at the door to the main tent; and something in the girl's face jarred him almost with the force of a blow. She was unusually pale and her wide brown eyes mirrored an unmistakable agony. Faint, tight lines marked the corners of her lips.

Wilton stopped a pace away from the door, aware of a sudden anxiety. "What is it, Helen?" he demanded.

"You haven't heard?"

Wilton shook his head, frowning.

"Arthur was arrested the night you left," Helen said swiftly. "He was accused of—of selling information to the Turks. Of—of being a spy."

James Wilton moved closer to the girl. He lifted his hands to her shoulders, looked steadily into her eyes; and then, as he could feel the trembling of her body, he drew her into his arms, not caring who might be watching them.

"Tell me about it, Helen," he said quietly.

"He had been gambling again," Helen whispered against his shoulder. "He was terribly in debt. I—I don't think he realized what he was doing. I don't want to think he did. He—Oh, Jim, why couldn't he have been killed? I would rather he had been killed than have father—"

"Where is he, Helen?"

The girl's body grew suddenly tense.

She hesitated, then muttered, "I—I don't know. He escaped. I don't know where—"

Wilton pushed the girl away from him so that he could see her face. He asked again, "Where is he, Helen?"

"I—I—"

"Where is he?" Wilton asked for a third time.

Helen Cavanaugh bit her lips. "He's here in the hospital. One of the wounded men died. I carried his body out at night, hid it. I helped Arthur get away, brought him here, put him in that man's place. There's only one doctor and I've been able to keep him away from Arthur."

Wilton drew a long, ragged breath. He knew how fond of her brother Helen was in spite of all his faults. To his mind there came a picture of Helen's father, that prominent, grand old man who was serving under the war secretary. Wilton knew what a blow this would be to him.

"Helen," he said abruptly, "go inside, take the bandages off of your brother and put him in a hospital coat. Send him out to my plane. Tell him to get in it."

Helen blinked at him, caught her breath. "You—you'll help him to get away?"

Wilton didn't answer that question. He said flatly, "Sooner or later he will be discovered here. I'll look after him, Helen."

"No! It's not fair. I—"

"Get him ready," Wilton said sharply. "I'll have Scott start the plane's motor."

He swung around, hurried over to the plane. There were several soldiers standing around it, talking to Scott. Half of the petrol cans which had been brought out had been packed into the storage space in the fuselage.

WILTON drew Scott aside. "We're taking a doctor back with us," he said bluntly. "Don't load any more petrol than you figure we'll need."

Scott shrugged. "It'll be plenty cramped in the observer's cockpit."

"What of it?" Wilton retorted. "Climb in and get the motor started. I want to get out of here as soon as the doctor shows up."

Scott called several of the soldiers to help him, finished loading in the petrol and then climbed into his seat. One of the soldiers swung the prop and the motor caught. The soldiers backed away.

Wilton hurried back to the hospital tent and Helen met him at the door. "He's ready," she whispered. "Jim, I—I don't know what to say. I—"

Wilton looked steadily at the girl. He had never lied to her. He couldn't lie to her now. "Helen," he said slowly, "I'm not helping Arthur to escape. I'm taking him to Lawrence. The whole Fourth Turkish Army has busted loose from Amman and is heading north. Lawrence has to stop them. Do you understand what I mean?"

Helen moistened her lips. "You will—"

Wilton nodded. "It is a better way than a firing squad."

The girl caught her lips between her teeth. A low moan came from her throat. Her eyes closed.

And then she suddenly leaned forward and her hands, clutching at Wilton's arms, fastened there with a grip which almost made him wince. "You will be there too," he heard her gasp. "No, Jim. No. I couldn't stand that. I—"

The girl's head was pressed against Wilton's shoulder and great sobs were racking her body. Wilton held her tight in his arms. The thought came to him that this was probably their farewell, that he might never see her again.

He knew what lay ahead. Lawrence would try with every force at his command to stop that Turkish army. Not many of them would last to see the end of the campaign.

He found that he could tell himself that matter-of-factly; his calmness was surprising to him.

He lifted Helen's face, looked down into it and smiled. He knew that he couldn't talk to her about what was to come.

He said, "Helen after all this is over and when people come to realize what Lawrence was able to accomplish in Arabia it's going to be very clear that he has a deep love for that country.

"But I discovered something else about Lawrence the other night. We were standing alone under the stars and he suddenly began to talk about England. His love isn't only for Arabia. It's for his homeland, too.

"And it's that deep love which has stood in the way of the imperialism which threatened the world, which will always stand in the way of any danger. It's so much a part of the English people that none of us is without it. Always remember that."

From the look in Helen's eyes Wilton doubted that she had heard a word that he had said. Over her shoulder he caught a glimpse of Arthur. He motioned to him to come on, bent and kissed Helen lightly on the lips. "Goodby, dear," he murmured. "We'll get along, Arthur and I."

He turned around, then, and dashed toward the plane while Cavanaugh followed. No attempt was made to stop them. Later, Wilton knew, men might wonder what doctor had left in that Handley-Page and an investigation might be started. But any investigation would come too late.

CHAPTER VI

SCOTT MADE A bumpy landing at the camp at the base of Mount Tell Ara. It was almost a disastrous landing. The planes wheels struck some obstruction on the rocky ground. It bounced into the air, tilted over and came down again, partially on one wing, crumpling it as if it had been paper.

Wilton boosted Cavanaugh out and then climbed out himself. He surveyed the damaged plane, glanced over at Scott and said flatly, "Anything to keep out of the air. You want to live a long time, don't you, Scott?"

A flush of anger showed in Scott's face. "That's a damn lie, Wilton. I didn't see that ridge."

Wilton shrugged, turned away, strode onward the Bedouin campfire a little distance away. A tall, slender figure arose from beside the fire and came forward to meet him. There was a bloody gash on the man's thin, dark face but his lips were smiling.

"Tabari!" Wilton cried.

"Yes, Sidi Wilton," said the Arab. "We would have been here sooner but a troop of the infidel Turks crossed our path."

As he spoke, Tabari's hand lifted to the cut across his face.

Wilton smiled. He could well guess what had happened to the Turks. "Where is the Sidi Lawrence?" he asked.

Colonel Stirling, at Briton, who like Wilton was serving with Lawrence and the Arabs, came forward. "Lawrence has gone to Azarak," he reported.

"To Azarak!" Wilton gasped.

Stirling nodded. "To meet several tribal *shereefs*. He feels that we must have more men. What's up, Wilton?"

In short, pithy sentences, Wilton told Stirling what he had observed from the air above Amman, what Allenby had said to him, what Allenby had asked of Lawrence. And as he spoke, Stirling's face grew grave.

"We can never do it," he muttered as Wilton finished.

"We've got to do it," Wilton answered.

He moved on to the fire, stared around at the Bedouins squatting near it. There were fewer than a score in this group, but here and there throughout the foothills were other camp-fires and other Arabs.

Stirling came up to him and said, "More troops have come down from Damascus. The Turks are making every effort to repair the railroad. A dozen patrols are scouring the countryside. We've been kept mighty busy. With what men we have here it's all we can do to keep the tracks cut and the way to the south blocked."

"If the Fourth Turkish Army gets up here that won't be

important," Wilton answered. And then, "How many machine guns in this crowd?"

"Six," Stirling answered, "And plenty of ammunition."

WILTON rubbed his hands together. "Stirling, do you remember that old medieval castle south of here, near the railroad, about half way to Amman?"

Stirling nodded.

"I went through it once," Wilton continued. "The place has about fallen to pieces but where the walls are still standing they are thick and are of stone. That castle commands the route along which the Turks must come. A few men with machine guns might hold it for a long time."

"Against an army?"

"Even against an army, Stirling. I want you to ride after Lawrence. I want you to tell him what I have told you, Tell him that those Turks must be stopped, that they must be held back for two days. Tell him that I will be at that old castle."

"And I with you. Someone else can ride after Lawrence."

Wilton shook his head. "No one else will do. You know the situation, the desert route to Azarak."

As if the matter were decided, Wilton lifted his voice and started addressing the Bedouins. He spoke to them in their own tongue, in the calm and yet impressive way which Lawrence had used so often and so successfully.

He did not go into any detail as he explained what must be done. He only said that the Turkish army now moving up from Amman must be stopped, must be held back for two days; that if that were accomplished, Lord Allenby and the British would reach Damascus and would deliver a death blow to the hated infidels.

"I go to stop them," he concluded, "I would like to have you go with me."

He had hardly finished speaking before Tabari moved over to his side and said simply, "I will go with you, *sidi*."

"And I," said another of the Bedouins.

A wrinkled old man with a long, flowing beard got to his feet. "I have lived too long already," he announced. "I will go too."

Here and there others were standing; land as he looked from side to side, Wilton felt a sudden pride in his friendship with these people. Not a one of them but knew the danger they were facing; yet without any hesitation at all each was signifying his willingness to go along.

Scott stood over to one side, scowling, and as Wilton's eyes fell on him he looked away.

"You, too, are going, Scott," Wilton announced. He glanced at Tabari. "See that he accompanies us."

A hand touched Wilton's arm. He swung around. A pale, perspiring Arthur Cavanaugh was blinking at him.

"May I—go along with you?" Cavanaugh asked.

Wilton nodded. "We will not come back, you know."

"Yes, I know," Cavanaugh said slowly. "That's why I—want to go."

Stirling grasped Wilton's hand, "I think you're crazy," he said thickly, "but I'd give anything to be in your shoes. Hang on until Lawrence and I can get there."

Wilton nodded. He took the reins of the horse Tabari brought him, made sure that the axe *Bretwalda* was strapped behind the saddle, mounted, and looked around at the others.

Scott was a miserable, huddled figure on the back of a horse near Tabari.

Cavanaugh was climbing into a saddle, He was still perspiring—trembling, Wilton thought. The Bedouins had finished breaking camp and most of them were ready to leave.

Wilton raised his arm in a signal, turned and headed south.

CHAPTER VII

THE OLD CASTLE stood on the crown of a little hill at the north end of a wide valley encircled by a rough, mountainous country to the east and to the west.

By its position Wilton knew that it had once commanded much of this territory. The railroad and the highway to the north turned around the base of the hill, close under its crumbling walls.

No one lived in the castle. Like many another landmark left by the Crusaders, it was thought by the Arabs to be inhabited by evil spirits; and for hundreds of years it had been neglected.

From the great gaps in the walls Wilton felt that this place had once been the scene of a long and bitter struggle. Who had erected it, he didn't know. Tancred, he thought, or perhaps Behemond who had come with Godfrey de Bouillon on the first great Crusade to the Holy Land and who had remained here in an effort to establish a Christian kingdom.

They had reached the castle in the early dawn after a night of hard riding; and now, as the first rays of the morning sun were stabbing at them from the eastern hills, they were making a hurried inspection of the place.

Beyond the crumbling walls and across a narrow courtyard was the donjon, or keep, the house in which the lord of the castle had once lived and where he had held court. The donjon walls were thick and were of almost solid stone.

Here and there around the place were narrow openings where archers had probably once been stationed, but they were high up where the second floor of the donjon had probably been, a floor which had long ago rotted away.

Finished with his inspection, Wilton sought out Tabari and drew him apart from the others. "Select the youngest of your men," he ordered "and have him take our horses and lead them away. I have a feeling that we will not need them again."

Tabari flashed a smile. "I will send my brother Yusef. I would like to know that my people still have a *shereef* after today."

"Send him, of course," Wilton nodded.

One of the Bedouins who had been staring to the south

called out a warning; and moving over to where he stood, Wilton looked that way. Far across the meadow he could make out a troop of Turkish cavalry. He shook his head.

"That is but a patrol. We must let them pass. We are here for bigger game."

During the next two hours, Wilton disposed of his men. With the huge stones which had once been a part of the wall, barricades were erected around the machine guns and the machine guns were so placed as to command each slope.

Yusef had left with the horses, cutting their force down to nineteen men: Tabari and fifteen of his Bedouin followers, Wilton, Scott, and Cavanaugh. Scott had assumed charge of one of the machine guns and Cavanaugh another.

"I can handle this thing," Scott had said through stiff lips. "I'm going to show you something, Wilton."

All throughout the night's ride and through the early hours of the morning, Scott had had little to say. Wilton couldn't quite make him out. The man was a coward, he knew; yet there had been a strange steadiness in his voice as he had announced his intention of taking charge of one of the machine guns.

Cavanaugh, too, had calmed down. There was a strange, glistening look in his eyes; but his hands did not tremble as he tore down his machine gun and reassembled it.

IN THE MIDDLE of the morning another Turkish patrol rode up the valley and around the foot of the hill, under the castle.

This patrol was larger, numbering several hundred men, but Wilton let it pass without revealing his presence. The main army of the Turks, he knew, could not be far behind.

He felt no excitement and was a little surprised that he should be so calm. They would never escape from here, any of them. Of that he was sure. And he decided that it was probably his acceptance of that fact which had steadied him.

Tabari, who had been standing near the wall staring toward the south, swung around and came over to where Wilton was resting. "They come, *sidi*," he announced. "So many that I could not number them."

Wilton stood up and went over to where Tabari had been. A great cloud of dust hovered over the southern end of the valley. In front of it he could make out a troop of cavalry and behind them foot soldiers. Sunlight flashed from their shouldered guns.

For the space of several minutes he stood there watching the advance. The cavalry troop drew nearer and nearer and the line of foot soldiers extended on back until it was swallowed by the dust cloud which was beginning to spread out over the valley.

He nodded and said under his breath, "Yes, here they come."

Then turning to Tabari who had followed him, he ordered, "Tell our men that those on horseback are to be allowed to ride past the castle. When those on foot are just below us, we will open fire. And Tabari, no shot must be wasted."

The Arab hurried off.

Wilton stared down at the axe *Bretwalda*. He had carried it with him since arriving at the castle—just why he didn't know. In this old medieval castle it had felt very natural in his hands. It had seemed to belong here. It had seemed to fit in.

Once, he knew, a Wilton had carried this axe through the Holy Land; and the thought had come to him that perhaps that ancestor of his had even wielded *Bretwalda* in defense of these very walls.

He wondered about that; smiled; swung the axe to his shoulder, carried it over to the donjon and leaned it against the wall.

On up the road came the Turkish army. The leading cavalry troop swept around the foot of the hill and the foot soldiers followed after them. Those in the front circled the hill and turned away from it. Wilton glanced from left to right. He raised a hand and said, "Now!"

The crashing rattle of the machine gun fire was answered by screams and loud cries and by a few scattered rifle shots. The column down below had been thrown into confusion.

Dozens of men were sprawled out on the ground, and from the way they were lying Wilton knew that they would never rise again. Some of the soldiers had turned and were racing away. Others had thrown themselves to the ground and were firing back.

Turkish officers rode back and forth on galloping horses, shouting orders and pointing up to the castle. More swiftly than he had thought it possible, a charge was organized and hurled against the hill.

But it was an ineffective charge. With a deadly precision, the Bedouin machine gunners mowed it down.

Wilton hurried over to the south wall. The advancing Turkish army had stopped and men were spreading out to the east and to the west. An armored car rolled up the road and several officers got out. Mounted officers rode up to where they stood, gathered around them for a moment, then hurried away.

And now the chattering of a machine gun sounded from the other side of the castle and Wilton moved that way. The cavalry troop which had passed, he saw, had turned back at the sound of the battle and was riding up the hill.

It was Scott who was stationed at the machine gun at that side; he was handling the weapon very effectively. Several Bedouins with rifles supported him. And that charge, just as the charge of the soldiers, was broken.

FOR A TIME, then, a period of silence settled over the valley. The soldiers who had moved out to the east and west circled north, and closed in where the road passed through the hills. They didn't advance but merely stood there, waiting.

From the south, great lumbering motor lorries appeared; and a few minutes later, cannons were unloaded from them and wheeled into position to fire on the castle.

Moe and more men filed up the valley and strengthened the lines on either side. One of the cannons roared and a shell screamed overhead.

The second shell was closer. The third struck the donjon wall, smashing in a section of it and sputtering Wilton with broken fragments of rock. He moved over toward one of the machine gun nests and squatted down by Cavanaugh.

Cavanaugh looked over at him and grinned. His round, plump face was perspiring again. "They're gettin' close to home," he shouted. "We can't stand much of that. I wish they'd try comin' up the hill again."

Wilton nodded. He lay flat on his face while the cannonading continued. The Turk gunners now had the range of the castle and were sending shell after shell crashing against its walls, tumbling them in and showering Wilton's men with broken rock.

Then after a while the cannons grew silent and Wilton sat up. He studied the encircling army for a moment, nodded and said to Cavanaugh, "They're going to come up the hill again. Wait until they're so close that you can't miss."

That same message he took from post to post. Several of the Bedouins had been cut by flying rock but none was seriously hurt. Though the donjon was almost reduced to ruins, the shells had had no other effect.

That second charge came from every side; and as the Turks reached the foot of the hill they started firing their rifles and screaming in defiance.

Wilton watched them come on. It did not seem possible, now, that they could be stopped. There were too many of them. By force of numbers alone they could surge on and over the place.

He lifted his arm and shouted, "Now!"

And again the chattering machine guns spewed destruction at the oncoming horde. Great gaps appeared in the Turkish ranks. Here and there the men in the front ranks fell to the ground to prove stumbling blocks for those who followed.

At one side a score of the Turks gained the level space at the top of the hill; but the Bedouins there rose up with clubbed rifles and swords and drove them back. In other places the charge broke a dozen yards short of its goal and once more the Turks fell back and drew away from the old castle, leaving their wounded behind.

THE SUN had crawled across the top of the sky and was sinking down behind the western hills. Wilton was a little surprised that it was so late.

That second charge had been more disastrous than the first one. Four of the Bedouins were dead; Scott and two more Bedouins were wounded.

Scott had a ball through the shoulder. Tabari had dressed it, binding the arm tight to the man's side and packing the wound so that it couldn't bleed. It must have been painful but Scott hadn't uttered a word.

Tabari prepared and brought food and said, "The infidels have set up their camp. We have stopped them, *sidi.*"

"Until tomorrow," Wilton answered. "It is not long enough."

... More cannonading started at dusk and continued intermittently for several hours. One shell struck directly on one of the machine gun nests, destroying the gun and killing three more men.

Two raiding parties tried to creep up the hill from opposite sides a little later but were detected and were driven back.

The night was long. Out in the valley Wilton could see the campfires of the Turkish army.

At one time during that night, Cavanaugh sought him out—a quiet, sober Cavanaugh, whose manner reminded him of the chubby, round-faced boy with whom he had played in his youth.

"I wanted to tell you this," Cavanaugh said to him. "I've figured out why it was that you helped me to escape. And it may sound funny, but I appreciate it."

Wilton didn't know what to answer.

"It was a rotten thing I did," Cavanaugh went on. "This won't make up for it, I know, but I can at least find a little satisfaction in this kind of a death."

Wilton was standing against a part of the old wall. He stared off toward the Turkish campfires and answered slowly, "I've been thinking again of England tonight, trying to remember what it was like back there, trying to face the fact that I would never see it again."

Wilton closed his eyes and his mind called up the picture of Helen Cavanaugh as he had last seen her.

CHAPTER VIII

THE CANNONADING STARTED again with the dawn; and with the first rays of the sun, the Turks again began their advance on the hill. They came this time not in any solid wall of men, easily broken by the machine gunners; but in single ranks, far apart.

And wave after wave was thrown against the slope, some gaining almost the top before they were driven back.

Wilton kept moving from one machine gun post to another. At the north wall, Scott sat grimly behind his weapon. His handsome face was marked by deep lines and there was a flush of fever in his cheeks. When Wilton reached him he glanced up and asked sharply, "Well, how am I doing? Could you handle this thing any better?"

Wilton shook his head. He looked down at this man whom he had thought a coward, to whom he attributed his brothers death. He said bluntly, "No, I couldn't do any better."

A hoarse laugh came from Scott's throat. He said thickly, "You were right, Wilton. I did run off and leave your brother. But the ghost of his ship has followed me through the air ever since."

A shudder gripped the man's frame. He looked over his gun, shook his fist at the Turkish lines and screamed, "Come on, damn you. I'm not afraid any more. Come on up here where this gun will reach."

They were coming again. Out in the meadows below the old

castle the Turkish officers were whipping their lines back into shape, were ordering the men forward. And now not only single battalions but the entire army was forming into position for the assault.

The cannons rained shell after shell on the old castle and at the walls; and another of Wilton's machine gun nests was wiped out. A little before that there had been twelve of them left. Now there were only nine.

As the cannonading stopped and as the Turks started forward again Wilton realized that this would be the last charge. He glanced up at the sun. It was only two hours high in the heavens.

His lips tightened bitterly. If they could have but held out until noon, he thought the Turks might have had to spend the rest of the day here, burying their dead and caring for the wounded.

But they couldn't hold out until noon. In another four hours the Turks would again be on their way north.

Grimly and steadily did that Turkish line move to the foot of the hill, start up the slope. Rifle shots laced the air and the staccato crackling of the machine guns spoke in answer.

The advancing line sagged but formed again and came on. One of Wilton's machine guns was suddenly silenced and then another stopped firing as the man who had been handling it slumped forward.

Wilton raced that way. He tilted the man's body aside, reached for the trigger and sprayed a circle of lead down the side of the hill.

The gun jammed. He reached for a rifle and emptied it. Out of the corner of his eye he could see that the Turks had gained the crest of the hill at the north side.

He caught a picture of Scott standing there. Scott, the coward. There was a clubbed rifle in Scott's hands and he was swinging it from side to side. The Turks closed in around him and he went down.

WILTON jerked erect. He felt a stab of pain in his side, knew that he had been struck by a bullet. Over near the old donjon he caught sight of Tabari, two other Bedouins and Cavanaugh.

Tabari was just lowering his rifle and now he clutched his sword, drew it, and with a screaming yell, charged directly at the men pouring over the hill top.

Cavanaugh waited where he was but the two Bedouins raced after Tabari.

Half stumbling and acutely aware of the pain in his side, Wilton moved over to where Cavanaugh stood. Near him, still leaning against a part of the donjon wall which had not fallen, was the axe *Bretwalda*.

Wilton dropped his useless rifle. He reached for the axe, swung it to his shoulder, jerked around—and a cry which he did not recognize as his own burst from his lips.

It was a loud, defiant, mocking cry, such as might have once sounded from the throat of an earlier Wilton in the Middle Ages. The pain in his side was forgotten and he was unaware of the great weight of the axe.

He saw Tabari go down, saw the two Bedouins who had followed him sink under the crackling shots of a dozen rifles. Cavanaugh staggered forward, swung his gun at the men who were closing in, tripped and fell. A slashing sword in the hands of one of the Turkish officers cut down at his head.

Wilton moved a step forward and struck out with the great axe. He slashed with it from side to side. Men screamed and fell back under its cutting blows.

Wilton turned to the right and then to the left, swinging *Bretwalda* as easily as if it had no weight at all. There was a strange, fixed smile on his face—such a smile as might greet the news that already Lawrence was on his way down here to take up where he had had to stop.

He couldn't have known that, of course. He couldn't have known that several thousand more tribesmen had joined Lawrence's forces and that even now they were lining the hills to the north.

He couldn't have known that from here on up the Turks were to blunder into a running battle with Lawrence's men which would result in their complete defeat. Nor could he have known that within a week Allenby and the British would enter Damascus; that this engagement would mark the breaking of the Ottoman Empire and the beginning of the end for Germany.

Yet even as the Turks again crowded in around him and as a score of shots drove him to his knees, he was still smiling. And though he did not understand it, the feeling of victory was surging strongly through his body.

A vision came to him in that last moment, a composite vision of all of his memories of England. It seemed to him that the green rolling hills lay just ahead, beckoning him, and that Helen was there, smiling and waving in greeting. He thought that he stood up and started running toward her.

ONE OF THE TURKS rolled Wilton's body aside with the toe of his boot, stooped over and picked up the axe *Bretwalda*. He looked at the bloody head of the axe and scowled.

He had thought that he had seen a flashing set there in the steel; but, now he decided that he must have been wrong. There were a dozen indentations in the head of the axe where jewels might once have been.

All of them, however, were empty.

ABOUT THE AUTHOR

I WAS BORN in Colorado in 1902 and attended various elementary schools all over the state, finishing up at Denver University, which I attended for four years without graduating. I married a Denver girl twenty years ago and am still married to her. We have an eighteen-year-old son who is six inches taller than I am, and who wishes I would write *literature*. We have a daughter of thirteen

Philip Ketchum

who is beautifully freckled, and who wishes I would write dog stories. My wife doesn't care what I write, so long as I enjoy writing it.

Half a dozen years ago when I gave up a rather good job for the precarious but free life of a writer, we were living in the Midwest. We flipped a coin to decide whether to move to Florida or California. Actually, of course, California lost. We like it here. We like the sunshine and the rain and the people. We like the lazy tempo of the life we have built. If I could write one page of *literature* for my son, and a really good dog story for my daughter, life would be almost perfect.

I have a passion for the truth. I must confess that I look nothing like my picture. I did pose for it, however, so it is the photographer who is the liar. As a matter of fact, I'm bald, haggard, Indian brown and need a shave.

THE ARGOSY LIBRARY ™

SERIES 1 INCLUDES:

* DENT * KETCHUM * KLINE *
* MacISAAC * ROSCOE *
* ROUSSEAU *
* SELTZER *
* TUTTLE *
* WIRT *
WORTS

THE BEST FICTION
FROM THE FRANK
A. MUNSEY LINE

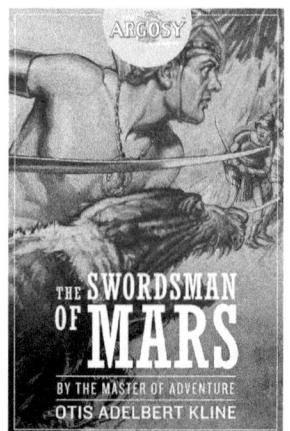

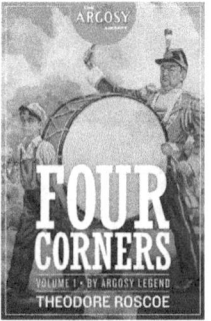

SERIES 1 • AVAILABLE SPRING 2015